FIRE BOUND

THE WHITE WOLF PROPHECY, BOOK FOUR

KAYLEIGH KING

Copyright © 2021 by Kayleigh King

All rights reserved.

No part of this book may be reproduced in any form or by any electronic or mechanical means, including information storage and retrieval systems, without written permission from the author, except for the use of brief quotations in a book review.

This is a work of fiction. Names, characters, businesses, places, events, locales, and incidents are either the products of the author's imagination or used in a fictitious manner. Any resemblance to actual persons, living or dead, or actual events is purely coincidental.

Cover Design by Qamber Designs https://www.najlaqamberdesigns.com

Copy Editing by Ellie McLove https://mybrotherseditor.netP

Proof Reading by Rosa Sharon https://mybrotherseditor.net

Epilogue Edited by Amanda at https://www.drafthouseeditorialservices.com

Beta Reading by G. Rivers, A. Ayala, B. Landers & C. Imb

ISBN: 978-1-7359304-3-5

For my tribe

Greer, Ramzi, Cat and Ash

I could write a novel about how much I appreciate and love each of you, but I'll keep it short and sweet.

I wouldn't be able to do all of this without you in my corner.

She looked my demons in the eye and smiled. She fell for the very thing I thought she'd fear.

— Vàzaki Nada

PLAYLIST

Fire Breather - LAUREL
Too Sad To Cry - Sasha Sloan
Flames - Tedy
Skinny - KALEO
I Want More - KALEO
Endgame - Talos
Feel Something - Clairo
Feel - FLETCHER
Part of Me - Isak Danielson
July - Noah Cyrus and Leon Bridges
Death of Me - PVRIS
Breaks My Back - Meg Myers
My Enemy - CHVRCHES

CHAPTER ONE
Remington

I was a happy person.

And I mean that. I'm not lying like so many others do when they slap a fake smile on their face and swear up and down their lives are great. I was *truly* happy. You know the old adage of the grass is always greener? My grass was the greenest.

Don't you get your panties in a twist, I'm self-aware enough to realize that saying this makes me sound like a condescending bitch. Before you come for my head for boasting about my pretty grass and perfect life, I'll warn you that life has already come for me. It came for me, knocking me on my ass and I haven't been able to get back up since.

My grass isn't so green, my smile isn't as bright and I'm no longer seeing the world through rose-colored glasses.

I took a lot of things for granted before the universe decided to give me a swift reality check. One of those being the ability to dream. Before my world exploded and the jagged pieces of it rained down on me like sharp glitter, I used to look forward to going to sleep. Not because I was exhausted and my body needed the rest, no I looked forward to the places my dreams would take me. They were always so vivid, so real. I was never one of those people who forgot their dream when they woke up, I remembered each and every one of them. They were a lovely escape.

Now, I dread going to sleep because I know when I close my eyes at night, I won't be met with the same kind of dreams I once had. Instead, I'm brought back to that moment that changed everything.

Do you know the exact moment when your life fell apart? Can you pinpoint the moment you knew nothing would ever be the same? Can you remember who stood next to you while it happened? Do you remember their face, their name?

I remember it all.

I remember every painful second as I stood there watching my world implode. I remember *his* face and the way his eyes stared into mine like he was looking into my newly broken, battered soul. I remember his name. I utter it like a curse now instead of the prayer it once was.

I remember it all and that is why I'm working so hard to forget.

Drinking away your pain isn't an easy task when you're a wolf shifter, our fast metabolisms mean the buzz from alcohol wears off fast. After three months of testing different methods and delivery systems, I've found the key to achieving a longer-lasting buzz. Large quantities in a short period of time. Not rocket science and it's pretty easy, especially when you're friends with the bartender.

Elsie lines up the shots in front of me, that grim look on her face firmly intact, just like it is every time I visit the club she works at. Which has become more frequent as of late. "I don't know how you manage to do this without needing your stomach pumped. I would be hungover until next Christmas if I drank all this. You're absolutely crazy."

"I'm a lot of things but crazy isn't one of them." I scrunch my face in dislike. "I believe the term you're looking for is *overachiever* or *existential crisis*, both are fitting in this instance."

Elsie laughs softly, her short blonde hair moving around her face as she shakes her head at me. She can laugh because she thinks I'm struggling to deal with the stress of midterms because she still believes I'm enrolled in classes. She has no idea the kind of things my family and I have had to face in the past year and a half. Elsie's poor human mind wouldn't be able to comprehend if I told her.

I was born and raised in this world, and I hardly believe what my life has come to.

A big part of me envies her. I wish I could live blissfully unaware of the dangers lurking in the shadows and the monsters that really exist out there. I wish I didn't know that sooner or later the biggest monster of them all is going to be showing up at our doorstep demanding our blood as payment for the monkey wrenches we've thrown into his plans.

"What are we drinking to tonight?" Elsie asks, picking up one of the shot glasses. She's not supposed to drink on the job, but she always makes an exception for me and has one with me.

I think it over for a minute, pondering the plethora of choices, finally I settle on, "To the boys that break our hearts and ruin our dreams."

My dreams take me back to the darkest moment, but they've also been infiltrated by *him*. He's the one person I want nothing to do with, but even in my dreams, I can't escape Jax Whitlock.

The burn of the alcohol running down my throat is welcome. Sometimes pain is the perfect distraction.

☾

Just like it's difficult for a wolf shifter to actually become drunk, it's very difficult and rare for us to have a hangover.

Difficult but not impossible. What I'm experiencing right now is proof of that. The humming from the heater is almost too loud for my sensitive ears and pounding head to handle. The thin stream of late morning light coming from behind the partially open blackout curtains makes my corneas burn. If I had the energy, I'd get up and shut the damn things, but I've elected to lie here and wallow in the pain a little while longer.

Last night is a little bit of a blur. After consuming the copious amounts of tequila shots Elise graciously provided me, it gets a little fuzzy. The faint memories of loud electronic music, flashing lights, and a mix of sweaty memories are all that I can recall at this time. That's probably for the best. No one needs to remember exactly what they did when they were blacked out. Some memories are best left forgotten, there are just some things that don't need to be replayed.

There is no reason to add to my embarrassing moment highlight reel. It's already extensive. My moments of greatness—as I prefer to call them—have been multiplying in the past six months. Every step and decision I make, are solidifying my role as the family screwup.

That role used to belong to Ryker, my oldest brother, but

since he discovered his long-lost mate is alive, he's really gotten his shit together. *What a fucking show-off.* He used to get brought home in police cars after vandalizing buildings and beating the crap out of people. He even disappeared for five years, didn't bother calling home once. Ryker would just send the occasional postcard to let us know he was still breathing. Now he's part of the alpha pair, leading the pack with his mate Pruitt. He's even going to be a *dad* in a couple of months.

Hell, all three of my brothers are doing better than me now. All mated and blissfully happy with their women. It's sick really how insanely in love they are with their mates. They always say you'll never understand the intensity of a mating bond until it happens to you, but my brothers have completely changed since meeting their mates.

Ryker is less volatile. Sure, he still loses his ever-loving mind occasionally and turns into a total rage monster, but it's happening less often. Especially since Pru is carrying his child. Ranger is no longer participating in underground cage fights and his dark gloomy cloud has dispersed since he found Winslow. Winnie is half brave and half *crazy,* a fun combo that keeps Ranger on his toes. And Ransom has finally stopped hiding parts of himself since Isabeau came into his life. Together they make a deadly pair, their bloodlust matching each other's.

Meanwhile, I'm here... alone in this hotel room and slowly watching the remaining pieces of my life rot.

Or at least I thought I was alone. The footsteps that stop in front of my room tell me that my solitude is about to end. I send a silent prayer that they'll go away, but the slow, methodical knocks ruin that dream.

I could ignore them, but it's not an option because I know who's out there. There is roughly thirty seconds on the clock before they break into the room. As it is, knocking was a courtesy.

Groaning, my stomach heaving and head spinning, I pull myself out from under the fluffy down comforter. My neck cracks when I glance down at my clothes. The short glittery dress I put on before going to the club clings to my body. The straps are hanging off my shoulders and the hem has ridden up to an—*inappropriate*—length.

I tug it back down because I don't need my newest sister-in-law seeing my bright pink thong. We are not *that* close yet.

With a glance at the mirror above the desk, I find that the dark makeup I'd applied last night is smeared all over my eyes. Walking to the door on unsteady feet, my fingers wipe at ruined mascara and eyeliner.

Opening the door, I lean against the doorjamb, blinking rapidly at the bright lighting in the hallway.

Eyes, the lightest—*coldest*—shade of blue I've ever seen stare blankly at me, and there's an equally unimpressed look on her face. "This is a good look on you," she comments dryly. "Trying something new with your makeup?"

My lips purse and my eyes squint at her. Deciding to play along, I tell her, "Yeah, I was going for *'hot mess Barbie'* meets *'sexy raccoon'*. I think I nailed it." Shrugging, as I attempt to wipe more of the makeup from my face, but I know it's no use. "What are you doing here, Isabeau?"

Of all the people to come showing up at my hotel room, she would be last on the list. My mother or Pruitt would be at the top, but I've been ignoring both of their texts and calls, maybe they finally got the hint?

"You've missed the past four training sessions." Beau cocks her head, her stare unrelenting. "I'm here to collect you since you've decided to act like a stubborn child and ignore all the phone calls."

I frown at her. "You didn't call me."

"No, I decided a more—*direct*—approach would be better. It's harder to *reject* me when I'm standing in front of you." The corner of her mouth tips up cockily. "You have ten minutes to get ready before I drag you out of this hotel by your hair."

"You wouldn't." I narrow my eyes. Isabeau is a highly trained assassin, being discreet is her thing. Surely, she wouldn't do something that would draw that much attention to her.

She takes a step forward, hand behind her back. Of course, she's dressed in head-to-toe black, a leather corset cinched tight around her waist. There're roughly five hidden weapons on her at all times. I've never met someone as lethal as her. *Wait.* That's a lie. There may be *one* other, but I don't want to ruin my day by thinking of him. "Wouldn't I? These training sessions are important and they're mandatory for all pack members."

Four months ago, Pruitt and Ryker gave Beau the beta female position of the pack. Seems the vampire is taking her new job very seriously.

Steeling myself, I shake my head. "I'll come to the next one, I don't feel good today." I already feel ten times better than I did when I first woke up, but still not well enough to go spar and train with my other pack members.

"Nope, that's not an option. You're coming today." Beau is completely unmoved by my compromise. "And you only have nine minutes now before I forcibly remove you from this building."

"Beau, *please*. I really don't want to go." I know who's been lingering around still. Why won't he just leave? He's never stuck around this long before.

"No, Remi." Isabeau's face hardens. "You know who's coming for us. We have to be prepared. This isn't up for discussion. Now go get cleaned up. Take a fucking shower, you reek of booze and cheap cologne. We don't need any bloodshed if you show up smelling like this."

"What? You think my brothers will lose it if I smell like a man?" That's ridiculous. They know I've been in a relationship before.

Cold eyes clash with mine. "It's not your brothers I'm worried about."

My stomach rolls again, but this time it's not the booze.

CHAPTER TWO
Remington

When I'm slammed into the mat for the third time in a row and the air momentarily leaves my lungs again, I decide I'm over this bullshit. I'm this close to either snapping at Isabeau who stands over top of me with an arrogant look on her face or getting up and stomping away like a toddler. The only thing stopping me from doing the latter is I've already been called a stubborn child today and I don't want to add any more fuel to *that* fire.

"I came here to train, not to have the shit beat out of me, *vampire*," I grit as I pull my aching body into a sitting position. My body now hurts from the absolute pounding I've gotten since I arrived back on pack property for the first time in a month. What was once my brother's backyard is now a vast training area. Various padded fighting mats sit among the forested area, different groups practice sparring with each of them. Across the way is the firing range Ransom built Isabeau, and Winnie is sitting there with a shockingly large rifle pressed to her shoulder, firing at a target fifty yards away.

I'm a wolf shifter, a pack animal by nature. I should feel at peace being surrounded by the chaos and noise of my pack, but instead I feel antsy. Antsy because I know *he* could show up here at any minute. I've gone a month without seeing him. While it hasn't been a great month by any means, it's been four weeks since I've felt the soul crushing *guilt* I experience when I lock eyes with Jax.

"You shouldn't have missed a month of training." Isabeau offers me a hand to help pull me up, but I brush it away, standing on my own. "You wouldn't be so rusty if you'd been here, *wolf*."

"Like that would do me any good fighting against *you*." I wave my hand lackadaisically in her direction. Beau has been trained since birth how to fight. Her first kill was at five years old. She had a much different upbringing than me. She can take on someone three times her size without much effort. Meanwhile, I feel like I've been hit by a bus. It doesn't matter how much I train; I would never be able to beat her. Which is endlessly frustrating.

"This is true." She nods once. "But you're not even trying."

"I told you I didn't want to be here." I yank the hairband from my shoulder-length hair, my ponytail has come loose from the ass-beating I've endured.

The hair I'd been trying to smooth out is abruptly messed up again when a hand ruffles the strands. Snarling, I whirl around to find my brother standing there, a stupid grin on his face. "Look who's risen from the dead." Ransom chuckles. "Are you finally done hiding from us?"

My fingers tangle in the newly formed knots in my hair, too frustrated to deal with it, I give up. Sneering at my brother, I snap, "I wasn't hiding. I was taking some time for myself and there is nothing wrong with that. If I recall, you went on a rogue wolf hunt for months and no one came and dragged *you* home."

"I was a thousand miles away. You've been stashed away in some hotel thirty minutes away from home." *Thirty-five minutes, but who's counting.* "I was also doing a job. You're running away because of what happened. I know you're grieving Gage but Remi, this isn't—"

I hold up my hand, cutting him off. "Stop," I order. "You want me here to train? Great, let's train, but *do not* bring up Gage again. The conversation of my dead boyfriend is off-limits, Ransom."

Grieving. I really wish it were that simple. It'd sure as hell be easier to blame my behavior on grief. Then I'd get a pass for jumping off the deep end like I have.

Ransom's ocean blue eyes, the same color as mine, flick to his mate who stands silently evaluating the exchange before he looks back at me. "Fine, but if you're here to train, you're going to put in some *actual* effort. No more of this half-assed bullshit I've been watching."

Blowing out a breath, I lift my chin. "Fine."

That's my only warning before I slam my fist right into his jaw. Beau laughs behind me, but I don't turn to look at her. My eyes never leave my brother as he stumbles back, caught off guard. Using his surprise to my advantage, I take the moment to deliver a punishing roundhouse kick to his chest. Just like Beau, Ransom is dangerously vicious. It will only be so long before he's slamming me into the mat under our feet.

Blood drips down his chin from his split lip. When he smiles at me excitedly, his teeth are coated in crimson, giving him an unhinged appearance. Ransom's wolf is wild, craves the fight. My wolf doesn't seek out violence, but if the opportunity appears, she's going to rise to the occasion. She was raised by alphas, after all.

Ransom's fist flies at my face, and I narrowly block it with my forearm before jumping out of the way. I'm subconsciously aware that the other pack members have stopped in their own sparring to watch ours. A Weylyn family fight is bound to draw attention. Someone almost always leaves with a broken bone.

His leg kicks out, swiping my legs out from under me. Landing on my ass, I roll out of the way just before his fist comes barreling toward me. It lands on the mat, inches away from my head. I kick my leg out and my foot connects with his knee with a satisfying *crunch*. His leg buckles and he falls forward. While he's down, I take the moment to spring back up.

Feeling confident that I was able to make Ransom fall, I hesitate just a moment too long to observe my handiwork before throwing another punch. His hand wraps around my fist so tight, bones crack. Ransom doesn't let go of my hand as he rises back to his feet. While he moves, he slowly, methodically, bends my wrist and my arm in the direction it's not meant to bend. My bones strain, my muscles scream in pain.

In an attempt to get him to loosen the hold on my limb, I bring my knee up, slamming it into his gut. He grunts and his hand loosens just enough for me to slip from his hold. With the hand that isn't still hurting, I deliver another blow to his smug face.

With a nasty growl, stemming from the wolf that lives within him, he charges me like a bull. His arms wrap around my middle, lifting me in the air. I bring my elbows down on his back repeatedly, trying to force him to drop me as he barrels us forward.

We land on the mat that was yards away from the one we started at. The crowd that watches moves with us but is mindful to not get too close. They don't want to get caught in the fray.

We roll as we land on the mat, I scramble to make sure I don't end up pinned under him. That will be the end of this little display if he gets that kind of upper hand. The delight that I'm able to pin Ransom to the mat before he can do the same to me is short lived. One second I'm feeling victorious, the next I'm being flipped over his head and landing on my back, promptly being put back in my place.

For the first twenty-plus years of his life, Ransom kept his wolf's strength hidden from us. We thought he was a docile, playful wolf, but that's what my brother wanted us to see. We had no idea that his wolf craved the fight, the bloodshed. His wolf is a warrior.

I've just gotten to my knees when his hand is wrapping around my neck. One-handed, he lifts me from the ground. Gasping for air, I shove at his hand, but it doesn't budge. Extending my claws, I dig them into his forearm and tear at the skin. It hurts like a bitch now, but he'll be healed in the next hour or so. He drops me and crumbles down into a crouching position. Momentarily distanced by his wounds, I snake my arms around his neck, effectively getting him into a choke hold.

My wolf howls in delight in my head that we are, for the moment, winning.

Grinning like a person gone mad, I apply more pressure to Ransom's airways. The sound of him choking for air only encourages me. People hoot and holler around us, cheering me on, but I ignore them all. My entire focus is on my opponent.

That is until the warm heat licks up my spine and every nerve ending in my body sizzles with awareness. A sensation that only happens when he's close. My body can sense him before I've even laid eyes on him. My head snaps up, searching him out. As if we are magnets, drawn to each other, I find him in less than a second.

He walks down the small hill incline from the house, Pruitt at his side, a content smile on her face. They're always together. My best friend has grown fond of the demon-wolf-shifter hybrid. He also has a smidge of warlock blood in him, but is such a small amount we hardly ever address it. He listens to whatever she's babbling on about, but he's not looking at her. His violet eyes are locked on me. The corner of his mouth lifts in a smirk as he assesses the situation.

Every time I see him, I feel like I've been punched in the gut. The guilt is so strong, there's physical pain. There's always a dull ache, something I've tried distracting myself from, but seeing Jax brings it rushing forward until it's a sharp, unbearable pain.

How can he be smirking right now? How can he seem so... unfazed? Doesn't he remember what happened?

The triumph I was feeling just seconds ago fizzles out, until all I can focus on is the man I've tried so hard to forget the better part of a year. Without thinking of the consequences, my arms loosen on Ransom's neck.

One second, I'm standing behind my brother, the next he's behind *me*. My effort to get away is unsuccessful. Strong hands wrap around my upper arms, keeping me in place. I bring my knee up just like I did before, but he saw it coming this time. One hand catches my leg, the other tightens its grip on my arm.

The look of anticipation on his face is my only warning before I'm airborne.

He whirls around once, gaining momentum, before hurling me twenty feet through the air. My body spins multiple times, blurring my vision, the distant sound of gasps fill my ears.

The tree in my direct path is what finally stops me. The wood cracks against the force of my body colliding with it, so do the bones in my right shoulder and ribs. Pain flares through my body when I finally return to the ground in a heap. Disoriented, I roll over to my back and blink slowly up at the tree branches above. All I can focus on is the ache in my bones, any other concern or sensation momentarily melts away.

It's a nice reprieve, but it's short lived.

I'm going to kill Ransom. As soon as I move, he's going to be roadkill.

Things come back into focus and the sound of shouting somewhere behind me has me turning my head with a groan. Back on the mat we were sparring on, Ransom and Jax stand toe to toe, yelling at each other. My brother's eyes have shifted into their glowing silver color and Jax's purple ones also glow as his own beast pushes to the surface.

What the hell is he so upset about?

Different pack members try to pull them apart, but they're both unmoved. Jax's hands are balled into fists at his sides, but from here I can see them shake in anger. He has no right to be angry. Isabeau finally steps in and pulls her mate back while Pru talks down Jax.

"What the fuck was that? You're supposed to be sparring!" Jax yells at Ransom. "How is she supposed to learn and improve if she's injured?"

"We *were* sparring, and she *is* learning," Ransom defends himself. "Just now she learned what happens when she gets distracted. She won't be able to let her guard down even for a second when the real fight comes. I just saved her from making that mistake when it actually counts."

I've heard enough of this.

Trying to pull myself up, I suck in a lungful of air, but immediately regret it when my broken bones scream in protest.

A small hand appears in front of my face, chipped black polish coating the nails. Following the arm up to her face, I find Winslow standing there, her weird two different colored eyes looking down at me. "I didn't know you could fly."

"*Ha ha*," I comment dryly before taking her offered hand. "You're *so* funny."

She grins while pulling me back to my feet. "I know, I'm thinking about taking this shit on the road, becoming a comedian or something."

I stagger a bit, unsteady on my feet, but with Winslow's steadying hands, I find my balance. "You could be like a traveling circus act. Talk to your ghost friends and after you're done helping them move on, you can tell bad jokes in dive bars."

Winslow's gift and sometimes curse is being able to see and communicate with the dead. She's basically a walking Ouija board.

She loops her arm around my waist and begins to lead me toward the house, leaving the yelling men behind us. "That actually doesn't sound so bad. Sounds a lot better than preparing to go to war."

The laugh that bubbles out of me, sounds sad even to my ears. *How did my life come to this?* For almost two years, my family has been fighting small battles against forces we never thought we'd face and now the final war is coming. I should be preparing for midterms right now, not preparing for battle. With a grim feeling filling my aching chest, I sweep my eyes over the sight in front of me and accidentally lock eyes with a set I try to avoid. My face turns to stone, my guard locking firmly in place, before turning away from him. "Yeah, anything sounds better than that."

CHAPTER THREE
Jay

Sixteen Years Ago

The cell feels bigger when she's gone, and it also feels so cold.

Nothing about the twelve-by-twelve room is warm or welcoming. The walls are bare of any pictures, just a shiny coat of white paint covers them. The floors are just as sterile looking, made of pristine white tiles. She is the reason this room ever has any warmth. She is the reason this room feels safe even when I know it's not.

Bad things happen here. Bad things are happening to her right now and I can't do anything about it. They keep saying that I'll figure out how to control it, that I'll learn to use the power coursing through my veins, but it hasn't happened yet. I wish it would, so I could use it on them. That way I could save my mom from the bad things they do to her.

Mom always tells me to be strong, to be brave, but I don't like when I'm alone in here. I'm afraid they'll come for me next. That *he'll* come for me.

He always tells me that I'm special, that he has big plans

for me, but I don't know what yet. I try to be brave, but he scares me. Sometimes when I dream, I see his face. Something about his eyes and the way he looks at me, makes my skin get goose bumps. The look is always so much more frightening in the dreams, because when he smiles, he has fangs and they're coated in blood. I think it's my blood, I always wake up before I can find out.

I hate those dreams.

The yellow ball bounces against the far wall before coming back to where I sit on the cold ground. I catch it and throw it again. I don't have many toys, but Mom says when we get out of here, she'll get me as many as I want.

She says that a lot, that we'll get out of here, but I'm not sure I believe her.

I want to believe her.

I want to believe one day Mom will take me to see the ocean like she always says she will. I want to meet the grandparents she always tells me stories about. I want to know if I look like my grandpa as much as she says I do. She tells me every night how thankful she is that I look like my grandpa and not my dad.

I'm thankful too, I don't want to look like the man who scares us both—the man who gives me nightmares.

Noticing Mom's bed across the room isn't made, I drop the ball and pull myself off the floor. Mom hates unmade beds, but they came for her so early this morning that she didn't have time to make it. They pulled her away before she could tell me goodbye.

She always tells me goodbye.

Tucking the sheets in and fluffing her pillow the way she likes, I step back and smile at my handiwork. She's been so tired and sad lately, hopefully this will make her happy. I think she's sad because there's something wrong with the baby in her belly, just like the last one. I'm not sure what happened to the last baby, but one day they took mom from our room and she came back with a flat tummy. She cried a lot after that.

I don't like it when she cries.

She tries to hide her tears from me because she doesn't want to make me sad, but I hear her when I'm supposed to be sleeping. She cries late at night under the blankets of her bed. I wish I could make it better, but I'm too small.

When I'm bigger, I'll be able to make it better. When I'm bigger, I'll make sure no one makes Mom cry again.

The metal door opens so abruptly, I jump away from the bed and retreat until my back hits the far wall. The bright lights from the hallway make the person standing in the doorway look like a dark silhouette. I can't make out their face, but the familiar cologne filling the room turns my blood to ice water.

Just like in my nightmares, he comes for me, but there is nowhere for me to go. Nowhere for me to hide. I want to be brave like Mom tells me to, but the voice in my head is telling me to run.

My heart beats hard in my chest and my hands shake at my sides.

"Jax." I don't like it when he says my name. "Come here."

My eyes dart around the room, looking for a way I could escape him, but he's blocking the only door.

"That wasn't a request." He gets angrier. *Darker*. He takes another step and I'm finally able to see the man I share half my blood with. Mom's right, we don't look anything alike.

His hair is light, or what's left of it is light. My hair is dark, just like Mom's. His eyes are also different than mine, but then again, I haven't met someone with eyes the same color as mine. Mom tells me they're special.

Special.

I'm really tired of being called that.

"*Now*, son."

Shoving my nervous hands into the pockets of the jeans that are two inches too short on me, I shuffle forward. Once I'm close enough, his big hand grabs my shoulder a little too tight, making me wince. He doesn't say anything else as he leads me down the bright white hallway. This hallway is familiar, it leads to the medical suites. I hate those rooms. They always stick me with needles and take my blood. They also have those loud machines that take pictures of my bones and whatnot. I hate those things too, they're too small. They make me feel like I can't breathe.

"Where's my mom?" I finally muster the courage to ask.

"I'm taking you to her now." His green eyes that don't hold an ounce of kindness in them slide down to me.

Not wanting to make eye contact with him, I look down. Each step we take, I count the tiles we pass. *One, two, three...*

He leads me through doorways, each one makes a buzzing noise when it opens. He has a special key card that opens each one. Mom always jokes about stealing one so we can leave. I know it's a bad idea, but still every time I see one, I contemplate taking it.

Fifty, fifty-one, fifty-two... "Jax, remember how I tell you that you are destined for greatness? That you're—"

"Special," I whisper before he can finish.

"Yes," he agrees. "Very special. You are the first of your

kind, a medical miracle. You are what I've been working toward for so many years. All the hours and deaths are worth it because you exist. Not many people are as great as you, as extraordinary. Some people are simply... *ordinary.* They have very little to offer and sometimes what they have to give isn't enough." He pauses by one more set of closed doors. "Do you know what happens to people who hold no value to me anymore?"

Eighty-five, eighty-six, eighty-seven...

I shake my head slowly but still don't look up.

The doors open and he pulls me through them, his fingers still dig painfully into my collarbone. I'm afraid he'll leave a mark. Mom won't like it if he does.

"People who do not add to the advancement of my work are deadweight. Completely useless to me. I do not have the time or resources to keep someone like that around." He talks about people like he's talking about an annoying fly that won't stop buzzing around his head. A nuisance. "I want you to remember this, Jax. I want you to remember that as long as you have something to give me, I will keep you around. I will allow you to keep breathing, but the second you turn into a burden, I will eliminate you."

Ninety-seven, ninety-eight, ninety-nine...

We walk around a corner into another wide hallway. When he jerks me to a stop, I finally lift my chin and take in my surroundings. I really wish I hadn't looked.

One hundred.

One hundred tiles, that's how many steps it took for my life to be forever changed.

When the hand on my shoulder slips away, so does every-thing else. All I can focus on is the sight before me. All I can feel is the crippling pain radiating from my chest as my heart breaks.

All the warmth, all the light, has been drained from her. Her skin looks too pale, her lips aren't as pink, her eyes that are usually a warm brown are dull, staring blankly at the ceiling. The white sheet is tucked all the way up to her chin, hiding the rest of her still body.

"*Mom!*" My voice comes out like a strangled cry. I hardly recognize it as my own.

"Your mother was deadweight," I hear him comment somewhere behind me, but it sounds like he's a hundred miles away. "So, she was dealt with accordingly."

The soles of my sneakers squeak on the tile floors as I take the timid steps toward her. The sound echoes around the eerily quiet space. I'm subconsciously aware that there are staff standing around where she lies. They stand back, giving her space.

"Mom?" I croak, my hand reaching out to shake her shoulder. Her skin feels colder than it should. I shake harder, but she still doesn't rouse. "Mommy, please wake up."

My plea goes unanswered.

As much as I fight them, I can't stop the tears from falling from my eyes. The sobs take over as I rest my head on her chest while I weep. She promised we would get out of here. We were supposed to go to the beach. She was supposed to take me home.

This isn't home.

She used to call it hell. At first, I didn't know what she meant by that, but I think I'm starting to understand.

"Jax," he calls my name sternly, but I ignore him.

He killed my mom. He said she was useless. She wasn't

useless. She was my mother. My protector. How am I supposed to survive without her? I shouldn't have to wonder this at the age of eight. I should have a lifetime with my mom.

My hands fist into the sheets while the grief feels like it might swallow me whole. I wish it would. Then the pain of losing her wouldn't be so bad.

I want to give up. I want my mom.

How can he just kill her like she's nothing? She was a person. She didn't deserve this. I don't deserve this.

An emotion begins to creep into my bones, eclipsing the monumental weight of her loss. It consumes me whole until all I can see is red. My hands no longer shake in fear but in pure rage.

I feel like burning the world down.

Whirling back around, I glower at the man responsible for this. "You killed her."

"Yes," he confirms apathetically. "She was brought here for a purpose. As she can no longer achieve such a purpose, she was eliminated. I'm sure you believe that she was important, but like I said, she wasn't. I have ten other women on standby who can do what she did, but hopefully for them, they're able to carry a baby to term. Or they'll end up like your mother. Another useless piece of medical waste."

Heat builds in my fingertips, the air around me begins to hum. My chest rattles and burns as something comes alive within me. A surge of power I've never felt rushes forward. "She wasn't useless," I whisper to myself.

"What was that, *boy*?" he presses.

"She wasn't useless!" I yell at the top of my lungs.

Like an explosion going off, the power that was building inside of me detonates. It flows from my fingertips and palms as I lift my hands at the man who ruined *everything*. It comes out like flames. Yellow and orange, they fill the room.

The distant sound of people screaming in pain registers in my head, but I don't stop. I let the anger and rage flow from my hands. This is what they've been waiting for, this is what they've wanted from me all along. I just don't think they were expecting to have it used against them.

People run and scream, the flames licking at their skin. Many of them are balled up on the ground. The man I want to see dead no longer stands in front of me, he sits in a heap against the wall. The outline of where he stood singed on the pristine white wall.

Like a battery, I run out of power and drop to my knees in the middle of the chaos. My whole body aches. My bones feel tired, my muscles are weak. My eyelids are heavy. I feel like I'm going to pass out.

The hollers and cries continue all around me, but he sits silently watching me. Half of his body is badly burned. His skin is red and blistered. Where hair used to sit on the side of his head is nothing but marred skin. His eyelid is so swollen I'm not even sure his right eye is still there. He doesn't make a sound, doesn't cry in pain.

Footsteps pound down the hallway. I blink rapidly, trying to stay awake as people rush in. A woman I recognize but don't know her name, kneels in front of him. She assesses his wounds, a look of confusion marring her features.

"Who did this?" she asks.

He slowly, almost lazily, looks at her before returning to stare at me. "He did."

The woman's head turns in my direction. "What? How—"

"*Hellfire*," he chokes.

Hellfire? I've never heard them say that word before.

"If he has the gift of hellfire, you know what this means." She eyes me skeptically.

I'm so tired, I just want to go to sleep.

His face cracks into a pained, evil smile. "It means he's even more special than we originally planned for, Nessa."

Her eyes flare with anger. "No, it means that one day he could burn everything you've built—*we've built*—to the fucking ground, Sterling. Look at you, look what he's already done."

He waves her off with his healthy hand. "Kaius will fix me up, he always does," Sterling croaks. "Jax won't be a danger to us. I showed him today what happens to the ones I have no use for. He knows that he has to be useful if he wants to live."

I want to live. I want to live so I can do exactly what Nessa said. I want to burn everything down.

I'll be brave and I'll be strong like she told me to be. I'll make her proud and I'll survive *because* of her. And then I'll make them regret it.

CHAPTER FOUR
Jax

Present

My body is drenched in a thin layer of sweat and my heart still beats erratically in my chest when I swing my legs over the side of the bed. Holding my head in my hands, I wait for the effects of the dream to diminish—for my body to return to normal.

I've been looking for the man who ruined my life for a long time with little to no luck. I may not be able to find him, but he's still able to find me in my dreams. Those nightmares I've had when I was a young kid locked in a cell, haven't stopped.

For the better part of twenty-four years, Sterling has been a part of me. Taunting me even while I sleep.

The looming threat that Sterling is going to make his final move soon has made the nightmare worse. They didn't used to happen every night, but they're happening more frequently. I dread sleep because of them.

I focus on my surroundings, grounding myself to what is happening now, not what happened in my dream. Birds chirp outside on the fire escape, car engines come from below and down the street, a car horn honks. The wind from the open window blows across my too hot skin, cooling me down.

My phone buzzes in my sheets, pulling my thoughts away from the nightmare and the woman I shouldn't think about as much as I do. Groaning, I search through the mess of tangled blankets until I find the obnoxious device. I know who's calling before I even look. There are only two people who contact me on this thing, and one of them only sends texts.

"Demon boy," she chirps. Pruitt Weylyn is the only one allowed to call me that. As the first friend I ever made, she reserves the right to use the stupid nickname. Anyone else would get their windpipe smashed. "Where are you? You're late. You're not bailing, are you? Jax, we agreed you'd participate in these training days. Beau and you know how to—"

"*Blondie*," I cut her off before she can ramble anymore. With a glance at the clock on the upside-down plastic crate that doubles as my nightstand, I tell her, "What are you going on about? I'm not late. There's still fifteen minutes before I agreed to be there. It's not like I have to account for *traffic*."

"You're always here annoyingly early." There's some shuffling and then a door closing. "You're never here right *on* time. So, what's wrong with you?"

The cons of hiding away with Pruitt for ten months while an assassin was searching for her means we had a lot of time to learn each other's quirks. I know this girl forward and backward, and she can almost say the same thing about me. There are some secrets I'm not ready to reveal to anyone. I trust her with my life, but there's still a side of *myself* I don't trust.

"Nothing is wrong," I lie easily. "I'll be there in a couple of minutes."

"Great," Pru says. "Ransom has everything set up at his place. Everyone should start showing up there shortly."

"Everyone?"

There's a pause. "I don't know. She's still ignoring my texts and calls. I'm not even sure where she's staying. She just up and left the house one night." *I know where she's staying. Hell, I even know the room number.* The hurt in Pruitt's voice is palpable. The past six months have been hard as it is, but the strain on her friendship with Remington has only made it harder for Pruitt. "Isabeau said she was going to find her and bring her today, so we'll see how that goes."

"You sent Beau after her?"

Getting out of bed, I shuffle around the loft, looking for the pair of pants I took off last night. Holding the phone between my ear and shoulder, I yank them on.

"Yes."

Grimacing, I mutter, "Bold choice."

Isabeau is a cut first, ask questions later kind of gal. Remington doesn't stand a chance telling the vampire *no*.

"I was out of options, Jax."

The sound of the toilet flushing comes through the line making me freeze in my search for a clean shirt. "Were you *peeing* while on the phone with me?"

"Desperate times, desperate measures. This kid is sitting *on* my bladder," Pru groans. "They're measuring a week ahead of schedule. Which shouldn't be a surprise, my mate is the size of the goddamn *Jolly Green Giant*."

Just a hell of a lot less *jolly*.

"I'm hanging up now," I announce. "I'm not answering

your calls anymore if you're going to pee while you talk to me."

"That's fair," she concedes. "See you in a minute."

I pull the clean black thermal over my head before shoving my feet into my well-worn boots. The leather is scuffed, and the ends of the laces that I leave untied are frayed.

Once dressed and my teeth brushed, I summon the power that makes me so *special*. In my head, I imagine Pruitt's living room at her house on the lake. My skin grows warm, but it doesn't burn. There aren't any flames.

There haven't been in sixteen years.

What happened in the hallway where I discovered my mother had been killed, was a fluke. For almost a decade they tried to get me to recreate that moment when my hellfire was a physical, perceptible thing. Sterling himself tried for a few months before he shipped me off to be trained and molded by his partner Nicolai. Nicolai put me through hell trying to get the flames to return, but they never did.

While I never learned how to create actual flames, I learned how to use my hellfire in different ways. One of those ways is traveling between the planes of this world. I don't like the word *teleport*. It reminds me of a bad fantasy novel from the eighties, but essentially, using hellfire I'm able to travel to places within seconds. As long as I have a clear location in mind, I can go anywhere. It works best if it's a place I've been before.

Like Pruitt's living room.

In the time it takes me to exhale the air in my lungs, I've left the loft apartment I've been staying in and now stand in front of Pru's fireplace.

Ryker, Pru's mate, sits on the couch hunched over a bowl of cereal on the coffee table. He doesn't look remotely surprised to see me anymore, the wonderment of my gift is long lost on him. He's never been a big fan of mine. The fact I was raised by the enemy rubs him the wrong way. He also isn't a fan of Pru being such good friends with me.

"You're making a better door than a window, demon," he grumbles around a mouthful of food. "Move your ass, you're blocking the TV." His tattooed hand gestures at the large television mounted over the fireplace.

Ryker Weylyn is covered in tattoos. Besides his face, every inch of his visible skin is covered in artwork. If he has bare skin, I've yet to see it and nor do I want to. Some things are best left a secret.

Leisurely, I shift out of the way and because I can't resist poking the beast with a long pointy stick, I plop down on the opposite side of the sectional couch from him. "Anyone ever tell you that your joy is contagious? I can feel it radiating off you in waves."

Without turning his head, he fires back, "Anyone ever tell you that you're highly irritating—like a gnat that won't stop buzzing?"

"Yeah, you did. Just last week I believe. I think you may need some new material."

"Or maybe I just need you to stop *buzzing*." Blue eyes, the same shade as the ones I shouldn't think about as often as I do, slice to me. "Why are you here?"

Footsteps come from the hallway as Pruitt enters the room. "*Boys*," she scolds. "You two are like oil and water, I swear." She finishes pulling her long white-blonde hair into a ponytail before sending her mate a look. "He's here because I asked him to be. We're heading over to Ransom and Beau's together."

Ryker drops the spoon in his bowl and stands quickly from the couch, concern crossing his face. "You're not training, Pru. You're five months pregnant, we talked about this, you need to slow down."

Pruitt's face hardens. The human side of Pru is calm but the wolf side is brutal. The alpha wolf living inside of her hates being told what to do. It doesn't matter *who's* giving the commands, she's not going to react well. "I don't need you to tell me I can't train. I'm not an idiot, Ryker, I know it's not safe. We already have an uphill battle with this pregnancy, there's no need to put additional strain on my body." No one knows why, but wolf shifters struggle to carry their pups to term. The population of wolf shifters has been dropping by the year. "I'm just going to offer support to my pack. *Jax* is the one who's going to help train."

Who better to help train Pruitt's pack than someone who was trained by the people we will be going up against? Sometimes being raised by the enemy comes in handy.

"Good." The hard line in Ryker's face softens as he moves around the couch to caress the side of his mate's face. Ryker was head over heels in love with Pruitt before he knocked her up, but now that she carries his child, he looks at her like she hung the moon. It's an interesting sight to observe. Ryker is harsh—unforgiving—but for his mate, he's a total pussy. "I have to go check something out with Sawyer. The fence on the east side of the territory went down again, we're going to see if it's something we need to worry about or just some deer being bothersome."

Playing with a loose string on the hem of my thermal, I

laugh dryly. "Sawyer went from hunting rogue wolves with Ransom to checking fences with you? That's a serious demotion."

Pru rolls her eyes while Ryker glowers at me. "Might I remind you the last time Sawyer was hunting a rogue with my brother, he got caught in an avalanche and almost died?"

Shrugging apathetically, my lips pull into a smirk. "Still better than checking fences with *you*."

The growl that comes from his chest is quickly soothed when Pruitt lays her hand on his shoulder. "Okay, as always, this is super fun. Let's do it again sometime soon. Jax let's go." She waves her hand at me.

Climbing to my feet, I follow her out of the house, saluting mockingly at Ryker as I pass him. His response is to growl at me again which only causes me to laugh. Ryker Weylyn isn't scary. I know scary, he doesn't come close.

"Why do you insist on pissing him off?" Pruitt sighs over her shoulder.

"Because, Blondie, he makes it *so* easy."

☾

IF SOMEONE HAD TOLD ME TEN YEARS AGO THAT ISABEAU Claremont would settle down and take a wolf shifter as a mate, I would have laughed in their face. Just like me, she was created in Sterling's lab to be nothing but a weapon for him to use as he sees fit. I'm skilled and deadly in my own right, but Isabeau is lethal. As she should be, she was the daughter of Nessa Claremont, the notorious vampire assassin after all. Not only was Nessa one of Sterling's right hands, she's also one of the original vampires, meaning Beau's bloodline is even more prestigious than mine. Not that I think being the son of a psychopathic mad scientist is prestigious. I am, however, envious that Beau was able to have her evil parent killed before I was able to do the same.

Don't get me wrong, I'm happy she was able to kill Nessa. The more allies we take from Sterling, the weaker he is. Pruitt killed Nicolai almost two years ago and now with Nessa gone, the only one that remains is Kaius. We have to get to him before we can even think about going for Sterling. Without Kaius, Sterling is vulnerable. Mainly because Kaius is the last full-blooded necromancer in existence and for decades, he's been the one to bring Sterling back from the dead. He's basically Sterling's twisted enabler.

After Nessa was taken care of, Isabeau mated *and* married Ransom before shacking up with him in the house he bought for her. I wouldn't go as far as to say she's been *domesticated*. No, she's still feral as hell but now she has a bathroom with two sinks in it so she can brush her teeth at the same time as her mate or some shit. I don't know. This world is foreign to me. Even the idea of calling a place my home is foreign.

Having a home or a family has been the last thing on my mind.

From the age of eight, I had a goal.

I was going to take down the man who ruined my life. The man who used my mother as a living incubator and then threw her away like a piece of garbage when she had nothing left to give. I had a plan. I was going to pretend to play the role I was given, the dutiful soldier, the pawn on a much bigger board. All while I was going to be fighting from the inside to get to my target. There was a time I didn't think I'd make it past the age of sixteen. Not to sound like a cliché, but I was going to kill the man who took everything from me or die trying.

The plan has changed, but the goal is the same.

I thought I was going to do this alone, but for the first time, I have allies. The entire Weylyn family has my back. Or almost the entire Weylyn family. One of them would like to see me beat into a bloody pulp and left for dead.

I know she's here before we exit Pruitt's white Jeep. I can feel it in my very bones when she's nearby. For a month I've kept my distance, never allowing myself to get too close, but it doesn't matter if I leave her for ten months or one month, I'd recognize that sensation anywhere.

Remington Weylyn is hard to forget. She crashed into my life like a wildfire, leaving burns that will never heal right. Each time those blue eyes clash with mine, they leave another scar.

Pru is talking to me about the plan for the weekend. While I'm sure it's a riveting topic, I lose interest the second I lay eyes on Remington.

As she glares up at me from where she holds Ransom in a choke hold, I feel more permanent marks slashed into my skin. She didn't used to look at me with hatred in her eyes, they were always so gentle and accepting. After all this time it still isn't easy to know I'm the reason the tenderness is gone. That it's my fault.

She's not as volatile as her brothers, never has been, but she can still hold her own. I've seen her do it multiple times.

Remi was doing well fighting Ransom, even though it was clear to me that he was going easy on her. Her tenacity and all-out stubbornness are what makes her so strong. She would argue with someone that the sky is purple before she admits she's wrong. Her unwillingness to be defeated by her brother is what kept her on her feet, or it was until she finds me watching her.

One split second of distraction has her losing whatever advantage she had over Ransom. In movements that are too fast for the human eye, Ransom has Remington in his grip. I know what's going to happen before he does it. The cocky bastard's face even splits into a knowing smirk before he sends her flying through the air.

I'm frozen in place watching her body spin uncontrollably. Next to me Pruitt gasps and moves into action faster than I do. I'm not sure what good she thinks she'll be able to do, but she runs down the remaining portion of the hill in the direction of where her best friend is thrown.

The sound of Remington's body colliding with the tree has the beast I keep caged tearing at the locks. His furious growls block out any other noise momentarily. His anger coupled with my own has me moving across the space before I can think it over.

The look of surprise on Ransom's face as I roughly shove him backward confirms what I already know. My reaction is out of character and inappropriate, but logic and reason mean nothing to me right now. I can smell Remi's blood from here, I heard her bones *break*.

"Watch it, *demon*," Ransom warns, his eyes narrowing, daring me to continue.

"What the fuck was that? You're supposed to be sparring!" I yell in his face. He has an inch on me height-wise but that doesn't mean jack shit. I could have him on his ass in half a second if I wanted to. "How is she supposed to learn and improve if she's injured?"

Pruitt appears at my side and her hand wraps around my wrist. She tugs at me, trying to pull me away, but I'm unmoved.

What the fuck was Ransom thinking? We can't afford to have people getting hurt right now. We need everyone at their best at all times, even with our advanced healing, those couple hours while we recuperate put us at risk. And to hurt his own sister?

"We *were* sparring, and she *is* learning," Ransom defends himself. "Just now she learned what happens when she gets distracted. She won't be able to let her guard down even for a second when the real fight comes. I just saved her from making that mistake when it actually counts."

"She needs to learn how to protect herself against Sterling. Beating her so bad she can't fight anymore for the rest of the day doesn't do her any fucking good!"

"*Jax*," Pru warns at my side. "That's enough."

I'm absentmindedly aware of Beau trying to pull Ransom away, but he too isn't budging.

"Maybe I just need to protect her from *you*." Ransom's wolf rears forward, his eyes shifting into their silver forms. Like pools of mercury. "We both know you're part of the reason she's been hiding from *us*. Her *family*." He pounds his hand on his chest. "What'd you do, Jax? What did you do that made her hate you so much?"

She needs someone to blame for what happened to Gage. The anger she already had for me made me the easy choice. I can bear her anger, it's for the best anyway. It just solidifies the wall I put between us.

"You have no idea what you're talking about," I snarl my warning.

"Maybe I would if my own sister wasn't avoiding me!"

Ransom is hauled back abruptly when his mate decides she's had enough.

He tries to fight her and return to his spot in front of me, but Pruitt quickly gets in the middle. She holds her arms up at her sides to ensure she keeps space between us. "That's enough!" The alpha power that seeps from her pores is almost suffocating. Her green eyes glow as her wolf surges to the surface. To any other wolf shifter, the power is strong enough to stop them in their tracks. My wolf is completely indifferent to it. A pack hierarchy means nothing to him. *No one* can control him. "Ransom, Remington's boyfriend, died in front of her, and she is *grieving*. We agreed to let her have space. That's not Jax's fault, stop acting like it is." Her head turns in my direction. "Jax, stop picking fights with the members of my family. One day they're going to snap and I'm going to have to stand over your dismembered body and say, *'I told you so'*. I don't really want to do that."

The corner of my mouth pulls into a smirk as I snort on a laugh. "It's adorable that you think that." Patronizingly, I pat the top of Pruitt's head before baring my teeth at Ransom, "I would honestly love to see them try." If my hellfire didn't take them out, my beast would.

Ransom's fist pulls back, but I'm nothing but a thin veil of smoke before he can make contact with my face.

☾

REMINGTON LEANS AGAINST THE COUNTERTOP IN THE KITCHEN, clutching her injured arm with her good one. Her face pulls in a wince when Winslow presses a bag of peas to her side. The shirt Remington had been wearing previously is gone, leaving her in only a bright orange sports bra. Dried blood coats the corner of her mouth and temple and her side is already bruised but healing. The ice compress will speed up the process, but her arm needs tending to.

She does a double take when I leisurely enter the kitchen, it's as if she wasn't expecting to be in the same room with me again. Remi thinks she's been given space, that for the past month, she's been alone, but I was closer to her than I am now just last week. She just didn't realize it. It helps that the club she frequents is always busy and she insists on drowning herself in cheap liquor. Her heightened senses are shit when she's in that state. She gets so drunk I could be one of the douchebags she allows to grind up against her and she'd never know it.

Her recklessness makes me want to burn shit down.

"You need to set that arm." I nod my head at her dislocated shoulder, the bone bulging from the skin.

Remington scoffs. "*Oh really*? I hadn't thought of that. I was going to just let it *hang* this way a little while longer."

Unimpressed with her lashing out, I cross my arms and lean against the fridge. "Your body is already trying to heal. If your bones fuse back while your arm is in this state, we will have to rebreak them to get your shoulder in place. I'm just trying to save you from some unpleasant pain in the long run. *Trust me*, it's not a fun time." The rebreak is always ten times more painful than the initial fracture. Nicolai at least got faster at it with time.

She shoves the frozen peas away from her side before taking a threatening step in my direction. "I don't need you to *save me* from anything. Just like I don't need you standing up for me with my brother. I've got everything under control."

My eyes flick over her, head to toe. She's thinner than she was, dark circles sit under her eyes, the happy spark that used to reside in those blue pools has been replaced with an angry glow. Remington looks like a shadow of the person I first met. "Yeah, looks like you've got it all figured out," I observe sardonically before backing away toward the door I'd entered through just seconds ago. "Well since you've got this all handled, I'll go."

My back is to her when she spits out, "Good. I don't fucking need you, Jax."

"So you've said." *Many times.* Yet I still don't believe her. She needs help. Not necessarily from me, but someone. She's found herself on a path that doesn't end well. "But..." Pausing in my halfhearted retreat, I hold up a finger before spinning back around. "Do you know how to reset a shoulder, Winslow?" I point my finger at the witch, who looks like she's been caught doing something bad with the way her big, doll-like eyes widen.

"Uhh, I'm afraid my area of expertise extends to talking to dead people and occasionally, shooting a gun, *but* I wouldn't consider myself an expert in the latter," Winslow offers reluctantly. Talking to the dead is putting it mildly. Like Isabeau and I, she too is a creation of Sterling's. More importantly, she's the biological daughter of Kaius. Winnie has necromancy powers but refuses to use dark magic like that. The price is too high.

Remington curses under her breath before instructing, "Winnie, go get Beau. That vampire knows how to do everything."

"Good idea," I praise, shuffling on my feet.

Winslow looks between us warily before sighing, "I'll be right back, there better not be any bloodshed before then."

"I wouldn't dream of it." I lock eyes with Remi across the room. "Cross my heart, hope to die," I drawl while dramatically making a crossing motion over my chest. "Besides, Remi here knows I'm very skilled at keeping my hands to myself." Low blow, but she deserves it. Her attitude sucks.

Winslow hesitates only a second before dashing out of the room.

Remi waits for the sound of the back door closing before glaring at me. "You think that's funny? You think what you did is something to make jokes about?"

Stalking forward, I shake my head. "No, I don't find any of this funny," I admit. "I usually find your unwillingness to back down—*to accept defeat*—as a strength. It's a trait I admire in you. Fuck, if I'm being honest, I also find it hot, but not right now. Right now, your stubbornness has made you ugly." She's so caught up in scowling at me, that Remi doesn't realize I've gotten too close for comfort until it's too late. She tries to get around me, but I've effectively boxed her against the kitchen island. "You have an entire family standing by to offer you help, but instead you're off rebelling against them. I'm standing here right now offering you help, just like I did six months ago, but you shoved me away then too." She literally shoved me into the dirt.

Defiantly, she lifts her chin. "I don't want your help any more now than I did then."

"I'm aware, love," I coo, a taunting grin splitting my face. "But I'm not giving you a choice."

Weak from the pain she's in while her bones heal, her

attempt to stop what happens is useless. It also works to my advantage that she only has one good arm at the moment. I have her body turned around and her hips pressed into the marble countertop before she can so much as make a noise. Using my own hips to pin her in place, I bend to talk low into her ear. "I'll make it quick. In and out, I promise."

Being this close to her is dangerous. It stirs the beast inside me.

She tries to free herself, but I'm unmoved. "What the hell, Jax! Let go of me or I swear to God I'm going to put your balls into a blender and—"

Her threat, while widely creative, is never finished. It dies on her tongue when I take her wounded arm and with a movement I've perfected over the years, twist the limb back into its socket. Remi's pained cry makes something in my chest ache, but I don't dwell on it. "There we go. All better."

My hand runs soothingly over her arm once before I step back, returning the space she so dearly wants. Wordlessly, I offer her the bag of peas Winslow had left when she turns around to face me once more.

She slaps the frozen vegetables out of my hand, and they go skidding across the dark wood floors. "If you ever put your hands on me again, I'll kill you."

"There was a time you were begging for me to touch you," I remind her. That moment—*that night*—will forever haunt me. A moment of weakness that would have had lasting consequences had I not stopped.

You did what was necessary, the rational side of my brain reminds me.

"I didn't hate you then." Fury burns in her ocean blue

eyes, the angles of her pretty face twist with wrath. "Do you hear me, Jax? I *hate* you."

"Yes, I hear you," I concede. "I just don't believe you."

Before she can slash me with more false, ugly words, I leave the room to let her cool off.

CHAPTER FIVE
Remington

It's an odd—*almost unimaginable*—thing when the people you once confided everything in are the ones you keep the most secrets from now. Or the people you once spent the most time with are the very people you now avoid. Or the people who once gave you the biggest smiles now cause the saddest frowns.

Pruitt was—*is*—my best friend. We shared everything with each other. Every secret, no matter how insignificant, was shared between us. Spending time with her was my favorite thing, but now as she tries to catch up to me on Ransom's driveway, I'm consumed by the overwhelming need to flee. I don't want to talk to her, I don't want to spend time with her. I really don't want anything to do with her.

"Remi!" The happy smile on her face is a genuine one. Despite the shit show that is headed our way, Pruitt has every reason in the world to be happy right now. "Wait up!"

I contemplate pretending that I can't hear her for a solid two seconds before I remember that excuse doesn't work with shifter hearing. *Goddammit.* After my encounter with Jax, I'm not in the headspace for this. There are too many emotions bubbling up in my body and I'm afraid one of them is going to escape right here in front of Pru.

With a steadying breath, I turn on my heels to face her. "Hey." *That's a normal thing to say, right?*

Pru gives me a puzzled look. "*Hey?*" she repeats like a parrot. "I haven't seen you in a month and all you have to say is, *hey?*"

"People are still saying that, right?" My brows rise in question. "Would you have preferred *hello* or maybe *hi* instead? How do we feel about *howdy?*"

"No, I would *prefer* if my best friend would actually talk to me." Her light green eyes are full of sorrow, a sentiment I can't deal with right now. I'm barely handling my own, I can't take on hers. "You've been gone for a month, Rem. You haven't answered a single one of my calls or texts. I'm worried about you." She reaches out to take my hand in hers. "I know you're going through a lot and you need time, but Gage wouldn't want you to suffer like this."

Each time I hear his name, my stomach bottoms out and my chest grows so tight I can't bring air into my lungs. I suffocate on the memory of him.

Harsher than I mean to, I retract my hand from her. "No, it's—" For a brief second, I almost explain myself, but the words won't form. The secrets I've been carrying, the guilt I've been harboring, are stuck inside of me. Stuck there to torment me. But the torment is my punishment, and I must bear it. "I know you want to help me, Pru, but this is something I need to deal with on my own. Your concern is appreciated, but not needed."

She wants to argue with me, I can see it by the way her

eyes narrow and her lips twitch with many unspoken words. "Fine, I won't push it, for *now*, but Remi, I miss you."

"I know, I'm sorry." I push the strands of my messy hair away from my face while giving her my best reassuring smile.

Her own smile forms, but hers is more believable than mine. "I'll see you this weekend, right? Winnie said she should have it all set up by noon, but I might sneak over earlier than that."

Pru all but bounces on her toes with excitement, meanwhile, I've never been more confused. "What are you talking about?"

The happy energy that'd taken over her melts away like a bucket of ice water crashed over her head. Hurt fills her eyes and she takes a step away from me. "You really haven't checked a single message from us, have you?"

My phone has been off for two weeks. The constant buzzing was making my hangover headaches worse. I'm not even sure it's charged at this point.

My silence is her answer.

She laughs coldly. "Well, I guess it's a good thing it's only my baby shower and not something really important we needed to tell you."

Her baby shower? Fuck.

When we first learned Pru was pregnant, I had planned on being there for all the important things. I was supposed to get over my shit and then be there for her. I'd intended to be the one who set up her baby shower. I wanted to do that for her, but in my own sick grief, I'd completely forgotten about it.

"Pru—"

"It's fine," she cuts off my apology. "You don't have to come. I know you don't want to be around us. Like I said, it's

Saturday, and it's at Ranger and Winslow's. I'll understand if you don't show up."

Clearing my throat of the emotion that'd bubbled up, I ask, "Do you want me to come?" I wouldn't want me there. I'm no longer the life of the party.

"Of course, I want you there, Remington. Don't say dumb shit like that."

"Okay, then I'll be there," I promise her even though when I say the words, I feel like I'm lying.

☾

IN MY HASTY RETREAT TO GET AWAY FROM JAX, I'D forgotten that I hadn't been the one to drive here. For a minute, I thought about just shifting into my wolf form and running back to the hotel, but it would be a little difficult to slip back into the building while a wolf. That's a sure way to get animal control called. I could shift back into my human form but walking around in my birthday suit in public is something I try to avoid.

I'd just pulled up the car service app when Isabeau appeared out of nowhere with her car keys in her hand. She didn't ask, just silently tilted her head in the direction of her parked Jeep. That's the thing about Beau, she doesn't talk a lot, but she doesn't have to. She knows what's going on at all times, nothing is missed by her observant eyes. I would bet money she knows more about me and what's going on than she's letting on.

We ride in silence through the back roads of our Montana home. Pack territory covers thousands of acres around the lake I grew up on. It gives us plenty of room to run freely in our wolf forms without any humans stumbling upon us. It's our safe haven and soon we will have to protect it with our lives.

Life was never this hard. The fighting is starting to become exhausting. The light at the end of the very dark tunnel is nowhere to be seen yet. With each person we eliminate, there's another one standing between us and Sterling. How he brainwashed so many people to follow him like some kind of fucked-up god, I'll never understand.

He's just another power-hungry male, desperate for control. There isn't a line Sterling won't cross to achieve his goals. His limits are nonexistent, as are his morals. No one with a conscience would kidnap women and forcibly impregnate them with modified embryos in an attempt to build the perfect genetic creation.

Sterling thought he'd created the perfect beings with Jax and Isabeau, but his perfect masterpieces turned on him. *Big time.* No one wants Sterling dead more than those two. Except maybe me. I want him dead so I can get my fucking life back.

When Beau slows the car down, I pull my mind away from the dark thoughts that consume me when I think of Sterling. Confused, I look out the window to see where we are and when I see the familiar wrought iron gate, my stomach sinks.

"I didn't know if you wanted to go home or back to the hotel," Beau comments from the driver's seat.

Behind those gates sits the home I was raised in. Up until a month ago, I still lived there. At twenty-two, almost twenty-three, I should have been dying to move out, but I wasn't in a rush. I was going to finish school and then figure out what I wanted to do.

A month ago, I couldn't get away from the house fast enough. I had to get away from it before it truly made me lose my mind. I would lay there at night and think about how different it all was and how nothing is ever going to be the same. I couldn't breathe there. The memories were suffocating me. The concerned looks from my parents were appreciated at first but grew irritating with time. The constant hovering and questions made me want to punch something.

I'd finally had enough and I left.

Without warning and without a word, I packed a bag and left. Went to the hotel and haven't been back since. All I offered my mother and family was a text telling them I was fine. That's *all* I could offer them.

I do miss the liveliness of the house. People are always there. My mom loves to entertain and insists on having all the events at her house. Pack members are frequently stopping by to talk to my dad, the now retired alpha of over fifteen years. The hotel is quiet and still, but I think that's what I need right now.

"No," I finally answer, tearing my eyes away from the gates that would lead me home. "I'm not ready to go home."

Beau nods once, her face unreadable. "Okay," she relents. "That's fine. Just let me know when you are."

Isabeau isn't someone I've ever felt close to. She's standoffish, hard to bond with, unlike Winslow, but right now I'm really thankful she's the one here. She won't push me like the rest of them. "Thank you, Beau."

We drive away from the gates. She doesn't say a word as she drives down the road that cuts through our small town. Not until we are two miles away from the hotel does she glance in my direction. "I'm not sure there's a right or wrong way to mourn. The concept is foreign to me and truthfully, it doesn't make complete sense to me, but I do know that at some point you have to let go. Or it's going to drag you down with it." *I already know this.* "If this is what you want, I'll be on your side and support your decision. Your family will fight it, but I'm not going to tell you what you can or can't do. You're an adult and you can make your own choices."

I shift uneasily in my seat, not sure how I'm supposed to respond to that. She's giving me what I want, but why does it still feel wrong?

"You just have to decide if this is really the path you want to go down. Take it from someone who chose the wrong path and had to fight like hell to get off of it, you should really think about what you're doing, Remington. Sometimes there's no going back. Some choices have lasting consequences we can't undo no matter how much we want to." Beau's past is covered in the blood of her victims. Ransom is the only one who truly knows what all Beau's done, but I know it's not a pretty sight.

"I don't know what I'm doing," I admit with a sigh while leaning my head against the window. "Everything I do feels wrong." The guilt isn't allowing me to move forward. It's like quicksand. Each movement I make only sucks me farther into it and seeing Jax today made me sink deeper. I'm barely keeping my head above the surface. He makes me feel all the emotions I've tried *too* hard to repress.

Beau pulls into the parking lot of the hotel and parks the car in a spot close to the entrance. Turning her head, she tells me, "I'm not going to sit here and tell you that I relate to what you're going through. I've never had to grieve someone like you have. When my brother and Nessa died, I only felt relief. I know how that sounds—"

Horrible? Reprehensible? Shameful? Take your fucking pick.

I can't help the laugh that escapes me as I listen to her. I lose myself in the hysterics, laughing until I can't breathe. My hand awkwardly undoes the seat belt across my chest so I can double over and laugh even harder. It's not funny, no part of this is funny and that's why as I laugh, sad tears run down my face.

"Remington." It takes a lot to rattle Beau, but right now as she watches me lose my fucking mind, there's concern in her voice.

I make the mistake of looking at her and the look of worry marring her usually impassive face only makes it worse. I laugh until they turn into choked sobs. I haven't cried in months. "It's not funny," I gasp while I try to steady my breathing so I can calm myself down. "I know it's not funny..." My hands wipe away the tears streaming down my face. "But it is." I snort another unwelcome laugh. Angry with my sudden outburst, I slam my hand against the dashboard in frustration, before throwing myself back in my seat dejectedly. "*Fuck!*" My hands clutch my head, my fingernails digging painfully into my scalp.

"I don't understand what's happening."

You and I both.

Wiping my tears away, I clear my throat. "Yeah, I've been saying that a lot myself lately." Grabbing my hotel key card from the cup holder, I reach for the door handle. "Thank you for the ride."

"Remi." Isabeau reaches out and grabs my arm before I can leave.

Looking over my shoulder at her, I say, "I never thought I'd have something in common with you, but here I am."

"You're being annoyingly vague."

With a sad smile, I admit, "You're not the only one who felt relief." With that, I tear my arm from her and escape from her vehicle. I can't breathe until the doors of the hotel lobby close behind me.

CHAPTER SIX
Jax

The building that once stood here has been resigned to nothing but charred rubble. What's left of it is almost unrecognizable, but I know what the burned establishment used to be. Nicolai used to bring me here.

It was one of Sterling and Kaius's favorite dumping grounds for the experiments that went wrong. The bodies they leave on the side of dark roads or in run-down buildings draw too much attention and because of that, they try to avoid it. Ideally, if they have the time and opportunity, they'd bring them here.

What better place to hide the bodies of their experiments than at a crematorium? No one would look twice at a body brought here, especially if they came with falsified documents. It also helps that this specific chain of crematories is owned by one of Sterling's confidants.

It's a little on the nose that Kaius would own a business that revolves around dead people, but it's benefited both him and Sterling immensely over the years. This specific one in Connecticut was their go-to location. It's far enough away from Sterling's breeding facility in New York that no one would draw a connection between the two, but it's close enough that bodies could be transferred over state lines within a few hours. Kaius and Sterling are fucked in the head, but they're smart as hell.

Their cleverness is what's kept us from finding them. Isabeau spent almost a year searching for Kaius and I've been trying to get to Sterling since I was eight years old, neither one of us has had much luck. Nicolai did an excellent job *of* keeping me away from Sterling. The last time I was in the same room as my father is when I almost burned him to death.

Every time I think I'm getting close, they're one step ahead of me.

Like now, I came here searching for clues on Kaius's whereabouts to find the place burned to the ground. They knew someone would come searching.

Despite everything being a burned mess, I shuffle through the remains. Hoping something survived the flames. I duck under another strand of caution tape left by the fire department, and travel farther into the building. Almost the entire roof is gone, only a few unstable pieces hang from the remaining bits of framework still standing. The moon up above casts soft light into the destruction.

In the room that was once an office, is a tape outline of a body, left by the arson investigator. It's no surprise Kaius set this place ablaze with people still inside. The man's psychopathic tendencies make it so he doesn't think twice about taking a life.

The kind of dark magic Kaius uses to bring people back from the dead has a price. Each time he uses his necromancy powers, he burns away a piece of his soul—his empathy. Kaius's soul is long gone.

The metal file cabinet in the corner has already been emptied, the drawers hang open like someone ransacked them in a rush. Same with the desk. Whatever paperwork that once sat on top of it is nothing but black ash now.

Stepping over the structural beams that had fallen, I make my way further back. There's a staircase that leads to the basement where the bodies were kept and ultimately cremated.

For the past six months, if I wasn't secretly watching over Remington, this is what I've been doing. I've searched through location after location, following any lead I can think of to get an advantage on Sterling. We know he's coming for us, but I want to stop him before he even has a chance to step foot in Montana. The bloodshed and death he's bringing can be avoided if I eliminate him first. And the best way to do that is finding Kaius. It wouldn't matter if we killed Sterling if Kaius is still out there somewhere. The necromancer would just keep bringing him back from the dead.

I'm just about to go down the damaged stairwell when I hear the scurrying noise come from below. Freezing in place, I close my eyes and listen hard. I can't pick up any scents, the lingering smell of char overpowers everything else. Just when I'm ready to chalk the whole thing up to a rat or raccoon, my beast awakens and emits a warning growl.

Whatever is down there, he doesn't like.

My eyes snap open as my guard goes up. There's another rustling sound followed by slow, lazy footsteps. Whoever it is has no idea I'm here, or they wouldn't be making so much noise.

I should have brought Isabeau with me for backup, but it would have slowed me down if I had to wait for her to fly or drive all the way to Connecticut. It's much easier and more fun to work alone. Plus, my wolf isn't a fan of sharing his kills.

Excitement fills me as I prepare for a fight. My wolf howls and bites at his confines to be let out so he can enjoy the fun, but I force him back down. There're very few places I allow him out and in the middle of a city isn't one of them. There are too many people around to allow that.

Summoning my hellfire, I disappear into smoke and reappear in the basement. The figure has their back to me, their head turned into the dark shadows. Their clothes are ragged, hanging off their thin body in dirty shreds. For a second, I consider the possibility they're a transient person, using the condemned building as shelter, but when they turn eerily slow in my direction, that thought vanishes.

His head tilts as he observes me with empty, non-blinking eyes. I haven't encountered that many people like this, but I can recognize Kaius's work anywhere. Whoever this poor man in front of me is, he'd been dead but was recently brought back. He was probably soundly at peace in his grave, but the necromancer came along and resurrected him. Based on the dated style of suit he wears, he's been dead a while which means whatever humanity he had is long gone. The longer a person is dead, the more fucked up they are when they're brought back. They come back angry, volatile, *monsters*.

If they're brought back within minutes of dying, there's little to no evidence they were ever dead. That's why Sterling doesn't appear like the man in front of me.

This guy should be nothing but bones, but Kaius's dark magic can also restore the body. The only tells that he was once dead are his grayish skin color and his eyes, they're pale blue and cloudy. *Dead.*

"*Shit.*"

He grins at me wickedly with decayed teeth. "He said you'd come. He said I just had to wait, and you'd show up."

It all clicks; this guy was resurrected to be Kaius's watchdog. How many more has Kaius made just like this one?

"Kaius talks about me?" I clutch my chest melodramatically. "Well, you go ahead and tell him I'm flattered he went through all this trouble for little old me, but it really wasn't necessary."

"He also said you were a little shit," he sneers.

I nod my head in agreement. "That's probably a fair statement."

He reaches for a soot-covered metal pipe to his left. It makes a loud scratching sound as he drags it off the metal table that survived the fire. "I grew quite bored waiting for you."

My face scrunches in confusion. "Why? You got a hot date or something waiting for you? Hate to break it to you, bud, but chances are, all your friends are dead. *Like you should be.*"

He runs the metal pipe along the concrete floors as he moves in my direction. "You really are annoying."

"You know, oddly enough that's the second time this week I've been told that." My head shakes in astonishment. "If people keep saying that, I'm afraid I'll develop a complex—" The smart-ass remark is never finished, because with an angry roar, he charges at me with the pipe raised above his head.

He's faster now than he ever could have been when he was alive. I shift out of the way just before the metal pipe comes down. He slams it against the ground so hard, the stone crumbles. It would be easy to reach out and infuse his blood with a healthy dose of hellfire, but the built-up frustration in my bones craves the fight. I want to beat something until I'm no longer able to think of Remington and all the shit that's happened between us. I want to slam this guy's face in with my fist until I'm too tired to crave her like I do.

The pipe comes swinging at my head once more, but this time, I catch it as I twist my body so I can slam my elbow into his face. Magically healed bones make the same satisfying crunching sound when they break. His nose is shattered and with a pained howl, he grabs his face with his free hand.

His dead eyes are full of anger when he charges at me again. Using the momentum he created, I grab hold of his dusty suit jacket and hurl him into the wall behind me. He bounces off the wall and chaotically swings the pipe at me. I don't move fast enough this time and the metal connects with my temple.

Pain sears through my skull, disorienting me briefly. My fingers wipe at the trickle of warm liquid running down the side of my face. Pulling my hand back, I find it coated in blood. My beast growls lowly, pissed I let myself get hurt.

Snarling, I catch the pipe as he swings it again. This time, I yank the damn thing from his hands. He charges at me again trying to get it back, but I kick my booted foot into his chest, sending him backward.

Grinning like a madman, I twirl the pipe in my hand like a batter stepping up to home plate as I stalk forward.

His hands fly up to cover his face, but it doesn't help him. Swinging hard, the pipe slams into his jaw, his gross rotted teeth fly from his mouth and scatter on the ground. He falls to his knees, his arm catching him before he falls forward. Bending down, I grasp his chin and force him to look at me. "If that fucker decides to bring you back a second time, tell him I'm coming for him. Tell him I'm going to burn it all to the fucking ground."

Like a kid at a birthday party, I make his body my pinata. I slam the pipe unforgivingly into his body over and over again. Blood sprays all over me, coating my exposed hands and face. When it gets in my mouth, I spit it back down on him. In my head, I imagine it's Sterling laying on the ground before me. I don't stop until the body is unrecognizable—nothing but a bloody lump on the ground.

Good luck fixing that mess, Kaius.

Breathing hard, I back away from my masterpiece. As the adrenaline fades, the pounding in my head becomes more evident. Cursing, I let the metal pipe fall to the ground so I can prod at the wound on my head. Head wounds always bleed like a motherfucker, but now that I've stopped moving, I'm pretty sure I have a concussion. I'll be fine once it heals, but right now, I'm afraid I might pass out.

Staggering back on my feet, I try to focus my disoriented vision, but it won't work. I need to get the hell out of here before I lose consciousness. The last thing I want to do is pass out somewhere I'm vulnerable.

Harnessing the last bit of my energy, I summon my hellfire and think of Montana. *Pru's... I need to make it back to Pru's house.* I picture the lake house and then her living room. Ryker will be pissed that I showed up this late, but Pruitt won't mind. At the last minute as I dissolve into smoke, the image of *her* fills my mind as does her hotel room. Before I can stop it, I'm careening—faster than light—through the planes of this world.

When I arrive at my destination, I make a less than graceful landing and stumble forward onto my knees on the carpet.

"What the hell!" the voice screeches. "*Jax!*"

I pass out knowing I've made a grave mistake. I was trying to get somewhere safe but ended up with the one person who might actually kill me.

CHAPTER SEVEN
Remington

My eyes are the same color they've always been, but something in them is missing. The light or shimmer of happiness is gone. Along with whatever innocence I once had. They look tired. *I am tired.* I'm tired of watching the lives of my loved ones threatened and I'm tired of fighting. We grow up knowing about monsters, but we never truly think we'll have to face them head-on. They're just a distant thought in the back of your head. It's a jarring new reality when you learn the monster is out there, craving *your* blood.

The things I've seen and the things I've done in the past two years have wiped away the remaining pieces of my innocence. I was going to nursing school to learn how to save lives, not take them. The blood on my hands is because of Sterling. I've been kidnapped and used as a bargaining chip because of Sterling. I've watched people I care about die because of Sterling. *All because of Sterling.*

With a frustrated sigh, I turn away from the mirror. The person staring back was unrecognizable anyway. With the white hotel towel secured around my chest, I leave the bathroom. Elsie said the club's packed tonight and that's exactly what I need. The sound and the chaotic energy will drown out the unwanted thoughts in my head.

Going back home yesterday did exactly what I feared it would. It made all the memories and emotions I tried to suppress bubble to the surface. Today I'm feeling everything. For the past month, I've been off tending to my emotional wounds. They were still tender and painful, but the bleeding had finally stopped. The two hours I spent back there tore open the sutures I'd placed and now I'm bleeding out.

Tonight, I'm going to start all over. Stitch by stitch, I'll mend the wounds again. I'll numb the pain and bury the feelings.

Running my fingers through my wet hair, I work out the knots as I rummage through my closet for something to wear. I don't have a lot of options since I left with only one bag of clothes, but I make do. Snagging the black dress off the hanger I turn to toss it on the unmade king-size bed behind me just as a dark figure appears out of thin air.

Jumping a foot in the air, I cover my mouth with my hand to stop the startled yelp from escaping. I can lock as many doors as I want, but that won't keep this demon out. The alarm I feel is quickly taken over by anger. "What the hell!" I yell at him. "Jax!"

How dare he come here? What is he thinking? I couldn't have been clearer when I told—the thoughts die when he stumbles forward, falling onto his knees and then the putrid scent of death and smoke hits me.

Confused, I watch as he crashes to the ground on his stomach. I stay where I am, head cocking to the side while I wait to see if he'll move. Jax is arguably the strongest among us, it takes a lot to really hurt him.

The first time I met him, he'd been shot in the stomach by Nicolai and his biggest complaint was the bullet ruined his favorite shirt. Meanwhile, I'd been frantically trying to stop the blood spilling from his gut. He heals faster than the rest of us, so why isn't he moving?

Warily, I shuffle forward and nudge his still form with my bare foot, but it doesn't rouse him.

I kept telling myself I want to see him bloodied and broken, but now as I stare down at him bleeding all over the carpet, my wolf is losing it. We've never disagreed more over something than when it comes to Jax. I want nothing to do with him while she misses him. *Traitorous bitch.* She claws and scratches at me, begging for me to help him.

Giving in this once, I hold my towel with one hand and kneel next to Jax. Gripping his shoulder, I shake him a couple of times, but he doesn't move. His head is turned away from me, but the blood that blossoms on the light gray carpet below his skull hints at a pretty nasty head wound.

Begrudgingly and in a manner I wouldn't classify as '*gentle*', I flip him over. Jax groans low in his throat, but his violet eyes don't open. His head just flops to the side. Gripping his chin, I turn his face so I can see what I'm dealing with.

I was right. It looks like he took a pretty massive blow to the head. A two-inch gash sits on his temple, disappearing into his hairline. It bleeds like a mother, but the good news for him is I don't see any brain matter. He'll live.

Goody.

Glancing down at the rest of his body, I find that his clothes are absolutely coated in blood. The head wound wouldn't have bled all over him like this. Shifting back on my knees, I search for another source of blood. I yank his black shirt up, exposing his torso. All I find is his annoyingly perfect body. Smooth, darkly tanned skin covers each of his lean muscles. He's not bulky like Ransom or Ryker, but he's just as strong.

Doing my best to shift him enough that I can check his back for injuries, I find nothing. Running my hand quickly down his dark denim-clad legs, I don't find any other wounds. It's only his head that's hurt. My guess is he has a severe concussion and that's why he's passed out, but that begs the question, who's blood is he smearing all over my carpet?

"You just *had* to come here," I grumble under my breath as I climb to my feet. I contemplate my next moves. Do I just let him bleed freely everywhere and let him heal on his own, or do I help?

I'd really like to get dressed and walk out that door, leaving him here to wake up in a pool of his own blood, but the aching pain that develops in my stomach at the thought has me stopping from following through with it. Plus, the cleaning bill from the hotel is going to be atrocious if I just let him bleed on everything.

Cursing, I jog to the bathroom and grab the remaining towels. On my way back, I grab two small bottles of vodka from the minibar before dropping back to the floor above his head.

Shoving one of the larger towels under his head to absorb the blood, I take a smaller one and press it to the actual wound. The white fabric quickly turns red. Holding the towel in place with one hand, I reach for one of the bottles. Using my teeth, I twist the lid and dump the contents onto the wound. Wherever Jax was, it was fucking filthy. His blood-stained clothes are also covered in grime. Surely whatever bashed his skull in wasn't sanitary. I don't know if he's completely unsusceptible to bacteria like full-blooded wolf shifters are. His DNA is altered and a total mystery to me. I don't know what species' traits Sterling was able to replicate when he created Jax in a lab. It's better to be safe than sorry.

Continuing pressure, I open the second bottle. This time, I pour the alcohol into my mouth and shudder at the unpleasant flavor of straight vodka. It won't do much, but it'll take the edge off while I wait for the bleeding to stop.

☾

THE WARM WATER WASHES OVER MY BLOOD-STAINED HANDS IN the sink. I scrub until the pink water runs clear.

It took fifteen minutes for the bleeding to stop. Once I knew Jax wasn't going to bleed out, I got up and left him to wake up on his own. It'll happen eventually, whatever damage his brain sustained is healing as we speak.

Taking that time to finish what I started when he first appeared, I dry my hair and apply my makeup, so I'm ready to go once he's awake.

I'm not going to let his unwelcome appearance change my plans. All he's done is made me late.

Stepping back into the bedroom, I grab the dress I'd left on my bed. Making sure Jax is still passed out, I let the bloodied towel drop from my torso and pool around my feet. I've just pulled the thin lacy thong out of my suitcase on the floor when the hairs on the back of my neck rise. Looking over my shoulder, I find a set of violet eyes roaming over my exposed body.

Shit.

I can either allow him to know I'm bothered that he's looking at my naked body or I can pretend I don't give a fuck. Going with the latter, I set my face into an unreadable piece of stone and turn boldly toward him. His eyebrows lift ever so slightly in surprise, but he doesn't say a word as he continues his perusal of my body. The adrenaline coursing through my veins is unexpected but addictive and when his eyes turn heavy with need, a surge of confidence hits me.

For the first time in a long time, I hold all the cards and the power is intoxicating.

"You bled all over my carpet, *hellhound*." It's a nickname I gave him a while back, he hates it which only makes it more appealing. The name itself is incredibly fitting given his mix of wolf shifter and demon blood.

"My apologies." His voice is gruff, and to my annoyance, it sends a shiver down my spine.

Forgoing the panties, I pick up the dress, slowly stepping into it and pulling it up my body. "I find you so much more tolerable when you're unconscious," I muse coldly. "It's a shame you can't be in that state all the time."

With a pained groan, he pulls himself into a seated position. He uses the dresser behind him to help prop himself up. "I'm sure there are people that would agree with that statement," he offers while pulling one of his knees up to his chest so he can rest his arm lazily on it. Not once do his eyes look away from me. They travel all over my body. Each pass they make over my curves leaves a trail of heat on my skin until I feel like I'm burning.

I don't want to feel this way, but just like my wolf, my body is a traitor.

"Who did this to you?" I ask as I waltz around the bed so I can sit on the end of it directly in front of him. The heels I wear to the club sit on the floor next to me. Bending, I take my time slipping my feet into them.

"Why?" Jax presses, the corner of his mouth pulling in a smirk. "You jealous?"

I look up from buckling the ankle straps of my heels. "*Immensely*," I tell him. "Don't you know if anyone is going to make you bleed, it's going to be me?"

"I'll be sure to tell my next attacker that they're not allowed to lay a finger on me because you've reserved the right for yourself," Jax plays along. "I didn't know you were so possessive, love."

With the buckles secure, I sit back up. Leaning back on my hands, I tilt my head and watch the man in front of me. There was a time that I wanted him so bad, but he pushed me aside and treated me as if I was a piece of garbage beneath his shoe. "When you figure out what you truly want, you don't let anyone else have it."

"Is that so?" His heated gaze slides up my bare legs until they reach the hem of my short dress. "Remington, you wouldn't be planning to go to that trashy club of yours with no panties on, would you?"

"How would you know about the club, Jax?" I narrow my eyes at him. I should have known that he was still watching over me after I left. It was too good to be true that he would agree to give me the space I craved. When I was home, he was lingering around every corner, his watchful eyes following every move I made. Even when he thought I didn't know he was there, I could sense him nearby.

"There's not much I don't know about you," he admits arrogantly. "You didn't answer my question."

The anger that he's been following me to the club fuels my next move. Without the anger, I never would have the balls to do it. I want to see him squirm, I want him to want me so bad it hurts and then I want him to regret ever thinking about me.

Blinking at him with false innocence, I skim my fingers down my bare thighs. When I reach my knees, I trace circles languidly before oh so slowly dragging my nails back up my leg so hard red lines form. Keeping my eyes locked with his, I slowly part my thighs until my pussy is fully exposed to him. The position in which he sits gives him the perfect view. "I prefer to not wear any to the club," I purr. "They get in the way of what I want."

He swallows hard as his eyes lock between my spread thighs. "And what's that?" Jax asks hoarsely.

Trailing my fingers back down my exposed leg, I slide them softly against the skin of my inner thigh. My oversensitive ears pick up on his quickening heartbeat. My skin grows warm knowing I'm affecting him, that I'm getting the reaction I desire. "I want to go to the club, find a man who knows *nothing* about me or my past and I want him to fuck me against a wall until I can't remember your name." My fingers delve between my folds and I'm shocked to find that I'm already wet. Jax has always had a hold on me I can't explain. "I want him to make me forget why my life has fallen apart and I want him to make me forget why I can't stand to be in the same room as you." One finger slips inside and I leisurely work it in and out of me. "And while it happens, I want you to watch."

Glowing violet eyes clash with mine and a low warning growl emits from his chest as his wolf pushes to the surface. This is the first time I've been able to sense his animal side, he keeps it locked away tight. I'm not even sure he's able to shift. He's always refused to go on pack runs with us. "*Remington...*" he warns, but I don't stop. He once lured me in, only to push me into the dirt, and I'm going to do the same now.

"I want you to watch him fuck me against a wall and while you watch, I want you to regret ever stepping foot in my life." My breath hitches as I circle my fingers against my clit. "As I come on another man's dick, I want you to hate me as much as I hate you." *As much as I hate myself.*

"I'd be careful if I were you. If you push me too far, you won't like what happens." Jax snarls, his eyes glowing with rage. "You're playing with fire, love."

"I know," I confess while pulling my finger from my hot core. "I don't fear your flames, Jax. I've already been burned. I've got nothing left for you to destroy." My heart is a pile of ashes, one strong gust of wind will blow what remains away. "So, do your worst," I challenge with a smirk before licking my finger clean.

Without a word, I stand from the bed and pull my dress back down. Jax remains in place, unmoving, but his eyes burn into my skin as he watches me collect my small purse. Pausing a few feet away from him, I flick my eyes at the bloody carpet. "You're paying to have this shit cleaned up, I'll be damned if I have to fix another thing you broke."

With that, I leave him to sit and think about what just happened. Or at least that was the plan.

The second my hand wraps around the metal handle to

leave, I'm abruptly whirled around, my back slamming into the door so hard I'm surprised the wood doesn't splinter. His arms rest on either side of my head, caging me in. His breath comes in angry pants, his chest heaving harshly. "Where the fuck do you think you're going?"

Tilting my chin up toward his face, I seethe, "I believe I just told you I had plans."

There's a wild, almost unhinged look in his purple eyes. Even this angry, Jax still looks like someone who walked off a runway in Milan. The perfect sharp angles of his perfectly symmetrical face make me want to punch him in the nose. Strands of his jet-black hair fall forward on his forehead as he dips his head closer to mine. He's so close to me, we share the air we breathe. "You're just going to leave after that little show of yours?"

I shove at his chest, but he doesn't move. "It's not fun when someone plays with your emotions and then leaves, is it?" I shout angrily in his face, giving no shits that the other guests of the hotel could hear me. "If you feel even a *quarter* of how I felt when you did it to me, then I did my job right." My wolf whimpers at the memory. She hasn't been the same since that night. He damaged her just like he did me.

His face turns cold, his lips twisting into a sneer. "You obviously didn't feel that bad since you wasted no time jumping into bed with Gage!"

Hearing Gage's name on his tongue floods me with an unbearable amount of shame. As the blood in my veins runs cold, my chest grows painfully tight. So tight I feel like I can't breathe. I need the hell out of here, but Jax's arms box me in. A mixture of fury and desperation powers me as I slam my fist into his gut so hard I hear the sound of ribs breaking. He finally stumbles away from me, clutching his side.

"You made your choice that night, and Gage was your consequence because of it." *He ultimately became mine as well.* "That's the shitty part of life, Jax. Sometimes we make the wrong choices and we're punished for it. So, grit your teeth and take your punishment like a fucking man."

Understanding crosses his face. "Is that what you're doing? *Punishing* yourself?" he questions, tilting his head to the side.

My air catches in my throat at his question. For the briefest second, I feel my face fall before I can stop it. Even though it was fast, I know Jax saw my slipup. Steeling myself, I lift my chin and boldly meet his eyes. "Our actions have consequences," I manage to bite out. "I'm learning to live with mine. I suggest you do the same and leave me the hell alone." This time when I leave, he lets me.

If I'm going to bear the weight of my actions, I can't do it with Jax around. Seeing him alive and breathing only reminds me of what I did and what it cost me.

CHAPTER EIGHT
Jax

Isabeau throws me the same bag of peas that Remi had just used yesterday on her ribs. Wordlessly, I press them to my pounding skull. The bloody gash may have healed, but the concussion-induced headache has yet to go away. If I'm being honest, I'm not convinced it's not a Remington Weylyn induced headache.

My encounter with her tonight left my body aching in all kinds of places. My cock had hardened painfully at her little display on the bed. Even as I contemplated killing her where she stood because of it, my body craved her. My wolf was deranged with the need to touch her. *Which is never going to fucking happen.*

With an unsettled wolf and semihard dick, I left the hotel and went straight to Isabeau's house. At this ungodly hour, I knew she'd be awake. The vampire requires very little sleep.

Sitting in the office chair, I spin in circles while holding the ice pack to my head.

"So Kaius is burning down his own businesses and resurrecting random dead people to watch over them?" she repeats slowly, like she can't believe it herself.

"It's a good plan," I reluctantly admit. "He's connected to each of the people he brings back, he'll know the second one of them dies." *Again*.

"They're like his own version of motion detectors," she surmises.

"Exactly, he'll be able to tell when we're getting too close to wherever he's hiding out and he'll move on." If he wasn't the enemy, I may applaud his plan for its ingenuity.

"How many of these places have you gone to with no backup?"

Continuing my spinning, I shrug. "Not sure. Five or six? They've all been dead ends though. This is the first place that was burned down and had a guard dog." I went to all the places I was brought to as a child, but they were all cleared out. Not a single piece of scrap paper remained in the buildings. "If they're resorting to burning shit down, it means they know they're running out of time. They know we're coming for them and they don't have the time to clean out each of the buildings anymore."

She's silent for a moment before in a low, authoritative tone, she bites out, "You went to six of these places *alone*? Without telling anyone?"

My foot digs into the carpet and my merry spinning comes to an abrupt halt as my beast snarls in my head. He claws at the steel door he's kept behind. His anger becomes my own as I meet Beau's arctic stare. "I don't need your permission to go, Isabeau. You may be the beta female of this pack, but your authority holds no weight with me. I'm not a member of this pack and you are not my boss. I can come and go as I fucking please." I point to the whiteboard bolted to the wall. For the past six months, we've been working on adding information about Sterling and Kaius to it. Isabeau's office is like our very own war room. "I'm working with you and this pack because I think it gives us the best shot at finding Sterling, but I am by no means *obligated* to report my findings to you. And I sure as hell don't need your *approval*."

My wolf bows to no one. Not even me. The years I spent being pushed around by Nicolai were the hardest I've ever endured. I did it because I thought it would allow me to get close to Sterling, but in the end, it was for nothing. By the age of ten, I was strong enough to kill Nicolai, but I allowed myself to be abused because I had my end goal in mind.

The goal is the same, but I no longer have to make myself seem small to placate the people around me to reach it.

"I don't think it's smart to go alone," she pushes. "We can't afford to lose anyone. We need every able-bodied person if Sterling is going to bring the fight here. We especially need you alive if we are going to stand a chance."

Grinding my teeth, I push my wolf back down, but after my time with Remington tonight, it's harder than usual. She has a way of riling him up. He wants to kill everyone he comes across, but she interests him to an extent I find worrisome. "Contrary to popular belief, I'm not an idiot. If I truly thought going alone was going to put me in danger, I wouldn't go." But if she continues to piss off my wolf, she's the one who will be in danger.

"Fine," Beau relents. "But I want it noted that I don't like it."

Standing from the chair, I toss the bag of peas onto the desk. "I want it noted that I'm not sure I care." I grin widely at her. "You missed out tonight though. It got bloody. *Gloriously bloody*."

She rolls her eyes. "That's where you and I differ, Jax. You like to leave a mess. Meanwhile, my kills are clean. *Organized*, if you will."

"Sounds boring." I scrunch my nose in distaste.

"Nicolai really failed in your training." She leans against the wall, crossing her arms across her chest. Even in her own home, she's dressed like she's going on a job with the black leather pants and the daggers strapped to her thigh. Her waist-length black hair is tied back from her face in a complicated braid. She used to hide her face with her hair, using it as another layer of armor, but since finding Ransom, she has to hide less. "Sterling's the worst, but he at least trained me right."

Sterling shipped me, his biological son, off to be trained by another but he kept Isabeau and her brother, Alexandre, around to train himself. She became his prized creation.

I think after I failed to harness the hellfire flames again, he grew frustrated with me and moved onto stronger prospects. I can't blame him entirely, Isabeau is half vampire and half fae, her unbridled strength and ability to melt into shadows makes her the perfect assassin.

"Yeah, he did a bang-up job with Alexandre," I remind her with an exasperated look. Her brother was a hot mess. He was overcome by bloodlust and became nothing but a hungry monster.

"That wasn't all Sterling. Nessa played a role in what he became as well."

Laughing coldly, I rake my hand through my hair. "We really got screwed over in the parent department, didn't we?"

"Yeah, we did," she reluctantly admits.

"At least your evil parent is dead," I attempt to lighten the mood.

"It's hard to believe that she's only been gone for six months. It should've happened years ago. I don't know why I waited so long."

"We were raised to fear them, to think that they were stronger than us." For many years, Sterling was the monster under my bed, the demon on my back, but as I got older, I figured out that he's just a man. He worked tirelessly to make beings like Isabeau and myself, but ultimately it will be his downfall. His creations are going to be the things that kill him. "They'll learn soon enough that they were wrong."

Once we fucking find him.

"Yeah..." Isabeau worries her bottom lip like her mind has suddenly wandered off topic. By nature, the vampire isn't a worrier and that's mostly due to the fact she's come across very few situations she doesn't know how to handle. Very few things scare her.

Shuffling slowly around Beau's desk, I snag the small dagger she keeps in her pen holder by her laptop. Only she would mix her writing utensils with weapons. Pressing the sharp pointed end into the fleshy part of my palm just hard enough that it hurts, but doesn't break the skin, I watch the way her brows pull ever so slightly. "What's wrong with you?" I finally demand.

She stares at me, not blinking like she's considering her next moves. Finally, she pushes off the wall and moves closer to where I stand. "I was dealing with Nessa and Alexandre when Gage died." The knife presses harder into my skin at the mention of his name. "I didn't see him die, I'm not sure anyone did."

"There was a lot going on," I remind her even though I know there's no way she's forgotten what happened six months ago. In an attempt to wipe out the pack, Nessa unleashed a couple dozen feral rogue wolves and starving vampires on pack land. A move that was no doubt authorized by Sterling. "I was too busy fighting to pay attention to what Gage was doing. One second, he was fighting not far from me, the next he was dead on the ground. What happened then is a mystery to me."

I was knocked to the ground and when I got back up, Remington stood over him in her wolf form. The sound of her pained howl is something I still hear when I try to fall asleep at night. That howl symbolized the moment she broke into pieces I don't have the right to put back together.

Beau's quiet for a moment, thinking over what I just said.

When she still hasn't said anything after a minute and her eyes have a faraway look to them, I stop twirling the knife between my fingers and I tilt my head. "What do you know?"

"Nothing," she answers quickly. "I just have suspicions."

"Are you going to share them with the class?" I drawl slowly.

"Are you going to tell me what happened a year ago that first made her mad at you?" she counters quickly, not skipping a beat.

What happened a year ago…

No, I'm not going to tell Isabeau what happened a year ago. Even though I know out of everyone, she's the one who would understand what I did the best, I can't tell her. Beau would probably support my choice and reasoning, but I'm not going to share it with her out of respect for Remington. Remi has gone to great extremes to keep it a secret and I'll do the same.

"I did what I had to do," is all I offer with an apathetic shrug, playing it off as if it's nothing important. I toss the knife back into the penholder and stuff my hands into the pockets of my jeans. "I didn't want to see her hurt and nothing has changed."

"But she *is* hurt, Jax."

Does she not think I know that? Remi's been slowly self-destructing for months. It's like watching a falling star speeding toward the earth. She's eventually going to crash and there is nothing I can do to stop it. I'm the one who pushed her after all.

"But she's not dead!" I shout, throwing my hands up in the air in defeat. "Yeah, she's hurting and acting out right now, but *she's alive*. And sometimes that's all we can ask for."

"What are you talking about?" She frowns. "Who was going to kill her?"

I was.

My lips part like I want to say my admission aloud, but the words never come. Snapping my teeth together, I grind them painfully as I meet Isabeau's stare with my own unyielding look.

"*Jax*," she presses me to continue, a tinge of urgency in her voice.

Shaking my head, I shove my fingers through my hair in frustration. "I have to get out of here," I announce. "I can't talk to you about this anymore." I leave before she can ask any more questions.

CHAPTER NINE
Jay

Two hours.

That's how long I pace the length of my scantily decorated, dark loft while trying to stop myself from doing something stupid. I thought after leaving Isabeau's I'd calmed down enough, but the silence of my temporary home made Remington's words scream in my head at a volume I could no longer ignore.

I want him to fuck me against a wall until I can't remember your name.

I now sit, watching the red numbers on my alarm clock tick by. Each minute that passes is time she has to follow through with it.

Those words—*that threat*—made my blood boil with uncontrollable jealousy as she said them, but now that there's a possibility that as we speak, she's truly letting a stranger inside her body, has my blood raging through my veins like lava.

She's willingly letting some random douchebag take advantage of her. That's how far she's fallen. That's how twisted her moral compass has become. And it's partially my fault.

No longer able to stand it, I stand from the mattress and hastily pull on the leather jacket I'd left on the rickety wooden chair in the corner. It's the only piece of real furniture in the entire loft besides my bed.

I'm not in Montana to build a home, this is all temporary until we take care of Sterling. If I somehow manage to make it out of that alive, I'll move on someplace else, but I don't allow myself to think much about where that could be. It'd be a mistake to set my heart on a future I can't have.

I leave the loft in a cloud of smoke and head to the place I know I shouldn't.

Appearing in a dark hallway near the emergency exit, I'm assaulted by the familiar smell of the club. It reeks of spilled liquor, cheap perfume, and sex. The music is deafening, the bass bounces in the walls and in my bones. I can understand how a place like this would be ideal for someone who's trying to not think. The music drowns out any thought you may have.

Even now, as I stalk through the dark hallway into the main part of the club, the voice of reason that should be screaming at me to leave is silenced by the loud music. It's for the best as I have no intentions of leaving until I get a visual on Remington. I need to know what she's doing. *Who* she may be doing.

I already killed one person tonight, I'm not against killing another if I find someone touching her.

After weeks of watching over her at this club, I know the building like the back of my hand. Climbing a set of stairs that lead to the upper level, I slip into one of the vacant VIP rooms that look over the dance floor and bar. Standing in the shadows, I sweep my eyes over the space. Remington usually enjoys sitting at the bar talking to the female bartender, but tonight her usual seat is taken by a blonde with a bad spray tan.

My wolf grows impatient as I search the crowd of dancers. For a weekday, this place is crowded, but it rarely isn't. It's the only source of entertainment for the college students nearby.

In the horde of people, I try to find her shoulder-length chocolate-colored hair, but once again, I find myself disappointed. I know she's in the building, my wolf can sense as much, but where continues to be a mystery.

With one last fleeting look at the crowd, I leave the room, tugging the velvet curtain closed behind me so hard, the rod is yanked from the drywall and hangs crookedly from the ceiling.

Prowling down the poorly lit hallway lined with the other VIP rooms, I head for the staircase on the other end. I pass one of the few rooms with a drawn curtain and freeze when a familiar scent assaults me. It's mixed with tequila and something sweet and fruity, but I'd still recognize it anywhere.

Grinning to myself, I back up with slow measured steps. Pausing by the curtain, I listen to what's coming from the other side. Two heartbeats, one beats more erratically than the other. Something clangs against the glass table before he speaks.

"Anyone ever tell you that your eyes are beautiful?" he slurs. "They're like a summer day. So blue."

Who the fuck is this guy?

Remington's eyes aren't like a summer day. Her eyes are

like the sky when a thunderstorm is rolling in. They're alive with chaotic energy. Lightning strikes every time she blinks.

He groans dramatically before saying the words that sign his death certificate. "Will they look like that still as you stare up at me from your knees?"

I'm charging into the room before he has a chance to finish his next sentence. I find him cuddled up to Remington on the leather couch, his face buried in her neck. His hands with sausage-like fingers wander over her body, caressing up her bare exposed thighs.

A look of boredom is etched across her face, there is no light in her eyes. They're dead—cold even. When her gaze locks with mine, it's like a switch is been flipped. The fire —*the life*—returns to her face.

If anyone could stop me from going after this guy, it'd be her. She could probably get me to do anything if she asked, but she remains where she sits, watching my movements with fascination.

He jumps to his feet to stand between Remi and me. Once I'm close enough, he pushes me back with both of his hands, but he'd have a better chance stopping a freight train than stopping me with his weak little human muscles.

"Hey, buddy, you lost? I think you've made a mistake—" The fucker doesn't get to say the rest because my hand wraps around his throat, effectively cutting off his oxygen and whatever moronic comment he's about to make.

"No, I'm exactly where I'm supposed to be," I snarl in his face, not caring for a second my tone is borderline animalistic. "You, however, have made a mistake that's going to cost you."

His fat fingers tear at my hand, but I'm not deterred by the scratches he leaves. "What is your problem?" he chokes out.

Pretending to ponder his question, I forcibly back him up until his lower back hits the guardrail of the balcony. "That's a bit of a loaded question, my friend." I chuckle softly. "But I believe the short answer is *daddy issues*. When I tell you that man did a number on me, I mean it." A low gasping sound escapes his lips as my hand clamps down harder on his throat. "He never did teach me how to share. From what I'm told, it's something kids learn at a young age, but he had other lessons in mind for me."

"*Jax.*" Remington's voice is a low warning coming from behind me, but I don't let him go. I can't yet. The red, angry haze has washed over me and I'm no longer in control.

"He taught me all kinds of things. For instance, I know right now your vision is starting to get a little fuzzy. Darkness is creeping in at the corners, right?" I pause, waiting for a choked answer, but all I get is a jerky head nod. "You probably think that's because I'm depriving you of oxygen, but in reality, it's not your airflow. It's blood. I'm *starving* your brain of blood."

With a snarl, I shove him farther back until his upper body is hanging over the balcony. I'm the only thing keeping him from falling backward onto the dance floor.

"Your parents really failed you by not teaching you to not touch other people's things. Surely, that's a lesson that comes soon after the sharing one. Don't worry though, I'll teach you it myself," I promise him. "When you touch something that doesn't belong to you, there are repercussions." My wolf thunders against his restraints and they fracture just enough that I feel his rage combine with him. "Do you know how long your brain can go without blood? Three minutes. You now have less than two minutes to learn what happens when you play with someone else's toys, after that you risk permanent brain damage."

I push him farther over the ledge and his hands cling on to my arm like a vice instead of trying to get me to release him. His face is red, and his eyes are wide with fear. Just when I think he's starting to learn his lesson, he has the audacity to open his dumb mouth again. "She's just a random... *girl*," he chokes out. "You'd do this over some easy *pussy*?"

This time it's Remington who growls. Looking over my shoulder, I find her eyes glowing as her own wolf pushes forward. Her hands are balled into fists, but if I had to bet, her claws are also out. She doesn't look at me. Her focus is on the man she was willing to let touch her just moments ago.

Turning back to the douchebag, I laugh coldly at him. "*Jesus*. You really are a dense motherfucker."

He glances down at the ground below him. Nervously licking his lips, he looks back at me. "Let me go."

"You want me to let you go?" I repeat, raising a brow.

"Yes." He nods awkwardly. "Please just let me go."

That's all I need to hear. "Okay." I nod once, shrugging before I release my hold on his neck.

He barely has time to open his mouth in a cry for help before he tumbles down a story. People yell in surprise as he falls toward them. The sound of his body slamming into the dance floor will be one I savor for a long time. Smiling to myself, I glance over the metal railing and find him splayed out on the ground. People stand all around him with puzzled looks on their faces.

Feeling pleased with myself, I turn back around and find

Remington standing with a dumbfounded look on her face as she stares at me. She doesn't look sad or remotely worried about the man, just shocked. "What did you just do?" she whispers.

"He said please."

"For you to *let* him go," she emphasizes while throwing her hands up in the air.

With a puzzled look, I thrust my thumb behind me. "*Yeah*, and I did." *Is she not paying attention?*

"He meant let him go, as in let him *walk* out of this room."

Shrugging halfheartedly, I move away from the balcony. "In that case, he really should have been more specific."

"Ja—" My name is cut off when I grab her arm and pull her with me as I stalk out of this godforsaken room. "What are you doing?"

She staggers behind me, the high heels and copious amount of alcohol in her system making her unsteady on her feet.

"They're about to come up here searching for the reason he fell," I answer over my shoulder as we move toward the back staircase. "Do you really want to be standing in there when they come asking questions?"

She tries tugging her arm from my grip, but I hold on tight. "Sure, why not? I'll tell them some fucking lunatic with no impulse control dumped the poor guy's drunk ass over the edge."

Tsking at her under my breath, I drag her down the stairs. "That's not very nice."

"How many times do I have to tell you that I'm not in the mood to be nice to you, Jax?" she snaps at me.

"I don't know. How many times have you said it so far?

I'm thinking multiply that number by five and it may start to finally click for me."

We finally make it down the stairs, but she's moving too slow for my liking. I pause so abruptly she slams into my back, but before she has a chance to recover, I'm turning around and lifting her over my shoulder.

"What the hell? Jax! Put me down right now!" Her hands slap repeatedly at my lower back.

My hand grips the back of her thigh, keeping her in place. "I bet right about now you're wishing you were wearing panties."

There's a startled squeal before her hands stop assaulting me and they try to desperately tug her short dress down to cover herself. The angle is awkward, and she can't reach. Chuckling, I yank the dress down for her. "I've got it," I assure with a pat on her ass.

She snarls at me, "I'm going to tie you to your bed and skin you alive!"

"*Kinky.*"

Her claws dig into my lower back and side as she slashes them at me. It hurts, but she can make me bleed all she wants. "What the hell are you doing here? I told you to leave me alone. *Repeatedly.*"

I ignore her question, but I don't know how to answer it. No response I give her will be okay.

Pushing open the back door with my shoulder, I carry her outside. She never stops fighting and thrashing around. Her claws have turned my lower back into a massacre by now.

I bring her down the alleyway farther away from the club until we reach a shadowy area blocked in by stacks of empty crates and boxes. She staggers on her feet for a second when I place her back on the ground.

Remi tugs her dress down and pushes her mussed hair away from her face. Breathing hard, she glares daggers at me. "Your inability to follow a simple instruction is going to be the death of you someday and with each passing day, I'm starting to think I may be your executioner." She spits her words like venom. "I don't know what just happened in there or why, but it was bullshit."

I look blandly back at the club we just left. "You really wanted that fucknut to touch you?"

"*What* I want or *who* I want does not concern you, hellhound." Remi marches closer until there are only a few centimeters between our chests. "You have no say in what I do. You gave up the opportunity to have a say a year ago. Or did you forget?"

My jaw clenches at the memory. "I remember."

"Do you?" She raises her brows in question. "Do you remember what you told me? What you said to me when I stood before you and bared everything to you?" Her hands shove violently at my chest as anger overtakes her. "*Do you*? Do you remember what my heart sounded like when you broke it? I do." Her hands turn into fists and she beats them against my chest. I stand there and let her.

If this is what she needs, I'll give it to her. There are a lot of things that I can't give her, but this is one of the few things I can.

"You broke my heart and I'm trying to fix it. I'm fucking trying," she bites out. I stagger back a step as her fist connects with my jaw, but I still don't try to stop her. "But you keep showing up and ruining everything! You left me and I found

Gage. I was healing but then you came back and *ruined* it. You don't get a say in how I choose to fix myself, not when you're the one who *destroyed* me."

"It was never my intention to hurt you, Remington." That's the truth. I thought I was saving her from getting hurt. Saving her *from* me.

Remington is more than hurt. She's broken, and she's started to self-destruct. She's a beautiful disaster, a piece of art falling apart before my eyes.

"No, you don't get to do that," Remi snaps at me. "You don't get to make what happened okay. Just like you're not allowed to keep showing up where I am. You can't watch me stitch myself back together because if you do, I won't ever be whole again. Every time you're near me, the wounds I just fixed split open, and I bleed all over again." My chest aches from her assault, each time her fist pounds into me, I swallow a grunt.

A year ago, when this first all started and I put the distance between us, I thought it would be easier to stay away from her. I thought I would be strong enough to do what is right, but the absolute primal need I have to be near her is hard to suppress. It doesn't help that my wolf is just as desperate to be close to her. I'm usually able to ignore him, but when it comes to Remington, I can't.

"I just want you to be okay."

"Well, I'm not okay!" She shoves me back a step with an angry growl. "Why do you even care, Jax? You're the one who started all of this. You didn't want me too close. *You* turned me away. Isn't this what you wanted?"

Her words sear into me like a hot poker. The next time she swings her fists at me, I catch them, halting her assault.

"*Wanted*? You think I wanted this? Fuck, Remington. You think if I truly had a choice this is what I would have picked?" I snarl at her. She tries to jerk her hands free, but I hold them up and away from her body. She attempts one more time, but this time I shove her backward until her back collides with the brick wall. "Do you think it's easy for me to sit back and watch you drown when all I want to do is offer you my hand." I pin her arms to the wall above her head. "I don't know if you've been paying attention, but I'm not allowed to have anything that I *want*."

I wanted a normal childhood, but that was taken from me. I wanted to see the ocean with my mother, but Sterling killed her. I want Remington, but the lingering fear I might kill her keeps me from claiming what I want.

She stops fighting against my hold and tilts her chin up to look at me. "Don't say that," Remi bites out. "Don't stand here and tell me that you want me."

"Even if it's the truth?" I ask against my better judgment.

"Yes, especially then!" she cries. "It's exhausting hating you. It takes every ounce of my willpower to keep that hatred alive and hearing you say that makes me want to give in."

Our chests heave in pained breaths. We stand so close to each other I can feel her rib cage expand with each breath. "Why do you insist on hating me?"

Ocean blue eyes lock with mine. "Because it wouldn't be fair if I felt anything else." My gaze locks on her mouth when the tip of her pink tongue swipes across her bottom lip.

"Wouldn't be fair to who, love?" I press.

Remi doesn't answer my question, she's too busy drinking in every inch of my face. It's like she's allowing herself to truly look at me for the first time in a year. "I'm so tired, Jax."

"I know," I tell her. "What do you need, Remington?"

Her body goes lax. Whatever fight that remains melts from her body as she releases a long, pained breath. It's like she's been holding it in for months. "For just a moment, can we pretend that you're not you and I'm not me? Can we pretend we don't have a past and that our future isn't so bleak? Just for a moment, let's pretend we're perfect strangers."

Remington Weylyn will never be a stranger to me. My soul will always recognize hers. A year or a lifetime apart wouldn't allow me to forget her. She's imprinted herself in my bones.

My hands loosen on her wrists, but she doesn't make any move to pull them away from me.

"And what happens after?"

"Nothing changes," Remi answers without hesitation.

Dropping one of my hands from her wrists, I brush my fingers down the side of her face until I reach her chin. It's then that I grab her face and force her to truly look at me. I need to be sure that she wants this. She's sobered up since I first found her. There isn't an ounce of haziness in those blue orbs. She's fully here with me. "You told me earlier you wanted a man who knew nothing about you to fuck you against a wall," I rumble lowly. "I'm not that man. I *know* you, Remington."

"Pretend you don't." Her eyes burn with need. "Let's play pretend for just a little while."

Every ounce of my body knows this is a bad idea, but the part of me that craves her like I crave oxygen drowns out the doubt. My wolf grins in my head with glee. He knows I'm going to cave before I do.

I see the flames in Remi's eyes and feel as they burn away my last bit of resolve.

Kissing Remington is like taking my first breath of air. My body soars to life, every nerve ending in my body comes alive. My blood burns as the heat of her body mingles with mine.

She tastes of whatever fruity drink she'd been sipping on earlier—like a piece of candy. When her tongue brushes against mine tentatively a low animalistic rumble comes from my chest. Needing her closer, I release her hands I'd been holding hostage. In one fluid movement, I bend down and grasp the back of her thighs so I can hoist her up.

Remington needs no instructions. Her arms and legs immediately wrap around me as I press her to the wall once more. She whimpers as I grind my pelvis into hers, with each lick of her tongue against mine, the harder my dick becomes in my pants.

She tilts her hips, grinding against my hardening length as our mouths devour each other.

Her short black dress has ridden up once more and for the first time tonight, I'm happy she elected to not wear panties. Her bare flesh rubs against the fabric of my jeans. Remington gasps against my mouth before she tosses her head back.

With the beautiful column of her neck exposed to me, I dip my head so I can swipe my tongue over where her pulse thunders. A shifter marks their mate by biting the juncture of their neck. Never in my life has my wolf been remotely interested in marking someone, but now as I lave her neck with open mouth kisses, I can't help the thought from crossing my mind.

The scent of Remi's arousal fills the dark alleyway,

making me groan in her ear. "You smell so fucking good." Like a forbidden dessert. "Touch yourself," I order her.

Without objection, Remington dips her hand between her thighs. I pull away from her neck just long enough to watch her play with herself. Her finger swirls around her clit, once, twice, three times, before she slowly slips one inside of her. Just like at the hotel, the sight of her touching herself is mesmerizing.

Groaning, I return to her mouth. She doesn't open for me immediately like I want her to, but that changes when I give her a warning nip to her bottom lip. She growls unhappily at me but doesn't protest as I sweep into her hot mouth.

She sucks on my tongue, making my own need increase as I think of what it would feel like to have her do the same thing to my cock. To have her hot mouth suck everything I have to give out of me.

Remington begins to pant harder against my mouth as she brings herself closer to her impending release. "Oh God," she whimpers, the nails of her free hand digging into my shoulder.

I want her to come, but I want it to be on *my* fingers.

I break my mouth away from her. "That's enough," I command. "Take them out."

Her eyes fly open and frustration fills them. "What? *No.* I'm so close."

Shifting her weight, I hold her up with one hand while the other reaches between us to snake around her wrist. She pumps her fingers inside once more and whines when I forcibly pull them from her core.

Her eyes heat as I bring her hand to my mouth. Remington's lips part as she watches me suck her fingers clean. I was so jealous she was the one who did this at the hotel room. This is retaliation for depriving me of the opportunity before.

"Your pussy might be the sweetest thing about you."

Even before her soul turned black and the light dimmed in her eyes, Remington was never sweet. She was sarcastic with a spitfire attitude. Her words could cut like knives if she wanted them to—hell, that's a skill she still has.

Remington's eyes flutter when I drag my fingers lazily down her stomach and then through her bare pussy lips. When I finally begin to massage her clit, her eyes close tight, as if her body is too overwhelmed to keep them open. "Open your eyes," I order. "I want them on me as you come."

Her eyes, like matching blue flames, snap open and connect with me.

"You want that, right?" I ask as I tease her opening with the tip of my finger. "You want my fingers inside of you, don't you?"

"Yes," she whispers.

I dip my finger inside, but quickly remove it, only giving her a taste of what's to come. She whimpers in frustration. "Yes what?"

It's not in her nature to be submissive, to give things over freely. Her chin tilts stubbornly, but when I roughly roll her clit between my fingers, she finally chokes out her answer. "Y-yes. I want to come on your fingers."

"Good girl." I reward her by sinking two fingers inside of her tight channel.

Her muscles clamp down on the digits as she releases a ragged breath.

I want to savor this moment because I know it very well might be the last, but at the same time, I want her primed and ready for my cock as fast as possible. It presses painfully against the zipper of my jeans, aching to be deep inside of her.

Remi's hips move in tandem as I thrust my fingers into her. Each time the pads of my fingers brush against that spot inside of her, she sucks in a shallow breath. When she starts to get close to falling over the edge, her muscles begin to shake around my waist.

"Come for me," I order, nipping at her chin with my blunt teeth. My gums burn, my elongated wolf fangs threatening to make an appearance, but I force them to stay back. I wouldn't trust myself to not bite her if they were out

With shaking legs and breathless pants, Remington shatters on my fingers.

Skimming my lips across her sweat-coated temple, I place her back on the ground in front of me.

She wastes no time before tackling the buckle of my jeans. While she unzips my pants, I tear off the leather jacket I wear, tossing it over one of the empty plastic crates around us. The crisp April air cools off my burning skin.

Remington just has the zipper down before her deft fingers are snaking inside. An almost pained sounding breath escapes between my teeth as she wraps her fingers around my hard length. My hips jerk forward, and I place my palm on the wall to keep from falling forward.

She looks up at me, a sly look on her face as she slowly begins to work my dick. With each brush of her hand, my control slips. Remi tugs the waistband of my jeans and briefs down until my dick springs out. Red and swollen, desperate for more of her touch.

Her thumb swipes across the crown, smearing the drop of precum around. Boldly, she holds eye contact as she brings her thumb up and places it in her mouth. Moaning low in her throat, she savors the flavor.

"Careful," I warn her lowly. "Or I'll force you to your knees in this dirty alleyway."

She removes her thumb from her mouth with an audible pop. "Who said you'd be forcing me?"

I caress my hand across her jaw and then down her throat. "I always told you that mouth of yours was going to get you in trouble." I bare my teeth at her as I collar her throat.

Her eyes flash as her wolf springs to the surface, I feel my own eyes shift as my wolf does the same. This is the closest our wolves have ever been to each other and if I have my way, the closest they'll ever be.

"And I always said you're not the one who gets to punish me," she sneers back while her hand picks up speed.

With a low growl, I have her turned around and move to stand behind her. Pressing her upper torso to the brick wall, I bend down to whisper in her ear. "You sure about that?" I slide my palm along her exposed ass cheek before giving it a slap.

She swings her hand back at me like she wants to claw me, but when the head of my dick swipes through her creamy folds, she stills. "That's what I thought." I chuckle.

Remi's back bows as she presses her hips back. Her arms lean against the wall, keeping herself up.

I tease her entrance with my dick, making her squirm before me, but she remains silent. "What? No more smart-ass remarks? Come on Remi, that's so not like you."

Her head turns so she can glare at me over her shoulder. "Either fuck me or get lost so I can find someone who—"

I'm thrusting deep inside of her before she can finish her

sentence. She cries out into the night air, the sound echoing off the building around us. I'm sure someone heard her, but I don't give a shit. Sinking into Remington delivers a kind of euphoria no street drug could ever replicate.

As her whole body shakes from the invasion, I brush her hair from her shoulder. "Threatening to have another man fuck you while my fingers still smell of your last orgasm isn't a good idea, love."

"Neither is this, yet here we are," Remi breathes out as her body adjusts to my length.

Painfully slow, I ease myself out of her. "What? You want me to stop?" I offer even though I know there's no going back. If we don't finish what we started, I may combust into flames.

Her muscles tighten around my cock, desperate to keep me buried deep inside. "Don't you fucking dare," she warns.

"Couldn't even if I wanted to."

I slowly build up my momentum, thrusting shallowly at first but as her soft sounds of need grow louder, I find it hard to go slow. My fingers dig into the curve of her hip, no doubt leaving bruises on her tanned skin as I plunge deeper into her.

With each thrust, my wolf bangs against his cage begging for me to let him partake. The scent of her arousal drives him mad. Gritting my teeth so hard I'm surprised my molars don't crack, I force him back down.

I want to focus on the woman before me, not the beast within. Those two things can never commingle.

Removing one of her hands from the wall, she delves it between her creamy thighs. Remington plays with herself as I fuck her from behind. Nothing about this transaction is sweet or romantic. There are no red roses or silk sheets. This is raw, primal, and *angry*.

She's angry at me and I'm angry at myself for something I can't undo. That I refuse to fix.

Snaking my arm around her, I roll one of her pebbled nipples between my fingers through the material of her dress. Remi hisses out a breath as the sensation makes her whole body quiver.

I want this to last, but this encounter is a long time coming. Months of angry glances and actions have been slowly bringing me to the edge. Watching her finger fuck herself on the bed earlier almost sent me over and now as her walls tighten and quiver around me, it's taking everything I have to not go off.

Her body is coated in a sheen of sweat and the gray T-shirt I wear clings to my own damp skin.

Removing my hand from her breast, I drag it up her spine to tangle it into the silky strands of her chocolate brown hair. Remington growls in protest when I roughly angle her head back so I can lick across the seam of her mouth. With little prompting, she opens for me and greets my tongue eagerly with hers.

Our breaths combine as we both race toward our climaxes.

When the walls of her pussy start to flutter and she begins to throw her hips back to meet each of my deep thrusts, I know she's close.

"That's it, show me how much you hate me," I order against her mouth before biting down hard on her bottom lip at the same time I thrust as hard and deep as I can.

I swallow her scream as she comes around my cock in a shaking, shuddering mess. Her squeezing me until my world tilts and I momentarily forget how to breathe. Pleasure rips through my body as I spill everything I have inside of her. I ride out the wave, continuing to move in and out of her in shallow movements until I have nothing left and we both collapse forward.

We stay there, catching our breaths. Her pussy continues to quiver around my dick and each time her muscles flex, I have to bite back a groan.

She rests her head against the brick wall, breathing hard while my forehead hangs on her shoulder. Our panting and erratic heartbeats are the only sound around us. The scent of our orgasms mingle in the cool night air.

For a moment, there is no anger and there is no remorse. We are just us; sweaty and spent. The storm that brews between us has calmed. The thunder and lightning are silent, the treacherous wind is still, but it doesn't last long. I know the second it all comes crashing back to her. Her muscles tense and her spine straightens abruptly, forcing me to stand up with her.

The walls of her pussy flex once more on my cock before she pulls herself off of me. Remington keeps her back to me as she silently pulls her dress back into place and smooths her mussed hair. She's not trying to make herself presentable. No, she's fixing the armor she had temporarily removed.

With each passing second, she's slowly putting the walls she's spent a year building back into place.

I follow her lead, shoving my semihard cock back into the confines of my jeans. "Remington," I try as I zip up my pants.

She doesn't say anything, keeps her eyes locked on the wall in front of her. She lets out a long breath before her chin tilts up and her shoulders go back. Like she's steeling herself to face me.

Wordlessly, she turns around and spears me with a cold stare. "Nothing changes," Remington repeats her earlier words, her tone lacking any semblance of emotion.

Remington pushes past me, the sound of her black heels clicking against the concrete echo through the alleyway.

My hand shoots out and wraps around her upper arm before she can get too far.

"Wait, Remi," I plead. "You're just going to walk away after that?"

She jerks her arm from my grasp and backs away from me. Remington eyes me up and down with cruel eyes before sneering, "You left me naked and heartbroken last time, it's only fair I'm the one who gets to leave you now." Her words have me freezing in place. "What was it you said last time?" Remington ponders this for a second as my stomach pools with dread. "Oh right! Now I remember." She snaps her fingers. "This was nothing but a meaningless fuck—something to scratch the itch. It meant nothing to me. You mean nothing to me."

It physically hurt me to say those words to her. Never in my life have I felt more disgusted with myself than I did when I spewed them at Remington. I've done some horrific things while involved with Nicolai and Sterling, but what I did to Remington a year ago will be something I'll never be able to forgive myself for.

I broke her heart after she laid it out bare for me. I'd stomped on it and then for good measure, spit on it too just to be sure she truly got the message. And while I did it, I felt a kind of pain I haven't felt since I discovered my mother had been killed.

As much as it hurt me, I can't take it back. After a year, nothing has changed. I'm still a danger to Remi and I don't trust myself to truly be with her.

I like to think that I've figured out how to keep the side of myself that scares even me at bay, but I haven't. Not really. All it would take is one wrong move before the beast in me is free, burning everything in its path. If that happens, Remi can't be anywhere near me.

I wanted to believe that if I told her that she meant nothing to me that I would start to believe it myself, but I never did. Ten months I spent away from Remi while I was in hiding with Pruitt and not a day went by that I didn't wish I could take back those words. That I could be with her.

Shaking my head slowly, I say, "I don't think you mean that any more than I did."

The only sign that she's affected by what I say is by the sound of her heart's quickening pace. Remi's face remains impassive, and her eyes remain cold. "I guess we'll never know," she finally offers before turning on her heels.

This time when she leaves, I let her.

CHAPTER TEN
Remington

It's been two days since I put my anger on pause and let Jax have his dirty, wicked way with me in that alley. For two days, I've smelled of him. No matter how many times I've scrubbed myself clean, his smoky, alluring scent clings to my skin—like it's now part of me. It permanently marked me as his, which is something I'll never be. He made that clear a year ago.

His scent was like a second skin on me the last time I let him touch me, but I don't remember it lasting for days. Maybe the absolute hurt and rejection I was feeling masked it, but now I can't get it to go away. Maybe it's because deep down I'm not ready for it to be gone.

For the past six months, I've spent every second pushing him away and lashing out when he got too close. That whole time I felt dead. I couldn't see the colors or feel the heat of the sun on my skin. I was simply going through the motions of living, but the other night when I allowed Jax to get close, I felt like I could breathe again. The blood in my veins that had been ice cold heated and I saw the colors again.

I really miss feeling alive, but how am I allowed to move

forward in life when Gage can't? I deprived him of the opportunity to live—to move forward. He's now nothing but a memory in the heads of the people that cared for him.

A penance I will never be able to repay.

I push through the double doors of the bar, Elsie stumbling out behind me. The poor human can't hold her liquor. To be fair, I'm also intoxicated, but I can at least walk in a straight line and touch my nose. This bitch doesn't even know where her nose is right now.

When her ankle twists, I instinctively reach out and catch her before she can smack her face on the pavement. "*Whoops*!" She giggles as I bring her back to her feet. "It's a good thing you're so fast, I can't afford a nose job right now."

"Don't you come from a family of doctors?" I loop my arm around her and lead her slowly toward the taxi we'd called for her.

"No, I said my dad *married* a doctor," she hiccups. "And I don't think plastic surgery is her specialty—*hey!* You should come spend the night with me, we can order pizza and find a horrible reality TV show to watch."

Her offer makes me long for my best friend. I miss Pruitt and miss when I felt like I could go to her about anything. She doesn't have time for my problems anymore and she definitely doesn't have time for such pointless activities such as watching mindless television with me. There was a time that I could show up at her house with a thing of cheap box wine and we'd sit in her bed, laughing and gossiping about nothing in particular. That was before she knew the truth of who she was and before she had all her responsibilities. She's mated and has a baby on the way.

I laugh off her request while I awkwardly fumble with the door of the taxi. Elsie wraps her arms around my neck and clings to me as I try to shove her into the back seat. She chuckles and sways the whole time like she's having the best time. Finally, I wrangle her into the car and strap her in with the seat belt.

Quickly, I rattle off the name of Elsie's apartment to the driver, Jeanie. She's a member of the pack, so I know she'll get my friend back to her apartment safe.

I stand there until the taillights of the taxi disappear as I contemplate my next moves. The bar is still alive with music and people, beckoning *me* back inside, but I'm tired. On top of Jax's scent permeating my skin, he's also found his way into my dreams. Instead of the nightmares I've had for months, I *dreamed* of the demon with the violet eyes. I *dreamed* of his touch and the way it eases the pain.

The pain he created.

It's twisted that the architect of my pain is also the one who can heal it.

I have no idea what I was thinking letting him touch me again, I barely survived it last time.

Looking longingly at the door of the bar once more, I turn on my heels and make my way toward my car.

I used to not think twice about calling one of my brothers to pick me up, but the idea of bothering them or pulling them away from the happy lives they've built for themselves stops me. Besides, being locked inside a car with them while I have nowhere to escape their worried looks or lectures seems like a special kind of hell. Why is it that conversations you don't want to have are always done in confined spaces?

I'm tipsy, not wasted. I can drive the twenty minutes to

my hotel. I've been making bad decision after bad decision lately, why stop now?

Climbing inside the electric blue 4Runner I bought myself when I got into nursing school, I snag the bottle of water I'd left in the cup holder earlier. I chug the contents before starting the car and driving away from the commotion of the bar.

All the streets around here are winding and curvy. Once you're away from the main part of town the roads are lined with thick forest. There aren't any streetlights. The only source this late at night is from the headlights of the passing cars.

The lingering scent of Jax that's clinging to my skin fills the confined space until I feel like I'm choking on it. Desperate for a reprieve from the demon, I roll down all the windows. The chilly night air floods the car, cooling down my skin and momentarily washing away the smell of him.

I relax into the leather of my seat, my hair whipping around my face as I navigate the roads I know like the back of my hand. Each curve, each crack in the cement I'm familiar with. That's what happens when you've spent your whole life in one place.

There was a time that I never thought I'd want to escape my home. Why would I? This is where my family is and before my life fell apart and I became the shell of the person that I am now, I couldn't imagine living far away from them.

I never used to think this way. While I wouldn't go as far as to say that I was the embodiment of positivity, I used to be more of a glass half full kind of girl. Now, I can only focus on all the things I've lost instead of what my family has gained since Sterling appeared in our lives. I only see the negative.

No longer wanting to think about the source of the ever-present impending doom I feel in my chest, I turn up the music and allow it to drown out my unwanted thoughts.

My fingers tap out the beat of the music and I focus on the lyrics of the song. Slowly, I begin to relax. I just want to get to the hotel and take a hot shower so I can climb into bed. I'm too tired tonight to dread the dreams I know will come. I'm too tired to fight them off. If Jax or Gage want to appear in my dreams tonight, so be it. Maybe just for tonight, some company won't be so bad.

A car comes around a curve ahead of me with its high beams on. My sensitive eyes burn as the headlights shine into my corneas. "*Asshole,*" I grumble under my breath while I blink away the spots in my vision.

As they get closer, I shield my eyes with my hands to ease the discomfort my poor eyes feel. It's only as they pass me do I realize just how fast they're driving and how close to the median line they are. To avoid being run into, I'm forced to abruptly jerk my car to the side. My tires on the passenger side grind against the gravel on the edge of the road, causing my car to rattle.

Shaken from nearly crashing, my hands tighten on the steering wheel as I right myself and return to the paved road. *Who the hell was that?* No one around here drives like that on these roads. Especially at night. We all know how dangerous they can be.

I glance in my rearview mirror quickly in hopes of getting their license plate to report to the sheriff but discover I can't see the tail of their SUV because it's making an illegal U-turn in the middle of the road. And turning back toward me.

Unease bubbles in my stomach and my wolf snaps to

attention in my head, her own warning bells going off. The last time I ignored my gut, I paid an excruciating price. I want to be wrong, but on the off chance I'm not, I increase my speed.

Whatever buzz I had going is long gone, the remaining alcohol in my system metabolizing as my body goes on high alert.

The black SUV catches up to me quickly, staying close behind me. Each time I pick up my speed, it does the same so it can maintain the space between us. My hands twist anxiously on the wheel as every nerve in my body comes alive with worry.

There's a four-way stop coming up in a mile. That will be the real test on whether they are just a random asshole with road rage or if they're truly following me. If they turn the same way I do, I'll plan my next moves.

As I speed toward the stop, I keep glancing between the rearview mirror and the road before me. Not once have they fallen back or granted more than six feet between our cars.

My headlights stream against the red reflective paint of the stop sign at the four-way stop. I stop and consider my options.

If I go left, it will take me down the road that will lead me into the other town where my hotel is. If I go right, it will lead me into pack territory where my family is.

If they're truly following me, do I want to lead them back to my pack? But on the other hand, I don't want to lead them back to the hotel where I'm alone.

So alone.

My body makes up its mind before my mind does. My foot slams against the accelerator and I race down the road that will take me home. I hold my breath as I wait to see what they'll do, but in my gut, I already knew they'd follow.

Remi, think, I silently order myself.

The sound of their roaring engine comes through all my open windows as they catch up to me. I'm not sure what they have planned but they're not planning on letting me go, that much is clear.

Holding the wheel with one hand, my other digs around in my purse on the passenger side. The phone I carry with me has been silenced for weeks, but out of habit, I carry it everywhere with me. Though now I'm cursing myself for turning it off because waiting for it to turn back on is costing me precious time.

I'm watching the screen, counting the seconds as it loads painfully slowly when I'm thrown forward unexpectedly, the sound of metal and plastic crunching accompanying the sudden movement. I drop the phone and return both hands to the steering wheel so I can straighten the car as it weaves on the street.

They're trying to run me off the road.

Shit.

In the passenger seat, my phone illuminates as my lock screen finally appears. With a fleeting glance in my rearview mirror, I dive across the middle console and grab the device.

The SUV tries to speed past me, but I quickly swerve to block them. If they get ahead of me and stop in the middle of the road, they'll be able to box me in.

I glance at my contact list and contemplate who I should call. When I see their name, I click on it without thinking it through. If anyone can get here quick, it's them. I just hope they actually pick up.

Behind me, they hit me again. This time on my left bumper. I jerk forward but my seat belt keeps me in place as the car swerves on the road again.

A harsh curse escapes my lips when they finally answer on the third ring. "Remington?"

"I'm five miles away from pack territory," I stammer out, not bothering with a greeting. Now isn't the time for pleasantries. "I have a black SUV on my ass. They're trying to run me off the road, Isabeau."

I don't know what made me call her, but after our exchange the other day, she feels less like a stranger and someone I can count on to help. And right now, I need help.

The phone is silent for a second and I pull it back to make sure that we're still connected. "Beau?"

"What do you mean they're trying to run you off the road?"

I veer to the side again, narrowly avoiding being hit again. "Someone is following me! They've already hit my car twice."

There's harsh whispering like she's reiterating the information to someone, but with the sound of my erratic heart pounding in my ears and the turbulent wind blowing through the window, I can't make out who she's talking to. If I had to guess, it's Ransom.

"We're on our way, Remi," Isabeau vows.

"Hurry, something is wro—"

The car starts to go around my passenger side. As I quickly angle my car to block them, they abruptly snake around the driver's side. I know what their plan is before they execute it. I even slam on my brakes trying to put distance between us, but it's no use.

They slam into me, sideswiping my car. There's the deafening sound of metal scraping together and crunching from the impact. My fingers wrap around the leather of my steering wheel so tight I'm surprised the whole thing doesn't bend in my hands.

The impact shoves me toward the edge of the tree-lined road. In a desperate attempt to keep all four of my tires on the pavement, I accidentally overcorrect myself. At the same time, the delinquent driver collides with me once more, this time they connect right into my back side panel.

The force causes the back end of my car to spin out. I try so hard to keep the car straight, but the momentum of the strike causes me to fly off the road.

The portion of the road we're at now doesn't have guardrails protecting cars from going into the ditch if, God forbid, they lose control. I don't know why I've never noticed it before, but now as I grapple to brace myself while my car rolls down the shallow ditch, it comes to mind.

My head snaps forward and then backward as my world spins around me. The vertebrae in my neck ache in pain from the force in which my head is thrown about. I've never wondered what it was like to be in a blender when it was turned on, but I imagine it's quite similar to this.

The seat belt digs into my chest and the shoulder that had been knocked out of socket just days ago screams in pain once again. At some point the airbags deploy. The angle in which my head is turned, and my body is positioned, means I'm hit headfirst by the deploying airbag. Had I been sitting normally in my seat, I'm sure it wouldn't have caused a problem, but being thrown about as the car rolls down the hill left me wide open for injuries.

With one last final plummeting turn, the car finally comes to a stop at the bottom of the ridge.

I blink rapidly, trying to clear my blurring vision so I can take in my surroundings. It takes a moment for me to figure out what the hell I'm looking at. It's not until the blood from my split lip drips down into my eyes do I piece together that I'm upside down. The seat belt keeps me suspended in the air.

One of my headlights still works, allowing light to fill the damaged cabin on the vehicle. It streams in through the shattered windshield. Smoke and a low hissing sound coming from the hood of the car.

You need to get out, the voice in my head orders.

The fire that Jax wields may not scare me but being caught in real flames seems less than desirable. I try not to think about how I'll die. While the idea of going out in a blaze of glory sounds ideal, I'd really rather not be burned alive.

My bruised and aching arm drops to my side, searching for the buckle. My thumb presses the red button to release me, but nothing happens. I try over and over again, but still, I hang upside down.

When headlights from up above the road flash over me, I hold my breath trying to slow my erratic heart so I can hear what they're doing. If I can't get the seat belt off, I'm basically a sitting duck just waiting for them to come down here and scoop me up.

My limbs shake with adrenaline as the brakes of the car squeak when it comes to a stop. I wait silently for the doors to open, but they remain still. Like they're waiting for something.

Releasing the breath I was holding, I focus on my hands. Learning to extend your claws and fangs is one of the first things we learn growing up. It usually comes easy, but for me and my wolf, we allow our emotions to dictate how fast we can shift. If I'm scared and panicking, a mental block is put up between us. It doesn't matter how much I want her to make an appearance, if I let my emotions take over, my wolf will get stuck.

I close my eyes and focus on calming myself enough to make my claws appear, but all I can think about is how it felt to tumble down that hill. This town has always been a safe place, because my pack keeps it safe. The people here leave their front doors unlocked and no one drives aggressively. Whoever did this to me isn't from around here. There's only one person that I know of that would want me dead.

Sterling has never met me in person, but that doesn't matter. I'm his enemy and he's mine. Sometimes you don't have to meet someone face to face to know that you hate them. How could I ever like that man knowing what he's done to hundreds of innocent women? He kidnaps them, sometimes right out of their beds, and forces them into his breeding facilities. A man like that is instantly unlikeable in my book.

A car door opens, and I hear the low voices murmuring to each other. "What the hell was that? She's no good to us if she's roadkill," a man's voice I don't recognize criticizes.

"She went off script tonight by leaving the bar early. I had to improvise," another deep voice assures.

They were watching me at the bar? How could I have not noticed? I was raised to pay attention to my surroundings, but I've been living in my own little bubble for months. Looking beyond myself was too much to handle. I could barely keep up with myself, let alone someone else. I've been in an alcohol-induced fog for some time now, but it was reckless.

I've been reckless with everything. My life more than anything.

There are footsteps. The way the soles of the shoes clack against the pavement, I would guess whoever is up there is wearing dress shoes. I think back to the bar and try to think if I saw anyone dressed in nicer clothes but draw a blank.

"Wait," the first voice orders. "We need to go."

"Why?"

"Someone's coming, I can smell them. They're getting close."

The second person pauses like he's considering his options. My ears strain to listen to their next move while I desperately try to keep unlocking the buckle. "She's *right* there. I'll go get her and then we can leave."

"*No*," the voice argues. "We don't have time. We'll find another way—he always has a backup plan."

"I'll go quick," they insist. "He needs her—"

"You're not listening to me. We do not want to be here when they show up. I've seen what they can do, we don't stand a chance."

There's a silent moment of hesitation before they finally sigh in defeat. "Fine, but this is on you. When he's angry at us for not following through with the plan, the blame will not be placed on me."

The dress shoes clack against the pavement as he retreats. When the door of the car slams closed, my claws finally make their appearance. *Better late than never, I guess.* In a mad scramble, I slice through the seat belt restraining me. My body aches as I fall unceremoniously into the ruins of my car.

On unsteady feet, I clamber out of the car and hurry up the hill back to the road. My black boots slip in wet grass and mud from the rain that fell days prior. My nails dig into the earth, trying to gain some traction so I can make it up the embankment before they leave.

I'm in no shape for a fight right now, but I want to see their faces, or at least a license plate before they disappear down the dark road. Had we made it down the road another mile, the security cameras placed around pack territory would have caught them, but out here, they'll be able to go on without a trace.

With one last push, I stumble back onto the road. Blood trickles from the cut on my lip and nose. I'm not completely sure, but I think there might be a gash on my forehead. Dislocating your shoulder twice in one week should be a record. It would be if I wasn't raised with my brothers. Those assholes were breaking bones every other day, usually from wounds inflicted by each other.

Cradling my injured arm with one good one, I watch the taillights of the SUV as it drives away. Squinting to clear my hazy vision, I look for the license plate number.

"Shit," I whisper under my breath when I see the plate is missing. Truly a smart move on their part. If I was planning on running someone off the road, I wouldn't want any identifying markers on my vehicle either.

From what it sounds like, they weren't just planning on making me crash. They wanted to take *me*.

But why?

My silent wondering is silenced when there's rustling in the trees behind me. Whirling around, my wolf surges forward, prepared to take on another assailant. When Isabeau's body appears from the shadows she can melt into, I relax, releasing all the air in my lungs in relief.

Her pale eyes assess the situation in front of her, from my completely demolished car to my banged-up state. She cocks her head in the direction of where the speeding car went. Her hearing is so advanced she can hear ants moving in the dirt below our very feet. She often wears headphones to help drown out the sounds around her when it becomes too much for her to handle.

In a move that even my advanced eyesight has trouble tracking, her leather-clad body is just a blur in the night, she moves to stand on the road with me.

"I don't know who they were, I didn't recognize their voices," I begin to stammer out, feeling rattled. "There weren't any license plates either, but I have the make and model."

She's quiet for a moment, just watching me with eyes that never miss a single detail. "Are you alright?"

I'm growing really tired of that question. The answer is always the same. I'm not alright. Haven't been for a long time. "I'll live."

Beau nods her head almost in an approving way. "Good. Ransom is running after the car. We'll know soon if he finds them." She shifts to stand in front of me. Without preamble or permission, her cold hands grab my arm and in one quick twist, places it back in the socket.

It doesn't hurt any less now than it did when Jax did the same thing just days ago. I grit my teeth and ride out the wave of pain.

Letting out a breath between my clenched teeth, I ask, "Did you tell anyone other than Ransom what happened?"

Isabeau walks the various skid marks left along the dark road, like she's replaying the events that happened in her head. She's so skilled at things like this I'm sure she can tell the second I lost control of my car. She stops at the edge of the road and looks down at the heap of metal that was once a car. "I just told Ransom," she finally answers.

"Thank God," I mumble, wiping the blood off my chin with my hand. "I don't need any more of my family showing up here tonight. I can't deal with their concerned stares and patronizing words. My mom will probably—"

She cuts me off, "*Remington*." Beau turns around and shakes her head tightly. "I said *I* didn't tell anyone else."

Understanding dawns on me after a second. "Oh." I grimace. "Ransom called them."

"Yes," she admits. "We're the fastest, that's why we're here before the rest."

I probably only have minutes before everyone shows up in full force. The little voice in my head whispers for me to run, that I still have time to get away, but truthfully, I'm tired. I'm tired from running from my problems and running from my family. The problem is, I know if I stop now, I'll have to face what's happened head-on and I'm not sure I'll be able to survive that. It's either I keep running or feel the pain I've worked so hard to avoid. Neither option feels ideal.

Shifting to the edge of the road, I stare down at the carnage of my car. I felt sober enough while driving, but if I hadn't been drinking, would I have had faster reflexes? Could I have avoided all of this by getting away from them sooner? If I hadn't been partying, maybe I would have noticed them watching me at the bar to begin with.

I could have died tonight.

Not just tonight. All the reckless choices I've been making lately have put me in danger. I'm willingly putting myself in positions where anything could happen to me. The amount of alcohol I've been consuming dulls the pain, but it also eliminates any sense of right and wrong. All those nights I drank so much I blacked out, anyone could have taken advantage of my state. I was foolish to think that Sterling wouldn't be watching all of us. I might not be one of the heavy hitters, but I'm associated with them. Of course, he'd still been watching me. He's watching all of us.

What have I been thinking?

I don't realize I've said those words aloud until Beau, without turning her head, simply says, "You haven't been. You're afraid if you do think, you're going to feel and you're trying your damnedest to not do that." Annoyingly observant as always. Both Winslow and Beau have an eerie way of knowing things that have never been admitted aloud. "Just remember when you refuse to feel anything, you're not only depriving yourself of pain, but also the good."

"Nothing has felt good in a really long time," I tell her, even though it's a lie. Being with Jax the other night felt good. For those few moments that I let go of the hurt and the anger, I felt good. My whole body felt at peace being in his presence even though I know it shouldn't have. The reprieve was short, but nonetheless, it felt good.

Beau finally turns and looks at me, but my eyes remain fixed on the flickering headlight of my car. "We're not close. That's partially my fault since I'm new to having a family or friends. I don't know how to be there for someone, but I can be there for you. You can tell me what happened. You can tell me what happened when Gage died."

My stomach pits out, the memories of that day filling my head. The visual of Gage fighting off rogue wolves and thirsty vampires. The way his eyes cut to mine when he realized he was losing...

No!

Closing my eyes tight, I fight to clear my head of him. "Nothing *happened*. Just like the others, he died in the battle. He was the head enforcer of this pack. It was his job to protect his pack and he died doing his job." If I tell the lie enough, will I start to believe it myself? "He was a hero." I might throw up.

"Remi—"

"I'll be right back," I announce, cutting her off. "I'm going to go grab my purse and phone from the car before everyone shows up." I want to be ready to leave as fast as possible.

I clamber back down the hill, the soles of my boots only slipping once in the mud. My eyes burn as tears threaten to fall. I don't want to cry here. I'm afraid if I start, I'll never stop. It's already going to be bad having my whole family show up here, I don't need them to see my tears. No, I reserve those for at night when no one can see them. I let them fall freely into my pillow.

Swallowing hard, I stuff the emotions back down where I need them to stay for just a little while longer.

Not wanting to be too close to the wreckage for too long, I make quick work of searching for my purse. Everything in it is replaceable, but I needed an excuse to walk away from the observant vampire. On my hands and knees, I peer through the open windows of my upside-down car. Glass digs into the palms of my hands making me wince and yank my hand away.

The familiar black leather strap of my purse catches my

eye. Reaching through the open window, I try my best to grab it, but my arm is too short. Pulling back, I sit on my heels and think about my next moves. It's *right* there and I've come this far already. I'm committed now.

Ducking low so I can fit through the window, I shimmy my head and torso into the remains of the car. My lips lift in a triumphant smile when my fingers wrap around the leather handle of the purse, but the smile instantly disappears when the scent of smoke fills the cabin of the car. My head snaps in the direction of where my engine sits, and I discover bright orange flames building.

Oh no.

CHAPTER ELEVEN
Jax

I stand in front of the wall, staring at all the pictures and documents I've taped up there while collecting information on Sterling. Most of it is the same information that's at Beau's house on her bulletin board, but I like to have my own copies. When I can't sleep at night, which is something that happens a lot, I stare at the pieces of paper, hoping I'll miraculously piece something together that we've missed before.

It's yet to happen but that hasn't stopped me so far.

In the middle of all the photographs of known locations, and people Sterling is affiliated with is a dark silhouette of a man with a red question mark on his face. Both Isabeau and I know what Sterling looks like, but we've yet to obtain a picture of him ourselves. It doesn't matter that it's been sixteen years since I laid eyes on the man, I would recognize him anywhere. His image is ingrained in my brain like an ugly tattoo. Or a scar. A scar would be more fitting since he left me with many, and I returned the favor.

I may not have inherited Sterling's looks, but I inherited his drive. He's stopped at nothing to accomplish his goal. His desire to create the perfect being has become an obsession. His goal is perfection. Each species has a weakness, and he wants to counteract or get rid of them entirely. Isabeau, for instance, her fae blood allows her to be in the sun, regardless of her vampire genes. I'm immune to the effects of silver that would usually harm my wolf side because of my demon genetics. The small amount of warlock blood in my system makes me resistant to most spells and witchcraft. Winslow is part necromancer, but her witch side counteracts the darkness necromancers carry with them.

He has, what we call, breeding facilities, all over North America. They're full of women he took. Just like my mother, they're forced to carry these so-called 'perfect' embryos, and just like my mother, when they're no longer able to carry these babies to term, they're terminated.

That's what drives him and what drives me is the idea that one day I'll slaughter him for the horrors he's done. I'm not going to let anything, or anyone stop me or distract me from what I need to accomplish.

Grabbing the folder I'd left on the cracked countertop of my small kitchen, I flip through the contents next. I can almost recite the documents word for word I've read them over so many times. It's all the same information I already know. Aliases Kaius has used over the many years he's been alive. God knows how old that fucker is. When you have the ability to steal souls—life—from others, you can probably live forever. Which is a problem, because that also means Sterling can live forever.

My phone buzzes in the back pocket of my jeans as I scan the addresses of the places we know Sterling has used in the past. Many of them are burned down or empty now. "What?"

I answer the phone distractedly, my focus still primarily on the information in front of me.

"Jax, something's happened with Remi." Pru's panicked voice comes through the line, making my heart seize in my chest. My hand drops the folder, the paper skids across the floor while I freeze in place as worst-case scenarios immediately start playing in my head. "Ransom said it was a car accident or something."

I took the night off from watching her stare at information I already know forward and backward. After fucking her in the alley, I needed to put space back between us or I was going to forget why it's a bad idea for me to get too close. She wasn't supposed to be at the club, I thought she would be fine for a night.

Fuck!

"Where?" My voice is unrecognizable to me as I bite out the word. It's the only thing I can manage to say as images of her broken body in her wrecked car fill my head.

"Five miles away from pack territory on the back road." The sound of a car slamming shut echoes behind her voice. "We're on our way there now."

"Is she alive?" I manage, my free hand fisting in the strands of my dark hair. Pruitt doesn't answer straight away, making my stomach bottom out. "Pruitt! Is she alive?"

"We don't know," she finally confesses, her voice cracking. "She called Isabeau, but the line went dead after she heard the car crash. We don't know what happened yet."

I take a steadying breath before releasing it slowly. "I'll meet you there." I hang up before she can respond.

Never in my life have I called up on my power as fast as I do now.

I materialize on the dark winding road fifty yards from where Isabeau stands with her back to me on the road. She's alone. From where I stand, there isn't any sign of Remington or her car. It's not until I focus my eyes do I catch the flickering light coming from the shallow ditch in front of her.

Taking off in a sprint, I run toward the vampire. *Why is she just standing there?*

I skid to a stop at the edge of the road next to her and follow her gaze below. The car is upside down, far beyond any repair. It's on the tip of my tongue to ask if Remington is still inside the vehicle and if she's alive, but movement beside the car silences me. Remington sits on her hands and knees as she attempts to fish something out of her car. Her back is to me, I doubt she knows I'm here yet.

"What is she doing?" I ask Isabeau once I'm able to breathe again.

"I don't think *she* can even answer that question," Isabeau answers, cutting me a bland look.

The tightness in my chest eases once I see that she's alive, but the lingering scent of Remington's blood in the air keeps my beast on edge. She's alive, but she's still hurt. A low growl escapes my lips as my wolf pushes forward.

Understanding my displeasure, Beau assures me, "It's superficial wounds. She's lucky considering she could have died."

"What the fuck happened?"

"She says someone was trying to run her off the road." Isabeau frowns, her voice turning angry. "Ransom is trying to track the car now."

Like a rabid animal, my wolf loses his mind. He throws himself against his cage with such force my whole body jerks, and the tips of my fingers burn as my claws extend. It's been many years since I've shifted even this much in front of another person. The last time was when I was poked and jabbed relentlessly with a cattle prod by Nicolai when he decided to put on a show in front of some of the other bigwigs in Sterling's organization. I was sixteen at the time, my wolf still a juvenile and not yet at his full size. In the span of ninety seconds, he had killed thirteen people. The number of tranquilizers it took to stop him actually ended up stopping my heart for a minute.

That was the last and only time Nicolai showed off that side of me.

Cold fingers wrap tightly around my wrist in a grip that makes my bones hurt. "*Jax*," Beau's voice cuts through the angry fog. "Not here."

Isabeau is the only one who knows the truth about my beast. It just so happened she was there that day, having been on an—*excursion*—with her mother, Nessa. She saw the damage my wolf can inflict. It's not very often that Isabeau allows herself to appear unnerved, but when I awoke covered in the blood of my wolf's victims, she was visibly rattled.

"Was it Sterling?" I bite out my question between clenched teeth once I have myself under better control.

"Who else would do this?" Beau responds. "Unless she's pissed someone else off recently, he's the only viable answer." I wouldn't put it past Remington if she did piss someone else off. She has a knack for that.

"He's going after anyone he can." We already knew he was getting desperate. He wouldn't be burning down or destroying the properties that have such high value to him if he wasn't starting to worry. "Remington can't stay alone at that hotel anymore. It's not safe."

"We both know she's seldom alone there." The vampire cuts me a knowing look and when I return it with a confused one of my own, she scoffs, "*What?* You think you were the only one keeping an eye out for her? I bet I knew where she was staying before you did." Not surprising. Ransom and Isabeau are the best trackers in the pack. "Pruitt told everyone to give her space, but Ransom and I agreed we weren't going to let her disappear completely. We kept tabs, though we learned fairly quick we weren't the only ones watching over her."

My arms cross in front of me as I return my attention to where Remington is now shimmying her body through the open window of her car. Her long legs shift back and forth as she slowly works herself *back* into the destroyed vehicle. "I know if I get too close, I'll end up hurting her, but I couldn't sit back and watch her be so careless with her life. I broke her to save her. If she went and did something stupid or got hurt, all that pain would have been for nothing."

"Both of you really need to stop talking in riddles." Isabeau shakes her head. "I'm incapable of getting a headache, but you two are making me fucking get one. Get your shit together, demon, and make it right—" Her face suddenly falls and her chin lifts, nostrils flaring. "Do you smell that?"

I inhale deeply, taking in the scent of trees and damp earth as I look around the quiet space. "I don't smell—" Then it hits me like a bullet to the chest. *Smoke.*

A small spark. That's all it takes for the hood of the car to come alive with bright orange flames. They dance and move like a living, breathing thing as the ground around the car starts to burn.

Isabeau's booted foot is barely lifted off the ground before I'm disappearing into my own cloud of smoke and reappearing at Remington's feet.

The sound of her sucking in a surprised breath comes from inside the car as my hands wrap around her ankles and I rip her from the car with a violent force. The second her head is free of the broken window I'm lifting her off the ground like she weighs nothing. The fluid from the car has leaked into the earth all around the car and with each passing second, inch by inch catches fire.

Moving faster than most beings can, I carry her far away from where the flames are roaring. Between some trees a safe distance away, I drop her to the ground. Her arms that had looped around my neck to hold on, move down my chest to grip the fabric of my black shirt as she tries to steady herself. Remi trips over her own feet and my hands fly out to her sides to help balance her.

It doesn't matter how many times I've looked into her eyes, the sensation that washes over my body never grows old. Almost like electricity, my body hums when she lifts her chin, and we lock eyes for the first time tonight. Blood coats her face, her hair is a mess, the delicate skin under her eyes is dark and swelling as black eyes form, but she's still beautiful. In every state I've seen her in, happy, sad, angry, bloody... she's always beautiful. They're different kinds of beauty, each one affecting me the same way. Like a hot knife through my heart.

"Are you okay?" The tone I use is reserved solely for her. The softness—*tenderness*—something I've never had a reason to use before. My hand leaves her side to cup her face, my thumb swipes across her swollen bottom lip, clearing it of the blood.

She blinks up at me before her lips pull in a sad smile. "I'm having a pretty rough night." Her whole face falls before she drops her forehead to my chest in defeat. It appears whatever energy she has left isn't going to be spent sparring with me tonight.

My arm loops around her waist while my other hand collars the back of her neck. Needing to just stand here and hold her for whatever time we have, I drop my head, resting it against hers. I breathe in her scent, letting it soothe me. My wolf cocks his head, observing this moment with curious eyes. Rage is his constant state, but right now he's still. *Silent.*

The silence is a reprieve I didn't know I needed.

Whatever amount of time we have now was never going to be enough, but it's cut far too soon when sounds of arriving vehicles fill through the quiet moment. Doors slam and footsteps pound. Panicked voices fill the air as they call for her. Between the trees we are hidden from view of the road.

At the first shout of her name, Remington's body goes stiff, but she doesn't yet turn away from me.

"We can pretend we don't hear them," I offer, referencing the other night when we pressed pause on everything. I just want another minute. One more minute and maybe I'll be able to let her go.

Her hands flex on my chest once, then, with a long breath, she pulls away from me. "No more pretending," she tells me solemnly.

Remi's eyes scan my face once before pulling away.

I stand and watch her move slowly away from me, her

body rigid from whatever pain she's in and with the anticipation of having to face every one of her family members again. I want to be at her side, facing them together, but that can't happen.

In Sterling's eyes, I'm the perfect creation. I'm stronger than any full-blooded shifter and my ability to manipulate hellfire in ways that are rarely done make me powerful. I'm the perfect *weapon*, but that's what he wanted. His idea of perfection is something that can wreak havoc on others. He didn't give a shit that, in reality, I'm like an unstable bomb. At any second, I can detonate and take out anyone close to me before they have time to pull the air they need into their lungs to scream.

I do my best, concentrating so much of my energy on keeping that from happening, but one wrong slip, it's game over for everyone.

Being at Remington's side would place her in my blast radius.

CHAPTER TWELVE
Remington

This night is slowly but surely becoming the night from hell.

The arrival of my hellhound just solidified that.

Jax has to remain the villain in my head. If I start thinking of him as a hero once more, I'll end up getting my heart broken again. And I barely survived the last time he broke it. *He broke your heart, but yet you still saved him,* the voice in my head reminds me of what I've done. As if I need a reminder. Seeing him breathing is reminder enough.

Jax was a hero tonight—*my hero*. He literally pulled me from the flames. When I was yanked from the car, I thought it was Isabeau, but the second I was lifted from the ground and his body heat mingled with mine, I knew it was him. I didn't have to look at his face. My body recognizes his like they've known each other for multiple lifetimes.

Despite how much he hurt me, or I hurt him, being in his arms still fills my bones with a sense of belonging. The first time he touched me—*really touched me*—I felt it and to this day, the sensation hasn't weakened or waned. It's only gotten stronger despite my best efforts to thwart it.

My whole body aches as I slowly walk up the slight incline of the road's ditch. Headlights from three cars blind me once my head peeks over the edge. The beams sear my eyes, making the headache I have from the airbag exploding in my face worsen. Wincing, I block as much light as I can with my hand as I make my way toward the crowd of people that now stand over the fiery car.

Winslow spots me first. The little witch is comically tiny standing between all the large male shifters. Her eyes, two different colors, widen, and she bounces on her toes, tugging on Ranger's jacket to get his attention before darting away from the group. She has a blanket in her hands and once she's close enough, she throws it around my shoulders. Funny that the girl who was never nurtured by her family has become such a caregiver for the pack. I firmly believe she's too good for my brother. It is my right as a sister to believe that after all.

"So nurturing and *motherly*," I muse halfheartedly, wrapping the blanket tighter around my shoulders. "Keep this up and you might be the next one knocked up."

Winnie gasps, appalled. "That's a terrifying thought." She pushes on my arm playfully. "So, *thanks* for that."

"All I'm saying is better you than me." I lift my hands in surrender, chuckling softly under my breath.

Her face turns serious. "I'm really glad you're okay. We've lost enough family this past year. We don't need to lose you too."

I attended three funerals in the past year. First was Pruitt's adoptive aunt, Addison. As a human, she never stood a chance against the cancer that infested her body. Then there was Noah, Addison's mate. After she died, he went crazy and ended up getting himself killed in the same battle as Gage. To say that I was pretty numb to the sadness of funerals by the time I buried Gage is putting it mildly.

"I'm hard to kill." If there's one takeaway from the past two years, it's that none of us are going down without a fight. "I like to be difficult like that."

"Difficult indeed." My mom's voice sounds before I'm abruptly pulled away from Winnie. In a flash, Mom's arms are wrapping tightly around my shoulders in a crushing hug. Her body shakes with nerves against mine as she squeezes the life out of me. My arms hang limply at my sides, my fingers flexing awkwardly. I never used to shy away from hugs from my mom. Before Pruitt, she was my best friend. We were the only girls in the house, and we had to stick together if we were going to survive living with four boys. While they were rough and tumble, breaking bones and destroying toys, we were having tea parties and playing dress-up. She was the only one who would play dolls with me. Mom played with just as much imagination as me if not more.

Margot Weylyn is a good mom—the best mom—but I know if I'm around her for too long, she'll look into my eyes —*truly look*—and know what I've done. She'll know what part I played in Gage's death and I'm not ready for her to look at me with disappointment.

Same with my dad.

Behind the quick tongue and attitude problem is a girl who wants to make her parents proud. What I did won't make them proud of me. They won't understand. *Hell, I'm not sure I do.*

Mom pulls back just far enough to take my face between her hands. Blue eyes that look like all of ours scan my injured face. I'm healing, but I'm sure it's not a pretty sight right now. "Look at you," she sighs. "You're a mess."

"Well, that's the understatement of a lifetime," I breathe out a light laugh, my lips tugging at the corners. The split in my lip pulls painfully, making me drop the small smile quickly. Mom doesn't look nearly as amused as I am by her comment. "I'm fine, Mom," I try to assure her, squeezing her shoulder. I'm subconsciously aware of the rest of my family moving closer. I can sense Jax hovering somewhere behind me.

"You say that a lot," Mom observes skeptically. "That you're fine."

"I have to believe if I keep saying it, that at some point it will be true."

Mom's about to step away from me, but freezes. Her eyes narrow and her nostrils flare. Confused, I jerk back when she leans forward and inhales deeply. The features of her face that had just a second ago been creased with concern, harden as she pulls away. "Remington, have you been drinking?"

My stomach drops as I feel the eyes of eight people boring into me. I open my mouth to answer, to tell her that when the crash happened, I was already sober, but she doesn't give me the chance to explain.

"Is that what happened?" she falsely deduces. "You were partying and then drove intoxicated? Did you roll your car off the road because you were *drunk driving*?"

My mouth snaps closed, frustration building in my chest. I'm frustrated that my mom would jump to that conclusion, but I'm more frustrated with myself that my actions the last few months have caused her to accuse me of this in the first place.

Taken aback by the accusation, my eyes shoot to Isabeau. My silent question must be written on my face, because she steps forward. "Ransom didn't tell them what you told me when you called. He just said it was a car accident. I wanted to see it for myself before we shared what you said." *Meaning...* she wasn't sure I was telling the truth until she saw the evidence for herself.

I was never a liar. Always believed in brutal honesty, even if it meant hurting someone's feelings, but I started keeping secrets and lying. It's on me that Beau wouldn't immediately believe what I told her.

My head nods tightly in sad understanding.

"And I was too busy telling them that you were alive and *where* you were." Her arctic eyes flick over my shoulder, presumably at Jax. "That I didn't get the chance to tell them."

Pruitt steps forward with her arms crossed, resting on the small perfectly round bump under her pullover. "Tell us what?" Ryker, her ever-present tattooed shadow stands vigil behind her.

My hand grips the edge of the blanket that Winslow had tossed over me. "I didn't crash my car because I had been drinking. Two men in a black SUV followed me and when I started to get too close to pack territory, they started running into me until they finally caused my car to flip."

My heart sinks when my mom looks at Beau for confirmation, that she can't blindly believe what I'm telling her. When the vampire nods her head, my mom returns her attention to me. "They were planning on taking me with them, but they heard Isabeau coming and fled. They were worried about what she'd do to them." *For good reason.* "We can stand around here and pretend we don't know who'd do something like this, or we can get straight to the point. Sterling is behind this."

I can't help but glance at my dad to gauge his reaction. He's been quiet the whole time, but that's the kind of man he is. The quiet, observant type. He's as straitlaced and level-headed as they come. How he ended up with four kids with varying degrees of control and anger issues, I'll never know.

"It's odd to me that he'd target you," Mom observes, almost sounding skeptical.

Instantly, her tone makes me bristle as defensiveness comes over me in a dark fog. Eyes narrowing, I demand, "What does *that* mean?"

Her face hardens, unimpressed with my attitude. "I just mean, out of everyone, you've had the least amount of contact with Sterling or his people." Is she forgetting about that time I was kidnapped by Nicolai and used as a bargaining chip? "Why target you instead of Pruitt or even Jax?" She gestures at the demon behind me.

"*Oh sorry,*" I remark, taken aback by her words. "I guess compared to the she-wolf who broke a one-thousand-year-old curse and the all-powerful demon, I'm pretty small potatoes." The worst part about this is I already felt that way about myself, but to have it thrown in my face by my own mother is a low blow. "Low hanging fruit if you will," I supply darkly.

"Remington Everett," Mom scolds. "That is not what I meant, and you know it."

Dad steps forward, silencing Mom with a subtle look. "Emotions are high right now, let's get back to the house and we can discuss our steps moving forward." It doesn't matter Elias Weylyn is no longer the active alpha. His voice will never lose that authoritative edge.

"Yes." Ryker nods his head in agreement. "We need to make some plans if Sterling is really starting to send people here to abduct our people."

I keep looking at my mom, her offhand remark still really bothering me. Whether she meant it how it sounded or not, it's not sitting well with me.

"Remi." My dad saying my name snaps my attention to him. "Let's go." He nods toward his waiting Escalade. Everyone around us has started shifting toward their own vehicles leaving us to stand off.

Pursing my lips, I look between him and the dark car. "I would really rather not."

"This isn't up for discussion. You're coming home."

Home. Cringe. "No, thank you."

"You can't be alone at the hotel anymore." Jax appears at my side, his violet eyes crossed with concern. "Or go anywhere alone anymore."

"I don't want babysitters," I argue. It's easier to keep secrets when no one is around to hear them. "And you don't make the rules, hellhound."

"No, he doesn't." Pruitt walks up from behind my dad. "But I do."

I raise my brows at her. "You're going to pull the alpha card on me?" Not once since she became the alpha of the pack has she treated me as anything but her friend. Her equal.

"I don't want to," she starts softly, but her voice hardens as she warns, "But I will if you make me."

We stand facing off. The woman in front of me now isn't my friend I used to talk about boys with. She's the alpha—my alpha. A job she's stepped into with such grace and ease.

"Fine," I finally relent with a snarl as bitterness burns

through my veins. "But I'm running there." No way am I getting into an enclosed space with both of my parents right now.

"What part of you can't be alone are you not hearing?" Dad asks.

"I'll go with her," Jax volunteers and for the first time in a while, I'm glad he'll be hovering around.

He's the lesser of two evils, I suppose.

Wordlessly, I remove the blanket and push it into the demon's chest, leaving my dad and Pru on the road. Jax follows silently behind me into the trees. As I walk, I start removing clothing, tossing it carelessly onto the forest floor. This is an outfit I'll never wear again. I don't need a reminder of this night.

"Are you going to shift with me?" I ask over my shoulder as I yank my tight sweater off. After all this time, Jax has never shifted in front of us. Some days, I'm not even sure he can shift. When asked about it, his answers are always annoyingly allusive.

His jaw tics as he watches me undo the strap of my bra. "No."

"Are you ever going to let your wolf stretch his legs? Have a little freedom."

"It's a nice sentiment in theory. I'll give you that, but in reality, that would be unwise." He laughs like it's some kind of inside joke with himself.

"What? He doesn't play well with others?"

"That's putting it mildly."

Interesting. Both Ryker and Ransom's animal sides are unpredictable and volatile, but they still shift around us. How much worse can Jax's wolf truly be?

"You better be able to keep up with me if you're not shifting," I warn. "My wolf wants to run and I'm not planning on holding her back."

"Good," he praises. "I hate it when you hold back."

I shoot him a look. "You were the one who held back first."

"That's true," he willingly admits, but doesn't elaborate.

I wish I knew why a year ago, in the span of a minute, Jax's entire attitude changed. He went from caressing me with a tenderness I didn't think he was capable of, to spewing those foul words at me. If I knew, maybe I'd understand and be able to move on. He's never once offered an explanation and after he broke my heart so viciously, I didn't have it in me to go back to him to ask.

Now we're both holding back. I know my reasoning, his remains a mystery.

I kick off my shoes before pulling the dark jeans from my body. Jax swallows once I'm standing before him naked. His beautiful, unique eyes heat as they scan over every inch of my naked skin. Nudity is something shifters get comfortable with quick, but no one has ever looked at my naked body the way Jax Whitlock does. "Stop looking at me like that," I order.

"Like what?"

"Like you want me."

His eyes collide with mine with such intensity that my chest tightens and my stomach clenches. "There are a thousand reasons why I shouldn't want you and why being near you is a mistake. A thousand reasons why I should walk away right now and never look back. Despite those reasons and all common sense, I'll never stop wanting you, Remington. So, I'm sorry I can't stop looking at you like that."

My heart pounds against my chest so hard it hurts. Girls dream of the day that a boy will tell them pretty words like this. They should fill me with joy and heal my broken heart, but they only cause more damage. The boy with the pretty words isn't one that I can have and his saying this only makes that fact hurt more.

Every fiber in my being wants to go to him, to yank his clothes from his body until he stands naked like me. I want to touch him and kiss him until his body heat becomes my own. I want his touch to heal the jagged edges of my soul. I want to allow myself to feel happy that he's alive without feeling the soul crushing guilt that follows quickly after. I want to look into those violet eyes and not see the devastatingly dark ones I sacrificed in their place. I want to feel at peace with the choice I made but don't think I ever will.

My eyes squeeze shut and my hands ball into fists at my sides. I take a slow breath in, forcing my defenses against my feelings for Jax back up. "You have to stop saying things like that to me. It's not fair," I plead. "Stop playing with my feelings like they're a toy put there for your amusement. We both know nothing has changed or will change."

Like star-crossed lovers, we are simply not meant to be. We're our own biggest obstacles and neither one of us is budging.

Before he can say anything that will only make it worse, I say, "Let's go. I want to get this over with so I can figure out where I'm sleeping tonight." There is no way in hell I'm spending the night at my parents'. I will sleep in my wolf form under a tree in the woods before I do that. "Keep up, hellhound."

Crouching, I call upon the shift. In the span of seconds,

my smooth skin melts away and it's replaced with dense silver and white fur. Shaking out my coat, I flex my paws in the dirt below. Living in the hotel means I'm not able to shift as often as I'd like. My wolf is ecstatic to be let out, even if it's only for a short while.

Jax stalks closer, his hand extends like he's about to brush his fingers over my coat, but my snapping teeth halt him. Just in time, he pulls his limb back before I sink my canines into his flesh. "Even in this form, you're feisty."

Chuffing out an unamused breath, I jerk my head in the direction of the house.

"Race you there," he responds before taking off in a sprint. Even in his human form, he's fast. There was clearly no reason for me to believe he couldn't keep up with me.

I follow after him, pushing my body to the limit because there is no way I'm going to let him beat me.

☾

IN A LIVING ROOM I'VE KNOWN MY WHOLE LIFE, EVERYONE stands around talking about what we should do to better protect ourselves against Sterling. We've already upped security and patrols. New security equipment has been placed all over pack territory. Motion sensor cameras now sit up in trees every few miles and people in the pack take turns watching the live feeds.

"We need to get another camera for the east fence," Ryker suddenly announces, causing me to perk up in the seat I'd been slouched in. The whole discussion bored me, everyone thinks they have a better plan or idea. At one point I felt like we were talking in circles. I'm dirty, tired and hungry. And

I'm tired of blatantly ignoring the glances my mother keeps shooting my way. I'm still mad at her. "The wires were bent again. I thought it was a deer, but now I'm not sure."

"East side?" Ranger asks. "The one by the pack cemetery?"

Ryker nods. "It's not far from there."

Crap.

Looking up from my lap, I anxiously glance around the room. When my eyes connect with a pair of two-toned ones, I freeze in place. Winslow stares at me with her highly perceptive gaze. Her ability to sense things isn't always limited to just ghosts. She can just *sense* things about people without spoken words.

Afraid if she looks at me too long, she'll be able to sense all my secrets, I jump from the cushioned chair, announcing, "I'm getting a snack." I leave the room before anyone can stop me.

Once in the safety of the kitchen, I release a worried breath. Not until my head is in the fridge, my hand digging through the produce drawer for an apple do I hear her walk into the room.

Without a word, she sits on one of the kitchen island barstools. "I like to go visit the cemetery. Especially after Addison and Noah were buried there. I like to go make sure that their graves are well kept and neat. While I'm there, I tidy up the other graves."

Around a mouthful of apple, I say, "That's very nice of you."

"I know they're at peace somewhere else, but I still like to go by and say hi when I have time," Winnie continues. "It's weird though. There are usually some weeds and leaves that need to be cleared from all the graves. All but one that is." Those eyes of hers peer into me once again from under the thick fringe of her bangs. "Gage's headstone is always pristine. Like someone was caring for it. At first, I thought it was one of his family members, but Ranger reminded me recently that Gage's family belongs to a different pack in Wyoming."

I swallow hard and wait for her to tell me she knows.

"How often do you visit Gage's grave?"

I could lie and tell her that she's wrong, but what's the point. She already figured it out. "I used to go every night when I was still living here." I would get out of bed, shove my feet in whatever shoes were nearby and walk the two miles from the house to the grave. Doesn't matter if it was the dead of winter with a foot of snow on the ground, I would make the trek out there. "And then when I left home a month ago, I started sneaking back every few nights. I figured out that spot on the east fence didn't have a camera and I cut back the wires so I could slip inside." I snuck in because if I came in the front gates, whoever was watching the camera feeds would see me and then alert my family I was back. And that was who I was trying to avoid.

Winslow nods in understanding. "What do you do when you visit him?"

My breath shutters as I tell her honestly, "I beg for his forgiveness."

"Why would you need his forgiveness?"

"It's my fault he's dead," I admit.

A single tear just falls down my face when Pruitt comes around the corner. Her face falls when she sees me. "*Oh Remi...*" she starts.

Clearing my throat, I swipe away the tear. In a second, I

have myself pulled back together. "I'm good," I mutter quickly. "What's going on?" I ask Pruitt.

"Ransom's back," Pru explains after a brief pause. I think she was trying to decide if she should push me for more information. "He wasn't able to track the car."

"Shit," I say under my breath dejectedly. "There has to be a way we can find it. Maybe we can get into the security cameras in town?"

"I don't have that kind of authority." Pruitt shakes her head. Doesn't matter, she's the alpha of the pack or the white wolf from a prophecy that dates back a thousand years, her authority means nothing in the human world. She's just a normal twenty-something female to the humans.

Winslow's face lights up. "I might have a way. My hacker friend who helped us before? He'll be able to hack into the cameras in town. If there are faces shown, he can also run facial recognition software on them. Whisper is incredibly talented like that."

"Just not talented enough to track Sterling," I offer dryly. Whisper has hacked into every government department and is on every kind of watch list, but he can't find jack shit on Sterling. Of course, the human computer savant doesn't know exactly why we want Sterling, he just knows it's dire that we find him.

"We don't even have a *picture* of Sterling to offer him," Winslow points out. "How is he supposed to track someone when we don't even know what he looks like or what his real name is?"

"I don't know." I shrug dramatically. "I'm just saying I'd tattoo Whisper's face on my ass if he could get me an address for that fucker."

"On your ass?" Winslow throws her head back, laughing.

"Oh yeah." I nod. "Like my *whole* left ass cheek too." I turn my body, grabbing my butt for effect.

"That's commitment."

"Hey, I can be a team player when I want to be." I find myself laughing along with her as Pruitt watches on.

"I'll make sure to pass that long to him when I call him later," Winnie jokes. "I'm sure he'd actually love it and have a few ideas for design."

"If he finds information on Sterling, I'll let him tattoo me himself." I'm that desperate to put an end to this. Chuckling softly, I glance at Pru and find her watching me.

I manage to give her a small smile which she returns. "Ryker and I are going to go home. I told Jax he wasn't allowed to sleep in that dingy loft of his alone anymore." Jax has a loft? I don't know why it never occurred to me to wonder where he's been living. "He's not a pack member so he just flipped me the bird but told me he'd take it under advisement." She rolls her eyes before giving me a pointed look. "*You*, however, are a pack member, so you need to stay on pack territory. If anyone leaves, it's with backup. No one goes anywhere alone anymore."

"I'm not staying here." I pick at the skin of the apple in my hand.

"You can come stay with me," Winslow announces. "But I have to be up early to start decorating for the baby shower tomorrow."

Oh shit, that's tomorrow? "That's fine. I can sleep through anything."

"Umm, no." Winslow frowns. "You're helping me."

"Interesting choice."

Pru laughs lightly. "Between the two of you, I have full faith you'll figure out how to hang a streamer." She waves her hand at us before leaving the room. "'Night guys," she tells us over her shoulder.

Winslow chews on her bottom lip before declaring, "It's decorating for a party, not rocket science. We can figure this out, right?"

My response is to give her a halfhearted thumbs up.

CHAPTER THIRTEEN
Remington

Turns out, Winslow and I may have had a better chance at understanding rocket science than setting up for a baby shower. By the time we are done putting the last of the pink and blue tiny cupcakes on a tray and the last balloon is inflated, we are both a sweaty, frazzled mess.

Halfway through the frilly affair, we had to call for reinforcements. Ransom and Isabeau showed up and were promptly put to work. I've never seen the leather-clad vampire look more out of place than she does in the middle of a bunch of pink and blue baby-themed décor.

Frowning at a table with a tray full of cans of baby food missing labels, she points at it and asks, "Are there actual babies coming?"

"No, that's for the adults," I explain. "We blindfold people and make them eat the baby food. They have to guess what the flavor is. It's a game."

"Why would anyone want to participate in such a thing?" she questions, still confused.

"Not a fucking clue," I confess. "I smelled a couple of the

options and am now truly appalled that this is what we feed children." Harvest squash and turkey? *Child abuse.*

Moving to another table, she gestures to the journal and bucket of pens.

"You write a note to the baby. Like a funny anecdote or some advice," I answer her silent question. Winslow should be in here explaining all this to her, but she had to run to town to grab the cake. So, it's now up to me to explain this weirdness.

Beau gives me a bland look. "Babies can't read."

"I'm aware."

"Why would you write a baby a note if they can't read it?"

Sometimes it's hard being around people who were raised in a lab. They missed out on so much of the real world. They're so good at so many things but are thrown for a loop so easily by everyday—normal—things. Isabeau would be more comfortable slicing someone into tiny bits than at this party.

"It's for when they're older, Beau," I deadpan.

"Oh."

Jesus Christ.

☾

IT'S A BAD DAY WHEN ISABEAU HAS BETTER SOCIALIZATION skills than you.

Rusty is putting it mildly. Pack members, some I haven't seen in months, keep coming up to me, asking where I've been or how I'm holding up. They try to talk to me about Gage, to tell me about happy memories they have of the man who died, but with each passing interaction, I want to scream.

I'm trying to pretend or forget it ever happened, but apparently the rest of these people didn't get the fucking memo.

A hand pats my arm in a way I'm guessing is supposed to be comforting, drawing my attention away from the piece of fuzz I'd been absentmindedly watching float through the air. Kody, one of the pack enforcers, stands in front of me with empathetic eyes. "How are you doing, kid?" Before I left the house and found the club, I used to frequent Kody's bar. He was there at the beginning of my downfall. First row seat at my meltdown.

I don't care how genuine his intentions are right now, I'm done having this conversation with people. I feel like a broken record. *I'm fine. I'm doing as well as can be expected. I'm just dandy. I'm still breathing. Blah blah blah.* "I appreciate your concern, but today is not about me. I know it'll be hard because I'm a wildly popular person and *clearly* the life of the party." My voice drips with sarcasm. "But please, return your focus to the people and the child we're here for." I mimic the pat he gave me on his arm before pushing past him and disappearing out the back doors that lead to the back deck.

I take the steps down to the backyard two at a time as I put distance between myself and the party.

The secrets and shame I've been carrying for months are choking me as they force themselves back up. I want to scream at the top of my lungs, telling everyone what happened. The weight is becoming too heavy.

Slumping against a tree, I drop my head and try to collect myself.

My break from the party is short lived when footsteps approach. My first thought is Jax followed me out here. He hasn't even been trying to pretend he's not watching me today. I've just filled my lungs with air to scold him when I find it's Pruitt. She looks pretty dressed in a pale blue dress and her white-blonde hair in a long braid over her shoulder. The glow of pregnancy means she requires very little makeup. Lucky bitch. I have a pound of concealer under my eyes right now to hide the hard wear and tear I'd put my body through as of late.

I stand there watching her in heavy silence for a minute before feeling my chest crack and my waning resolve fracture. "I'm happy for you."

"What?" she asks, clearly caught off guard.

"I'm happy for you—I truly am. You and Ryker have beat every single one of the odds and together you're living the best life. Well, if you ignore the impending doom of Sterling that is." I add the last part quickly. "You deserve everything this world has to offer you. I'm happy for you, but in the same breath I am so incredibly jealous of you."

Pru's face drops.

"You have the perfect mate who literally worships the ground you walk on. You have the perfect house he built for you. And now you have, no doubt, the perfect baby on the way. I mean, there's no way they won't be perfect. They'll have you and Ryker as their parents. That kid is going to be amazing." My voice cracks as I say, "You have everything I didn't know I wanted. I guess I didn't know I wanted it until I learned I couldn't have it. I've been sitting back watching you build this life and I'm cheering you on, but God, Pru, I'm jealous."

"Remi…"

I push off the tree, standing up straighter. "And you know what? The house or kid thing? Those are things I could take or leave. I would live alone in a cardboard box under a bridge somewhere if it meant I could be with the man I love. I'm more jealous that despite every single one of the hurdles Ryker and you were thrown, you were able to overcome each one of them. It didn't matter how impossible it felt, you still fought for each other. You have a man that will fight for you and do anything to have you. Why can't I have that?"

Pruitt wraps her arms around me before I can stop her. I'm not sure I would have had the mental energy to stop her if I tried. "Remington... I know you loved him." My stomach rolls. "But that doesn't mean you can't be happy. I know you wanted to build a life with Gage, but he isn't the only man out there for you. He wouldn't want you to be miserable without him. You're allowed to move on." Her hands smooth down my hair. "He died knowing you loved him."

That's a lie. He died watching me save a man who broke me.

I choke on a sob before I admit something I never thought I would. "I wasn't in love with Gage." my voice is just barely a whisper, but I know she hears me because Pru pulls back so she can look at my face. "I thought it'd happen eventually, that if I just stuck it out, I'd fall for him. I *wanted* to love him. It would have been so much easier if I did. We'd fall in love and the mating aura would appear, we'd settle down and things would work out." The mating aura only appears when shifters truly allow themselves to fall in love. It won't appear if one of the parties is holding back. Both of them have to be fully committed and deeply, irrevocably in love. "I could see it in his eyes when he looked at me that he loved me. He was just waiting for me to hand my heart over to him, but I couldn't. I miss him and

I'd give anything to give him back his life, but I didn't love him."

Pruitt wipes away the tear that falls down my cheek, her eyes full of sympathy. For the first time in six months, that look doesn't make my skin crawl with unease. I'm pleasantly surprised how much lighter I feel being able to admit this to Pruitt. It's lonely work keeping secrets.

"I already gave it to someone, but they broke it." My bottom lip wobbles. "A perfectly good man wanted me and loved me, but I couldn't love him back because I was still in love with the person who *destroyed* me. How pathetic is that?"

Pru's eyebrows pinch in confusion, her lips pulling down. "Who—" she begins to ask but the rest dies when her eyes suddenly widen and her hand drops from my hair. "I thought it was just an innocent crush," Pruitt starts. "I didn't think it was more than that." She doesn't say his name, but we both know who we're talking about.

I laugh sadly to myself. It was never supposed to be more than a crush. It was no secret that, since the beginning, Jax and I had a flirty relationship. Tormenting and trying my damnedest to make the demon blush was my favorite hobby. It was innocent. Something fun to pass the time with. Until it wasn't.

"I didn't know it was more or that I even wanted more until the very second he told me I couldn't have more. That nothing was ever going to happen between us," I sniff. "I never wanted to be this person that cried over a boy. It's pathetic. *I'm pathetic*, letting some dumb man hurt me like this, but *fuck*, Pru, it really hurts. It's been over a year since it happened, but it still hurts."

"A year ago," she repeats as a thought dawns on her. "This all happened before I had to leave and Jax went with me."

I nod my head in a jerky movement. "I've never needed you more, but there was no way to communicate with you. Gage started hanging around and I selfishly clung to him as a lifeline." *I'm a horrible person.* "I wanted to tell you when you came home, but then the battle happened…"

"And then Gage died," Pru finishes for me.

"Gage died." Repeating those words feels like swallowing razor blades. "The man I want, I can't have and the man who wanted me is dead." Telling her about my feelings for Jax is about all I can offer her today. I'm not ready to disclose what led to Gage's death. That's a shame I'm not ready to share with someone else. I reach out and take her hand in mine. "You did nothing wrong, but I treated you like you did. It was really hard being around you when my life is falling apart. I felt bitter and angry at something you had no control over. Like I said, you deserve to be happy. You've literally broken curses and overcome certain death to get where you are. I can't apologize enough for my absolute *horrific* behavior."

Pruitt and Ryker's love for each other is so epic, it's part of a thousand-year-old prophecy. The white wolf prophecy, to be exact. Long story short, a thousand years ago a witch was upset when her son wanted to mate with someone that was a different species. The witch, a total weirdo who wanted to keep the bloodlines pure, cast a curse. For hundreds of years, species couldn't mate outside of their own species. Didn't matter if they truly loved each other, they could never be mated. All the right stars had to align for the curse to be broken, but by Pru mating with Ryker, the curse was broken. Now, no matter what species they are, if the love is strong and true, the mating aura will appear, and they can be mated. Like I said… it's an epic love.

"You don't have to apologize for hurting, Remi."

"I do," I insist. "Because I've been a monster bitch."

That's putting it mildly.

Pruitt wraps her arms around me and this time I return the hug. "I've just really missed my best friend."

"I've missed you too."

"I need you to get your shit together though," Pruitt remarks suddenly after a moment of silence. I guess we've moved on to the tough love portion of the segment. "It's okay to be sad and to be angry, but I need you to pull it together. We're still in the dark with Sterling and his plans. I can't be worrying about you *and* him. There simply is not enough time in the day to do both."

Last night was a wake-up call that I really needed.

"I'm working on it."

I'm tired of playing the passive part in all of this. Whether she meant it or not, Mom was right. I'm a small player in this deadly game, but that's changing.

After we pull away from each other, her face turns serious. "Do you want me to kill Jax for you?" Pru asks. "I'm so mad at him right now for hurting you."

"Oh, don't you worry your little pregnant head, I'm carrying around enough anger for the both of us." Angry at Jax for breaking my heart, angry at myself that despite what Jax did I still did horrible things to keep him alive, and angry at Sterling for being a big fat dick. The anger in my veins has been burning in disorganized chaos. I've let it cloud my judgment and consume me, but not anymore. I'm going to harness that emotion and let it fuel me. "Come on, we need to get you back to your party."

"You're probably right." Her hand smooths across the growing bump. Maybe it's because I'm growing accustomed to seeing sadness in my own eyes that I recognize the fleeting look of it in hers.

"What's wrong?"

"I know I don't remember my mom and dad, but I still want the baby to know about them," she starts, a sad smile on her lips. "I only have a small handful of pictures of them. I guess, I wish I had more information about my side of the family that I could tell the baby about. I just won't have anything to offer my child if one day they come asking questions."

"All that matters is that it knows that it is loved, Pru," I assure her. "It's got an entire baseball team of aunts and uncles that will be fighting to be its favorite. Which is going to be *hilarious* to sit back and watch because we already know I'm going to be the favorite."

We start walking back toward the house. For the first time in months, we stand side by side.

"Can you find out if the baby is a boy or a girl so I can stop calling them an *it*?" I plead.

"No." Pruitt laughs. "We want it to be a surprise."

"Shit, don't you think we've had enough surprises?" I grimace. "I'm one surprise party or jump scare away from checking myself into a psych ward. Do you think Winslow can get me a deal at the one she was at?"

CHAPTER FOURTEEN
Jax

Climbing into Pruitt's lifted Jeep, I find the passenger seat already occupied with a box of donuts. I smile happily at the sight of them before moving them so I can sit down. While we were in hiding for ten months, we bonded over junk food. Every day I would use my hellfire to travel all over the continent to get different kinds of donuts from all over the place. It was a happy spot in an otherwise very dark time.

"*Ooh*," I praise, lifting the lid of the pink box. "Come to daddy."

Junk food wasn't something I was ever allowed to have while living in the facilities. I was fed a very nutritious, clean diet in the hopes it would make me healthier and subsequently be stronger. Turns out, it didn't matter how many plates of kale I choked down, it still never helped me harness the flames.

My metabolism is so high, I'm basically hungry all the time. Using my powers or shifting only makes it worse. After allowing my wolf out, I swear I can eat an entire cow. It takes so much energy from being in that form.

With one donut around my finger like a ring and another one shoved in my mouth, I freeze when I feel a heavy stare on me. Turning my head, I find Pruitt's green eyes locked on me. Swallowing the food in my mouth, I ask, "These were for everyone, right? You're not about to go all hungry-pregnant lady on me, are you?" When she doesn't answer, I continue. "Come on, Blondie, the baby would want you to share with me."

Still, she just stares at me instead of answering me or pulling away from the loft. We're supposed to go back to Isabeau's to train again. Usually, I'd just flash over there myself, but Pru was running an errand in town and offered to pick me up. I don't usually do the whole 'car thing', it's a slow and confined way to travel, but sometimes it's good to humble yourself. Or so I've been told.

"We're going to be late," she finally grumbles, pulling away from the cracked curb.

We ride in weird, heavy silence to Beau and Ransom's place. It's never been awkward between Pru and I. For all intents and purposes, Pruitt should hate me. When we first met, I was working with Nicolai and was tasked with torturing Pru with hellfire. At the time her wolf was bound, and Nicolai thought pain would help entice it out. It didn't work, but that's not the point. The point is from our very first meeting we clicked. I hadn't felt a connection to someone in a long time. No one had been on my side since my mom died, but Pruitt had my back from the beginning. She kept my secret from everyone—even Ryker—for over a year before finally letting it slip that Sterling is my dad last fall. She was the first person I felt like I could trust with that knowledge.

And then there was Remi.

The connection between us is so strong, it's dangerous.

I trust Remi—that's not the problem. The problem is I don't trust myself.

Once parked on Beau's U shape driveway, Pruitt gets out of the car without a word. She's never been mad enough at me to not talk to me completely. We were stuck together in a small house on a beach for ten months, there were definitely times I pissed her off during our stay there, but she never used the silent treatment on me before.

Jogging around the car, I catch up to her. Yanking playfully on the hood of her jacket, I make her stop. She whirls around, an angry snarl on her face, and bats at my hand.

"Who pissed in your cornflakes this morning?" I chuckle, truly thinking whatever's got her bent out of shape is something insignificant.

"I'm mad at you," she grumbles.

"Yeah, *I know*," I deadpan. She glares at me, and I hold my hands up in surrender. "*What?* Was it supposed to be a secret? Hate to break it to you, but you're not exactly *hiding* your emotions right now."

"I'm not trying to hide them," Pru snaps. "I want you to know that I'm mad at you. No, I'm *disappointed* in you."

"Disappointed?" I repeat. "What the hell did I do?"

Her green eyes cut to where pack members loiter around not far from us. Without a word, she snags my shirt by the collar and drags me away from any overhearing ears. With a less than gentle shove, she pushes me into the bed of Ransom's silver truck. "If you knew you didn't want to be with her, you shouldn't have humored the flirting. Leading her on only to break her heart was a dick move, demon boy."

That was not what I was expecting to come out of her mouth.

My jaw snaps closed, molars grinding. Unease building in my body. "She told you?"

"Not everything. I don't know exactly what happened, but I know whatever it was hurt her *really* bad. What were you—"

I hold up my hand, silencing her. "I'm going to stop you right there," I snap. "You just admitted you don't know the full story, so you don't get to stand here and draw conclusions. Usually I value your take on things, but I had ten months where I spent every waking moment with you. Don't you think that if at some point if I felt like this was something I needed to discuss with you, I would have?"

"Jax, I'm just trying to understand what the hell happened. You're both my best friends, but whatever you did *changed* her. I can't help her if I don't know what happened." Pruitt isn't backing down. "What. Did. You. Do?"

"Fine, you want the truth?" I challenge, nostrils flaring. "I fucked her and then while she was still sweaty and naked, I told her it meant nothing to me. That *she* meant nothing to me," I hiss out in an angry whisper. "She admitted she had feelings for me, and I basically laughed in her face."

Pruitt's face pales and for the first time since we met, she looks at me like I'm the monster Sterling always wanted me to be. I *hate* that look coming from her. "Did you mean it?"

"It doesn't matter if I meant it or not. It needed to be done," I grit out.

"Why? What possible reason could you have to do something like that? Why was it so necessary that you hurt her like you did?"

I shove a hand through my hair, pulling at the strands. For

a second the pain in my scalp distracts me from the pain in my chest as I replay that moment a year ago in my head. "I needed to make sure that whatever feelings she had for me went away. Breaking her heart was the fastest and most effective way to do that." Letting her down easy or admitting what we'd done was a mistake would have left room for argument or debate. I couldn't risk that. I needed it to be final.

"Jax," she starts to argue. Of course, she would argue, to her, this situation looks like it could easily be fixed. In her mind, I just need to crawl to Remi on my hands and knees and beg for forgiveness. If it were that simple, I would have done it the second I saw Remi again after ten months away. Anger bubbles in my blood. Angry at myself for not being strong enough to control the side of myself that's keeping Remington and I apart. And angry at Pruitt for sticking her nose in a place it doesn't belong. "You need to talk to her. You need to make this right. You can't just hurt her like that and—"

Before her eyes, I dematerialize into the faintest cloud of smoke before reappearing behind her, effectively switching our positions. No longer am I the one cornered against the truck.

Pru's green eyes flare as I box her in. There's only a hair's width between us. I don't touch her. I don't need to get my point across. Pruitt isn't the only one that can emit their power to the extent that people gag on it. I don't usually have to do this. My reputation alone usually stops people from fucking with me. Pru is a powerful alpha, she's not going to back down without a little nudge.

"You've been told since you were reborn into this world that you are powerful. The strongest even. You've been told that you're the alpha and you must lead your people, but I am *not* your people." I jab a finger into my chest. "I am your friend, but I am not your people. You do not get to demand answers from me. You do not get to interfere in matters that do not concern you. You are not privy to all my secrets." I feel my eyes shift into their wicked wolf's form. "And you are not stronger than me. One wrong slip of the hand, one second of distraction, and I could settle the whole fucking state. It would be wise to remember that there is a reason that I keep secrets. There's a good chance I do it so I can protect *you*." I flick my eyes over her shoulder toward the area where I know Remington to be sparring. I sensed her the second we pulled up like always. "*And her*. So, the next time you try to question me or my motives, remember that I'm doing my fucking best to keep her alive."

Pru shakes her head in jerky movements. "I know you, Jax. You wouldn't hurt her."

My head tilts back as I release a cold, almost manic laugh. "I never took you for stupid, Pruitt," I tell her coldly. "Believing I'll never accidentally hurt her is foolish."

"*Accidentally*," she repeats with emphasis. "You'd never hurt someone you care about on purpose, Jax. Stop trying to make yourself seem like the evil people who created you. You're not them."

"Half of my blood is *his*," I remind her. "Just because I don't want to hurt people like he does, doesn't mean I won't."

Whatever words that are on her tongue are cut off when the front door of the house is torn open and thundering footsteps pound down the wooden stairs. Moving around the truck, I find Ranger and Ransom charging toward us. Both of their features are pinched with concern. As identical twins, their different hairstyles and personalities are the only things that differentiate them. Ranger is calmer, thoughtful, much like his dad. He thinks before he acts. Ransom is volatile and impulsive. Something I can relate to.

Instantly on guard, Pruitt meets them halfway while I loiter a few feet back. "What happened?" she demands.

"The cameras at my house went down," Ranger explains as he anxiously presses his phone to his ear. "Kody was watching the cameras today and he said all of the ones we placed around my property are out."

"Winslow is here, right?" I question. Since things with Sterling have heated up, Ranger very rarely allows his 'little witch' out of his sight. Usually, she works at the psychic shop in town with her aunt, but she hasn't worked in months.

"She's out back, Beau was showing her something," Ranger confirms, still looking at his phone. "I'm trying to access the cameras in my house, but they're not working either."

"I'm going," Ransom declares, his shirt already over his head as he prepares to shift.

"I'm going to get Winnie, and then I'll meet you there," Ranger tells his twin.

Appearing seemingly out of nowhere, Remington comes around the car. "I'll go with, Ransom." Her blue thunderous eyes clash with mine, a hurricane of emotions in them. That storm would scare any mortal man, but it fills me with relief. The fake unemotional mask she's been wearing for months is starting to break. She's allowing herself to feel again.

Even if I'm not the reason she's healing, I'm glad to see the improvement.

"No, we don't know what's waiting there." Ransom shakes his head in disapproval. "I'll scope it out first."

Remington pulls the tank top she wears over her head and kicks off her sneakers. "I don't know who died and made you the boss of me, but I'm going."

"I outrank you," Ransom reminds her heatedly. "I'm the beta male."

Remington flicks her gaze over him with an unimpressed look, before she snaps her fingers and mockingly grimaces. "*Oh darn*. Looks like I left all my fucks to give in my other pair of pants." She pouts out her bottom lip. "Better luck next time, butt munch."

Ransom gives a warning snarl, but it goes unanswered as Remington shifts into her stunning silver wolf.

"Hardheadedness runs in the family," Ranger remarks, sounding resigned to the situation. He gestures flippantly at Pru's growing tummy. "That child is going to give you a run for your money. Best of luck with that."

Remington makes an impatient chuffing noise at her brother. Ransom only hesitates a second before shifting into his own wolf form. Remi's size isn't small by any means, but standing next to her brother's massive wolf form, he dwarfs her.

"I'll meet you guys there," I announce to the wolves as I back up from them, calling upon my power.

"What? Jax no—" Pruitt starts but I don't hear the rest.

With a cocky salute, I hurtle through the planes of this world to Ranger's house.

CHAPTER FIFTEEN
Jay

Winslow and Ranger's house looks like a modern treehouse built up into the trees. A unique design I haven't yet decided if I like yet. All I know is it fits the quirky witch's vibe to a T. When Winnie first met Ranger, he was living in a sixty-year-old silver airstream trailer with no running water. The weird treehouse that sits in front of me with no signs of life or movement is a serious upgrade.

I stand on the gravel driveway, observing the dark house. If I were Isabeau, I'd be slinking around the dark shadows, trying to be as sly as possible. Her whole schtick is sneaking up on her enemies without them even knowing she's been there.

I'm not as shifty, I prefer for my enemy to see me coming. My wolf likes it when he can smell the fear seeping out of their pores and see the fear in their eyes.

Nothing has been disturbed. The only signs that someone unwelcome is here right now are the fresh tire tracks left on the unpaved road and the lingering scent of cigarette smoke. I can't think of a single person in the pack that smokes.

Unhurried, I peruse around the building, looking for signs that something has been tampered with. Things like trip wires or freshly moved dirt, just any sign that traps have been laid out for us.

Odd that they'd start at Winslow's house, but like Remington, they're just going after anyone they can. The house was empty since everyone was away at Isabeau's. They saw an opening and so they took it.

Or so I thought at first, but now that I'm closer to the house, the scent and heartbeat alert my senses. Both are *human*.

Sterling sees humans as a means to an end. Expendable. The gum stuck to the bottom of his shoe. That's why he prefers to use them as hosts for his modified embryos. If the woman dies, there's always another human female there to take their place. He'd never send a human out on such an important job. He'd never trust them to execute his plan.

My curiosity piqued; I waltz up the staircase to the porch that wraps around the entire house. Leisurely, I walk in slow paces around the building. At the French doors at the back of the house, I find the electronic keypad has wires sticking out of it. *Interesting.*

Almost every wall of this house is made of floor-to-ceiling windows. Who would take the time to pick a lock when breaking the glass is so much easier? I sure as hell wouldn't have the fucking patience.

Tires grind against the driveway out front. With one last look at the door, I turn around and meet Ranger and the witch as they pull up in Winnie's black Mercedes SUV. I'm not overly concerned about whoever is inside. If they truly meant any harm, I'd be bleeding by now.

"Ransom and Remi are doing a perimeter check," Ranger tells me before I can ask why he and Winnie beat them here.

"You made good time," I remark as I descend the stairs.

Ranger jerks his thumb toward his mate with an unamused face. "That's because she drove. She thinks speed limits are mere suggestions and/or scores that she should try to beat. All I'm saying is if you're ever in the mood to go on a rollercoaster, just sit in the back of a car with no seat belt and let Winslow drive. You'll think you're at fucking *Six Flags*."

Winslow flips him the bird before looking at me. "Why are you just standing there when there could be strangers in my house sniffing my pillows and licking my spoons?"

"Of all the things to be concerned about, your *spoons* are what come to mind first?" I question, sounding dumbfounded. "Personally, I'd be more concerned about your more *intimate* belongings. Who knows what they're doing right now with your thongs."

Winslow's eyes widen as she stares in disgust at her house. "People are in there right now?"

Ranger emits a low, pissed-off growl, his eyes glowing silver. Wolves are incredibly protective of their homes and someone is trespassing in his.

"Just one person, a human," I clarify nonchalantly.

Her jaw drops. "Why are we standing here!" Winslow shrieks. "Humans are by far the worst! Have neither of you ever seen Dateline? They're probably up there touching my panties as we speak!"

The front door swings open and a man I've never seen before leans against the wood railing of the balcony. "Winslow, I'm disappointed. You know I don't wear underwear." He waves a hand around his groin area. From here I can see his nails are painted black and spiked leather bracelets wrap around his thin wrists. "The bits like to breathe."

Who. The. Fuck. Is. This. Man?

When Winslow's eyes light up and she gasps out a name, I get my answer. "*Whisper?*" In a flash, she's pulled away from Ranger's protective grip and is charging up the stairs to wrap her arms around the man dressed head to toe in black.

His pants have various buckles and zippers on them, I'm not convinced they're actually there for functionality. His arms are thin and incredibly pale. It's like he hasn't been outside in months. His hair is a spiky black mop that hangs forward into his eyes; eyes that sit behind a pair of thick black-rimmed glasses.

"Whisper?" I repeat.

"The hacker friend," Ranger answers with an uninspired tone.

Confused by his tone, I look between the newcomer and the wolf shifter. "I thought we liked him?" The last I heard Whisper was an ally.

"We do," Ranger confirms. "I liked him more when he wasn't breaking into my house."

"There are worse things than an emo hacker letting himself into your house," I remark with a smirk. "It could be an emo hacker *with* a panty fetish. Bullet dodged, my dude."

"I hate you."

☾

IN THE HOUSE, WE STAND AROUND THE KITCHEN. THE KITCHEN island that had once been bare is now littered with various computer equipment. How long has this dude been here? The setup looks advanced enough to launch a rocket into space.

"After we talked the other night, I thought you may need some more help," Whisper explains after taking a drink from the water bottle Winnie offered him. "You were so vague about that car you wanted me to track, and I could tell that something else was going on, so I got my ass on a plane. Not a fan, by the way. Too many people and security, but a bus would have taken too long."

"Yeah." Winslow nods sheepishly, eyes darting nervously to Ranger. "There's a lot going on here right now."

"Well, that's putting it mildly," Whisper scoffs. "I hardly doubt life is uneventful when you're shacked up with a goddamn *werewolf*."

The room gets so quiet we could hear a pin drop in Alaska.

I don't know a lot about this hacker, but one thing I know for sure is Winslow has never told him the truth of what we all are. He only gets vague information. So, this begs the question, what the hell does he know? And how does he know it?

Instantly uneasy, my arms drop to my sides from where they'd been crossed against my chest.

Winslow tries to play it off at first, laughing nervously. "What? *Werewolf*? That's funny, Whisper. How'd you come up with that?" She used to be good at lying, being blissfully in love and happy with her mate has *ruined* her.

"You've never asked me for help," Whisper starts. "I had to practically *beg* you to let me help you when you were hiding from your adoptive parents in New York. In the past year and a half, you've come to me on three separate occasions for help. I knew something was wrong. Plus, that man you wanted me to find? Silver, was it?"

"*Sterling*," I instinctually correct.

Whisper points at me, nodding. "Yeah, Sterling. That whole situation bugged me. I couldn't find anything from his name or the small amount of information you gave me. That never happens. So, I got worried about you and hacked into the cameras to make sure you were okay. You really need a new system, by the way, it was *embarrassing* how fast I got into them. A teenager with a Nokia could get access to those."

"You hacked my camera feed?" Ranger repeats slowly like he can't believe it.

"Don't worry." Whisper grins. "I won't tell anyone you turn into a giant flea-ridden wolf." Winslow puts her hand over her mouth and snickers, but when Whisper points at her with an accusatory finger, the laughs halt. "Don't act innocent. I'm offended you didn't tell me you were a *witch*. *What the hell, dude?*"

Winslow shrugs meekly. "I told you I saw dead people years ago."

"*Yeah*, but I didn't think it was true. You were on a lot of drugs at the time. You also thought the blind man in the apartment across the street was a fed."

Winslow's mouth opens like she wants to argue, but she snaps it shut after a second. "That's fair." She sheepishly looks at Ranger. "Turns out, it was in fact, a seeing-eye dog and *not* a drug dog."

In Winnie's defense, if I suddenly started seeing dead people without any explanation, I too, would have turned to drugs as a way to cope. Good news is, she's been clean and sober since before she met Ranger. It's amazing what a guiding hand and some clarity can do for one's health.

Ranger shakes his head at his mate's admission. There is no judgment in his eyes, only acceptance. "So, you know all of our secrets," he deduces, looking back at the hacker, skepticism still written across his face.

"I wouldn't say all of them." Whisper's eyes cut to mine from behind his glasses. "I still have *no* idea what you are."

"Depends on the day and who you ask," I offer vaguely. "I think I'm awesome, but if you were to ask Pruitt today, she'll say I'm an ass."

"If you ask Remi, she'll say he's a hellhound," Winslow supplies unhelpfully.

"Hellhound?" Whisper repeats, eyes lighting up with wonderment.

"Don't get excited," Ranger cuts in. "Have you ever met one of those yippy chihuahuas with a pink studded collar? He's about as tolerable as that. They have similar personalities as well."

"What? Like he's clingy and slightly annoying?"

"No," I interject. "It's more like on a dime. I will turn on you and bite your fucking finger off, but then I'll want tummy scratches. You know, just to round out my day."

Whisper looks at Winslow, giving her a look that screams *'what the hell did I get myself into?'*.

Footsteps pound up the stairs and the front door flies open. Ransom and Remi, dressed in the loose sweats and T-shirts they presumably got from the back of Winslow's car, on high alert. They've yet to learn the threat is a skinny human with a fondness for guyliner. I'll be the first to admit, it's not a look I'd go for myself, but it works on him.

Ranger gestures with his hand to his brother for him to chill out, silently telling him that everything is alright. Remington's eyes dart around the room, bouncing between each of us as she waits for an explanation.

"Is someone going to make an introduction, or are we just going to pretend he's not here?" she finally questions. "If that's the plan, it's fine. I can get on board, but I gotta be filled in first. I don't know if I'm allowed to make eye contact."

"Remington, this is Whisper," Winnie begins introductions. "Whisper, this is Remington and Ransom."

Behind Winnie, Ranger adds, "The hacker," just to clear up any confusion.

"*Yeah, I figured.* Strangely enough, I don't actually know that many people named Whisper." Remi passes her big brother an unimpressed look before returning her attention to the newcomer. "Bold of you to show up here unannounced." What she really means is '*it was really fucking dumb to waltz onto a wolf shifter's territory.*'

"I have almost every government looking for me. *That's scary.*" Whisper waves his hand around at each of us in a blasé manner. "A bunch of werewolves, a witch, and a hellhound don't scare me."

"Hellhound?" Ransom repeats like a goddamn parrot.

"What? Is that not actually what he is? At this point, one of you could tell me you're a unicorn and I'd believe you," Whisper says.

"I'm half wolf shifter and half demon."

"Hellhound is still a better explanation," Remi says under her breath. "Of Satan's lapdog," she adds with a sarcastic smirk.

☾

WHISPER USES THE LARGE FLAT SCREEN TV MOUNTED ON THE wall to mirror his computer screen so we can all see what he's looking at. In all fairness, he moves so quickly, I'm not completely sure what I'm looking at. We moved to the living room after we gave him the quickest rundown of what's been happening. A couple of times I thought he was going to lose it, but he kept it together as he learned about all the insanity of our world.

The SUV that ran Remi off the road was found at a chop shop a hundred miles away from here. The black car—or what was left of it—still had scrapes and skids of Remi's blue car's paint on it. A dead giveaway. The men that were driving that night are long gone, but Whisper tracked them all the way back to the car rental place they acquired the car.

"I've got the name they placed the car rental under," Whisper mumbles to us, but I'm not completely sold he doesn't talk to himself. Hey, who am I to judge? We've all got quirks.

The name on the screen is small but it stands out to me like a glowing neon sign. Reading it is like a punch to the gut with a pair of brass knuckles. I haven't seen it written down in a long time, but I hear it in my head often.

Before he can start digging any further, I stop him. "That's not going to lead you anywhere," I warn him.

"How do you know?" Whisper questions from across the room on the low black velvet sectional.

"Because she's dead."

"Are you sure?" Ransom asks, not sounding convinced.

"If we've learned anything this past year, it's that the dead don't always stay dead."

In the corner of my eye, I see Remi narrow her eyes at the screen before her head turns in my direction at a neckbreaking speed in shock. "Simone Whitlock." Her voice is just a whisper.

My chest tightens hearing it said aloud. "I'm sure." I answer Ransom's questions, my tone devoid of any emotion. "That's my mom and Sterling killed her a long time ago." Like Sterling said, she was useless to him. There would be no reason he'd have Kaius resurrect her. "He's using her name to send a message. He knows I've been trying to track him and Kaius."

For the first time in over a year, Remington's eyes soften with sympathy when she looks at me. For the time being the contempt and anger is put on hold.

"What do you mean, trying?" Whisper elects to blow past the whole 'dead mommy' portion of the conversation which is more than okay with me. I'm not exactly keen on an impromptu therapy session. Stabbing myself in the forehead with a fork *repeatedly* sounds more enjoyable than talking about my *feelings*.

"I figured out that Kaius and Sterling have been burning down buildings. Kaius is starting to leave undead guards at the sites to make sure I don't come poking my nose in things. Met with a particularly strong one just last week." I rub the spot on my head as if I can still feel the pain in my skull. "I took care of him, but now Kaius knows I've been there."

"*That's* what happened to you?" Remi gapes at me. "Some dead dude split your head open like a cantaloupe? Why didn't you just tell me that?"

"I didn't realize we still shared secrets with each other," I challenge her with a pointed look. "Show me yours, I'll show you mine."

Her eyes narrow, like she's considering accepting the challenge, but finally she scoffs with an annoyed eye roll. "No, you won't. You cling to your secrets like you're a child holding their baby blanket."

Our eyes lock, silently daring the other to look away first. Like two battling storms, thunder and lightning crackle in the air around us. Neither one of us is going to break, whether it's to prove a point or to spar for dominance, our stares are unwavering. This silent battle has been going on for a year. I started it but I think she's going to be the one to finish it.

Whisper clears his throat awkwardly, interrupting the heated moment. "So, are we going to sit here and choke on their sexual tension a little longer, or shall we move on? I just feel if we stare any longer at them, it'll get awkward for all of us *real quick*."

Remi finally looks away to glare at the hacker. "There's no sexual tension."

"*Right*," he drawls. "And if I were wearing panties, they wouldn't be a pile of ash right now."

Ransom chokes on the water he'd just taken a sip of. "*Gross*," he heaves out between a fit of coughs. "You're talking about my sister."

"Well, she's not *my* sister." Whisper shrugs. "But don't worry. She's pretty, but if I had to pick, I'd much rather be chasing the hellhound's tail. *He's* more my type."

"Jax is everyone's type until he opens his mouth and ruins it for all parties involved," Remington warns Whisper with a laugh. A laugh that's at my expense, but damn, it's still good to hear again.

I cock my head in mock confusion. "I don't remember you ever complaining about my mouth before."

The pale blush that forms on Remington's face might be the prettiest thing I've ever seen. "Jax!" she scolds, eyes darting between her two brothers. "He's kidding. He's just trying to get a reaction," she quickly pacifies them with lies.

Ranger and Ransom's matching faces turn into scowls as their eyes narrow at me. Before things can escalate too far for my *slightly* out-of-pocket remark, Winslow steps in, drawing all of our attention back to the task at hand. "Is there any way we can track which buildings are going to be burned down before they're destroyed. Does Kaius have a system?"

I shift forward in my seat, resting my elbows on my thighs. "The only way I can think to track Kaius is by following cases of grave robberies. I don't have that kind of access to information, so I haven't been able to do it myself."

"Enter Whisper, stage left." The hacker rubs his hands together over his keyboard with excitement. Beating the shit out of someone is how I get my rocks off, but to each their own.

"People rob graves more often than you think," Winslow interjects. "People get so desperate they don't think twice about defiling a final resting place. I heard about it when I was living on the streets in New York."

There's a moment of defeat before I remember something crucial. "Yes, but not all grave robberies have a perfect black circle scorched into the ground." The room falls silent as everyone stares at me with puzzled looks on their faces.

"When Kaius resurrects someone, the dark magic he uses leaves a perfect black circle around the bodies. If he can, Kaius prefers to resurrect people in their final resting places since the energy there is stronger."

"I can work with that." Whisper smirks cockily.

CHAPTER SIXTEEN
Remington

Two days later and I still haven't gone back to the hotel or my parents' house. Pruitt, without me having to ask, went to the house and packed a bag full of my clothes for me just so I didn't have to.

I've stayed at Ranger and Winslow's house which is a lot more fun now that Whisper is here. I no longer feel like the awkward third wheeler. Plus, it's fun being around someone who doesn't know everything about you. Whisper doesn't ask how I'm coping or how I'm doing. It's refreshing to spend time with someone without them looking at you with worry or sympathy.

Leaning against the kitchen counter, I stare at Whisper where he sits at the bar top working on his computer. I'm not convinced this dude sleeps. The steady stream of energy drinks I've seen him consume help keep him upright.

"I finally figured it out," I announce around a mouthful. "I know who you remind me of. An emo *Sonic The Hedgehog*."

Without skipping a beat, he replies, "And you remind me of the girl in every early 2000s coming of age movie. She's hot but behind the pretty face is a tragic backstory."

Blowing past the tragic backstory comment, I dramatically clutch my chest. "Did you just call me the pretty popular girl?" My lips pull up in a grin.

Whisper finally looks over the edge of his laptop at me. He sighs before finally relenting, "The prettiest." He's smart and figured out I didn't want to talk about my trauma. "But only if I get to be the quirky sidekick that ultimately steals the whole show."

"Deal." Laughing, I rinse out the bowl and move across the room to sit down on the barstool next to him. I stare at the screen and don't recognize a single window that's open. Awkwardly, I clear my throat. "I know you're busy looking for suspiciously empty graves, but I could actually use your help on something."

"Name it."

"I didn't get Pru a baby shower gift yet." Because of the before stated trauma. "I could be boring and go off the registry, but I want to get her something she never thought she'd be able to have."

"That wasn't cryptic or anything, Remi."

I push the strand of hair that's fallen from my ponytail behind my ear. "I want to get her information on her family. Specifically, her mom's side. Her dad used to be the alpha of this pack, so we have adequate info to tell her about him, but her mom is a pretty big mystery to everyone. I have her name and her birthday. I know it's not much to go on, but any information at this point would make Pru happy."

Whisper is quiet for a moment before pushing a blank piece of notebook paper over to me. "Write down what you do know, and I'll start running a search."

"Thank you."

He smiles, the corners of his eyes crinkling. "I think it's sweet how much you all care for each other. I'm glad this is where Winslow ended up."

"We're glad too," I agree. "Plus, I really like how she doesn't make me look like the crazy one."

"Oh sweetie, I can smell the crazy coming off you like a cheap perfume."

"I've earned my crazy."

Whisper chuckles. "Haven't we all."

The buzzing of my phone in my pocket interrupts the moment. Isabeau went with me to town yesterday to replace the one I lost in the car wreck. Two weeks ago, I wouldn't have been in a rush to get a new one, but since being back and feeling a little bit like the angry fog has lifted from my shoulders, I've wanted to have it on me just in case someone needs me.

The phone number that reads across the screen isn't saved on the phone, causing me to consider not answering it for a moment, but a lot of numbers aren't saved on the new phone. It could be someone I know, and I'd never know, because who the hell remembers phone numbers anymore? More importantly, who calls instead of texts.

"Hello?" I answer, pressing the phone to my ear.

"Remington?" A voice I don't recognize comes through the line. Feeling Whisper's eyes on me, I get up from the counter and move to stand by the back French doors.

"That's me."

"H-hi," the woman's voice stammers. "I know this is out of the blue and I'm sure you're busy. I don't know if you remember me, but I'm—I'm Gage's mother."

Whatever weight that had been lifted off my shoulders in

the past few days crashes into me, making my bones creak and my muscles shake under the heaviness.

Instantly I'm catapulted back to six months ago when I had to make the hardest phone call of my life. Telling someone that their child has died is something no one should ever have to do. Pruitt and Ryker had offered to make the call, but I insisted it be me that tell Gage's parents. At the time, I was numb. The weight of what had happened hadn't yet settled in. When the horrific sound of Gage's mom screaming in unbearable pain at the news is something I hear at night when I close my eyes. In the blink of an eye, I forever changed this poor woman's life. It happened faster than Gage died.

She didn't see it coming any more than Gage did.

Neither one of them saw *me* coming.

"Of course, I remember you, Lorena." I'm barely able to get those words out without them sounding strangled. With one last glance at Whisper, I slip out the back door away from prying eyes and ears. This isn't a conversation I want to have, but I sure as hell don't want an audience.

"I hadn't planned on calling you," Lorena says quickly. "I promised I wasn't going to call and ask you questions I'm sure you don't want to answer, but I saw my phone lying there. Before I knew what I was doing I had dialed your number. I've been thinking about him a lot today. As I should be, I suppose. He might not be here anymore but it's still his birthday," she rambles, not once does it sound like she's taken a breath. I'm not sure I have either since I answered. "It's his birthday today, I'm not sure if you knew that." *I didn't.* "I've spent all day thinking about my boy. I've also spent all day thinking about what you told me. That phone call? I memorized every word you said, I repeat it over and over in my head when I need to remind myself that my son died a hero." I'm going to be sick on Winnie's deck. That sugary cereal I just ate is going to make an unholy encore performance. "I know you said at the time that you told me everything that happened, but I don't know. I guess I just wanted to know if you remembered anything else that you could tell me. Selfishly, I think I'm just looking for ways to make this... *excruciating* grief... easier."

I force the bile back down, swallowing hard. Inhaling multiple shaky breaths, I try to steady myself before I speak. Even hundreds of miles away, I'm afraid she'll be able to sense my lies. I haven't admitted to anyone what happened, I'm not going to start with his *mother*. "He died protecting his pack." *The good ol' company line.* "We tried our best to have each other's backs, but the battle was chaotic; we were all fighting for our lives. Gage was so strong, he fought for his pack—*for his people*—until his last breath." That's not a lie.

"Gage cared about all of you so much." Her voice cracks. I'm not sure how this conversation is helping her. It feels like we're pouring salt into our open wounds. "He wasn't always the easiest person to be around, but he really did care about that pack."

"I know." I nod, even though she can't see me. She's right. Gage was a total prick occasionally. He was cocky and arrogant. At times, he was even wildly condescending. His inability to read the room got him into trouble more times than I can count, but he took his job as head enforcer seriously. It was the ultimate honor to him to have that job. Beneath the abrasive surface was a good man. "I never doubted that about him."

"I just wish there was something you could tell me that would make it hurt less."

I release a long breath. My hand rests over my chest, my racing heart beats hard against my palm. "Lorena, nothing I tell you is going to take away the pain. You lost someone you loved, and it *hurts*." I'm hurting in a different way than her, but the pain is the same, nonetheless. If I tell her the truth, it'll only make it hurt worse and I want to spare her as best as I can. She deserves whatever reprieve I can offer her. If lying to her will help, I'll lie like it's my fucking job. "I wish there was something I could do to take away your agony but nothing I say is going to magically make the grief go away. They say it gets easier with time, that eventually one day when you think about your son, it won't feel like this. Hold on to that. I am desperately clinging to that thought like it's my life raft in this sea of pain." We just have to keep our head above water and eventually we'll make it to dry land.

I don't know if I'll ever think of Gage and not feel the stabbing pain in my chest as guilt floods my body. More importantly, I don't know if I'll ever deserve to feel at peace.

"I wish he was here."

And I wish I could have saved them both. "Me too." My voice is just barely a whisper. Even outside with the fresh air cascading over me as the wind cuts through the trees, I feel like I'm suffocating. My world is closing in on me. The panic attack I've been putting off for weeks is barreling toward me like a freight train.

If I don't get off the phone with this woman, she's going to hear my breakdown. If I've learned anything in the past six months, it's that these moments are best done in private.

Where no one can witness the shame written across my face. Where no one can judge you harder than you judge yourself.

My chest is so tight that I can't even muster a proper goodbye to Lorena. I'm pressing the off button on the device before the line is dead.

Maybe I was wrong. Maybe I'm not ready to have my phone back.

On shaky legs, I rush down the stairs and into the forest behind the house. These woods are my home. My wolf is usually at peace here. If I'm going to make it through the hurricane of unwanted emotions roaring through my bones, I need whatever peace I can get.

On instinct and muscle memory alone, I make my way through the trees. Each fallen log and each rock on the trail I recognize. If I had to, I could navigate these woods blind. Right now, I basically am blind. My head is so clouded by the duress I'm feeling that I can barely see what's in front of me.

I don't know how long I walk, but eventually I make it up to the bluffs that overlook the lake. From here I can see my parents' and Pruitt's house that sit along the lake. The unique treehouse Ranger lives in sits hidden in the trees somewhere behind Pruitt's lake house. Ransom and Isabeau live farther away from the lake, but their home is out there somewhere. Perfectly happy homes my brothers have created for their mates that could be torn apart any day now by Sterling.

At least if that time comes, they'll have their unbreakable bonds to rely on. Meanwhile, I feel like I'm broken.

Burned and broken beyond repair.

Hands on my knees, I bend at the waist and force air into my reluctant lungs. Everything hurts. Lorena was looking for a way to ease the pain. She wanted to talk about her son.

Meanwhile, the way I've been trying to cope is by avoiding it all. Avoiding my family, avoiding talking about Gage, even trying my best to avoid thinking about him.

I'm not sure which way is better because either way you're going to eventually feel the pain. You can feel the pain now, or you can feel it later. Either way, it's going to knock the wind out of your lungs, I'm finding.

My fingernails dig into the skin on my knees so hard it breaks the skin. Red, half-moon-shaped marks mar my skin now, but I don't care. The small burn of that pain distracts me from the soul-deep ache I feel now.

For the first time ever, I'm wishing for tears to fall. The emotional release of them might help and I'll take anything at this point. The lightweight hoodie I wear feels like too much, too confining, the hair tie in my hair feels like it's pulling at my scalp. I tear at both, letting them fall into the dirt at my feet.

Eyes squeezed shut and the wind blowing through my now loose hair, I try to breathe. The second I feel him walk up behind me, my body tenses but my wolf's agitation is instantly sated. She doesn't understand that he *rejected* us. She wants him on a level that is embarrassing to admit. It's borderline obsessive and it's only gotten worse since we've been actively avoiding each other the past year.

"Remington," he says my name. His smooth voice washes over me like liquid fire.

I don't turn around. "I need you to leave, Jax. Please just go. I begged you to stay last time, but this time I'm begging you to leave. I need you to listen to me now."

Of course, the fucker doesn't listen. "What happened?"

I contemplate lying, but what's the use? He's not going to

go away. When I want him here, he leaves me, but the second I don't, he becomes a level fourteen clinger. I can't keep up with this man. The emotional whiplash is causing my brain to bruise and my walls to crack. "It's Gage's birthday. I had no idea. His mother called me and told me." Gage and I never talked about birthdays or holidays. It wasn't that kind of relationship. At least for me it wasn't.

Behind me, Jax shuffles slowly toward me. "Okay, what do you want to do? What will make it better? Do you want to celebrate it?" He shocks me by asking. "We can light a candle or pour a beer over his grave? Whiskey maybe? He seemed like a whiskey guy."

"*What?*" I shout, dismay clear in my voice. I'm whirling around and stalking toward him before I even realize I've moved. "No, I don't want to celebrate his birthday!" I throw my hands up in frustration. "I can't celebrate the life that is no longer here because of *me*. I can't celebrate the life I *sacrificed*. I can't celebrate the life of a man who looked me in the eyes and watched as I didn't choose him. And I sure as hell can't celebrate him *with* the man I chose over him." At this point I'm yelling at Jax. Months of repressed secrets and guilt are spilling from me like a burst water line. "For the life of me, I couldn't tell you why I'd choose you over him. All you've done is hurt me and break me, but still I picked you, Jax. And the saddest fucking part is that I'd do it again. I'd bear all this pain again if it meant that you were alive. I don't know what kind of sick masochist that makes me, but here I am picking you over and over again, when you don't even *want* me."

Jax's violet eyes scan my face like he's watching all my neatly stitched up emotional wounds split open before him.

He watches me bleed for him. "What happened, Remi? Just let it out."

I wipe at my face even though there still aren't tears. "You're possibly the strongest person I've ever met, but you were losing. You *both* were." While Isabeau and Ransom were off dealing with Nessa and Beau's brother, Alexandre, we were left to deal with dozens of feral wolves and vampires. For months, these monsters had been locked in storage containers. They were starved and taunted until there was nothing but savageness left. Their hunger and anger made them stronger than they should have been, but that was Nessa's plan all along. "You were taking on three wolves, at some point you were knocked over. Each time you tried to stand or use hellfire to slip away, you were taken back to the ground. Ten yards from you, Gage was battling a couple of vampires. One of them had their arms around his middle. I could hear his bones breaking. I was equal distance between you both. I looked around to see if anyone else could help, but everyone was busy with their own monsters. His bones were breaking, his insides being crushed, and you were being torn to pieces by fangs and claws. The snow was so red beneath you. Gage locked eyes with me. They silently begged me to help him, but I—" I choke on a sob that rattles my chest. "I turned away from him. I turned my back on him and I saved you."

Jax's face drops. The sharp, blade-like angles of his face softening. The shiny, mischievous glint that is permanently in those purple eyes of his dim. For the first time in six months, he's finally understanding the demons I've been carrying around.

"Do you want to know the worst part?" I ask before he has

a chance to say something, because what could Jax say that could possibly make it better? Even if those words were, *'I'm sorry, I love you'* it wouldn't make it better because how am I supposed to be happy with Jax when it took Gage dying to get there? How the *hell* is that fair? "I tried to get to Gage after I killed the wolf that was on your back. I gave you just enough time to get to your feet and kill the other two. You didn't even notice that I'd helped you because it happened *that* fast. I was five feet away from Gage when the vampire's arms crushed his vital organs and his spine snapped." The pained yelp that came from Gage's wolf form replayed in my head for weeks. I heard it in songs, and I heard it in crowds. It *haunted* me. "As I stood there between you and Gage's body, all I felt was relief. I was so relieved that you were alive and standing that I couldn't process what had just happened. What *I'd* done. But you were breathing and for that minute all I could feel was *relief*." My hands shake at my sides. "Don't worry, the all-consuming, soul crushing guilt eventually came. It's too much. Feeling this way is just too much and I just want to…" I trail off because I'm not sure what I want.

Jax finally steps into my space and grips my face between his hands when I try to look away from him. "What do you want? Tell me what you need."

"I just want to… *scream*."

He smooths my hair away from my face. "So, scream," he whispers. "Let it all out, the guilt, the anger, the pain, let it out," he coaxes. "Give it to me. I'll carry it all for you. It's my fault, anyway, let me bear the weight now. If you really want it back, I'll give some of it back later, but you don't have to carry this all on your own anymore."

I shake my head.

Jax drops his head, resting it against the side of his as he whispers in my ear, "Scream, Remington." Body trembling against his, I give in to the emotions I've been fighting for months. They break free at a speed I have no hope of stopping.

"Scream."

And I do.

CHAPTER SEVENTEEN
Jax

Soul Crushing.
    Earth shattering.
Haunting.

These are the only ways I can describe the sound that comes out of Remington as she finally lets go of the tight restraints she's had on her emotions. Every bottled-up feeling, every repressed moment where she didn't allow herself to feel the pain she's in, comes out of her as she screams in my arms.

The sound splits through the trees and glides across the lake's surface below us. The noise pierces my eardrums, but I can take the splintering pain for her. I'd let her slice me with hot blades if it made her feel better. It's the least I can do since I'm the reason she feels this way.

I never wanted this for her. I thought by breaking her heart I was saving her from me. Despite my best efforts, I still ended up causing her more damage. She saved me even after I rejected her. Rejected the idea of us. She still fought for me after I told her I didn't want her. This is just proving once again that Remington Weylyn is too good for me and I'll never deserve her. Even if I found a way to control my beast, I never could deserve to call her mine.

She screams until her legs can't hold her any longer. When her knees buckle, I cradle her against my chest as I lower her to the ground. She's limp in my arms as she gives every bit of her strength into the screams that rip through the air. Months of sorrow and grief escape her while I hold her.

As she screams, the pieces of her shredded soul come apart so they can mend once again.

She screams until her voice cracks and breaks, until she has nothing left. Her cries fall silent, and her forehead drops to my shoulder in defeat.

Smoothing my palm down her clammy back, I ask, "Feel better?"

My response is a small, silent nod.

"You shouldn't have saved me," I tell her softly after another moment of deafening quietness. "This guilt and regret aren't worth it. *I'm* not worth it." I was a number on a test tube and then I was nothing but a living experiment for Sterling and Nicolai to poke and prod. Eventually I became their weapon. And now I'm nothing but a man who wants vengeance. I'm not worth anything to anyone.

Remington pulls away from me, the redness in her eyes makes her brilliant blue eyes look even bluer. "I never said I regret saving you, Jax. I regret that it cost the life of someone else for me to do it. I regret that I saved the man, who despite everything, I still want even though he made it clear he doesn't want me. I've said over and over again that I hate you, and I regret that each time I said it, I never fully meant it. God, it would be so much easier if I did, but I can't." Her eyes search my face. "Why can't I hate you?"

"Probably for the same reason that I can't stay away from you," I admit. "You keep saying that I don't want you. If that were the case, it would have been so easy to say those things I said to you. None of it was easy because just like you, I was lying. I do want you, Remington. I want you with each breath I take, but I can't have you. I can't have you because if I do, I'll hurt you." *More than I already have.* She can heal from a broken heart, but she'd never survive my beast. "You said I was the strongest person you know, if that were the case, I would be strong enough to protect you from me. But I'm not. Your life is something I'll never risk and each second you spend near me is a gamble."

The only other person my wolf has even been this fixated on is Sterling and he wants him dead. The same level of interest he has for Remington is terrifying. His emotions have never been easy to decipher, but nothing good can come out of this obsession with Remi.

"Even though you don't hate me, I still can't offer you more, Remington," I reluctantly tell her. Just like she said the other night. Nothing has changed. "I will help carry the weight of your pain and I will let you scream in my ear until it bleeds, but I can't give you more." Reluctantly, I pull away from her. Slowly we climb to our feet and the space between us now feels like it's miles long. "You were right, it's not fair for me to keep playing with your emotions. You deserve someone who will give you the world, who will hand over every single piece of themselves to you freely. That's not me. No matter how much I wish I were that man, I'm not. I have pieces missing and the pieces I do have are damaged beyond repair. You deserve someone who's whole." Filling in the space we'd just created, I lean down and kiss the corner of her mouth because I'm unable to walk away without one last touch.

I thought by sticking around this past year that I was doing it so I could have help finding Sterling, but I was lying to myself. I was lingering because I couldn't walk away from Remington. I need to be the strong one now. She's been the one carrying that burden for months and it's not fair. Just like it hasn't been fair of me to linger when my presence causes her pain. I thought she needed me to watch over her while she healed from Gage, but I've been hindering that healing. I'm disappointed in myself that it took me this long to figure out, but I'm going to make it better now.

"Give me your pain so you can be happy again, Remington," I plead to her softly against her cheek. "I'll take it and I'll burn it all away."

"Do we deserve to be happy?"

No. I don't. "You deserve every ounce of happiness in this world, and I'd sacrifice everything if I thought I could be the one to give it to you."

Her head tips back so she can look me in the eye. "Can we pretend for a minute that you are?"

"We agreed no more pretending."

"I just need a minute longer." It's a lie. We'll always need a minute longer. "Just give me this, Jax. *Please*. Let's pretend that we're not broken and damaged. Let's pretend that we haven't said the ugly things that we have, and let's pretend that everything is going to be alright. Kiss me and pretend the world isn't burning down around us."

How am I supposed to refuse that request? How am I supposed to tell her no when she's looking at me with those beautiful storm-like eyes?

With only a second of hesitation, I meet her lips halfway.

This kiss isn't angry like the last one. The hot fury that fueled our last exchange has been dampened and replaced with remorse and sorrow.

We kiss each other like it's the last time we'll ever do this because it should be. If I'm strong enough to do what I need to, this will be the last time I taste Remington's mouth and feel her tongue sweep across mine.

Our mouths work together in a slow rhythm like we are both desperately trying to commit this feeling to memory. With each brush of our lips across each other's, we are memorizing the sensation.

My fingers thread into the soft shoulder-length waves of her hair as her hands knot into the front of my shirt. We cling to each other because without having to say the words aloud, we both know what's coming. Remington isn't an idiot. She's smarter than most give her credit for. I'm sure she figured out I'm leaving before I'd fully made the decision myself.

Pressing my lips against hers in one last punishing kiss, I inhale her before I muster the strength to pull away.

"I'm going to take care of everything," I promise her, burning the vow into our very souls. "I'll make sure you can smile again, Remington. That's all I want. You know that, right?"

"*Jax...*" She reaches for me, but her hand is met by the faintest cloud of smoke as I dissolve into nothing with a singular thought in my head. *Find Sterling before he finds Remington and her family.*

This is my purpose.

CHAPTER EIGHTEEN
Remington

Covered in sweat and blood, some mine and some Ranger's, I walk into the kitchen and grab a bottle of water from the refrigerator. Every single one of my muscles hurt and my bones ache, but I'd take the physical pain over the emotional pain any day. At least with a sore body, there are easy remedies. A little ice, some pain relievers, and maybe a hot pad, you're good to go. It's not that easy with emotional pain. Those wounds aren't visible, there aren't any physical reminders of what caused you to bleed, but somehow they find a way to hurt more.

He just left.

Without a word to anyone. Not even Pruitt and those two have become pretty buddy-buddy. She's called or texted me every day asking if I'd heard from him and every day it's the same answer. No, I haven't talked to him. I'm not sure he ever plans on coming back. The way he slipped away from me makes me think he isn't coming back.

It's been four days since he walked away. For those four days, I've thrown myself into training. For months I craved the solitude of the quiet hotel room, but now the idea of sitting in that cold, impersonal room makes my skin crawl. Silence isn't my friend right now. It makes me sit there and replay those last moments up on the ridge.

He was telling me goodbye without saying the words. That kiss it felt so... *final*. Like a breakup. Not that we were ever truly together, but it hurts just the same if not more. Instead of thinking of all the things I've actually lost, I'm mourning the idea of what could have been and that hurts more. The what-ifs replay in my head like a movie I'll never get to watch.

While I train with my brothers, I don't think about anything but what's right in front of me, and that's what I need right now. I can't sit here and worry about where Jax is. If he's doing what I think he's doing, he's a fucking idiot. He can't find and fight Kaius and Sterling alone. If he could, he would have done it years ago.

It's only been a few days of really focusing on training, but I already feel stronger. My mind is also starting to clear, my instincts are getting sharper with each training session. The dark haze I've been living under is clearing just enough that I can see a path in front of me again. I'm trying my best to fight against the sad cloud that has settled in since Gage died. It doesn't hurt any less, but I'm so tired of it weighing me down.

I'm leaning against the counter, bottle of water in my hand when Whisper comes lurking around the corner with a look on his face. "You look weird," I tell him. "Well, weirder than normal. You kinda always have that odd *'don't get too close to me, I might sniff your hair or feet'* vibe to you."

His eyes roll behind his glasses. "I'm not going to *sniff* your feet."

"I'm relieved to hear I can now wear open-toed shoes around you," I joke before taking a sip of water. "What's really wrong with you?"

He trails a finger over the pristine white marble countertop, looking away from me. "Have you seen Jax?"

"Why does everyone keep asking me that?" My hand squeezes the plastic bottle in my hand in frustration. It makes an obnoxious crinkling sound. "I'm not Jax's keeper and he's not mine."

"So that's a *no*?"

"No, I haven't seen or talked to Jax," I grit out.

"Okay..." He trails off, but it's clear he has more to say. Whisper doesn't come across as someone that holds back but right now it's clear to me that he's holding back.

"Just spit whatever it is out already," I demand. "I don't have the patience right now to wait for you to find your words, *Hot Topic*."

He holds his hands up in surrender. "*Okay, jeez*. I'm still trying to figure out how all of this works. Pruitt and Ryker are the alphas, so information is supposed to be brought to them, but I'm not a member of the pack. Technically, I don't have to tell them jack shit. Right?" The more he rambles, the closer he is to being punched in the throat. "But I like to think that you and I have become friends, or we're well on our way to being friends, and I feel like I should tell you. It is about Jax after all and he's your... *Jax*."

"*Whisper*," I warn when he doesn't immediately continue. At the mention of Jax's name, I'm freezing in place as alarm bells start to go off in my head. What could the hacker possibly know about Jax?

"Last night a grave was robbed in Seattle," he finally

admits after an annoyingly long pause. "I did some digging and that black circle that Jax warned us about? There was one around this grave."

"Kaius."

Whisper nods his head in confirmation. "Unless there's another necromancer out there raising the dead."

"There isn't," I confirm. The only other one we know of is Winslow, and she's only half. Her powers aren't like Kaius's. "He's in Seattle."

"As of eight hours ago, he was."

"Eight hours? Why are you just telling me this *now*?" That's eight hours the necromancer has to get away from us again.

"Because Jax threatened me with an extensive amount of bodily harm if I told anyone else." Whisper rolls up the sleeve of his oversized and ripped-up sweater. Dark bruising wraps around his thin, pale forearm. The marks are clearly fingerprints. *Jax's fingerprints.* "I don't know a lot about this world yet, but from what I know about these guys, Jax is going to need backup. If I'm right, he'll be thankful I told you because he lived, or it won't matter because he'll be dead. After eight hours of agonizing over what I should do, I decided I'm okay with either of those outcomes. Obviously, I'd prefer the first one, but I'd rather not have a pissed-off demon on my ass."

I feel my eyes shifting into their glowing wolf forms as my animal side surges forward. "Would you rather have a pissed-off wolf shifter? Because if something happens and I could have been there with him hours ago, I'm going to shred your body into pieces and then post it on your fucking *blog*."

"*My blog*? What the hell do I look like? A bored soccer mom who ignores that her husband is having an affair by writing up muffin recipes and DIY shiplap projects? I think the fuck not," he sniffs like he's offended. "I have a message board that can only be found on the dark web. It's *different*."

I stand there imagining what it would be like to string him up like a pinata and beat him with a stick for a second before announcing, "I'm going after him. I need to get to Seattle."

If this is our only chance to get to Kaius, we can't risk Jax being there alone, and I can't risk something happening to Jax. I didn't go through six months of hell for him to be so cavalier with the life I risked everything for.

For reasons I'll never be able to understand, I need that jerk to stay alive. I need it more than I need air.

"Do you want me to find you a flight?" Whisper offers. "If I had time, I'd prefer to get you an alias to travel under just in case Sterling is monitoring things like that. Ideally, it would be better if you could drive, but I don't think we have time for that."

"I have a way there," I assure him. "Or I think I do. I just have to go ask my sister-in-law if it's okay." Whisper looks at me with a confused look. "Remember all that money you helped steal from Winslow's adoptive dad? She bought a plane with it."

Now I have to find a way to ask her if I can borrow it. It's a lot like asking someone if you can borrow their car, only it's a few *million* dollars more expensive. Easy-peasy.

☾

WINSLOW WAS THE EASIEST ONE TO WIN OVER. I'D BARELY finished explaining myself before she was on the phone calling the pilot and crew to get the plane ready. The rest of my family, however, weren't as easily persuaded, it wasn't until I reminded them that they were better off here, they reluctantly agreed.

Ryker and Pru can't leave because they're the alphas. Pru argued at first, but when she was not so gently reminded by her mate she's carrying a *child*, she conceded. Ranger won't leave Winslow here alone. Isabeau offered to go with me, but if Sterling shows up while she's away, the pack won't be as strong without her here. The pack needs both Isabeau and Ransom here to keep them safe.

As I wait for the small crew to finish getting the plane ready, Winnie and Whisper stand on the small tarmac with me. Ranger waits by the car in the distance, his vigilant eyes scanning the area around us just in case.

While Whisper is busy typing away at one of the three phones he carries around with him, Winslow cocks her head and stares at me. "What?" I ask, feeling self-conscious.

"You seem… lighter." She waves her hand around my frame. "Not quite yet yourself, but you're getting there."

"I've… uh…" I clear my throat nervously as I try to find the words. "Well, it turns out that every one of those self-help books is right. Keeping secrets and shoving feelings down will help for a minute, but not in the long run."

Winslow laughs softly. "I could have told you that months ago, but it wouldn't have mattered. You weren't ready to listen or let go. You needed time to figure it out on your own. I didn't know I was ready to tell my secrets until I met Ranger. At the time I thought admitting my past to him was the worst thing that could have happened, but it turned out to be the best. I've never felt *freer* than I did after he knew everything. Every dark detail I told him was a weight off my chest. So, if you've relieved some of your own weight, I'm happy for you." She grins at me. "Plus, I'm excited to have you back because Beau doesn't always understand my jokes and she really takes the fun out of it when I have to explain them to her. A hamster would understand a knock-knock joke better than her."

"I'm trying to get back to normal," I tell her. "Or at least I'm trying to figure out what my new normal is."

"Good." Behind us, the door of the black jet opens and a short staircase is released. "So, if you do find my sperm donor, kick him in the nuts for me." A gleeful look lights up her face. The intensity of it is almost terrifying. "Or better yet, cut them off and bring them home for me in a doggie bag."

"You're more bloodthirsty than we give you credit for," I observe as I stare down the tiny witch. "I *like* it."

She shrugs innocently before leaning up and kissing me on the cheek before *skipping* away to her waiting mate.

Shaking my head I look at Whisper who has finally put away his phone. He's traded his usual pair of glasses for a pair of comically large black sunglasses with silver studs on the side. "Are you hiding from the paparazzi?"

"Several governments, actually," he answers without skipping a beat. He takes a phone out of his pocket and hands it to me. "Use this to contact us. I've put software on it that makes it untraceable. I've also put the addresses you need to go check out when you get there."

I hike my leather backpack up farther on my shoulder before taking the offered phone. "Thanks."

"I'll keep you updated if I learn anything else while you're in the air." He shocks me by leaning in and giving me a brief hug. "I haven't forgotten about that information you asked me to look into. The second I find something, I'll let you know."

I can count on one hand the number of times I've left Montana. Two of those times were to help my brothers and I've never gone alone. The nerves I feel are unexpected as I climb the stairs of the plane, but they're also welcome. They're new and after six months of feeling the same dull way, it's a fun change.

Settling into the seat by a window, I think about how this moment is so full circle for us. I never wanted Jax's help, but he ignored me and watched over me anyway. He doesn't want my help now, but I'm coming for him whether he likes it or not. This is also the moment I finally understand Jax's side of things.

It doesn't matter we can't be together; nothing is going to stop us from being there for each other—from protecting each other when we don't think we need it.

CHAPTER NINETEEN
Jay

I can't imagine how unnerving it is to be abruptly brought back to life. One second, you're off somewhere in the afterlife hopefully at peace, and the next, you're shoved back into your earthly body with energy that is foreign to you powering your existence. Especially for those who have been dead for decades, they're going to have it really rough when they discover their humanity has been burned away after all this time.

Sterling is lucky that he's always had Kaius there to bring him back within minutes. If he hadn't, Sterling would be even more of a monster than he is now.

Two sets of footprints lie in the fresh dirt around the empty grave. One set, a pair of men's dress shoes, the other much smaller. This grave isn't the one I originally came to Seattle for. This one is new, it only happened about an hour ago. The groundskeeper at the other cemetery told me about it when I was questioning him earlier. No surprise, he didn't have any information to offer me. He was just more perplexed by the perfect black circle seared into the ground.

He's pointed at the mark with a gnarled, old, finger.

"Witchcraft, I tell ya!" He'd wheezed through cigarette corrupted lungs. "These kids come in here and play with those damn Ouija boards." He gripped the rosary beads hanging out of his jacket pocket like they'd save him from evil. "I swear, they'll summon a demon if they're not careful."

At that point, I had doubled over in laughter because he truly didn't see the irony in what he said. A demon *was* summoned here. I wiped the tears of laughter off my cheeks as I stood back up to my full height. Slapping him on the shoulder, I thanked him for making me laugh. "Demons? Come on, old man. Those don't exist." I had slowly backed away from him, heading toward the metal gate not far away. And because I'm an asshole who finds humor in things I shouldn't, I'd let my eyes shift into their glowing animal form. "Or do they?" The look of terror on his face is something I'll laugh about for years. "You better say your prayers tonight," I warned before mockingly crossing myself.

After that I'd casually walked down the street, following the muddy footprints left on the sidewalk and the lingering scent of death in the air. Doesn't matter that Kaius brought them back, that scent will cling to the undead until they're cleaned up.

The footprints eventually vanished but the scent remained. It led me here, to the abandoned and decaying textile factory located in the heart of the industrial part of the city. Standing in front of the dark building, my beast lifts his head and emits a warning growl. Whatever is in there, he can sense, and he isn't a big fan of it.

I don't bother going in quietly and stealth-like. My palms slam into the boarded-up front doors, breaking them open with a loud *bang*. The chains around the door handles snap at the force and clatter to the cement floor. Bending down, I snag a piece of the cold metal and swing it around in the air a few times before allowing it to wrap up my wrist and forearm.

The farther I walk through the building, the more I start to think this place isn't as abandoned as I had originally assumed. A lot of work had been put into keeping the rundown appearance, but the new wiring hidden in the beams of the ceiling and discretely placed cameras tell me otherwise. When I spot a familiar-looking keypad hidden behind a stack of leftover factory supplies, it dawns on me. I'd accidentally wandered into one of Sterling's buildings.

Whether this is a breeding facility like the one I was raised in or just an outpost he uses while it town isn't clear, but it's the first establishment I've been in that is still intact. He's been systematically destroying the other ones. If Kaius is resurrecting bodies nearby, that means this building is the next one that is going to be cleared out or burned down. It also means I got here just in time.

We should have brought in the hacker sooner. At some point I'm going to have to apologize to the whacky little human. I'm ashamed of how I acted with him, but he had information that I needed.

Walking down a long corridor, I swing the chain back and forth, letting it clank against random objects lined up against the walls. "I smell dead people," I sing loudly, my voice echoing down the vast space. "Come out, come out wherever you are." The farther into the building I travel, the stronger the scent becomes.

They're somewhere close, I just hope their maker is with them.

As I round the corner, a secret door that blends seamlessly

into the grimy wall swings open and a man built like a brick shithouse charges out of the dark space. His dead eyes are wide and unblinking as he opens his mouth in an angry roar, his teeth are almost black from rot.

I jump into the action, backing up just before his giant fist swings at my head. Twisting the chain in my hand, I swing it at him. The metal collides with the side of his head, splitting the skin above his right eye open.

While one hand covers his bleeding eye, the other swings wildly at me. His knuckles collide with my chin, the force of it making me stagger back a bit. The pain of the blow fuels me and my wolf. He rages inside my body, craving the taste of his enemies' blood on his tongue.

The large man charges at me once more, but this time I'm prepared. Just as he reaches me, I vanish into smoke and reappear behind him. Before he can figure out I'm now behind him, I loop the chain around his sizable neck. Throwing every ounce of my weight behind it, I pull the metal taut.

His hands tear at the chain as he falls to his knees in front of me. With him now below me, I have better leverage and I pull tighter. He gargles and gasps for air loudly.

I can't hear the footsteps over his pained noises until it's too late. Like a freight train, another body collides with mine, sending me sprawling onto the dusty concrete floor. Before I have a chance to recover, a booted foot slams into my ribs, knocking the wind out of me.

With a pissed-off roar, the next time the foot is slammed into my body, my fingers wrap around their ankle. As I infuse the body with hellfire, the new assailant screams in pain and falls to the ground.

While they writhe in pain, I clamber back to my feet, one

of my hands holding my now broken ribs. The new attacker, a scrawny woman dressed in an outfit fresh out of the fifties, tries to get to her knees. Before she can stand up, I grip either side of her head.

Her mouth parts in a silent scream as hellfire fills her skull. Her pupils dilate until they look like they explode while blood pours from the corners of them. Blood begins to leak from her mouth and nose as her brain slowly melts in her head.

The faint sound of the metal chain scraping across the stone floor as it's picked up behind me is my only warning before the cold metal wraps around my neck and I'm roughly pulled away from my new victim. As I'm forced to let go of her, she falls to the ground in a heap. Her dead eyes stare lifelessly at me as I struggled to pull the chain from my neck.

My power is just starting to hum in my veins as I prepare to vanish, but just before I do, the tension on the chain is released. The metal falls completely away from my body as the large dead man makes pained gasping noises, followed by an unpleasant gurgling sound.

When I turn around, I'm so shocked to see the sight in front of me that I have to blink a couple of times to make sure it's really real and not a trick my mind has conjured up for me because it knows how much I want her here with me. But no matter how many times I blink, nothing changes or disappears. She doesn't disappear.

She's here.

Remington, wrapped around his back, has her claws in the dead man's throat. With one flick of her wrist, she tears through all the vital arteries. Blood pours out of his jugular like a water faucet. His hands try to put pressure on the wound, but Remi only tears it open farther. His eyes widen and he falls to his knees. The weight of his large body hitting the ground causes objects around us to rattle. Remi holds on to him as he falls and doesn't let go until he finally succumbs to his injury and falls forward on his chest.

Silently, Remington looks at her blood-soaked hand and without a second thought, she wipes the residue on the back of the dead man's jacket. She finally lifts her head and looks me over for any wounds. When she deems I'm okay, she's charging at me with a pissed-off look on her face. Her hands slam into my chest as she violently shoves me back. "What in the *Disney Prince Charming* was that shit!" she yells at me. "You kiss me goodbye on a *literal* cliff and then gallop away on your white horse to *what*? Almost get taken out by André the *fucking* Giant." Her hand waves at the very large dead man at our feet. "Tell me that wasn't your plan, Jax!"

"If you'd just given me a second, you would have seen I had it perfectly under control," I reassure her, but her response is to roll her eyes at me in pure Remi fashion. "You're not supposed to be here, Remington."

"And you're not supposed to be here alone," she argues instantly. "You're *definitely* not supposed to threaten our new human friend with bodily harm either or leave bruises on their body. That was a dick move, dude."

"He had information I needed, and he wasn't inclined to give it to me at first," I sniff unapologetically.

"Maybe because he's smarter than you and knew it was a bad idea for you to go alone." Her eyes jump from me to her hand as she discovers there's still blood on it. With a grimace, she bends down and uses the hem of the guy's dated jacket to clean her fingers off. *"Jesus,* what the hell is this man wearing?"

"I think Kaius gets a kick out of bringing back the people who've been dead the longest," I theorize. "I think it makes him feel strong knowing he's bringing back someone who's been dead for over fifty years. He's always been a little bit of an egomaniac."

Remington looks between the two dead bodies and their dated clothes, before nodding in understanding. "Are they the only ones here? I can't tell if there's more, that ungodly smell is masking everything else."

I look around the empty space. "Not sure. I haven't gotten that far."

"I'm assuming this is one of the buildings they haven't had a chance to clear out yet?"

"Based on the short amount of time those assholes have been alive," I gesture at Kaius's dead goons. "Kaius is getting his ducks in a row before he does just that."

Her face sets like she's preparing for battle. "Alright, so let's keep going and see if we can find anything else."

"*I'll* keep going. You're going to turn that cute little ass of yours around and go home where your family needs you."

"My family doesn't *need* me right now," she argues. "They're all watching each other's backs, but no one is here watching yours. I want to find Kaius as much as you do." She pleads before her face pinches like she's in pain. The expression goes away as fast as it flashed upon her pretty face. "We can't ever be together. *Fine.* One day I'll come to accept that, but that doesn't mean we have to stop being there for each other. Since the very first day we met and you jumped in front of a bullet for me, we've been protecting each other. I'll admit I didn't always see that, but I do now. So just let me help."

If I had the time, I would lift her up and put her on a goddam bus back to Montana right now, but this mission is time sensitive. As we speak, Kaius could be setting aflame important documents. One particular document I want is one that has all the breeding facilities on it. I've only ever been to a couple and those have been cleared out, but there is no way Sterling would have terminated all those viable experiments. He just moved them to a new location, and I want to know where. If and when we kill Sterling, someone will have to go to those facilities and save all those souls.

"Fine," I relent. "But if I tell you to get out—*to run*—you have to listen to me."

She blinks slowly at me before shaking her head. "Nope." Remi pats my back mockingly as she walks past me. "But that was a nice try. Your tone… very convincing. Bravo, well done," she praises over her shoulder before making her way down the corridor.

Catching up to her, I ask, "How the hell did you even find me?"

"I put a GPS in your dog bowl, and I had Whisper ping your location." When I stare at her with wide, confused eyes, she laughs under her breath. "Kidding. Whisper gave me the address of the cemetery, so I went straight there from the airstrip. There I found a groundskeeper who was pacing around by a headstone, mumbling about a demon" —she gives me a pointed look clearly not as impressed by my joke as I was— "I knew I'd just missed you. The poor man pointed me in the direction you headed, and I eventually caught your scent and followed it here. And you know the rest."

"*Come on.* The man had rosary beads in his pocket! How many times am I going to get an opportunity like that?"

"I'm assuming you missed this lesson when you were a kid as well, but our kind has only been able to survive this long because we keep our existence a secret from the humans. Can you imagine how they'd react if they found out their monsters and horror movie villains were in fact real? It would be chaos. You know how humans react when they're afraid. Violence is always their first response."

"Sterling always had an issue with humans," I tell her. The sound of our matching footsteps bounces off the concrete walls and metal ceiling. "You should have heard the way he talked about them. I've never heard someone talk about something with so much disdain as how he does with humans." The only thing that rivals it is the manner in which I talk about Sterling.

We come to metal double doors. The glass windows in them have been broken and the shards crunch under our feet as we walk over them.

"Well, this isn't creepy or anything," Remington comments dryly at my side as we both pause and look around the vast room we'd entered. Mannequins, some fully intact and standing while some are in pieces in bins lining the walls, fill the dark room. The only light comes from glowing red exit signs posted above the doors. Plastic hangs from the ceiling, blowing slightly from some kind of airflow streaming into the room. "Seems a little on the nose as well. Sterling and Kaius might as well have spray-painted *'villain lair'* on the freaking walls because this place is straight out of a scary movie."

"If you were trying to keep nosy people out, wouldn't you make it as unappealing as possible?" I question as I pick up a broken mannequin hand. When I poke Remi in the back with it, she swats her hand at it and glowers at me.

"Well, five stars to the criminal masterminds because if I didn't have to, I wouldn't come within five hundred yards of this room." She waves her hand in front of her face, nose wrinkling. "It smells in here too."

"Like death and chemicals." It's so strong, it almost makes my nose burn.

She turns around like she's about to say something, but her face drops and her head tilts. "Do you hear that?"

"Hear what?"

"I swore I heard someone whisper something." Remi's voice is low as she tries to listen once more. "It was almost childlike…"

"I didn't hear anything," I tell her as I continue to look around the unsettling room. It's just as my eyes lock on the faint red flickering light in the corner that Remington gasps and grabs my arm.

"There!"

Looking away from what is no doubt a camera, I try to find what she's looking at. "What?"

"Something moved."

"It's the mannequins and moving plastic. They're playing mind tricks on you." I try to calm her nerves but when my wolf lifts his head and bares his teeth, I realize I may have spoken too soon. Instantly on high alert, I step closer to Remington just in case something else is planning on ambushing me in the building. It wouldn't be a surprise if it happened again.

"No, I'm telling you, it was something else," she presses,

her spine rigid and hands balled into fists at her sides as her blue eyes dart around the space.

She jumps abruptly and her hand points to the other side of the room where the open doors to another hallway sit. "There it is again," Remi announces just as light footsteps slap across the floor. There's the smallest flash of movement, whatever is out there is tiny.

"What is it?"

On cue, a child's whimper echoes through the cold and dark space sending a cold shiver of unease down my spine.

"It's a kid." Remi's eyes fill with sympathy when she looks back at me before starting to pull away from me. "We have to help them."

This all feels so off to me. "No, something's wrong."

"Jax, it's a kid," she tries to reason. "What if this place is actually a breeding facility and they escaped? They need help." With a harsh tug, she pulls out of my grasp and takes off like a rocket through the various pieces of plastic.

As I call her name to order her to come back, I remember something I'd foolishly looked over earlier tonight. The small footprints at the gravesite.

Oh shit.

CHAPTER TWENTY
Remington

For various reasons, I'm not sure I'll ever be a good mom if that time ever comes. For starters, I've killed every houseplant I've ever owned. Even those ones that are supposedly easy to take care of and you only have to water them like once a week. Poor little guys. I also have burned every meal I've ever tried to cook that wasn't frozen. I also sometimes forget to wash my toothpaste out of my sink. Those are some basic adult skills I'm going to need to master before I procreate.

But just because I'm not ready to care for a child doesn't mean I don't like them. Every child I've ever met I've felt fiercely protective of. This child is no different. I don't know if it's because the kid that's in here with us could be from a breeding facility and that possibility makes my heart ache for the little boy that Jax once was when he was raised in a medical hellhole, or just my pure instincts, but either way, I run. I ignore Jax when he tells me to stop.

If I can save just one of the children who are subjected to this world tonight, maybe I won't feel like such a failure for not doing anything to help for the last six months. So caught up in my own misery, I hadn't had enough energy to put toward helping the women and children stuck in places like this.

Saving someone tonight isn't going to miraculously make up for my behavior, but it's a start. And God, I want that start. I sacrificed a life and maybe in my sick way I'm trying to make up for that by saving this one.

Just like the eerie room we were in with the mannequins, this corridor is devoid of windows. The red exit signs above the few doors remain the only source of light. My advanced eyesight allows me to see in the dark, but I'd still prefer if there were some overhead lights that could cast away the unnerving shadows around me.

"Remington!" Jax yells behind me. "Stop."

Far ahead of me, I see the tiny figure disappear when it makes a turn down another hallway. The faint clacking of their shoes from their light footfalls fills my ears. I'll give the kid credit, they're fast.

Picking up speed, I bolt through the dark hallway until I reach a small room. It's full of industrial-sized laundry hampers. Rows and rows of them make for perfect hiding places.

"I'm not going to hurt you," I call out to them in a soft, calm voice. "I just want to help." *Please let me help.*

At the very last row, facing the wall, I find him. He's curled into a ball and facing the wall. As he hears my footsteps behind him, a small, scared whimper comes from his tiny body. His hair is cut in a perfect bowl shape around his head. The strands look dirty, grease and grime cause the strands to stick together. His white collared shirt has also seen better days.

Crouching low, I slowly approach him as to not startle him any more than he already is. "It's okay," I coo. He shifts and presses himself tighter against the wall.

As slow and as gentle as possible, once I'm close enough, I reach out to grasp his shoulder to encourage him to face me. I just want to show him I'm not here to hurt him—to show him a friendly face.

Just as my fingers grip his boney shoulder, Jax barges into the room. "Remi! Get back!" his warning has just escaped his lips before the small boy in front of me is whirling around, showing me his face for the first time.

I barely have time to process his cold, dead eyes before there's a flash of silver cutting through the air. On instinct, I lift my arm to protect my face. My forearm burns in pain as something slices through my flesh.

Gasping in shock and pain, I fall back on my ass on the dirty floor. My hand covers my bleeding wound as I stare at the little boy in disbelief. He's dead. Or he was dead.

Whatever childlike innocence he had was sucked out of him and replaced with wickedness when Kaius brought him back. He can't be more than five years old, but here he is, a knife coated in my blood in his hand as he comes toward me with a warped grin on his face.

I attempt to back away as he charges at me once more with the blade held high, but before he can slash me, I'm abruptly yanked up from under the shoulders and lifted out of harm's way. A noise, more animal than human comes from him. It's one I've never heard before and it sends a shiver down my spine. My wolf's ears perk with interest instead of fear. Jax dumps me behind him and places his body between me and the possessed child.

The boy laughs almost manically as he attempts to cut Jax. The next time he swings wildly, the demon takes hold of his tiny arm and jerks the knife free. The blade skids across the floor out of sight as it disappears under one of the clothing bins.

Jax dangles the kid in the air by its arm. The child fights and thrashes in the hold, but it's no use against Jax's strength. As he tries to fight, his manic laughs turn into pissed-off screams. The haunting sound bounces off the stone walls.

"Remington." Jax's tone is cold, and it immediately sets me on edge. "Go stand outside by the door but stay where I can see you."

Holding my hand over my cut, I shake my head. "What? No. I'm staying."

"No!" he roars, his purple eyes flashing as he turns to look at me. "For once, just do what I fucking say. I don't want you to see this."

It takes me a second to figure out what he's referring to, but when I do, my stomach sinks. "*Jax...*"

His face is completely impassive, not a single emotion written on his devastatingly handsome face. "Leave, Remi," he pleads over the screaming child.

With one last look at the pair, I slowly back out of the room. Sorrow and remorse follow me like a black cloud. This shouldn't have ever happened. He might not be in any pain, but no one should ever subject a child to this.

Once I'm out of the room and I'm turned away with my

back pressed to the doorframe, I hear the slight struggle. Not once does the frustrated screaming stop. At one point I heard Jax make a grunting noise, making me think the kid was able to land a blow at some point.

It's so faint, I almost miss it but through the shrieking, I hear my hellhound whisper, "I'm sorry." Then there is a cracking sound that makes my stomach roll and my throat tighten as nausea works its way through my body.

Just like that, the screaming stops and the silence becomes deafening.

I stand there, breathing hard for a moment, before I force myself to turn back around. Jax doesn't want me to see what he's done, but I told him I'd be there for him, and I know without a doubt, he needs some support and empathy right now. He can deny it until he's blue in the face, but I know him better than either of us are willing to admit.

Reentering the quiet room, I find Jax searching through the bins. He doesn't turn to look at me, but I know he knows I'm here by the way his muscles go stiff. When he finally finds a large piece of fabric that's almost bedsheet-like, he takes it over to where he left the boy. I can't see the body. Only a tiny set of dated dress shoes stick out from behind the bins.

Without a word, Jax covers the boy with the sheet. He stands over the small body for a second longer before finally turning and looking at me. "He wasn't a kid," he explains to me like he somehow needs to justify what just happened. "Not anymore, anyway. "

"I know."

"It had to be done."

"I know," I repeat.

He stands there staring at me like he's still expecting me to lose it on him or to freak out. When I don't, he finally gives a curt nod before his hands grip the hem of his black shirt. With one quick yank, he rips the fabric. Stalking toward me, he takes my wounded arm in his gentle grip and ties the fabric around the cut. "It'll be healed soon, but this will help stop you from bleeding everywhere."

"Thank you," I tell him.

"Let's go."

Side by side, in heavy silence, we leave the room and journey farther into the building. I don't push Jax to talk, whatever is going on in his head he needs to work through himself. There aren't any words I can offer him right now. He already knows I don't judge him for what just happened, he just needs a second to come to peace with it himself. I want to kill Sterling and Kaius for continuously putting Jax in these kinds of positions. How many times has he had to do such ugly deeds because of them?

He hasn't told me about them in detail, but the way he and Beau talk about their time in the organization, I know they've been made to do horrific things.

We climb a metal staircase. At the very top, we come to a metal door with a high-tech security panel that looks completely out of place on it. Jax rubs his fingers together before pressing his palm to the device. I can't see it, but the slight hum of power in the air that makes the hairs on my arms rise lets me know he's using his power.

The panel makes a high pitched buzzing noise before all the lights begin flashing in disarray, before finally the whole thing begins smoking as the wires are fried by hellfire. After a second, the locking mechanism buzzes, and the door opens for us.

Side-eyeing him, I mumble, "Show off," before walking through the door, not bothering to let him go first.

The light I had so desperately wanted just twenty minutes ago blinds me as I enter the brightly lit portion of the building. Without a doubt, this is what we've been looking for. There isn't any discarded textile equipment, or ominously dark rooms. No, instead I feel like I've walked into some fancy office building. Everything is made of glass and the bright white floors and walls make the place feel bright. It's clean. Sterile.

Instead of the disgusting smell of death that polluted the air downstairs, this space reeks of gasoline. Like someone has dumped gallons of it out all over the space.

Straining my ears, I listen for any movement, but it's so quiet.

We pass multiple empty offices and what look to be medical exam rooms. As we pass the rooms full of exam tables, Jax's body goes stiff next to mine. When I instinctively reach out my hand for his, I have to silently scold myself. Jax is so distracted by what's around him, I'm almost positive he missed it.

Seeing this place really puts in perspective how different our childhoods were. I already knew they were, but having the visual of just how different they were is like a gut punch. The things I would complain about as a child or even now are so inconsequential compared to this.

"They probably cleared out everyone a while ago and they're only back now to clean up loose ends."

Flicking my eyes toward the stream of gasoline that

puddles on the ground around us, I nod in agreement. "Setting the whole place on fire is definitely the easiest way to do that." We pass rooms that are jail cells disguised as hospital rooms. Some of the beds are still here, white sheets neatly tucked in them. "The arson investigators are going to be so confused when they discover there was a medical facility hidden in this shithole building."

"There will barely be any of it let for the humans to figure anything out," Jax explains as we move through a rounded room made up of more jail cells. Instead of metal bars, they're glass boxes. "They'll think it's weird, but there won't be anything for them to track or investigate further."

There's a loud switching sound as the lighting all around us changes as every glass wall that we're surrounded by changes from see-through to a shiny reflective surface. *Mirrors.*

"We like to keep things tidy," a disjointed voice I've never heard before suddenly answers. "You don't get as far as we have by leaving loose ends."

Jax's eyes begin to glow as he whips his head around looking for the source but based on the low ominous growl coming from his chest, he knows that voice.

"Jax, my boy, how you've grown," the voice praises. "Did you like my presents? I thought the boy would be a fun little… addition to the party." A man appears out of nowhere. His reflection is plastered on every single one of the mirrored surfaces. I suddenly feel like I've found myself at a funhouse. "We were so close to having a good time, but you had to ruin it," he scolds, tsking under his breath. "Couldn't you have let him play a little longer? I wanted to see what he'd do to her."

My eyes dart around, bouncing between each of the

reflections. With the weird lighting, I'm struggling to figure out where the actual man is.

I'm about to ask who the hell this guy is, but before I have the chance, Jax is spitting out a name like it's coated in venom. "*Kaius.*"

"In the flesh," Kaius purrs before bowing slightly at us.

CHAPTER TWENTY-ONE
Remington

Whether I was searching for him or not, if I walked past Kaius on the street I wouldn't be able to stop myself from staring at him. His hair is longer than mine and is dark brown like Winslow's. It's stick straight, and he has a pretty severe widow's peak. His eyes are pale blue, the same color as one of Winnie's. She definitely looks more like her mother, but unfortunately some genes are hard to shake. All the men in my life are over six foot, the necromancer looks shrimpy compared to them even though he's technically medium height. His thin body is dressed in an elaborate, almost ornate, black suit. The silk vest he wears under his embroidered jacket is patterned in a floral design. A chain hangs from his pocket, presumably attached to a pocket watch. He even has a cane. His palm rests over the decorative metal top.

Having caught me looking him over, Kaius twists and turns like he's showing off his outfit. "First impressions, Remington?"

"Honestly?" I ask, pursing my lips. "You look like a

rejected member of *The Addams Family*. I feel like you really need a top hat or a monocle to complete this look."

Kaius stares at me with a pensive look on his face before his lips slip into a creepy, gleeful smile. "How *fun*. I see why you like her, Jax. She's *riveting*," he muses. "Even if she did kill one of my little birds. Those take a lot of power to make you know, you can't just go around ripping out throats willy-nilly like that."

"Why are we having this conversation through mirrors?" Jax interjects angrily, staring at one reflection instead of trying to look at them all. "Why are we having this conversation to begin with? This isn't a fucking meet and greet. Get out here, Kaius, I've been waiting months for this moment."

Kaius begins pacing. As he moves, it's like the reflections begin to circle us. "*Patience*," he chastises. "I want to talk to you about something first, but if you still feel the need for bloodshed after, we can arrange that."

"What the hell are you talking about?" I demand.

Kaius stops pacing so he can look me in the eye. His head cocks as his gaze looks over me. "Do you know how old I am?"

"Should I?"

"No, but I suppose I probably should. I have walked this earth for a very long time. Well before witches were creating curses and vampires were hiding from the sun, I was here. I've tasted all the foods, I've heard all the songs, I've watched the technology progress. And do you know what happens after a while? You become bored. Dreadfully bored. Nothing is new or exciting, there is nothing keeping that spark inside of you lit." I knew Kaius had the ability to steal souls from others and keep them for himself. Stolen life force keeps him going and if he keeps it up, he's basically immortal. I just hadn't realized just how long he's been at it. "That's what happened to me. Nothing caught my interest, but then Sterling came poking around and for the first time in centuries, my curiosity was piqued. I wish I could stand before you and tell you I truly believed in Sterling's scientific advancements or his uninspired mission, but the truth is I was bored and I wanted to see how far Sterling could go with all of this. So, I stuck around, I used my power for his gain, and I allowed him to use me when he needed." Kaius yawns like he's exhausted. He scrapes his hand over his open mouth before continuing. "I'm no longer amused. It was fun for a minute seeing what he was capable of doing, but once again, it's all grown old, and I no longer have a desire to participate. It's time I move on to my next adventure."

Jax and I look at each other, confused, before looking back at the necromancer. "So, what are you saying? You're prepared to walk away from Sterling? To turn your back on the man you've been loyal to for almost thirty years?"

"Loyal is a strong word." Kaius's thin lips purse. "It was more of a..." He snaps his fingers until he finds the word. "*Symbiotic* relationship. He kept me entertained and I kept him alive. The relationship is no longer working for me."

"You're here to burn down one of his buildings, you're obviously still team Sterling," I remind him. "And you had dead bodyguards waiting downstairs."

"I had to keep up appearances before I got what I wanted." He shrugs unapologetically. "As for my little birds, I don't have claws or teeth, dear, and I left my sword in the seventeenth century. Plus, I do find great joy in watching others fight for their lives. I really miss the gladiator times," Kaius tells us, sounding almost wistful that the days of the arena are long behind us. "Oh, but watching you try to save the boy was truly thrilling to watch. Bitter end but fun while it lasted."

Only a man with no soul or empathy could find enjoyment in resurrecting a child only to have him killed a few hours later. Only a psychopath like Kaius could find *entertainment* in what Sterling has done.

"What is it that you wanted?" Jax asks, not sounding convinced.

Kaius pulls out a piece of paper from his jacket pocket. "This..." He sounds almost proud of himself. "Sterling has been a busy boy, moving all his pieces around on the chessboard. He's also foolishly tasked me with doing the same. Divide and conquer, I think was his plan. On top of destroying our buildings, I've also been moving his test subjects to different hidden locations. Although, I'm not exactly moving them to the locations we'd agreed on. I thought it may be wise to have a couple bargaining chips on the off chance I needed some *leverage*. You know, just in case things turned south after he discovered I was no longer fascinated with his experiments." He pauses and looks over Jax before glancing my way with inquisitive eyes. "Though, even after all this time, you still manage to keep me captivated. You are a curious creation indeed, Jax. Not even Sterling could have predicted you'd become this when he created you. A fun surprise for all parties. None of our other demon hybrids were remotely like you, and trust me, we tried. Sterling spent over a decade trying to create another being that can control the flames, but alas, there isn't anyone like you."

A snarl escapes from Jax. "Well thank hell for small miracles. The world and its people are thankful for his inability to replicate me."

"*Jax*," Kaius scolds. "Don't talk about yourself with such contempt. You're special."

"Don't call me that."

My eyes continue to dart around the room as I attempt to find where the real Kaius is, but the whole thing is so disorienting, I can't even remember what side we entered this room from. My right and left are completely twisted. From what I've seen, Jax hasn't even bothered looking around. He's barely moved since we found ourselves surrounded by mirrors.

"What is it you want from us?" I ask, interrupting the intense moment.

"Who says I want anything from you?" Kaius questions.

I roll my eyes. "You think because you're the oldest that you're the smartest?" I challenge him. "If you didn't want something from us, we would have bypassed this whole conversation and you never would have shown us that bargaining chip you keep stuffed in your jacket pocket. You wanted us to know you have it, and I'm asking why."

"You really are a smart girl, aren't you?" Kaius's lips lift in a wicked grin, his slightly yellow teeth shining. "You're right. I do want something from you. I'm looking to create another *reciprocal* relationship. I'll scratch your back if you scratch mine, so to speak."

"What the hell could we possibly have to offer you?"

His dull, uninspired eyes light up in excitement as he says,

"I want you to kill Sterling and dismantle his little empire. I think seeing everything he's built go up in flames would be an enjoyable spectacle to watch."

"Anything to get your kicks, right?"

"That," Kaius agrees. "But also, Sterling seems to have forgotten that I'm not one of his devoted servants and he's started to treat me as such. Especially when your family started wreaking havoc on his plans. Kudos, by the way, I haven't seen that man that frazzled in decades." He holds up the piece of paper with the addresses on it. "Anyway, back to my position. This list is all the places where Sterling is keeping all the people he's taken. There's another list with the locations of where I've been stashing away people. They're mostly women and children. If my guess is right, your poor little bleeding hearts will never allow these people to suffer even after Sterling is dead. You couldn't sleep at night if you didn't save them. A truly *exhausting* dilemma." He's right, we've long wondered how we were going to find all the breeding facilities and free the people in them. "I will give you the lists on three conditions. The first one is obvious; I want you to kill Sterling. The second one is where things get a little sticky. After our encounter today, you're going to let me go—"

Jax laughs coldly, cutting him off. "That's not fucking happening."

Kaius holds up his finger to his lips, shushing Jax. "If you'd let me finish, you'd know it's not forever. I have a couple loose ends I need to tie up before I go. As you may recall, I told you I was ready for my next adventure. I've decided I'm done with this world. I've walked every continent, seen and done everything I can or want to. It was fun until it wasn't. It's time I see what kind of mischief I can get into in the next life."

"You want to die?" I ask confused.

"And I'm going to allow one of you the absolute pleasure of doing it."

CHAPTER TWENTY-TWO
Jax

I should be rejoicing at the thought of killing the necromancer, but every nerve in my body is screaming at me that this is a trap. No man as old and powerful as Kaius would want to die. But then again, I've only been alive for twenty-four years and I already feel like I'm a thousand in my bones. In my short life, I feel like I've lived many lives. Maybe he truly is just ready to move on.

Unfortunately for him, I'm not prepared to take that risk right now. The only thing I want to do right now is get these fucking mirrors to go away and to get that list in Kaius's pocket. Saving those people in those facilities aren't at the top of the priority list right now, but one day, after Sterling is killed one way or another, those people are going to need to be freed. Those poor children who are being trained as weapons need to be protected like I never was. They deserve a childhood that Isabeau and I were deprived of.

"So, what do you say?" Kaius's reflection grins at me. "Want to make a deal?"

There are a dozen different Kaius reflections around us, but I haven't pulled my eyes off the one directly in front of me. He thinks he's smart, that we wouldn't be able to figure out where he really is. He's been boasting about how foolish Sterling has been, but here he is, being just as dumb. "I would love nothing more than to rip your head from your shoulders and use it like a soccer ball for a bit, Kaius, but unfortunately, unless it's sex, I'm not into delayed gratification. I'm not going to wait for you to do your laundry list of things before you're ready to kick it. I'll kill you, but I'm doing it today."

Kaius pulls his pocket watch from his pocket and looks at it dramatically. "You see, I have plans already. A later date really would work better for me. How do we feel about the third Friday next month? Do you think you can wrap things up with Sterling by then?"

My power hums through my body, warming my limbs.

One second I'm standing next to Remington, the next I'm standing behind Kaius in the glass cell he'd been hiding behind. He coyly looks over his shoulder at me, not an ounce of fear or concern on his face. "Well, that's just cheating."

Without a word, I press the button on the wall in front of him, turning off the mirrored effect on the surfaces. On the other side of the glass, Remington turns around so fast she almost falls over. Her eyes fill with confusion when she realizes Kaius has been standing right behind us the whole time. With my overly advanced hearing, better than any other shifters, I was able to pick up the faint heartbeat behind the soundproof glass.

Kaius's fun little trick was completely futile against me. Hellfire burning in my palms, I shove the necromancer with so much strength that his body crashes through the glass. It shatters all around us. Shards fly through the air and cover the ground at our feet. Kaius skids through the disarray, the scent of his blood instantly filling the air. Remington backs up a foot when he almost collides with her legs. The small amount of hellfire I'd infused his body with makes him whither in pain on the ground for a minute before he finally settles and leans up on his elbows. Spitting blood from his cut lip, he grins wildly at me, blood coating his teeth. "I'm strongly advising you to reconsider my offer."

"And I'm strongly advising you to shut the fuck up," I seethe between clenched teeth as I charge for him. As he tries to pull himself off the ground, I shove him back down, filling his body with hellfire again. This time with three times as much.

Watching him groan and shake in pain on the glass-covered ground isn't penance enough for the role he's played in all of this, but it sure does make me feel better.

I'm so distracted, loving the way Kaius is hurting, I'm not paying attention to what Remington is doing until it's too late. She bends down over top of him, her hand reaching for the pocket of his jacket. Alarm and fear scream inside of me as I shoot forward. "Stop!" I yell at her in desperation. "Don't touch him!"

The hellfire coursing through Kaius's body will transfer to Remi if she touches him now.

My hand wraps around Remi's shoulder as her hand abruptly pulls away from Kaius's chest with a surprised gasp. I pull her away and bring her back safely up against my chest. She cradles her hand against her chest. The sound of her spiked heartbeat beating wildly against her ribs fills my ears.

"Are you okay?" I ask, spinning her around. "How bad does it hurt?" I've never felt the pain of hellfire myself, but from my growing list of victims, it's not a pleasant experience. It's a burning, soul-deep pain. "You can't touch them when they're filled with hellfire. It's like touching an electric fence. The power will transfer to you." She doesn't look at me, just keeps staring down at her hand where she's rubbing her fingertips against each other. Worried that she hasn't spoken yet, I give her a gentle shake. "Remington, are you hurt?"

She was quiet for a second longer before her head shakes and she slowly looks up at me with an odd emotion in her eyes. "I didn't actually touch him before you pulled me away. Nothing hurts."

I could have sworn I saw her palm rest on the necromancer's chest, but if that were the case, she'd be on the ground crying in pain just like he is.

"Are you sure?" I look at her skeptically.

She holds up her palm for me to see, not that I've been able to see any physical marks left by my hellfire for a long time. Not since I controlled the flames when I was eight. I can still smell the scent of burned bodies if I think about it.

"I'm fine," she promises before stepping out of my grip, replacing the space we so desperately need between us.

"Thank God." I shove my fingers through my hair in relief. "I don't think I could handle you being in that much pain. You'd turn into a total baby about it, I'm sure. Tears, snot, maybe some vomit. Pruitt threw up when I used hellfire on her." This is my poor attempt at lightening the mood.

The amount of hellfire I used on Pru should have killed her. I've used that much, sometimes even less, on other people and it's made their heart stop, but not Pruitt. She gritted her teeth and made it through it like a fucking rock star. No, like an alpha.

Brows furrowing, she glances down at her hand once more before lifting her chin defiantly. Not one to back down from a challenge, Remington smirks cockily at me. "I drank a bottle of *Tito's* and used those trailer trash Lime-A-Rita's as chasers, and I didn't puke once. If I can make it through that, not so much as gagging once, I can handle your hellfire."

I'm inclined to believe her. Her pure stubbornness would get her through it. I'm convinced that trait will and can get her through a lot of things. I'm sure that it's part of the reason she's still standing today after a year of hell.

"We need a plan for him." Remington ends the lighthearted conversation by pointing at the now passed-out necromancer.

"I have a plan," I remind her, blinking slowly at her. "Did you miss the decapitated head soccer ball thing?" My foot kicks out like I'm passing a ball to someone.

"You can wear his intestines as a fucking scarf for all I care, Jax. If that's going to make you happy, I'm all for it, but before we begin dismembering him, we need to see if he's telling the truth. Get the list in his jacket."

I snag the folded piece of paper from Kaius's jacket, making him slowly stir awake. Reading the neatly printed words across the page, I begin to frown before glaring down at the necromancer. "These are only partial addresses." Numbers and town names are missing, strategically left out of the document. "What the fuck is this?"

Kaius's eyes open. "Did you really think I'd been idiotic enough to have the actual list on me?"

"Do you really want us to answer that? Or was it more of a rhetorical question?" Remington asks flippantly.

He ignores her cynicism, still looking in my direction. His

already pale skin looks grayish right now and the whites of his eyes are red and bloodshot. "You don't carry vital information around in your goddamn pocket, kid. Don't you know anything?"

"I know I'm this close to dumping your body in a tankful of piranhas if you don't shut up," I snap at him without hesitation.

"Where the *hell* are you going to get a piranha in Seattle?" Remington remarks, completely taking the weight out of my threat.

"I don't know, I'm fucking resourceful. I'll figure it out," I scoff, before stalking toward Kaius. Gripping him by the lapels of his fancy jacket, I haul him back up to his feet. Glass sticks in his disheveled hair and blood seeps out of the wounds on his body from all the glass.

Remington steps forward, tugging the end up my ripped T-shirt. "Jax, I really think we should discuss this. If he's telling the truth, we can't risk letting those people rot in jail cells just like this one. If we don't help them, who will? It's not like we can send in an anonymous tip to the human police."

"I have been searching for him for over six months. Isabeau spent a year before that looking for him to no avail. He's now standing before us, and you want me to let him go?" I ask slowly as if I'm talking to a child. "You're really going to take the word of a known psychopath? Why?"

Her eyes flood with emotion. "Because I'd hope if someone had the chance to save you and your mom from the facility when you lived there, they would have taken it too."

I stare at her, thinking over her plea, before my face turns stern and I nod once. "Fine," I relent because it appears, despite my best efforts, I can't say no to her.

Holding Kaius by the back of his neck, I jerk him forward, silently ordering him to start walking. "We're going to chat more about these lists somewhere else." I don't want him on his own playing field. He has the advantage here. "If you try anything while we go there, I'm going to fill your head with so much hellfire, your brain will turn into mush. Do you understand me?"

"Loud and clear," Kaius mumbles. "You really do remind me of your father at times."

My fingers clamp down around his neck until he winces and raises his hands in surrender. "Too far?"

"Shut up."

☾

THE RAINY SEATTLE SKY DRIZZLES DOWN ON US AS WE PUSH open the back metal doors of the building. The alleyway is silent and still, but I still don't trust that there aren't any prying eyes observing us from somewhere. Remington followed quietly behind as I led us out of the building. The room with the mannequins wasn't any less eerie the second time we went through it. Kaius had mumbled something about getting a kick out of it and when we walked over the two dead bodies we'd taken out, he'd pouted out his bottom lip and droned on about how it was such a waste.

"Whisper booked me a hotel room not far from here," Remington offers as we make our way to the dark street. "We can take him there."

"That's fine, I just want to get there quickly. I don't like being out in the open with him like this."

"Ashamed to be seen in public with me?" Kaius questions.

"I do look rather rough right now with all the blood and glass. I'm bound to draw some attention."

We walk down the quiet street. Luckily, it's not a main road and we don't pass many people or cars.

The farther we get away from the building, the more restless Kaius becomes. "I know you don't believe me, but watching Sterling lose everything would be the best thing to witness before I died. I'm more than willing to tell you where all those poor helpless souls are once Sterling's taken care of."

"Nope," I bite. "You're going to tell us tonight."

"Like I said, I'm afraid I do have plans..." he mutters like he's truly put out. A blacked-out van suddenly makes an illegal U-tern on the road next to us. My wolf growls low in my head warning me of danger even before the vehicle comes to a screeching stop next to us on the sidewalk. "And what do you know, there's my ride."

The side doors are ripped open, and something is thrown toward us. There's the sound of metal as it lands on the sidewalk. Unsure of whether or not it's an explosive, I release Kaius and dive for Remington. I just barely have her tucked protectively against my chest when there's a loud bang and a burst of blinding light.

Flash-bang.

CHAPTER TWENTY-THREE
Remington

Even though Jax shielded me, I'm still affected by the stun grenade. There's a high-pitched ringing in my sensitive ears and when I pull away from the safety of Jax's chest and open my eyes, my vision is spotty. Jax is hunched over with his hands on his knees as his eyes blink rapidly. While he was busy protecting me, he failed to fully protect himself from the flash-bang. I call his name out, but he doesn't turn his head to face me. Even to my own ears, my voice sounds too quiet.

With unfocused vision, I turn toward the black van. Two men dressed in protective gear are standing by the open side panel door, ushering Kaius into the back of it. The necromancer looks over his shoulder at me with a sly smile. "My offer still stands. Kill Sterling and I'll get you those lists." He waves his pale hand at us. "It's been a pleasure. I'll be in touch."

I spring forward in an attempt to pull the man from the car, but one of the two bodyguards interferes. He tries to grab me, but I duck and turn before his fingers can so much as brush against my clothing. When he comes at me again, I slam my fist into his sternum before he can try again. As he doubles over, I wrap my hands around the back of his head and force is downward as I bring my knee up. My hearing is slowly coming back, but even muddled, I can hear the sound of his nose cracking on my kneecap.

He falls onto his hands and knees on the cement in front of me. Kicking my foot into his ribs, I knock him completely onto the ground before stepping over him and stalking toward the open van door again.

"Go!" Kaius orders.

"What about him?" The other guard looks nervously between Kaius and the security guard at my feet.

"What about him? We're leaving." Kaius shoves at the remaining security guard's shoulder, ushering him into motion. As the door slides closed, he calls out to me. "You'll see me soon, Remington." I don't know if that was a threat or a promise.

The van speeds down the dark, rain-soaked street and when I step off the curb, intending to run after them, a gloved hand wraps around my ankle and jerks my leg, sending me flying forward. My palms and knees burn as I land on the rough asphalt of the road. With a groan, I roll over onto my back just as the guard pulls himself off the ground. He clutches his ribs with one hand while his nose is bleeding down his face. With a pissed-off smile, his free hand reaches for the gun on his hip.

He holds the weapon up, pointing it directly at my head. Before I have time to come up with a plan or even have time to move a muscle, a dark looming figure appears behind him. Hands are placed on either side of his head and with an inhumanly fast twist, the guard's neck is broken. He falls to the ground with a harsh thud.

Jax, still blinking and rubbing at his poor eyes, stumbles forward and extends his hand and pulls me back to my feet with one quick tug. Without looking at me, he looks down both directions of the road. "Which way did they go?" he asks.

"That way." I point to where the van had disappeared.

"To the main highway that leads right into the city," Jax mumbles unhappily under his breath. "We'll never find them," he declares with an angry bite in his tone.

"Jax..." I start to say, but trail off because would *'I'm sorry'* or *'this is all my fault'* really make anything better? I settle for, "You were right," but it still feels wrong as I say it.

Without a word, he turns and delivers an angry blow to the dead man's abdomen with his booted foot. With my hearing finally returning to normal, the sound of Jax's ragged breathing and low constant growl are deafening. And the way he's refusing to look at me hurts more than it should.

I watch helplessly as Jax delivers kick after strong kick to the corpse on the sidewalk. When this starts to not be enough for him, Jax straddles the guard and begins to beat the man's face in. I can hear bones breaking, it's either the guard's facial bones or Jax's hands, maybe both. A couple of times, Jax's fists miss the head completely and slam into the hard concrete instead, each time I cringe, but I don't make a move to stop him. Based on the unhinged, deliriously angry face he wears, he needs this outlet right now. It's disturbing and bloody, but if this is what he needs to release some of the rage he's feeling, I'll sit back and let it happen.

But I don't have to like it.

As the man's head begins to concave from the multitude of harsh blows, I have to turn my head and cover my mouth with my hand. I'm not a squeamish person, blood doesn't bother me, but the sight in front of me makes my stomach roll.

With an angry roar, Jax slams his fist once more into the mess before he hangs his head and his chest heaves with angry breaths. I look around the dark road, making sure the sidewalks are still empty of people. Explaining this mess to a human would be borderline impossible.

Slowly, I walk up and place my hand on his shoulder. "Jax." I just barely softly say his name when he's ripping my hand away from his body.

"Don't touch me!" he roars, his head turning just enough that I'm able to see his glowing wolf eyes and elongated fangs. In the almost two years that I've known this man, I've only ever seen his eyes shift forms, so seeing those sharp canines is an alarming sight. He climbs to his feet and when he stands in front of me, with his head still slightly turned away from me, he seems taller than usual. "I don't know how you do it. You have the ability to make me do things I know I shouldn't, and each time they bite me in the fucking ass," he snarls, but I don't miss the slight grimace as his body heaves. Jax's shaking hand clutches the fabric of his T-shirt over his chest as he turns completely away from me. "I had him and I could have..." His words die out as he lurches forward like he's going to throw up. His hand presses against the brick wall of the nearby building, catching himself as he stumbles away. "Killed him, but *you* stopped me."

Ignoring his cruel words, I ask, "What's wrong?" instead.

His skin looks pale and clammy in the full moon's light up above.

I move closer but a terrifying noise I've never heard him make rips through his chest as he snarls, "Don't come any closer."

I don't recognize his voice, it's deeper and raspier than usual and it causes me to freeze in place. *Something isn't right.* "Jax, what's going on? Are you hurt?" Did the flash bang hurt him more than I realized? "What can I do to help you?"

"I have to get out of here," he groans like he's in pain. "Don't..." Jax chokes out. "Don't follow me, Remington. Go to your hotel room and lock the door."

"What? No, I'm not going to leave you..."

"Remington!" The roar that comes out of him sends cold shivers down my spine. "Fucking listen to me! No matter what, do not follow me. Do you understand me?" Each word he speaks sounds like he's fighting to say them, like it physically hurts him to speak. His whole body is shaking now. When I don't answer him fast enough, he repeats himself harshly, "*Do. You. Understand. Me?*"

No, I think but instead I manage to stammer, "Y-yes," to him.

Without so much as a word or a look back at me, he takes off like a bullet down the dark alley wall. I stand there watching him run off until I can't see him anymore. Every fiber in my being screams at me to follow him, but his warning plays on repeat keeping me locked in place.

I rub my scraped-up palms nervously against the fabric of my black jeans, as I think over my next move. I haven't ever seen Jax in this state before. Not even when he was shot in the stomach did he break a sweat or become pale. If he can make it through that pain without so much as a curse, it means whatever is happening to him right now is bad.

He told me to leave, but how am I supposed to leave him out there alone when he's in this state?

He's made it this far without you holding his hand. He'll be fine, do what he said, the logical part of my brain pipes in.

I'm just about to listen to my own advice when I hear it and it instantly changes my mind.

A howl.

The sound cuts through the night air like a cry calling to me. It fills my body and spreads to all the cold pieces in my bruised and broken soul. My wolf is going mad in my head, desperate to go to the source of the noise. That howl, while I've never heard it before, I know it. I would know it in the symphony of millions, I could pick it out without a second of hesitation. It's like I was born knowing that howl.

I have to go to him.

My body is moving, feet splashing through the puddles left on the sidewalk and streets as I race for the noise.

☾

JUST LIKE HOW I TRACKED JAX WHEN I FIRST ARRIVED IN town, I follow the lingering scent of him in the air through the edge of town until the brick and concrete buildings are replaced with tall pine trees and the wet asphalt turns into muddy earth. The forested area is smaller than we are used to back on pack territory but it's still big enough for a wolf to roam for a short time.

In the trees, the scent changes and shifts from human to

animal. As I walk farther into the wooded area, I find pieces of Jax's clothes that he had ripped from his body. I pluck them off the ground and shake the pine needles and mud from them the best I can as I go. In the wet mud, I follow the footprints left.

Eventually the man's footprint turns into the very large paw prints of a wolf shifter, but these are different from mine or anyone's in my family.

They're not just normal paw prints left in mud, they've been burned into the ground. Scorch marks accompany each of the outlines left in the earth. Bending down, I trace one with my fingertip, the dirt still feels warm to the touch as I drag my finger around the smoking ground.

"What the hell?" I whisper to myself as I lift my head to look for more. To my side, there's a trail of them leading farther into the trees. Leaving Jax's clothes in a neat pile at the base of a big tree, I begin to follow the prints with my heart racing. Unease fills me as I worry about what I'm going to find.

Up until I heard that haunting howl split through the night, I still wasn't convinced that Jax could even shift. I never allowed myself to imagine what his animal side would be like and now I'm about to face it head on.

A loud yelp cuts through the trees. It's followed by a few whimpers before the noise is completely cut off. As the wind picks up, the scent of blood fills my nose. Picking up my pace, I jog toward the source of both.

When I find him, I skid to a stop because nothing I could have imagined in my head would have prepared me for what I see before me. His fur is the darkest, deepest black I've ever seen. The moonlight that shines through the trees does little to light up the dark coat. If anything, the thick hair absorbs the darkness around it until you can barely see him. Unlike mine or another wolf shifter's, the coat isn't smooth and neat. It's spikey in places, but mainly down his back. Almost like a rabid-looking mohawk. He's also less bulky than a normal wolf, but he's taller than any wolf I've ever seen. Up until this moment, Ryker was the tallest, but Jax's wolf has inches on him. His thin, but powerful legs are attached to giant paws. From here I can see the faint glow. As if the pads of his feet are made of the embers left in a dying fire, they flicker as they scorch the ground beneath them.

I was right. He does look like something directly from the depths of hell.

His head is bowed as he tears at the flesh of the small fox he'd killed. A constant unhappy growl comes from his chest as he devours his meal. When my feet crunch on dry leaves when I shift my weight, his head tips up ever so slightly and glowing purple eyes collide with mine. They look so much like Jax's but I know the second I look into them that they're not Jax. There isn't a hint of kindness or warmth in these eyes. These are the eyes of a bloodthirsty predator and they're not staring at me like I'm their next meal.

My body is filled with the urge to turn around and run from the beast in front of me, but my wolf's calm demeanor keeps me in place. There is no fear coming from her, not even a twinge of unease. She is completely at peace being stared down by this dark creature.

She's finally lost it. After a year of such varying emotions, the whiplash caused by them has left her with permanent damage. She's finally cracked.

I really am going to have to ask Winslow for some psychiatric facilities recommendations, because I'm no longer afraid of things I should be terrified of. Even as he disregards his prey and steps over it, moving toward me, I don't flee. I stand strong and boldly meet the gaze that holds cold flames.

He moves painfully slow across the space, his head low as he observes me with keen interest. As he comes closer, I raise my hand out toward him, even though I know I'm risking my fingers being maimed. I send a silent prayer to whoever might be listening that my intuitions are right and he's not going to attack me.

His giant head extends toward my hand and his nostrils flare as he breathes in my scent. He comes to an abrupt stop, his lips curling up, exposing his very sharp teeth. There's a low rumble in his chest as he slowly begins to circle me with precise methodical steps. I mimic him, making sure I never have my back to him. The last thing I want to do is give him an advantage over me. As it is, I'm pretty sure I'm already at a disadvantage. The power that radiates off him is palpable. It reminds me of the alpha power that comes off of Pruitt when she's upset. It's thick in the air, suffocating.

Meeting this side of Jax makes it clear why he'll never be willing to submit to an alpha and be part of a pack hierarchy. His wolf side is more alpha than any other wolf I've met, but Jax's lack of interest in being a leader would never allow him to be in such a position.

We silently continue our dance with each slow circle, it's like we are trying to figure each other out. The wolf never turns his violet eyes away from me. I'm not positive he ever blinks. My muscles and bones are stiff, my body on edge, prepared for the chance that this will turn south at any second.

The energy between us is tense with anticipation, like we

are both waiting for the other to make a move. His inquisitive and dubious appearance vanishes the second the phone in my back pocket begins to buzz as someone calls me. Like a switch being turned, the beast's body pulls back, and his head lowers as a terrifying snarl cuts through the air. As he bares his fangs at me, saliva drips from his muzzle.

There isn't a second to react or try to run. The best I can do is put my arm over my face as he lunges at me. His large front feet slam into my chest as he brings me to the ground. My breath momentarily leaves my chest as the wind is knocked out of me. I expect to feel the pain of his fiery paws searing into my flesh, but it never comes.

Just like when I touched Kaius when he was full of hellfire, all I feel is a warm buzzing sensation humming beneath my skin. There isn't any pain.

There should be pain. Excruciating pain.

The wolf stands over top of me, keeping me pinned to the cold muddy ground. Saliva drips onto my chin as he growls above me.

When he attacks again, his sharp teeth aiming for my face, I'm able to get my hand up in time to shove at his neck and I just barely keep him at bay. His teeth snap together with such force, I'm shocked they don't crack and break.

"Jax!" I cry his name in an attempt to plead with his human side, but the cry falls on deaf ears. The wolf doesn't even register I said anything, let alone its name.

He lunges for my face once more but this time his canine clips my jaw. Instantly, the spot burns in pain and the sensation of warm blood blossoming and then dripping down my face follows. When he tries again to bite me, his muscles lock and he comes to an abrupt stop halfway to my face.

I hold my breath and force myself to stay still as the rage in his eyes melts away again and the curious look returns. Painfully slow, he lowers his head toward the wound he caused. I have to stop myself from pushing him away when his scary teeth get too close for comfort as he presses his cold, wet nose to the small bite mark.

My eyes flutter closed before I'm too afraid to watch what he's going to do next. I send my second silent prayer of the night that this doesn't end how I think it will. Although, it would be divine retribution if I were killed by the man I sacrificed everything to save. Just the universe's way of saying fuck you and laughing in my face.

But the pain never comes, what does is even more shocking

CHAPTER TWENTY-FOUR
Remington

My heart lurches in my chest when I feel the warm swipe of his tongue across my jaw instead of the painful bite of teeth. My whole body shakes with nerves, still too afraid to move as he cleans up the blood. When he's done, he moves his head lower and presses his snout into the juncture of my neck, I hear his lungs expand as he takes in a deep breath. A low whine comes from the beast. A sound that is the complete opposite of the vicious growling that was coming from him just minutes ago.

With shaking, apprehensive hands, I raise them slowly to sink them into the thick coat at his neck. This time instead of pushing him away, I softly caress the coarse fur. It's wiry compared to a full-blooded wolf shifter's, but it's not unpleasant by any means. Just different.

Then again, everything is different when it comes to Jax.

When the beast pulls away and gazes down at me with content violent eyes, my lips pull in a small smile. "Hello," I greet him. He may not look like Jax, but the same content energy I feel when I'm around him is there. If not stronger. The connection I feel to this animal is stronger than anything

I've ever experienced and each second I spend in his presence, it grows stronger.

My wolf pushes forward underneath my skin, desperate to join in on the introduction. Without having to be told, as if he can sense her desire to be free, the wolf backs away, allowing me room to sit up. He grants me just enough room to sit up into a crouching position. It's clear he doesn't plan on giving me any more space and insists on sticking close.

Standing to my full height, I begin to remove my clothes. His watchful gaze observes my every move as well as the area around as if he's checking for onlookers or threats while I disrobe. Fully naked, the light drizzle of the constant rain in this state makes my skin prickle in goose bumps. Shivering, I step away from him to drop my clothes on a spot devoid of mud, but with a warning snarl, he jumps around me and stops me from moving another inch away from him. As if he's herding me, he paces around me, keeping me in place.

Attempting once more to move a couple feet away, he shoots forward, his teeth nipping at my fingers in warning. It doesn't hurt and it doesn't break the skin, but the message is clear. *Don't leave.*

"Hey!" I scold. "Don't be rude. I'm not going anywhere. I just need to put my clothes over there where they won't get wet, you clingy motherfucker."

I move again and this time when he lunges for me, I lift my hand away before he can nip my fingers. Instead of scolding him once more, I sink my fingers back into the fur at his nape. His body relaxes at my touch, as if it soothes the agitation that lives in his veins. This time when I move, I lightly tug at the fur, coaxing him to move with me. He's unsure of what I'm trying to get him to do, but when he gets it, he follows at my side without complaint.

"Of course, you would be a big terrifying monster, but have abandonment issues," I mumble mostly to myself because the longer I'm around him, the more it becomes clear the human side of Jax is nowhere to be seen. When I'm in my wolf form, my wolf is free, but I'm very much still present and in control. We coexist. I'm not convinced that Jax and his wolf work the same way. It's like they're two completely separate entities. "A walking contradiction just like your human side."

With my clothes protected from the rain, I turn and give him a pointed look. "I'm trusting you to not be an asshole. Don't come at me with those teeth again," I order before crouching low and allowing the shift to come over me.

Within seconds, I'm standing before the tall hellhound in my wolf form. Elation washes through me as my wolf greets him like a woman greeting her husband who's returned from freaking war. I thought she had a crush on Jax's human side, but nothing compares to the deep-seated fixation she has for the wolf side of him.

The pitch-black wolf stands rigid at first as if he's never been around another wolf, but with gentle cajoling, he relaxes and begins to understand. When I reach up and lick the side of his muzzle tenderly, he jerks back in surprise as if he's never once been shown affection like that. It's then that I realize he probably never has. The only people in Jax's life to show him any form of kindness or compassion has been my family. The last person to do that was his mother and from what I know, she's been gone for a very long time.

No one has been around to show Jax or his wolf any kind

of love and that thought alone makes my heart break. It makes my heart break that when I was willing to give him my love, he acted like he didn't want it.

I don't know how much more time I'm going to be able to spend with his wolf or showing this side of him affection, but I'm going to make the most of the time I do have.

Yipping happily, I dance around him, trying to get him to play with me. He looks at me with confusion in his violet eyes. When I lunge forward and nip at his shins playfully, his lips pull back in a warning growl. *He's not getting it. He doesn't know how to play.*

I do it again, and this time I run away from him before he can retaliate. His ears perk up with interest before he quickly follows after me at a slower, unsure pace. With a wolfish grin, I take off through the trees, forcing him to follow after me.

It takes a few more minutes, but it finally starts to click.

For an hour we play in the rain and the mud, chasing after each other and hunting small animals. The hellhound begins to relax and the aggressive edge fades, but never does it disappear. The anger and aggression are a part of him, but it doesn't scare me or my wolf because somehow, I know he'll never purposely hurt me.

I may not know if I can or want to trust the man with my heart, but I know I can trust both him and his wolf to keep me safe.

☾

I WANT TO KEEP PLAYING IN THE RAIN WITH JAX'S WOLF. IT'S no surprise I've found yet another side of Jax that I love. Even the sides of him I hate, I love. The ugly, broken, mean sides I love and unfortunately want them all. I've become addicted to him even though it hurts.

He fights me when I usher him back toward where I left my clothes, but begrudgingly he eventually follows me. I'd love to spend another hour in the woods, neglecting our real-world problems, but we've already wasted more time than we should out here.

My wolf pouts for a second before finally allowing me to shift back. The cold wind blows against my bare skin, making me shiver. The black wolf standing next to me releases a low whine, not happy I've changed back. "I know," I tell him, running my hand over his head. He leans into my touch immediately. "We have to go. Can I have Jax back now?"

His eyes narrow as he makes an indignant, chuffing noise before he turns away from me. Confused, I jog ahead of him and stop him from going any farther. He tries to get around me, but I hold my ground. Kneeling in front of him, I smooth my hand soothingly over the side of his face. "I promise I'll see you soon, but right now I need Jax." I lean my forehead against his as he grumbles in displeasure. If Jax keeps him locked away, like I'm starting to believe he does, it's no wonder his wolf is reluctant to go back. He doesn't know when the next time he'll be free is. Living locked away isn't healthy for a wolf. "Come on, Jax," I whisper even though I'm not sure he can hear me. "Come back to me."

The wolf backs away from me, making a low, unhappy noise in his chest. His head shakes back and forth, and he snorts, as if he's fighting to maintain control. Eventually, the man wins, and the wolf is locked back inside. The black fur melts away and is replaced with perfectly smooth, tanned skin.

Once again, Jax appears in front of me on his hands and knees. His chest heaves and his fingers dig into the mud underneath him like he's confirming he's once more human. His head is bowed and he's yet to look up at me. I'm not even sure he knows that I'm here.

When I say his name softly and his head snaps up in surprise, my theory is confirmed.

Blazing violet eyes widen and his lips part in a silent gasp when he finally sees me kneeling before him. All of the color drains from his face. "Remington?" My name comes out as a croak.

"Hi," I answer with a small, nervous wave.

His gaze looks over every inch of my naked body like he's looking for something. "Why are you here? Are you okay?" Jax looks more confused than I've ever seen him.

"I'm fine," I assure him. "Am I not supposed to be?"

His head shakes back and forth. "No," he rasps. "You should be dead."

CHAPTER TWENTY-FIVE
Jax

Shifting always makes me feel like I've been run over by a steamroller. Every fiber of my being is in pain after I've spent time in my wolf form. I think it's my wolf's way of punishing me for keeping him so tightly locked up and only allowing him freedom once every few months.

I can't believe I lost control tonight. It's been so long since I've last done that. When I shift, I methodically plan it out months in advance. There are a few small uninhabited islands off the coasts of America that I like to shift on. The only things that are in danger there are the wildlife. There aren't any human lives there that might accidentally fall victim to my wolf's wrath. I lucked the fuck out tonight that I was able to get to the wooded area we're in now, but what I don't understand is how I managed to stay within the parameters of the trees. Usually, my wolf would have just run off into the town and started wreaking havoc on the citizens. Not that I'd remember doing it.

I never remember what happens while I'm in my wolf form, which is why I have no idea what Remington is doing naked in front of me right now or how she was able to be around my wolf without being killed.

"*What?*" she squawks. "What do you mean I should be dead?"

I bring my hand up to shove the hair that has fallen into my eyes out of the way but stop halfway through when I discover my hands are covered in mud. *Better than the usual blood.* "You were around my wolf?" I ask.

"You don't remember?"

When I don't immediately answer her question, her unyielding stare finally breaks me down. "I... black out when I shift," I reluctantly admit. "I never remember what horrors I've inflicted when my beast is in control."

"Oh," she mumbles while she ponders what I've said for a second. "Yes, I was around your wolf," Remi finally confesses. "Well, it was more than just being '*around*' him. We got to know each other, and I shifted and let my wolf play with him for an hour or so. Took us a minute to figure each other out, but no surprise, just like you did, he grew on me."

I feel like I'm in the Twilight Zone. I'm hearing what she's saying but I'm not believing a word of it. "That doesn't make any sense."

"What doesn't?"

"How you're alive right now when you shouldn't be." I sit back on my haunches and stare at her in disbelief. "Remington, there is a reason I've never shifted in front of you or your pack before. Hell, there's a reason I've never confirmed if I was even able to shift."

She cocks her head to the side, clearly perplexed. "I don't understand, he seemed a little testy... intense even—"

My cold, cynical laugh cuts her off. "*Intense,*" I repeat, shaking my head in awe. "Intense is putting it mildly."

"Jax, what are you saying?"

I release a long breath. "All this time, I haven't been protecting you from me, I've been protecting you from him, Remington. Every single person I've ever shifted in front of my wolf has killed or attempted to kill. From the very start, my wolf was disturbingly fascinated with you which concerned me because every other person he's ever been captivated by he's wanted dead. I couldn't risk your life by letting him get too close to you."

She crouches there silently, like she's trying to process what I'm telling her, as her eyes take on a confused look. "Jax, I feel like we're talking about two different animals. Yeah, we got off to a little bit of a rocky start, but after that, he was completely fine. Sure, he's got a quick fuse, but so do you so it wasn't that different." Her fingers trace along a healing mark I'm just now seeing on her jaw. In a flash, I'm kneeling right in front of her, taking her face in my muddy hand so I can examine the wound. "It's fine. Like I said, we had a rocky start, but he felt bad after he did it. Just like you, he can be gentle when he wants to be."

"He's never gentle," I argue, still not understanding what's happening. "There isn't a second—a moment of peace—where I'm not fighting him for control. With every breath I take, I'm forcing him to stay in the binds I've placed on him. We share a mind and a body, but we don't share souls. Mine is dark and corrupted, but his is pure black."

As if Remi's putting together the pieces that have been missing, her eyes search my face, but they're not truly focused on me as she thinks. Finally, her lips part in a soft gasp as she jerks her face out of my hands. She clambers to her feet and backs away from me while her hands sink into the mussed strands of her hair. Remi paces for a beat before her head snaps in my direction once more. "So, this is why then?" she begins to question. "This is why, since the very beginning you've kept me at arm's length and why when you finally did let me in, you brutally turned on me?"

I climb to my feet so I don't have to look up at her from the muddy earth. "Every single time I've woken up from shifting, I've been covered in blood. Sometimes I'm still laying in the pools of my victim's blood. It's like my wolf gets so tired from his reign of terror that he can't help but fall asleep right there in the middle of his carnage." Even when I'm far away and the only things out there for me to hunt are other animals, I still awake coated in their blood. "When I didn't know how to maintain control over him and I accidentally shifted with other people around, I've killed more people than I'll truly ever know. And I don't *want* to know." For the sake of my already unstable sanity, some things are better left unknown. Knowing the official total isn't going to do me any good now. I can't undo what I've done. "Very few people have lived after meeting this side of me. Tonight is the first time I've ever lost control and there isn't a trail of bodies behind me. So yes, Remington, I lied through my fucking teeth and told you were a meaningless fuck and kept you at a safe distance because the idea of waking up covered in your blood was fucking unimaginable. I also said I'd do it again if it meant I kept you safe, but now…" I trail off as I allow myself to consider what I thought to be impossible.

"But now…" she prompts, with an ushering hand motion.

When I take a step toward her, she eyes me skeptically.

"Now I'm not sure I ever had to do it." Even as I say those words, I feel like I'm dreaming, but my dreams are never this happy and that's how I know for a fact it's real life. "I was protecting you from something that wasn't going to hurt you. I should have known that if anyone was going to tame my wolf, it was going to be you."

Instead of her face softening at my words, her features harden, and her lips pull back as she sneers at me. "I could have told you that a year ago, Jax, had you just fucking talked to me. We could have avoided all of this if you'd just confided in me about your wolf's temperament. I would have told you that every time someone warned me to be careful with you, that you were dangerous, I didn't believe them because in the very fiber of my soul I knew you'd never hurt me. My wolf has trusted you since the first time she laid eyes on you and now I know it wasn't you she trusted; it was your wolf. But instead of trusting *me* like I trusted *you*, we went a whole year doing nothing but hurting each other for no reason!" Her eyes slash across me, no doubt leaving more invisible scars. "And now you're standing here staring at me like we're suddenly supposed to raise our white flags and *what*? Be together because you've miraculously gotten over your issues? That's not how it works, Jax."

"Why not?" I find myself asking. "For most of my life, I've had people telling me what I can or can't do. They've taken everything and they've deprived me of both the things I want and need. Even when I was free of them, I still ended up implementing rules and placing myself in chains because I thought it was the right thing—*no*, the safe thing, to do. And now I'm learning I was wrong." When she turns her head, I step forward and return my hands to her face, forcing her to look at me. "So, I say fuck the rules and fuck doing what's safe. They've robbed me of enough, and I refuse to let them take anything else from me. I *want* you and I *need* you, Remington."

"Jax," she starts but I cut her off.

"I'm the reason there's a wall up between us. I started all of this, and I know it's my fault." I take responsibility for my actions and until the end of time I will be apologizing to her for the horrific year we've had and what it's taken from her. "Our future is uncertain and there are still a lot of wounds that need to heal but drop your walls for just a second. Allow the walls you built to protect yourself from me to come down, and imagine what it'd be like to have everything you've ever wanted. Imagine what it'd be like to wake up in the morning and not feel like you're missing something. That's how it is for me, Remi. Every day I wake up without you, I feel like a piece of me is missing." She looks up at me with uncertainty. "Close your eyes and let yourself imagine it all, love."

After a moment of hesitation, her eyes finally flutter closed. It takes a minute for the tense look on her face to smooth out and for her stiff bones to relax. I don't know what she's seeing, but I hope it's as perfect as what I'm seeing.

I will never be able to forgive myself for all this wasted time I've inflicted on us. For two years I pushed her away to keep her safe. I broke her heart to keep her safe and it was for nothing. The hold she has on me is strong enough to tame my beast. If she can keep him from creating a bloodbath, then she truly is capable of anything.

As she stands there with her eyes closed, picturing what I hope to be perfection, the air around us starts to buzz, almost like there's an electrical energy humming between us. The hairs on the back of my neck rise and my wolf's ears perk as he stands at attention, like he's anticipating something important. My fingertips tingle and something in my chest tightens painfully before, like a rubber band snapping, a surge of power explodes all around us.

Remington gasps and her eyes snap open in shock.

When those blue eyes collide with mine, my world comes to a screeching halt and everything around me ceases to exist. I can no longer feel the soft drizzle of rain across my warm skin and the cold breeze that has been whipping through the trees stills. I'm not even sure if my heart continues to beat or if my lungs are capable of bringing in air as I take in the sight in front of me.

Never in a million years did I think I would experience this. I thought it was just another thing that I was going to be deprived of, but now as I take in the shiny gold aura that gleams brightly around the most beautiful woman I've ever encountered, I'm hit with a wave of peace and contentment that I've never experienced before. My life up to this point has been a turbulent storm, but Remington is the eye of my hurricane. The lightning in her eyes and thunder in her soul has found a way to calm mine. Her chaos counteracts mine—always has. I didn't know why, but now that I'm staring at the golden mating aura shining around her, I know why.

She's my mate.

"Is that..." Remington stammers out as she searches the air around me. To know that she sees what I'm seeing fills me with even more relief. "Does that mean what I think it means?" there's a slight edge of panic in her tone, but I make it my goal to ease it.

"It means you're fucking *mine*, love," I confirm, holding

her face tighter between my hands. "It means that no matter what happens, every single piece of you belongs to me." One of my hands drops down to rest over her bare chest. Her thundering heartbeat slams against my palm. "This heart that I broke? It's mine and I'm going to spend the rest of our lives mending it. I'm going to stitch it up and protect it with my life." I trace down her collarbone, down her arm, until our fingers intertwine with each other's. "These hands are mine to hold and I will hold them during our darkest days." Those days are coming quicker than we think. Finally, I remove the hand that holds her face to brush my thumb over her plump lips. "And these lips?" I bend my face to brush the softest of kisses across them, but still, her breath hitches like the sensation is too much. "They're mine to kiss and to savor. Even when you use them to talk back and argue with me, I'm going to savor each one of those words, because they're mine too," I tell her, just a breath away from her mouth. "And as much as you are mine, I'm yours. Every dark and twisted piece of my soul, it belongs to you. Always has. I'm sorry it took us this long to figure it out, but I'm yours."

Emotions flash through her eyes like an earthquake. The impenetrable and cold foundation she'd built cracking in front of me. "Fucking finally," she barely has time to whisper before my hand wraps behind her head and I slam our mouths together.

Kissing Remington has always been the highlight of my life, but kissing her now and knowing this is what I was always destined to do, it's different. It's like each swipe of my tongue and each ragged breath between kisses is solidifying the connection between us.

For the first time since we met, we are more than stolen moments and lies. We're no longer pretending.

This is real. This is us.

We are people with flaws and we've both made mistakes, but regardless, somewhere—someone—decided that we were meant for each other—that we are stronger and better together.

"*Mine*," I growl across her lips as we back up into the nearby tree. The combination of her sweet mouth dancing with mine and the knowledge that she truly is mine, already has my cock growing hard. Without a stitch of clothing on either of our bodies, the red, swollen tip presses against her soft stomach.

"*Yours*," Remi agrees easily and without complaint, a phenomenon that doesn't happen often, so I savor it.

My hands hold her hips in a punishing grip like I'm afraid if I let her go, all of this will disappear. Her arms wrap around my neck, holding me close as our tongues tangle for dominance.

My wolf sits quiet in my head, observing. There's an air of smugness coming off of him because he knew this would happen all along. The obsession he had for Remington wasn't because he wanted her dead, it was because he just wanted his mate.

We're both covered in mud, but neither one of us seems to mind. Nothing is stopping us. Sterling himself could walk up on us now, but I still wouldn't stop. I'd let him simply watch as I claim my mate.

Trailing hot, openmouthed kisses down her neck, I reach the juncture of her neck and scrape my teeth across the place I'll leave my mark. My gums burn and my fangs threaten to descend just at the thought, but I keep them at bay for just a little while longer.

Remi's hands grip the strands of my hair as I continue to nuzzle her neck. I feel her shiver against me, and her body relaxes as I suck on the sensitive spot. "You're going to look so beautiful wearing my mark."

"Jax," she says my name like a plea.

I nip at her earlobe before asking, "Tell me what you need, love."

Her body moves restlessly against mine. "I need more," she begs. "Touch me."

"And to think not that long ago, you were threatening to kill me if I touched you again," I muse cockily, staring down at her beautiful face. Even with the mud I'd transferred from my hands to her cheeks, she looks stunning in the light of the full moon. "I knew you'd eventually beg for it once more."

Her eyes narrow in challenge. "I'll kill you now if you don't touch me. I've waited too long to have this, Jax. Are you really going to deprive me any longer?"

"Wouldn't dream of it."

Swooping low, my hands grip her behind her thighs and lift her. Instead of having her wrap her legs around my waist, I bring her up higher until her legs rest over my shoulder and her perfect pussy is exactly where I want it. My wolf purrs in contentment seeing how she's already wet and glistening for me. The scent of her need is intoxicating, and I inhale it greedily.

Mine, I think possessively before taking her pussy in my mouth.

She whimpers as her fingers sink into my hair, clutching

my head to her body. At the second lazy swipe of my tongue through her folds, her back relaxes farther into the tree.

I suck her clit, bringing it into my mouth over and over again, making her breath come in short pants and her hips squirm. It's like the sensation is too much for her to handle but in the same breath, not enough.

Licking her up and down, I swirl my tongue around her opening, teasing her, but I don't yet delve inside. Each time she thinks I'm about to give her what she wants, and I don't, she pulls harder on the strands of my air in frustration and an adorable desperate noise comes from those sweet lips of hers.

I could get drunk on the sounds she makes and the way she tastes.

Remi arches her hips toward me, silently begging for more. I don't give in until I have her right where I want her, delirious with need and dripping for me.

I lap at her enthusiastically, taking and savoring it all.

Finally, I spear my tongue inside of her and lick those sensitive walls for her. She's so close. I know it won't take much to bring her over the edge. The way she moves against my mouth and her soft moans make me lose control. I begin to kiss and nibble her everywhere in a frenzy.

When I clamp my lips around her clit once more, she finally breaks. Her thigh and stomach muscles quiver and shake. The noises she makes fall silent as she momentarily loses the ability to breathe.

Not once do I let up. I tongue her until the very end and when she finally comes back to earth, I press tender kisses to the apex of each of her thighs. The fleeting desire to mark her there as well flashes through my mind. It's only customary and necessary to leave one mark, almost always located on the neck, but I want to decorate Remington's body with my marks. A bite for each month we weren't together when we should have been.

Carefully, I bring Remi back down until she is once more standing on her own, albeit shaky, legs. Before she has a chance to say something or even more, I'm bringing my mouth back down to hers. I thrust my tongue inside of her parted lips roughly, forcing her to taste herself.

My cock jerks when she moans greedily and sucks the taste of her pussy off my tongue, I groan and gasp at the same time when her hand snakes between us and her nimble fingers wrap around my hard length.

She starts off soft, gentle even, but it's all a front. Not giving a fuck about the mud, she clambers to her knees before me, and with a devious look twinkling in her eyes, she lightly flicks her tongue along the crown of my dick, licking up the pearl of precum.

Remington takes me into her mouth, her wet and hot tongue making me hiss out a breath between clenched teeth. While her mouth sucks and licks at me, her hand wraps around the base and slowly and methodically moves up and down.

She sets the perfect rhythm and knows exactly what I need without needing to tell her. Her tongue glides against the sensitive spot underneath and I almost come right then and there. My balls tighten and shivers run down my spine.

"I would love nothing more than to spill down your throat," I tell her tersely as I fight to regain composure. "But not right now. I have a sweeter place in mind instead." My hand, wrapping around her chocolate brown hair, tugs at the strands until her lips leave my achingly hard cock.

While she climbs back to her feet, my eyes dart around the space looking for the perfect place for us to do what I want to do.

"What are you looking at?" she questions.

"I'm not leaving these fucking woods without you wearing my mark, but I'm not going to fuck you in the mud," I explain. "The mating bond can only be created during a full moon, and I'll be damned if I have to wait another month to make you mine. I don't think I have it in me to wait for us to find another location either."

Remi twists her head around, joining the search before her eyes light up and her fingers intertwine with mine. As we run by her pile of clothes, she swoops them up in her free hand.

"I don't know where we're going, but if I'm not buried inside of you in exactly one minute, I'm going to burn shit to the ground," I warn her as I allow her to lead the way.

"You think it's any easier for me to wait?" she questions over her shoulder. "I would have done this a year ago if you'd let us." Remi weaves around a couple more trees before coming to a stop in front of a secluded area of dense trees, but at least the ground isn't made completely of mud.

Good enough for me.

Like a goddamn heathen, I all but tackle Remi to the ground. She grunts from the impact but as I fall on top of her, she squeals and laughs. Music to my fucking ears. "That sound..." I murmur. "I like it almost as much as the sound you make when you come. *Almost*."

She grips my chin before dragging my face down to hers. She nips at my bottom lip with her blunt teeth before licking the spot to soothe the burn, little does she know I like it.

When I devour her mouth, I taste both myself and her on her tongue and the flavor is delectable.

I fit myself between her long, tanned legs. My hand roughly wraps around her thigh, hiking her leg up. I slide my length through her folds, coating my shaft in her wetness. When the head of my dick glides across her clit, she moans softly in her throat.

Shifting lower, I align myself at her entrance, but don't thrust inside yet. Breaking our kiss, I pull back just enough that I'm able to look at her. Nothing but trust and love sit in her eyes as she stares up at me. She brings her hand up to lightly trace her fingertips along my face. First, she makes a circle around my orbital bone before running the pad of her finger across my bottom lip.

"Tell me you want this," I plead. "Tell me now to stop if you have any doubts, Remington, because once I'm inside you, there's no turning back. I'm making you mine. This is forever."

Her heart thuds wildly in her chest as she says, "I want this, Jax. I want you forever," Remi vows. "I don't know how long our forever is because our future is so unsure, but I want to spend every second of it as your mate. Every obstacle that is coming our way, I want to face it together as mates. So shut up and make me yours. *Officially*."

"Why would anyone want to tie themselves to me?" I can't help but wonder aloud.

Remi smiles up at me. The darkness that's occupied her features for the past six months is gone. Not even the shadows that surround her can dull the light that's coming off her in waves right now. "Because my beautiful broken boy, you are perfectly imperfect. In each one of the flaws you see in yourself, I only see strengths. You're reckless and impulsive, but I will still follow you anywhere because I know I'll be safe as long as you're there. You're unhinged and your wolf side is uncontrollable, but you are so strong. The strongest person I've ever met. You're distrusting, but once you let them in, you'll protect them with your life even when they swear up and down that they don't want your help." She laughs quietly at the self-deprecating comment. "Why wouldn't I want a man like that as my mate?"

I turn my head and kiss the inside of the wrist of the hand that still rests on my face. Her words wash over me, solidifying my decision. Not that it's really a choice at this point. I don't think I'll survive if we stopped, and she walked away from me now. I'd let her, but it would hurt like a motherfucker to do it.

"That's all I needed to know."

Holding her eyes and gripping her hip, I thrust inside of her. Immediately I feel like I've found euphoria. She arches off the ground, head back, exposing that beautiful, unmarked column of her neck. Her pulse is so fast, I can see the flutter in her jugular as she tries to find the ability to breathe again.

My body shakes as I fight for control, I want this to be a tender moment we look back on but the animal inside of me is urging me to take her hard and fast. The overwhelming, almost primal need to do just that is really difficult to fight.

I thrust again, slowly building up my pace as her body adjusts to me. She can take every inch of me. Her pussy was built to be filled with my cock after all. With each thrust, I sink deeper inside her slick heat, and I become closer to snapping—to allowing the animalistic side of me to take charge. Each time I pull back leaving just my tip buried in her, she makes a shuddering, gasping noise when I thrust back inside.

"Oh fuck... Jax!" she cries when I slam into her harder than I mean to. Fear grips my chest that I hurt her, but when the walls of her pussy tighten around me and her hips tilt up to meet my next move, I realize I was mistaken. "Again," Remi pleads. "I want it just like that."

And with that, the restraint I was holding on to by a thin thread, snaps. My wolf surges forward, but for the first time since I can remember I don't instantly try to shove him back down. I allow his need to mix with mine as we take the beautiful woman below us.

With deep, almost punishing thrusts, I fuck her into the grass below us. She takes everything I give her with enthusiasm.

Collaring her throat with my hand, I apply pressure to the sides of her jugular. Her blue eyes blaze up at me with excitement and desire. "You like having my cock inside your pussy, don't you?" Her response is a jerky head nod and a long, agonizing moan. "Good, because it's going to be there a lot. I'm going to be reminding you every chance I get who this pussy belongs to." I pull almost all the way out before thrusting deep back inside.

Keeping my pace, I dip my head to take one of her pert nipples in my mouth. I swirl my tongue around the peak before clamping my teeth around it until the pleasure is borderline pain. She holds my head and arches into my touch, telling me she likes a bite of pain.

I lick up her chest, dipping my tongue in the divot where her collarbone is. The closer I get to the juncture of her neck, the more my gums burn as my fangs threaten to descend. This time instead of fighting it, I allow it.

Remington turns her head and when she spots my elongated fangs, the walls of her pussy quiver in anticipation. Silently, she tilts her head to the side, giving me access without having to ask for it.

I swipe my tongue over the spot that will bear my mark. Everyone who looks at her neck will know that she's mated and unavailable. They'll know she's mine.

"Do it. Bite me," Remi whispers. "I love you and I'm yours."

I love you. It's been sixteen years since someone has told me that and I hadn't realized how much I missed hearing it.

With one more deep stroke inside of her, I sink my teeth into her perfect skin as deep as I can to ensure that even when the mark is healed, the scar will remain. Shifters don't typically get scars from wounds, but that rule goes out the window with mating marks.

Remington's body seizes up as the pain of the bite slices through her, but as quick as the pain comes, it disperses and is replaced with pleasure. The sensation is so powerful, it sends her over the edge, and she comes violently with my fangs embedded in her.

When her body stops shaking, I pull my teeth from her so I can swipe my tongue over the wound. Seeing my mark on her body fills my soul up with a sense of belonging. Never in my life have I had a home or known where I belong. Remington Weylyn is my home. Wherever she is, that's where I'm supposed to be. I'd follow her to the edge of the world if that's where she wanted to go.

With one last look at my mark, I roll us and transition into a sitting position. My cock is still buried deep inside of Remi, and she continues to ride me. At this new angle, she's in control and she sets the pace. "Come on, love," I encourage her. "Your turn. Bite me hard and make me bleed."

Her arms snake around my head, turning it to the position she wants before her warm mouth covers the spot she's picked in an open-mouthed kiss. She sucks lightly on it before her fangs plunge into me. Pain followed by the most amazing euphoria I've ever felt sends me over. I come powerfully inside of her with a shouted curse.

I haven't come down from the high before it happens. It's as if the world explodes around us. The trees bend and bow as the wind blows violently through them. Like a dam giving way, there's a rush of power that washes over us. Every single one of my nerves feels like it's been electrocuted, and by the way Remi tenses in my arms, I know she feels the same thing. As if all the power surrounding us rushes into our bodies, there's a lightning storm inside of us before the entire world falls silent and the only thing that can be heard is the drizzle of rain hitting the tree leaves and our labored breathing.

Remington pulls her head away from my neck and smiles at me, blood still coats her lips. "We're going to burn the world down together."

"Like an uncontrollable wildfire," I confirm, wiping the blood from her mouth with my thumb before leaning forward to capture her lips with mine. "I love you more than you'll ever know, Remington Weylyn, and I'm going to prove to you every day that I'm worthy of your love."

CHAPTER TWENTY-SIX
Jax

When you can use hellfire to travel to places within seconds, traveling by airplane is a tedious and confining event, but when it's the only way your new mate can get back home, you grit your teeth and climb aboard the luxury jet with her. Even if by the twenty-minute mark you're so antsy and jumpy you're about to call upon your power and dip the fuck out.

I'll meet her at the airport with flowers or something, but this isn't working for me.

Remington, picking up on my nerves through our newly developed mating bond, lifts her head from the magazine she's been calmly flipping through. "Don't even think about it," she warns.

"Do what?" I grit, my hand tightening on the armrest. I'm pretty sure I'm going to leave a permanent mark in the leather.

"Use your power to leave this plane." *It would seem she's a mind reader.* "It's just some turbulence. Phillip has flown a thousand times."

I blink slowly at her. "Who the fuck is Phillip?"

"The pilot" Remi gestures toward the closed door of the cockpit.

Still not convinced, I question her further. "How do we know Philip and how do we know he's a 'good' pilot?"

"Winslow hired him when she purchased the plane. Don't worry, he's good at his job."

She is clearly far too trusting. I would leave this plane now if she wasn't on it with me. I can't just go leaving the life of my precious mate in the hands of fucking *Philip*. "I've met many people who were, in fact, not good at their job. They were just good at bullshitting people into thinking they were."

"Drama queen," Remi mumbles under her breath before finally putting her magazine away and giving me her full attention. "Would you like me to distract you?"

Color me intrigued... "What did you have in mind?" I ask slyly, with a smirk.

Once we redressed last night in our dirty and ripped clothes, we'd returned to the hotel Whisper had booked for Remington. We got many worried and appalled looks when we waltzed through the lobby covered in mud. Remi was embarrassed, I found it hilarious. After taking a shower, we'd climbed into bed to go three more rounds. By the time the sun had risen over the horizon, our bodies were so coated in sweat we had to take another shower which led to more shower *activities*.

"I was thinking we could talk about your hellfire." Remi's face is oddly serious as she turns in her seat to look at me.

"My hellfire?" I repeat, feeling disappointed. "Are you sure I can't offer you a more *stimulating* conversation?"

She winks at me. "I'll take a rain check on that."

"Fine," I reluctantly agree. "What do you want to know about my hellfire?"

She twists her lips as she thinks over what she's going to say. As I wait for her to finally say what's on her mind, my eyes zero in on her neck. The white hoodie she wears covers a majority of the mark I left, but I can still make out a piece of it. The mark, still pink and healing, looks beautiful in contrast to her tanned skin. Unable to help myself I reach out and caress my thumb over the mark. A move I have a feeling I will be doing often.

I haven't had a lot of things in life that I could call 'mine'. There was the yellow ball, my only toy growing up, at the facility I was raised in and then I have my favorite pair of leather boots that are scuffed, and laces frayed, but they're mine.

And now I have Remington and I know without a doubt I'll never need anything more than that.

She relaxes under my touch and leans into it. "Does your hellfire affect everyone the same way? Does it always hurt?"

I frown at her question. "For some people it takes larger doses, but yes, in the end, it always hurts." Always. Pruitt needed more than anyone else for it to truly take effect, but in the end, she still screamed just like the rest of them. "Why do you ask?"

Remi turns and reaches for my hand, tangling our fingers together. "Do you trust me?"

"With my life." I learned the hard way what happens when I don't fully trust her and I'll never do that again.

What she says next nearly knocks me over in shock. "Use your hellfire on me."

She's been begging me for years to try it on her. She's

always been morbidly curious about what it feels like, like a crazy person. What part of soul-deep pain does she not understand?

I look at her like she's grown a second head. "I just swore to you last night that I was going to spend the rest of my life keeping you safe, and ten hours later, you want me to *hurt* you?"

Remi shakes her head. "No, that's the thing. I don't think you'll hurt me." *No, it will without a doubt hurt her.* "I lied last night. I did touch Kaius when he was full of hellfire, and Jax, it didn't hurt."

I pause and stare at her, thinking over her words. There's no way it didn't hurt. "Maybe you were confused and didn't actually touch him."

"No, I definitely did," she insists.

"Remi..."

"It felt warm, but it didn't burn. At most my skin just... *tingled*," she explains, a look of wonderment reflected on her face. "I want to know if it was a fluke... or if it was something else." Remi rotates her wrist so that our palms and fingers are pressed flat against each other. "Try it again."

"Absolutely not," I answer immediately without having to put so much as a second of thought into it.

But then she says the one thing that can make me change my mind—that can make me do anything. "I love you and I trust you. Trust me that it's not going to hurt me."

Even though everything in me pleads for me to not do it, I give in with a defeated sigh. "I'm not going full power," I warn her. "We'll start small."

She nods her head, her face lighting up, as if she's excited at the possibility of being in pain. *Jesus Christ... this woman.*

It's true. Her crazy fits mine.

Slowly, as if I'm turning a faucet, I allow my power to trickle through my body and out my palm. At first, I think her hand is shaking, but I quickly figure out that it's my hand that is quivering with anxiety as I wait for her to feel the effects.

Her eyes stay locked on our joined palms as the power fills my hand. I keep waiting for her to pull away from me and start crying in pain, but she doesn't so much as flinch. Even with the small amount I'm using on her, there should be excruciating pain accompanied with it.

I feel my jaw drop as I observe her. "Nothing?"

"No," she breathes in awe. "Use more."

Needing to see how much she can handle, I push more of my power into her body. Bit by bit, I increase the amount, but she never moves.

"It's just warm and my body is humming, but it doesn't hurt."

With one last push, I infuse her with as much of the hellfire as I can. This amount would kill even the strongest person. It could easily take out Isabeau.

It's the amount I plan on using on Sterling.

"Can you feel it?"

She presses her palm harder against mine, but still shakes her head. "It's hotter than before but no, it doesn't hurt."

Reining in my power, I take her hand in mine so I can examine her skin for any signs she's fallen victim to my power, but there's nothing. Her skin isn't even red. She should have been rendered to a screaming puddle on the ground as her organs were overcome and destroyed by the hellfire.

I can't find the words yet so I keep staring at her, as I go through all the possibilities as to why it wouldn't work on her.

When my eyes slide over the mark on her neck once more, it clicks.

"The hellfire is an extension of me. A piece of me," I announce as it all comes together in my mind. "Just like you are. As my mate, you're part of me and my soul." My other half. "It can't hurt you because you're a part of me." A very important part of me.

She looks thrilled by the knowledge, but I don't miss the flash of *remorse*. Hidden behind the joy. "You're upset it won't hurt you."

Remington sits back in her chair with a pout. "I still wanted to know what it felt like."

Laughing, I sling my arm around her shoulders and bring her to me. "You're twisted." I tilt her chin up. "Just like me," I tell her before kissing her.

It starts off tender, but just like every other time, it quickly heats up until she's moaning into my mouth and I'm gripping her waist, pulling her into my lap. As I lick into her mouth, she grinds herself into my quickly hardening cock with slow, measured movements.

Without breaking her mouth away from mine, she reaches between us and tackles the fly of my distressed jeans. She has my dick free and in her hand before I have time to register what she's up to. Teasingly, she trails her fingers softly over the hardening flesh. It's just enough for me to hiss out a breath.

Remington smirks against my lips before she slips off my lap and spreads my legs wide so she can kneel in front of me. Scraping her nails across my jean-clad thighs, she looks up at me with liquid fire in her eyes. Holding my gaze, she grips the base of my dick before leaning forward to flick her tongue across the sensitive crown.

"Think Philip can see us?" Remi asks tauntingly. "Do you think he can see me on my knees for you?"

"I don't care if he can," I grunt out as she wraps her lips and sucks the head, tongue swirling. "I want him to be jealous of me. I have something that he'll never have." Or anyone else will ever have. "He can watch all he wants, but I'm the only one who gets to touch you. I'm the only one who gets to know what this hot mouth feels like or what it feels like to have that tight pussy of yours milk every drop from me."

When she has me so close to the edge that my world starts to tilt, I pull her violently off the ground.

"What—" she begins to ask, but when I start to rip her leggings off her body, the question dies on her tongue. "Kick off your shoes," I order with a gruff voice.

She does what I say while I shove my jeans farther down my thighs. Once she's bottomless, I'm pulling her back onto my lap.

Remington just barely has herself straddling my thighs before I'm gripping her hips in a painful hold and slamming her down onto me.

"Sucking me off makes you so wet, doesn't it?" I groan as I glide fully into her, bottoming out at her cervix. She whimpers and nods her head in jerky movements.

Holding on to the back of the seat, Remington rides me and while she does, I begin to think maybe flying isn't so bad.

CHAPTER TWENTY-SEVEN
Remington

I didn't realize just how big the piece of my missing soul was until Jax became mine. It's like my whole life I've been walking around missing a vital organ or something, but now that he's mine and I am his, I feel whole.

And happy.

I never really understood what people meant when they said they couldn't describe the feeling of being mated and that I'd have to be mated to understand. I always thought they were full of shit and didn't know how to articulate their emotions or something, but they were right. The level of contentment I feel being mated isn't something I'll ever be able to put into words.

For the rest of my life, I will have him with me. There's an invisible tether tying us together and through that, I can feel him. Like his soul is now embedded with mine. For the rest of my life, as long as that might be, I'll never feel alone. I feel ashamed of myself that I ever resented my siblings for spending more time with their mates than with the pack or with me. I understand now that they weren't able to stop themselves. Jax has been at my side for the past twelve hours, but the idea of being somewhere he's not makes my chest tighten.

Oh great, being mated just makes you wildly codependent and a stage-five clinger. Not a good look.

But regardless, I'm blissfully and unapologetically happy and I want to protect that feeling from everyone and everything. I want to continue to live in my perfect bubble with my mate. I don't want to have to let everyone in on our secret and I definitely don't want to have to go back to our dark reality where our monster is lurking somewhere in the shadows.

A part of me isn't ready to tell my family or pack because I'm worried about the questions. For months, most of them think I've been mourning the loss of my boyfriend, but grief wasn't what I was feeling. To them, it looks like I bonded myself to the first man to show me interest. They have no idea what mine and Jax's history is. Hell, Pru is the only family that knows, and I think that's why when Winslow's house comes into view ahead of us, my palms start to sweat.

Winnie and Ranger had picked us up from the airport and they'd called the rest of the family to meet us back at their house after Jax and I gave them a short recap of what'd happened with Kaius. Even though Jax and I aren't acting like anything is different between us, Winslow has been sending me weird looks through the rearview mirror the whole time.

Jax and I aren't hiding what we are, but I'd rather not have to explain everything to each family member one at a time. This is a conversation best had once, done quick and dirty. Like pulling off a Band-Aid.

Walking around the car, Winslow stops me before I can start heading toward the stairs of her house.

Knowing eyes lock with mine and her lips tip in a grin.

"And just like that, the rest of your light has returned." *God, she's so observant it's scary.* She gets up on her tippy-toes so no one else can hear her as she whispers, "I'm glad you finally figured out what he means to you."

Stunned silent for a second that she'd sensed the change already, I finally find the ability to ask, "Did you know the *whole* time that we were..." I trail off.

Smiling smugly as she backs away from me. "I only had strong suspicions." Winnie shrugs nonchalantly. "And it was another thing you needed to figure out on your own. You wouldn't have believed it coming from me anyway. That denial tends to run deep."

"You could have saved us a lot of time if you'd just said something." A lot of wasted time and a lot of hurt.

"I don't know, I'm a pretty big believer that things happen the way they're supposed to. Just look at how all of us found each other. The universe is a sick bastard, but there's a plan in place and sometimes we just have to suffer along until we find our person." None of my siblings met their mates under normal circumstances, that's for sure. "It's a tough journey, but the final destination is so, *so* worth it, Remington." Winslow looks behind her where Ranger talks to Jax before turning back to me. "And you've made it and you're allowed to be happy about it. Don't feel like you have to hide it from us."

Not needing to say anything back, I wrap my arms around her tiny body and squeeze her tight. She showed up like a stray at our door a year and a half ago and I'm so glad she did. Our family needed someone like her.

Pulling back, I smile when I see her bangs are mussed. Remembering something important, I push her hair off her forehead and expose her hairline. Keeping my face straight, I fix her hair without giving her any explanation, then I head toward the house.

Jax, now waiting for me by the end of the stairs, stares at me with purple flames in his eyes. I feel the heat of them licking on my skin the closer I get to him. He reaches for me, and I let him wrap his arm around my waist and pull me close. Winslow's right, we shouldn't hide. My heart skips in my chest when Jax presses a kiss to my temple.

"What the *fuck* was that?" I hear Ranger shout somewhere behind us, clearly not missing our moment. He suddenly grunts like he's been hit by something. The noise is followed by a harsh, whispered warning from his mate.

Jax laughs against my hair before whispering, "This should be fun."

☾

EVERY SEAT IN THE WINSLOW'S LIVING ROOM IS TAKEN BY A member of my family when I walk inside. Even Sawyer is here, at this point the longtime friend of my brothers' is basically an honorary member of our family.

As if I'm holding a press conference, I stand before them. Jax leans against the wall behind me. Through our bond, I can feel his support. After Ranger and Winslow have taken their seats, I look around at the expectant faces of my family.

"Alright!" I clap my hands before rubbing them together. "There's a few things we all need to discuss before we talk about Kaius and Sterling. First and foremost, let's talk about the giant pink, moody elephant in the room. And no, I'm not talking about Pruitt." I pass my pregnant best friend a joking glance. I've missed months of precious time where I could have been joking about her being knocked up and I'm making up for lost time now. "I'm talking about me. I'm not sure if you guys noticed since I was doing *such* a good job at hiding it from you all." When in doubt, go with sarcasm. A life motto I live by. "I was going through a rough spot. There were a lot of things going on and maybe sometime soon I'll fill you all in." I'm not sure I'm ready to admit to everyone what happened with Gage. That's a wound I'm afraid will take more time to heal from. "I apologize for pushing you all away when you just wanted to help. I was an ass and hope you all can forgive me for disappearing like I did."

Pru smiles at me from across the room. "We're just happy you seem to be doing better." Ryker, who sits next to her, nods his head in agreement.

Ransom shifts forward in his seat. "Yeah, Rem, don't take this the wrong way, but you've been looking *hella* rough, but you look better now, so that's good."

Isabeau, who sits on the arm of his chair, rolls her eyes and slaps the back of his head. "Ignore him."

"I've spent twenty-two years around him, I'm well versed in that skill," I assure her.

Mom clears her throat. "I know we weren't always helpful in the way you needed us to be, so we apologize—I apologize —for the things we did that only made it worse."

Behind me, Jax scoffs under his breath like he's still not overly thrilled by how she talked to me that night on the road, but I need to forgive her and move on if I'm going to one day fully heal from this year of hell.

"It's okay," I tell her. When no one else has anything to say, I move forward. "Okay, to the next important thing we need to discuss and this one is crucial." When I glance at Winslow, her eyes light up expectantly thinking I'm about to share my news with everyone, but that'll come in due time. "It is now each and every one of our responsibilities to make sure Winslow never grows out her bangs. She has, unfortunately, inherited Kaius's widow's peak and that simply won't work." *Obviously, this is a joke... for the most part.*

Ryker doubles over in his seat, laughing while Ranger fights his own fits of laughter.

Winnie simply shrugs and says, "I wasn't going to grow them out, mainly because I don't like my forehead, but now it's definitely never happening"

"What was Kaius like?" my father asks, ignoring the noise coming from his sons.

"Let's see... *what was Kaius like?*" My mind fills with flashbacks from my short time around him. Hard to believe it was just last night that all of this happened. Since everything happened with Jax, meeting Kaius feels like days ago. "He was great. Dresses to kill. Good conversationalist. I especially liked when he brought a five-year-old back from the dead because he thought it would be *fun*." My stomach twists when I hear the sounds of the small boy's screams in my head. "I think the logical next step would be to have Winnie invite him over for the next family barbecue. I think he'll make a wonderful addition to the evening," I deadpan.

"A five-year-old?" Pruitt blanches, her hand going to the growing life in her stomach.

I nod in confirmation. "In all honesty, Kaius is twisted just like Sterling, but I think he may be easier to understand than we originally thought, but we'll get into that more later." Even though he ran from us, I can't help but think he meant what he said. His only desire in life is entertainment. Like a junkie looking for a fix, he's just searching for the next thing that interests him. What better source of entertainment is there than to watch Sterling and my pack battle it out? If he's being truthful about wanting to watch Sterling fall, he'll follow through with his side of the deal.

"I can't believe we're related to these people." Winslow looks between Jax and Isabeau. "How did we make it this far with them being our biological parents?"

Whisper who's been sitting quietly, pipes in, "For you specifically, I believe the answer is a copious amount of drugs." Winnie flips him the bird as he turns his attention to Beau. "For you, I'm not sure yet how you did it."

Blinking at him, the vampire says, "I turned off my emotions and didn't allow myself to feel anything for almost my entire life."

"*Alrighty then.*" Whisper nods slowly, lips pursed like he's trying to hold back some kind of remark. "You do you. Whatever works, am I right?"

Isabeau looks at the hacker like he's a puzzle she hasn't quite figured out.

Ranger sits higher in his seat before asking, "Is there anything else you want to tell us before we talk about our next moves?" I don't think he's even bothering to hide the knowing tone from his voice.

I pretend to think it over while counting my fingers, like I'm going through the list of speaking points I want to cover. Shaking my head, I tell him, "I think that about does it." I go as far as to walk a few feet toward an empty love seat before I hold up a finger and spin around on my heels. "Nope, you're right, I did forget something." With a steadying breath, I glance once more at Jax before confessing. "Jax is my mate. We completed the mating ceremony last night." I tug at the collar of my hoodie to expose Jax's mark to them, so they know I'm not joking while I back up a few paces to stand at Jax's side. A united front. "I'm happy which is something I never thought I'd be able to say again, so unless the next words out of your mouth are, *congratulations, we're happy you're happy or where are you registering? I'd like to buy you a present,* I don't want to fucking hear it. I'm not going to let you ruin this for me."

Jax's warm fingers intertwine with mine as he stands stiffly at my side as we wait for someone to say something, but so far, it's crickets. Everyone but Winslow, Ranger, and Isabeau are sitting there with their mouths gaping open. Even if the vampire was truly shocked by this news, she wouldn't show it externally like the rest. She's too reserved for that, but I get the feeling that just like Winnie, she knew something was up between us for a while now.

Everyone's head turns in the direction of my dad when he stands from the armchair he'd been sitting in. Jax's muscles go rigid as if he's preparing for a fight as my dad walks toward us with an unreadable expression on his face. He pauses a few feet away to look back at everyone. "The white wolf who was long prophesied about." He gestures at Pruitt before moving on to Winslow. "A witch with necromancer blood in her veins that can communicate with the dead." Isabeau is next. "A vampire-fae hybrid who can become one with the shadows." Finally, he looks at Jax. "A demon-wolf who's more powerful than any of us will probably ever know." He stares at Jax a little longer than the rest before saying, "I never could have guessed that my children would end up with you four, but I can say with complete certainty I wouldn't change it for anything. You are the ones that my children needed. You are giving them something no one else will ever be able to and for that I am thankful for each of you."

I'm not sure I've ever heard my dad say so many words in such a short time if he wasn't addressing the pack as the alpha. Regardless, his words wash over me and ease the anxiety that was heavy on my shoulders.

I slump into Jax's side in relief.

CHAPTER TWENTY-EIGHT
Remington

The house is quiet when I get up the next day.

We'd stayed the night at Ranger's because Pruitt's rule about pack members staying on pack territory is still in place. While sleeping three doors down from your older brother with your new mate isn't ideal, we found a way to make it work.

Only mere hours later, after Jax had let me pass out from exhaustion, did he kiss me on the forehead and tell me he was leaving to help train at Isabeau's house. I'd started to get up to go with him, but he had told me to get some more sleep and he'd be back in a couple of hours. It'd felt weird being left here without him, but I reminded myself that he could be back here In just seconds if I really needed him. With that thought, I'd fallen back asleep.

Dressed and ready to go meet everyone at Beau's, I walk onto the wraparound deck of the elevated house to find Winslow feeding her raven blueberries. Most people have dogs or cats, but Winnie has a raven named Poe. The two of them have a special connection since Winslow accidentally brought the bird back to life many years ago when she didn't know she had powers. The raven has literally flown across the country to be with her.

"Morning," the witch chirps as the black bird snaps a piece of fruit out of her fingers greedily.

Eyeing the animal warily, I walk closer to her. "Morning. Why aren't you training with everyone else this morning?"

"I'm going to head over in a bit," she explains. "I just wanted a morning where it didn't feel like I was at bootcamp preparing to go into battle. Plus, Isabeau is picking up a new rifle today that she thinks will be a better fit for me, so I'm waiting for her to bring that by before I go."

I still can't believe we trust this woman with an armed weapon. When I first met her, I wouldn't have trusted her with a pair of children's scissors.

Leaning against the railing, I look into the trees, thinking about how everyone reacted to what happened with Kaius. The room was split evenly by who believed the necromancer was telling us the truth and who thought he was just yanking our chains to get a reaction out of us. Either way, we all have to just wait and see if he shows up after we take care of Sterling.

And we will take care of Sterling.

We've been through too much and lost too much because of that man. It has to end.

I know if Gage were here, he'd have been riling up and motivating the enforcers, getting them primed and ready to fight. He was many things, but he was good at his job. It's a shame he won't be here fighting with the rest of us.

"Where'd that mind of yours go?" Winslow's voice brings me out of my thoughts.

I look at Winslow, a question I never thought to ask her until now on my tongue.

"What is it?"

Clearing my throat, I tuck a piece of my hair behind my ear nervously. "I'm not sure if I'm even allowed to ask anymore because I'm with Jax and I'm ecstatic to be with him."

"But?"

"But I want to know that Gage is okay," I admit. It's probably totally selfish of me to want this, but I need to know. "I mean, I know he's not okay, he's dead, but do you know if Gage is at peace?"

Winslow closes the container of fruit, prompting the large raven to fly off to a nearby tree. She watches him for a second before turning back to me. "Spirits that linger after death are the ones that have unfinished business. They don't move on until they find closure," she explains. "I know what you're trying to ask me, but you're afraid to say the words aloud. You want to know if Gage is upset that you're with Jax now. You want to make sure that he's not angry at you for choosing Jax." Winnie doesn't know that I have and always will choose Jax over everyone. "In the months that Gage has been dead, I haven't seen or even felt his presence lingering around. Not even when I'm at the cemetery or around you. If Gage was upset and not at peace with your choice, he would be here, but he's not." Winnie reaches out and places her hand over my arm. "You can move forward without worrying about him."

Whatever I was about to tell her is cut off when the front door violently swings open and Whisper stumbles outside like a man emerging from a dark cave. His pale hands cover his eyes, and he groans. "Oh my God, *the sun*. I think I'm blind.

I've been staring at a computer screen in a dark room for fifteen hours straight, my eyes don't know what to do with all this *light*."

"You act more like a vampire than the actual vampire we know," I comment, watching him push his glasses up into his mess of hair so he can rub his sensitive eyes. "I'm surprised you didn't walk into the sunlight and burst into flames immediately."

"Joke's on you, bitch, I only do that when I walk into a church."

Winslow laughs before telling us, "There was this guy at the hospital when I was locked up who tried to light himself on fire because he thought he needed to repent for his sins. He ate a cheeseburger or something when he wasn't supposed I guess. He got fully naked in the middle of a *Big Lots* and doused himself in gasoline. Luckily he forgot his matches."

Whisper stops rubbing his eyes long enough to look at Winnie with a flabbergasted expression. "I really do love your stories and I definitely want to hear more about that guy because I'm sure there's a whole backstory you're not telling us, but I need to borrow the new bride for a second."

He reaches for me and ushers me toward the door. "The new bride? I'm not a bride."

"And what a shame that is because I really am a joy to have at a bachelorette party."

☾

Whisper has turned Winslow's other spare bedroom into a hacker-like cave. The curtains are drawn tight, keeping any light from entering the room. A dark sweater is thrown over the bedside table lamp, hindering the amount of light it produces. The dresser is littered with different computer equipment. Each time I'm around him, he has more. I don't know where he's magically getting them all because I know for a fact he didn't travel here with them.

Papers are littered across the bed and taped to various places on the wall. Knowing Whisper, there's a method to the madness, but to the untrained eyes, it looks like a mess.

"Don't mind the chaos," he tells me over his shoulder as I follow him to the desk he has set up across the room. "I'm looking for a thousand different things, so shit is just kinda everywhere right now," Whisper explains as he picks up a few pieces of paper so he can sit down in the desk chair.

"Everything is a mess right now, so this is just par for the course." I point to the end of the unmade bed. "If I sit here, I'm not going to accidentally sit on a forgotten frozen burrito or something, am I?"

"What? No. I don't bring food in here."

I glance around the wrecked room. "It's good to draw the line somewhere, I suppose."

He spins in his chair and faces me. "Okay, smart-ass, do you want to keep criticizing or do you want me to tell you what I found on Pruitt's mom's family?"

"I'm fairly good at multitasking," I joke, but when he gives me an impatient look, I sigh and relent. "Fine. Show me what you found."

He grabs a blue folder off the desk and hands it to me. "The only member of the family that I can still find records on is William Axton, Genevieve's brother." He taps a couple of times on the keyboard in front of him until William's DMV picture appears. He looks just like he did two years ago when we kidnapped him from his penthouse in Vancouver after we discovered he'd been the one working with Nicolai to help abduct Pruitt. "As we already know, he worked for Nicolai's medical company. Which was a legit business and very lucrative." That's why Sterling teamed up with Nicolai. Nicolai wanted to breed a pack of powerful wolves he could be the alpha of, and Sterling wanted a financial benefactor with access to the medical equipment he'd need to run his breeding facilities. A true match made in hell. It helped that Nicolai was just as twisted as the rest of them. "Or it was until Nicolai mysteriously vanished." Pruitt ripped out his throat and he's now buried in a shallow grave in the middle of the Canadian woods. "William was in charge of finances and when Nicolai died, what was left of the crumpling company went to him. After he takes every dime he can get from the company, he shuts it down and disappears. Goes completely off the grid. All the bank accounts in his name have been closed and all his property and assets have been sold. Which I would think was odd if I didn't discover it was a common occurrence in this family."

"What do you mean?"

"Around thirty years ago, Genevieve's father, John, did the same thing. One day he just ceased to exist."

"So, there's nothing I can give to Pru?" I ask, feeling disappointed. Pru already knows her uncle has played a small role in the dangers we're facing. That's information she's not going to want to pass along to her child. "What about Gen's mom? What happened with her?"

He taps the folder in my hand. "That's where this comes in."

Opening the blue folder, I find a few printed-out pieces of

paper. On the very top is a scanned page of a newspaper dated over thirty years ago. Reading the first headline, I frown at Whisper. "What does a random animal attack have to do with Gen's mom?" A *brutal* animal attack is more correct. It says five hunters were mauled to death by something.

"Read down farther." Scanning the page, I find the obituaries. "Gen's mom was named Claire," he tells me before I have to ask.

At the very bottom of the obituary section is a small little blurb.

"For Claire Axton. It wasn't supposed to end like this. - John"

"What happened to her?"

"I don't know." Whisper rubs his face in frustration. "This newspaper article and this"—he flips the newspaper clipping up to show what's underneath—"this family picture from when Gen and William were younger was all I could find. Someone went through a great deal to wipe everything there is about them out. I'm lucky I found the few pieces they missed."

The picture looks like it was taken at one of those mall photography places. Where everyone wears matching white shirts and blue denim jeans. Except for the happy, smiling photo you'd expect of a family, the parents look stiff and their expressions are bland. Unemotional. The two children that stand in front of them have tight, almost pained smiles on their faces.

This wasn't a happy family.

"Genevieve looks just like Pru when she was a kid," I observe. Gen's hair is just a couple shades darker than Pru's white, blonde locks. Everyone in the picture is blonde, although John's hair looks a little sparse. It seems William has lucked out with being able to keep his hair. Sighing, I take the picture from the folder. "It's not much, but at least Pru will know what her grandparents looked like."

Whisper nods solemnly. "I'll keep looking, but something is really weird about this family."

"I bet when William got involved with Nicolai, he had his family's history wiped so they couldn't be tracked if things went south." I grasp at straws for an explanation.

"Yeah, maybe."

I leave Whisper to wallow in his mess.

CHAPTER TWENTY-NINE
Remington

I'm on my hands and knees rummaging around through boxes of various décor and knickknacks in Winslow's storage closet when someone abruptly clears their throat behind me, making me jump and hit my head on the shelf.

"Fuck!" I moan as the back of my skull throbs. Carefully backing up so I don't accidentally do it again, I turn around to glare up at Isabeau. She leans against the wall, an impassive look on her face as she watches me. "You were a really good assassin, weren't you?" I ask dumbly while rubbing my head. As a wolf shifter, my senses are heightened, but I still wasn't able to hear or sense Beau approaching.

The vampire lifts a shoulder in a noncommittal shrug before pushing off the wall and stepping closer to me. "What are you doing?"

"I need a frame to put a picture in for Pru," I explain while climbing back to my feet. It's not the kind of picture I'd typically want to frame for someone, but I still want it to look somewhat presentable when I give it to Pru later today when I go train with the rest of the pack. "I kinda screwed up and forgot to get her a gift for her baby shower, so I had Whisper try and track down some information about Genevieve's side of the family."

"That was thoughtful of you. I just bought the first thing I saw on the registry. What is a *Baby Bjorn*?"

Isabeau can tell you a million facts about guns and knives and tell you the easiest and cleanest way to kill someone, but she is still learning about real world things. Ransom has her in what he calls *'pop culture'* bootcamp because before meeting him, she'd never watched TV or seen a movie. He got tired of none of his movie references working on her, so he now forces her to watch Netflix and whatnot with him.

"It's something you strap to your chest and pop your baby into so you can use both your hands," I explain to her while looking through the upper shelves of the closet.

"So, it's a baby... *carrier*?"

"Pretty much," I answer over my shoulder. Standing on my tippy-toes, I try to see what Winnie has stashed on the very top shelf, but it looks to be just leftover gallons of wall paint and painting supplies. "Hey! You wouldn't happen to have an extra picture frame, would you?"

She quirks a dark brow at me. "Do I look like someone that would have an extra picture frame? I have one framed picture in my house and it's from when I married Ransom in Vegas and it was included in the package for the ceremony." While shifters don't typically get married, Ransom decided to elope with Beau in Vegas. It's a really classy affair when an Elvis impersonator marries you.

"You know what? That's on me. I forgot that your idea of decorating is mounting weapons on walls."

She scoffs. "Ransom only let me do that in *one* room."

"Whatever, it still looks like a serial killer dungeon." I roll my eyes. "Want to go with me to town to pick a frame up before we head back to your house?" I snag the picture off the side table I'd left it on. "I really want to give this to Pruitt today," I explain while handing the photograph to Beau.

She takes it from me with little to no interest in her eyes, almost as if she's looking at it just to humor me. Her arctic eyes scan the picture really quick like she's going through the motions before starting to hand it back to me. I reach out to take it from her, but just as I'm about to touch it, her eyes narrow and she snaps it back to her.

Thinking she's seeing the same thing I see, I cross my arms and frown. "I know, not exactly the happiest of pictures."

Beau ignores my statement before asking harshly. "You said this is Pru's mom?"

"And her parents and brother," I confirm, standing up a little straighter because of her change in tone.

"Whisper found this for you? Did he find any more pictures or just this one?"

"Just that one. It's super weird, it's like Genevieve's family has been wiped from existence. They went off the grid or something thirty some odd years ago," I tell her, sounding disappointed we couldn't find more out. I shouldn't really be surprised that we hit a roadblock. We've been hitting them every way we turn lately. Why should this gift be any different.

Isabeau shakes her head. "No, it's not weird at all. It's smart." *She would think that* I think flippantly. "Especially because of who *he* is." She points at the picture.

I can't see exactly where she's pointing from my angle, but it looks like it's at the little boy. "Yeah, that's William.

We've already had a run-in with him in the past. He was working with Nicolai." He was also the one who masterminded Nicolai's obsession with Gen. "After Pru killed Nicolai, William fell off the face of the earth again. I'm sure he's off licking his wounds—"

"Remington," Beau snaps impatiently. "I know who William is and he's not who I'm talking about. I'm talking about *him*." I look down again at where she's pointing and at this adjusted angle I finally see who she's talking about. "I don't know how I never saw it before. I was never in the same room as both of them, but now as I'm staring at this picture, I can't believe I missed it. The resemblance is glaring. I should have figured out William was his kid."

"I'm not following, Beau."

"William is not who we need to worry about. He's nothing but a pathetic child looking for approval. His father is the one who's been pulling the strings all along. He's the one we're looking for." Pulling my gaze away from the picture, I stare wide eyed at Isabeau as she finally says, "Pruitt's grandfather is—"

"*Sterling*," I breathe out

"Yes," she confirms. It takes a lot to make the vampire look shocked, but right now her eyes are as wide as mine and I swear she's paler than usual.

"You're positive? We need to be sure, Beau, before we tell anyone anything."

"This picture was taken a long time ago, well before the accident, but even without the scars all over his face, I know it's him. This is Sterling. I'd recognize him anywhere, but if you don't trust my judgment, take this to Jax."

"No, I trust you," I assure her. Isabeau was trained personally by Sterling. Jax may be Sterling's son, but he spent way more time with the vampire than Jax. "What accident are you talking about?"

"Sterling was badly burned sixteen years ago in a fire." Beau begins to pace the room "He was never able to get rid of the scars."

"He's a wolf shifter, we can heal from a burn."

"Yes, you can when it's a normal fire, but not when it's *hellfire*."

Jax.

Taking the picture back from Beau, I stare down at it, committing it to memory before folding it up. The idea of framing it and giving it to Pru no longer seems like a good idea. I shove it into the pocket of my jeans for safekeeping. "I need to go," I announce. "I need to go tell everyone." I need to tell Pruitt *and* Jax. They need to know how they're related.

Beau nods. "Go now. I'll drive over with Winslow." She fishes the keys to her Jeep out of her leather pants. "Take my car."

I snag the keys from her hand before sprinting out the door.

☾

THE LAST TIME I DROVE THESE ROADS, I WAS RACING through them because I was being chased. I'm not being chased now, but I'm driving just as fast, if not faster. I know we aren't going to be able to do anything immediately with the information, but it's been the first real information we've gotten on Sterling since the start of this and I want to tell everyone as soon as possible.

I also want to be the one to tell Pruitt and Jax. Even though we have the picture now as glaring proof, I still think it will be easier for them to believe and wrap their head around if they hear it coming from me.

We always knew this all tied back to Genevieve, but we thought it was because of her history with Nicolai. William orchestrated for Gen to be given to Nicolai. Nico wanted to breed a powerful pack and if he was going to do that, he was going to need a powerful she-wolf to carry his pups. Before Nicolai could force a mating bond on Gen, she found her true mate. Once a wolf is mated, they can never be impregnated by another and just like that Gen became useless to Nico.

Now that we know who Sterling is, I can't help but think that it wasn't William setting up Nicolai with Gen, but Sterling pulling the strings like he always is.

After coming around a curve of the road, I floor it because I know the next mile of road is perfectly straight with no stop signs. Just as I'm getting to the speed I want to be at, I'm forced to slam on my brakes as the sight in front of me comes into view.

It must have just happened, there's still smoke coming off the destroyed motorcycle in the middle of the road. Putting the car in park, I search the accident for signs of people or another vehicle. With no other car or motorcycle to be seen, I deduce the rider must have lost control or it was a hit and run. The latter doesn't seem likely as we're still on pack territory and no one in the pack would do that to another member.

Climbing out of the car, I race toward the destroyed motorcycle. It's bent and scraped up. Just like the night of my wreck, fluid leaks out of it onto the road. I look for signs of the rider, a trail of blood or footprints. *Something*. But the road is devoid of both.

Alarm bells go off in my head as the hair on the back of my neck and arms rise. Not until my wolf begins to growl low in her throat do I see the familiar sticker on the motorcycle. My body freezes in place as I figure out who this bike belongs to. I'm ashamed it took me so long since I've ridden on the back of it many times, but it's not supposed to be here. It was supposed to have been shipped back to his parents with the rest of Gage's belongings.

Scanning the trees and empty road around me with a watchful eye, I search for who or what could have crashed Gage's bike. Or, what's starting to feel more likely, this bike was left here for me to find. But who would do this to me?

The whole thing feels offs and like a trap.

Warily, I turn back toward Isabeau's matte black Jeep so I can call her or Ryker about what I found. I want to call Jax, but the burner phone he had he destroyed before he went on his poorly thought-out solo trip to Seattle.

My back is just turned to the bike crash when the explosion happens. My first assumption is that the bike has blown up, but the sound is too far away. Whirling back around, I search for the source and find black smoke billowing up from the trees many miles away on the other side of pack territory.

My blood runs cold, and my wolf bares her teeth and steadies herself. She knows what's happening just like I do.

It's time.

Over a year of waiting, planning and training, *he's* here.

If I didn't already know it in my bones, the symphony of warning howls cutting across our land would. Forgetting completely about the weirdness of the motorcycle, I sprint toward the car. From this vantage point, I can't tell where that explosion happened, but I need to go make sure everyone is okay.

The only thing keeping me from fully panicking is I can still feel the link between Jax and I. It's alive and strong. As long as it remains that way, it means he's okay.

My hand just brushes the metal of the door handle when I hear the whooshing sound behind me. Before I have a chance to turn around and see what it is, a hand is tangling in the strands of my hair. I cry out as they yank me backward just to shove me forward.

My face slams against the glass of Isabeau's driver's side window. I can't hear the sound of my bones breaking over the sound of the glass shattering, but I can feel them break. Instantly I taste blood and my face screams in pain.

Disoriented from the head trauma, I drop to the ground on my hands and knees. My attacker releases my hair but continues to stand close. I can see the red heels in my peripheral vision as they're leisurely joined by a pair of men's dress shoes. Spitting a mouthful of blood into the asphalt before turning my head, I look up at the man.

When I see him, I can't help but choke on a laugh. "I should have known." I spit more blood onto his shoes. "Only a pussy like you would attack from behind."

"You didn't give me much of a choice." He grins at me. He tries to be sinister like his associates, but he just can't seem to pull it off. Even the woman with the fairy-like features that stands next to him in a red dress is more intimidating than him. "I tried to get you that night, but you called for help before I could get you out of the car."

"Another embarrassingly weak move, *William*. You

couldn't face me yourself, so you resorted to running me off the road with your car? Genevieve really did get all the strong genes, didn't she?" William also had to resort to traps like leaving Gage's motorcycle out to get an advantage over me.

With an angry snarl, he shoves his foot into my side and forces me to roll onto my back in a heap. "I'm surprised you didn't recognize me that night on the road, Remington. I thought for sure you'd recognize my scent at the very least. I remembered yours."

Holding my ribs, I grimace as I sneer up at him. "Of course, you did. I'm a very memorable person. You, however, are about as memorable as a piece of chewed bubble gum stuck under a park bench."

William hauls me off the ground, his fingers digging painfully into my arm as he drags me to my feet. His woman companion stands silently at his side. When my eyes collide with hers, I find they're glassy and unfocused. "Let's see if you've still got a mouth on you when you meet Sterling," William growls in my face. Now that I know Sterling is his dad, I find it really odd he refers to his own father by that moniker. I don't call my dad *Elias*.

Off in the distance, another explosion echoes through the air. William turns his head to stare at the new cloud of smoke rising above the trees. While he's momentarily distracted, I kick my foot out. My boot collides with his kneecap. The blow makes him holler in pain and loosen his grip on me just enough I'm able to slip away.

I only get ten feet away before William is screaming behind me. "Go after her!"

The same whooshing noise from before comes up behind me and before I have time to do anything about it, the woman in red is standing in front of me. She holds her hand out, palms up. As I collide with her, her palm is pressed to my heart.

When Jax touches me with hellfire, it feels like he's transferring something to me. I can feel the steady stream of power as it enters my body even though it doesn't hurt. What she's doing now doesn't hurt, but it feels wrong, like she's stealing the life from me. I can feel my energy and power being pulled out of my body from where her palm presses to me.

Her facial expression stays the same and her eyes remain that glossy, dead looking pair.

Feeling incredibly weak, I stumble forward. I try to keep myself upright, but my knees have become wobbly, and my vision has started to blur. When I fall toward her, I half expect her to reach forward and stop me from falling onto the dark ground, but instead she just stops and watches me fall.

"Mina, that's enough," William warns the girl. I have no idea what kind of species she is. "He doesn't want her dead yet."

Without a word or pushback, Mina lifts her hand off of me and moves back a foot like a soldier stepping back into line.

Back on the ground, I try to shake off whatever she'd just done to me, but no matter how many times I blink or take slow measured breaths, the exhaustion and threat of passing out looms over me.

Another explosion goes off as William steps in front of me. "What are you doing?" I slur out.

William waves his hand in the direction of the clouds of smoke. "We're just making sure your people know we're here," he answers casually. "And we needed to keep them distracted for a short time while we collected you. I have no idea what Sterling has planned for you, but he said you were important."

I want to tell him to get fucked, but my body becomes so tired I lose the ability to form words. My only hope is Jax feels my distress through our bond, because my world is quickly turning black

"Close your eyes, Remington," William orders. "It'll all be over soon."

And with that, everything goes dark.

CHAPTER THIRTY
Jax

I'm impressed by the level of fighting skill Pruitt's pack has been able to develop in these past months. They are already the strongest pack in North America, but with the help of these grueling training sessions, they've become stronger. Their instincts are sharper, and they've learned tips and tricks on how to take down certain species from Isabeau.

She's fought and killed everything, and it's a wealth of knowledge for her pack.

We have no idea what Sterling has been cooking up in his lab and what mutations he's bringing with him. The pack needs to be prepared to fight everything.

I'm still holding out hope that we'll be able to find Sterling and I'll be able to deal with him one on one without having to bring the entire pack into it, but I don't think I'll get that lucky.

The sound of Ransom's fist connecting with Ranger's jaw makes me grin. Watching any of the Weylyn brothers fight is always a sight to behold. They don't hold back. They fight like they are truly each other's enemies, but when the match is called, they instantly go back to acting like brothers.

Ranger doesn't have the savage edge that Ransom has, but Ransom doesn't have the patience that Ranger has. It's an interesting dynamic watching these twins fight. Their styles couldn't be more different.

"Stop pussyfooting around each other and fucking fight!" Ryker yells at his brothers from his position next to Pru. "Get him, Ranger!"

Smirking, I lean around Pruitt so I can talk to him. "You're cheering on Ranger and not Ransom?"

Ryker's eyes cut to me just long enough to scowl at me. "Ransom kicked my ass last week on these mats. I want Ranger to do the same to him."

"Hmm..." I think it over before a brilliant idea comes to mind. "This just got exciting. Ransom! Stop holding back and finish this!" I grin wildly when I find Ryker glaring at me. "It's no fun being on the sidelines, I needed something to entertain me. One hundred dollars says Ransom beats Ranger."

Pruitt holds her hands up between us. "No, we are not going to wager—" she begins to order at the same time Ryker nods his head and says, "Deal."

Pru rolls her eyes as we shake hands on our bet before mumbling, "Holidays are going to be interesting for us moving forward."

Holidays. The first Christmas I've ever celebrated was last year, and I only stopped in for a second. It will be an interesting learning curve to celebrate holidays with a real family and with a mate. And birthdays. I wonder how Remi and I will celebrate those. Preferably, I'd like if we could somehow arrange that she'll blow me while I blow out my candles. I make a mental note to broach the subject with her. It could be our own special tradition.

Definitely can't invite the whole family over for that kind of party.

I'm lost in thought, thinking about eating frosting off Remi's body when I hear Ryker shout something incoherent at Ranger. Focusing back on the fight in front of me, I watch as Ranger tries to dive at Ransom, but no surprise, Ransom saw the move coming and sidesteps him.

Ransom is just about to pin Ranger to the mat when the ground underneath us shakes and the trees rattle as something explodes.

In a second, every single member of the pack that is here is standing at attention, their bodies rigid like they're ready for an attack at any second. Everyone's expression is a mix of dread but also determination. Which is the right combination of emotions to have if this is what we're all thinking it is. If Sterling has finally come, we're going to need both of those emotions if we're going to make it out alive. The dread will keep them from doing something reckless, but the determination will keep them going even when it gets bleak.

Ryker is standing in front of Pru, guarding her and their unborn child in a flash and the twins are standing back-to-back, searching the surrounding area for the threat. When they don't see anything like the rest of us, they give each other a silent look before they begin to jog away from the training area.

"Where the hell are you going?" Ryker yells after them.

"Our girls are alone at my house," Ranger hollers back. "We need to get to them."

My chest squeezes uncomfortably tight when I remember

that Remi is there too. I kick myself that for a few seconds my mind was so overcome with thoughts of battle that I didn't think of where she was. I'm only a few days into this mate thing, and I'm already failing.

"Remi's there too," I announce while pushing through the crowd after the twins. "I'll meet you there." there is no way in fuck I'm going to get into a car that travels fifty miles an hour when I can get to her in seconds.

As I call upon my power, another loud boom comes from the distance. My eyes squeeze shut as I turn my power to full force and allow it to wash over me at neckbreaking speeds. I've never traveled between locations as fast as I do now.

I'm moving so fast that when I land in Winslow's kitchen, I stumble forward multiple feet and have to catch myself on the countertop to stop the strong amount of momentum in my body.

Her name is on my lips as I prepare to call for her when Isabeau and Winslow come around the corner. Each of them are armed to the teeth and wearing tactical gear. Winslow wears a black beanie on her head and there's a bulletproof vest strapped to her chest. Just like every scary situation I've ever seen her encounter, her chin is lifted while bravery comes off her in palpable waves. She's always faced each challenge head-on. Her lack of a fight-or-flight response makes her strong, but reckless at times.

"We heard the explosion," Winslow tells me while she adjusts the strap of her rifle on her shoulder. "Is he here?"

Isabeau glances up at me quickly while she continues to strap weapons to the various holsters on her body. She's as calm as can be. You'd think she was planning a trip to the local coffee shop based on her demeanor. "Do you know someone else who would set explosives off on our land?" the vampire asks the witch.

"No, but I was kinda hoping they were just fireworks," Winslow mumbles before walking down the hallways yelling, "Whisper! I've got good news and I've got bad news. Good news is you can stop searching for Sterling. Bad news, we might all die." Glad to see that the imminent battle hasn't taken away from her humor. "Whisper? Where are you?" There's a pause. "Are you hiding under the bed?"

My wolf nudges at me and bangs against his cage, demanding I pay attention to him. When I figure out what he's trying to tell me, I narrow my eyes at Beau. "Where's Remi?" I can't sense her in the house. Her scent is too faint as well.

While she checks the clip of one of her guns, Beau frowns at me. "What do you mean, where's Remi? She left fifteen minutes ago to talk to you at my house."

"She wasn't there when I left," I tell her as fear creeps into my bones.

"She should have been," Beau insists. "It's only an eight-minute drive to my house from here and she was hauling ass because she had something important to tell you."

"Then where is she?"

Beau shakes her head lightly. "I don't know, she should have been there."

As the third bomb explodes, so does my control.

My eyes shift into their wolf form and my fangs and claws descend as my wolf pushes forward. My skin is too tight and too hot, Winslow's spacious home is too confining. My palms burn like my hellfire is close to exploding from them.

"Jax." Isabeau tries to get my attention but I'm slowly being consumed by my wolf rage.

"What was she coming to tell me?" I ask, my voice sounding rougher than usual.

"We figured out who Sterling is."

☾

THE WIN OF FINALLY DISCOVERING WHO STERLING IS, IS LOST on me. I couldn't give a shit we finally have a name, or I now know where the other half of my DNA truly comes from. I don't even feel anything knowing I'm related to Pruitt. That knowledge should probably make me feel some sort of way, but now as I stand on the road staring at the drops of my mate's blood, I'm consumed by the feeling of rage. Rage and complete and utter helplessness.

My mate has been taken and she's bleeding.

I don't care if the sky started flying and Lucifer himself emerged from the depths of hell in front of me, I would still only care that Remington isn't where she's supposed to be.

Which is with me, at my side. *Forever*. That's what we promised each other.

"How did this happen?" I bite out. "How were they able to get onto pack territory. I thought we had it locked down tight."

"We did," Ryker, who had joined us after getting Pru to her parent's house, says at my side. "We do," he corrects.

I turn on him so fast, he jerks back a step. "No, you clearly don't. If you did, your sister—*my mate*—wouldn't have been taken!" I snarl as I invade his space with fury seeping out of my pores.

Isabeau, suddenly the voice of reason of the group, gets between us, her cold hands pressing into our chests. "Jax, you're forgetting who we're dealing with. This is Sterling. He's a cockroach and can find his way into anywhere."

I know she's right, but the rational side of my brain isn't dictating my emotions. My wolf is and he wants blood. He doesn't care if it's Sterling's or Ryker's at this point. Until his mate is returned, he's going to crave the bloodbath.

Ransom's truck roars down the road and skids to a stop by the Jeep Remi had abandoned. My eyes stay locked on the glass from the broken window that's littering the ground. The shards are caked in Remi's blood.

"What did you find?" Ryker questions his brothers. After they knew their mates were safe and well, they'd taken off to check out what the explosions were.

"There were definitely bombs being set off, but they didn't damage anything. Only some trees on the west side of the property were affected. The fences there are fully intact still," Ranger explains quickly. "There were tire tracks on the edge of the fence line. Looked like they used dirt bikes to ride out there. We followed the tracks but lost the trail when they hit the main road."

"What was the point of the bombs if they didn't ruin anything? Why go through the trouble of setting them if they aren't going to actually hurt any of us?" Winslow asks the group the question we're all thinking.

Isabeau steps away from the huddle and walks into the middle of the road. Instead of looking to the west side of the territory where the bombs were, she stares off to the east. Her head cocks to the side. Due to her advanced hearing, I know without having to confirm with her that she can hear something. After a minute, she stops and turns her head toward me.

All it takes is one curt nod from her to figure out what she's heard.

"They weren't trying to *hurt* us," I clarify, my voice full of frustration. "They were trying to distract us." A trap that we fell perfectly into. "While we were busy running around getting our mates to safety or checking the explosion site, they were invading the east side of the territory." The lingering scent of Remi's blood fills my nose as I grit out, "And taking Remington right from under our noses."

Winslow stands up straighter and pushes her shoulders back in an attempt to make all five feet of her look bigger and stronger. "How many are there?"

Isabeau's head tilts again as she's listening to distant noises before answering. "A lot."

"I don't care," I tell her. "There could be a hundred or a thousand of them here, but I'm still getting to Remington."

"You don't need to worry about the hundreds or thousands, you need to worry about the *one*," Beau reminds me. "The numbers don't matter if he's gone. Without their leader, they'll crumble."

I vowed when I was eight years old I was going to kill my father and burn everything he's worked for down. I've waited patiently for sixteen years, but today is finally the day. When he took my mother from me, I barely survived it, but now that he has my mate, I know I'll never recover from that loss.

Either way, one of us won't live to see tomorrow's sunrise.

CHAPTER THIRTY-ONE
Remington

Like I've been held under water for a long time, I wake up gasping for air. My body feels wrong, like I'm still missing my energy, but I'm strong enough to hold my head up and keep my eyes open. A small victory, but one I'm thankful for as I wheeze for my next breath.

When I try to bring my hands up to my chest while I catch my breath, I discover I can't move my arms. At first, I think it's still a lingering effect from what that Mina bitch did to me on the road, but when I try to move them again, metal bites into the skin at my wrists.

Blinking rapidly to clear the remaining haziness from my eyes, I look down at my arms. Handcuffs made of silver are locked around each of my limbs, effectively keeping me locked in place on the cold metal chair I sit on. That's why I still feel weird. The silver in the cuffs is affecting my wolf's strength.

We are immune to all diseases, and we can survive most wounds, but if those wounds are inflicted by a silver blade or a bullet it's extremely difficult to heal from. When Ryker was shot with a silver bullet, it took him weeks to fully recover.

The only thing that saved him was the fact the gunshot was a through and through. Had the silver lingered in his body much longer, he would have died.

Silver cuffs like the ones I'm wearing weaken the body, the silver permeates the skin and then the bloodstream until it makes the animal side of a shifter ill.

Even though I know it's no use, I yank on the confines. All I succeed in doing is making them unbearably tight. Cursing, I lift my head and look around the room I'm in. The single light in the dark space hangs above my head. It sways slightly like there's a breeze in the air that I can't feel. Every time I shift in the chair, the wooden floors below me creak and moan. The walls of the room aren't insulated or dry walled.

It smells musty, almost like mothballs and old people's clothes.

An attic maybe?

The pounding on what sounds to be stair steps before the door to the room I'm in opens, confirms my theory.

The figure that enters the attic keeps his head turned into the shadows and away from me. Even with my ability to see well in the dark, the angle in which he keeps his face, keeps him hidden from view. Slowly and quietly, he begins to walk around me like a shark circles its prey.

The fact he hasn't said a word makes me more nervous than the dark energy rolling off him like a heavy fog. "Are we going to make some introductions? Or are you going to walk in circles until you get dizzy?" I snap at him, my anxiety coming off as bitchy sarcasm. I'm tied to a chair, it's my only defense right now.

"You're an interesting individual, Remington." His voice

is odd sounding, almost like something is hindering his speech. "You're not as strong as your brothers, but you act as if you are. Your attitude and how you choose to carry yourself make people perceive you as stronger. It's a clever move," he praises. "You almost had me fooled, but I saw through the strong façade. Those eyes of yours, they give you away. Everything you feel is reflected in them. You know what they say about eyes being the windows to the soul."

He steps into the light and finally allows me to see his face. Isabeau undersold it when she talked about Sterling having scars. Jax seriously fucked his face up. Right down the middle of his body, he's gruesomely burned. The entire right side of his face, bald head, and neck are nothing but scarred and uneven flesh. Deep lines run through the skin like at some point they tried to stitch him up, but it didn't help. His nose is extremely disfigured as well is half of his mouth. The skin around his lips on that side are long gone, and his teeth are exposed because of it. Where his right eye once sat is now an empty dark socket. The burns disappear under the black turtleneck he wears, and his fingers are covered with black leather gloves, but I have to assume the damage covers more of his body than just his head.

The half of his face that isn't damaged is weathered from age. He has to be in his mid to late sixties. I'm not stupid enough to think that his age has made him weak though.

His remaining eye, a deep green, peers into my eyes as he leans in close and asks, "If that's true and eyes are windows to the soul, what do you think my soul looks like?" He rests his hands on either armrest of my chair as he continues to invade my space. "Look and tell me what you see."

I do what he asks, mainly because I'm finding it hard to

look away from his face. I feel like one of those idiot people that hears a tornado siren and then goes outside to look at it. I know it isn't safe, but I do it anyway. I search his eye for a glimmer of something, but I'm met with nothing but darkness. "This is a trick question," I finally answer him.

Curious, he pulls away and grants me some breathing room again. "Oh? And why's that?".

"We both know it's been a very long time since you've had a soul, *John*." I make a point of using his real name. I don't know how he came to be known as Sterling, but regardless, I know it's not his birth name. "Did you lose it when you started all this madness or when you lost Claire?" I bring up his mate's death for two reasons. The first one being I want him to know that I'm not as in the dark as he may think I am. I know *who* he is. The second is he's going out of his way to make me uncomfortable, it's only fair I return the favor.

"Looks like someone has been doing their research," he muses coldly, not sounding remotely impressed by my knowledge. "Don't get too smug, Remington. I can assure you that you do not know the full story."

"You're right," I concede. "I'm not sure I want to know it either. I have a feeling that, like your face, it will give me nightmares. I don't need to hear the gory details of what you've done to become the monster you are."

He paces as he listens to me. "You're right, you don't need to hear the story, but you want to. You want to know how this all came to be. You want to know how a mated, father of two, could have turned into what I am."

Yes, he's right. I want to know what brought all this on and what was the event that made him become the monster from a bad B movie, but I'd rather be tied to the stake and left for the crows than admit that to him. "I am handcuffed to a chair with silver slowly infusing itself into my bloodstream. If you want to do an impromptu story time, it's not as if I'm in a position to tell you no." I tug on the chains of the handcuffs for effect. "But we both know this is how you like your women, isn't that right?"

"Truthfully, I prefer when they're sedated so they can't speak to me or plead for their lives. I find those exchanges tedious and obnoxiously time consuming. I don't have time for their tears or cries for help."

"You're disgusting."

I can't believe that Jax and Pruitt both come from this man. Jax looks nothing like him. Pruitt shares the blonde hair and green eyes, but even then, their energies are so different, you'd still never know they were related. The only thing I can think of that Jax inherited from this man is his tenacity and strength, both things he will need if he stands a chance against the fight Sterling is bringing.

I keep checking in on the link between us, ensuring I can still sense Jax. As long as that bond is alive, I'll be okay knowing he's alive.

"Scientific advancement isn't always pretty." Sterling laughs mockingly, his destroyed lips pulling in a way that makes me uncomfortable. "You know who first told me that?" He turns serious once more. "My mate. You see, this" —he gestures around with his gloved hand— "whole thing started because of her. Although, we both had better intentions when we first started our experiments."

"I find it hard to believe that Genevieve's mother could be responsible for any of this," I argue. What kind of woman could sit back and allow the things Sterling has done to other women? I have to believe that she never would have allowed something like this to happen.

"I'll admit, it wasn't this... *extreme*... when Claire was alive, but after she was killed, I saw no point in holding back or following the rules," he explains. When he talks about his mate, the normal side of his face pinches as if after all these years, he still feels the weight of her death. I'm sure he does. No one handles the loss of a mate well. It's like losing the other half of your soul. Many wolves don't survive it. "Before my granddaughter went and made that prophecy come true, the wolf shifter population was falling. Birth rates were declining rapidly as more and more she-wolves struggled to carry their pups to term. If someone didn't intervene, we were going to be extinct in a few hundred years. Claire believed if she was able to genetically modify a wolf shifter embryo, she could find a way to save the species. As you know, we're the only species that struggle with fertility rates. Claire thought that if she could find a way to splice in just enough DNA from another species, we could ensure the wolf embryos continued to thrive and grow. We had to find the right amount of foreign genetic material to use because we didn't want the characteristic from the donor species to be present. At that time, we weren't—or I should say, *I* wasn't—interested in cross breeds or hybrids. We just wanted to save our people from dying out."

So selfless, someone get this man a medal.

"Well, your priorities have obviously changed."

"When your mate is unexpectedly killed in a shocking and senseless way, you tend to reevaluate your thinking." His weird voice turns into a low growl. "I thought I could live beside humans in harmony, but when they hunted my mate for sport and then got away with killing her, I decided humans didn't deserve to live in peace or in power. We allow these inconsequential beings to dictate our lives. We have to follow their rules and live in hiding as to not spoil them, while they go unpunished for their crimes against us. They slaughtered my mate and cheered about it because they thought they'd simply killed a wolf. They had no idea what kind of life they'd just taken. These *hunters* took pictures of her body and put it in the newspaper. They were applauded for their 'record-breaking' kill. In order to remain a secret to the human world, they could never be held accountable for what they did."

At the mention of a newspaper, the clipping that Whisper had found comes to mind and so does the heading I'd read. "You got your revenge though, didn't you? You tracked them down and ripped them apart in your wolf form."

His gruesome mouth pulls in an evil smile. "That I did."

"But you couldn't leave it at that, could you? You needed more."

Sterling leans against the wall by the door, his arms crossing in front of him. "My mate used to say, why settle for sterling silver when you could have gold." *Ah, and the question of the hour is finally answered.* Sterling is a sentimental name. Odd, considering I didn't think he was capable of being sentimental. "I wasn't going to settle for just killing the humans responsible for my mate's death. I won't be satisfied until every human knows they belong on the bottom of the food chain. They will know when they see what I've created that we are the true gods." He stands up straighter as if what he's saying is lifting his twisted ego. "It took a lot of trial and error, but I took the science my mate had started to develop, and I changed it. Nicolai had been funding our research on wolf shifter embryos, but when he learned of my plans, he was more than willing to invest in that as well. There was a small price I had to pay him in exchange for his financial assistance of course."

"Genevieve."

I knew William wasn't the one pulling the strings. He's not a planner or a mastermind like his dad. He just does what his father says.

"Yes, she was strong and would have been a perfect match for him to breed with. When William introduced her to Nicolai, he took an immediate liking, but of course, as you know, that all fell apart when Gen met that other man." Sterling doesn't even attempt to hide the contempt from his voice.

"That man she met was her mate. *Archer* was her mate. Nicolai was never going to be that. Even if you'd let him force a mating bond on her."

"*Forcing*," he scoffs. "Believing we had the luxury of waiting for our true mates was what got us into this mess to begin with. Wolves waited and waited for their fated mates to come along, but they never did, and our birth rates dropped because of it. Of course, that's something we no longer have to worry about now that *Pruitt*" —he spits her name out like its poison on his tongue— "has broken the curse. In one way, she went and made all my hard work obsolete now that species aren't confined to mating within themselves. Now hybrids will be something that is natural. Something I was upset about for some time, but then I reminded myself of what I'm creating. I'm creating perfection and if nature has proven anything, it's that it's rarely perfect. Everything has a flaw. A weakness. Each day that passes, I'm figuring out how to make those flaws disappear. Only the strongest traits from each species are selected and used. One day soon everything I create will be as perfect as Isabeau and Jax. Those are the ones I'll unleash on the humans." Sterling grins wickedly at me. "But first I need to eliminate your pack. With your *irritants* constantly sticking your noses in places it doesn't belong, and killing my benefactors, you are interfering in my search for perfection and when I finally find it, you will stand in my way of executing my plan just as you are standing in my way now. I have worked too hard to get to where I am. I have sacrificed the lives of many in the name of science. I've even lost my own life a time or two to achieve my goal. It's not an easy road and it's not one that everyone has the stomach to handle, but it is my road and I'll be damned if I'm going to let you or your pack destroy it."

This isn't new information. We knew he'd come seeking revenge for all the things we've done to ruin his business, I just thought I'd be there to help fight, not held hostage by him.

Feigning indifference, I tilt my head and flick my gaze over him. "That was quite the speech, John. I feel like now is when we'd cue the dramatic change in music and lighting, You know, so it'll fit the mood," I mumble to myself, imagining I'm in a movie scene right now as the evil mastermind divulges his whole backstory. Why do they always do that? Don't they have a confidant they can tell? Surely, Sterling has a friend—*Nope*, wait, all his friends are dead. Well, Kaius is still alive, but according to him, he's no longer team Sterling.

"Do people actually enjoy your sarcasm?"

I shrug my shoulders. "I'm a very likable person, John.

So, if you don't like me, I suggest you look inward at yourself and reflect a little, because it's definitely a you problem."

"It should be no surprise that you are my son's mate. He's got a mouth on him too," he grumbles.

Smiling slyly, I wink at him. "That he does, and I'm a big, big fan of what he can do with it, so if we could wrap this up in a timely manner so I can get back to him and that tongue, that'd be great."

"You're crass."

"You're ugly," I shoot back immediately. "This is fun, shall we keep going? I'll go first this time." I lean as far forward as my chained wrists will allow. "You're a sadistic fuck who is going to pay for what you've done. Jax is going to burn you alive, and I will dance in the ashes he leaves your body in. I'll do goddamn snow angels in them." I sneer at him as my wolf, despite being affected by the silver, surges to the surface.

I see it coming, but there's nothing I can do to stop it. The back of Sterling's hand whips across my already bruised face as he growls violently at me.

Letting the pain fuel me instead of stop me, I calmly spit the mouthful of blood at him before grinning wildly at him. "How does it feel to know that your most perfect creation is going to be the one that kills you?"

Sterling's gloved hands grip my chin as he yanks my face harshly up so I can look at his mangled faced as he says, "The second Jax turned on me and my plans, his perfection ceased to matter. He became nothing but a problem for me. I have no use for him now. I warned him what would happen if that ever happened. And after everything he's done, I could never let him live. He needs to be punished for his acts against his *father*."

"You're *hardly* his father."

"You're right, I'm more than that. I'm his creator. I gave him life and gave him his power." Sterling swipes his gloved thumb over my lip that is now bleeding again. With that evil gleam on his face, he brings the blood-covered finger to his ruined mouth and licks it away. I feel my face pull in disgust as I watch. "I know just how strong he is, and I know that getting rid of him is my first priority if I'm going to get rid of the rest of you." He runs his hand fondly down the side of my face. "And that is why I worked so hard to get you here. You have been his weakness since the first day he met you. I've kept tabs over the months, I knew what you meant to him before he did."

I snarl and bare my teeth at him as I jerk my head away from his disturbing touch.

"That bond you share that you think makes you so strong?" he starts, the corner of his mouth on his good side rising. "It will be the reason Jax dies tonight. You will be the reason I come out victorious like I always have."

With one last look at me, he leaves the room. Before the door closes behind him, he tells me, "Thank you for your sacrifice, Remington."

CHAPTER THIRTY-TWO
Jax

The waiting and not knowing is the worst part of all of this.

For hours, we've been standing in the forest, half a mile away from where Sterling's army of people are literally waiting outside the gates. Just like us, they've had plenty of time to make a move, but they stand unmoving right outside the fence. While we wait for them to make a move, it's like they're waiting for something else.

Or someone else.

Sterling isn't here and neither is Remi. I would be able to sense them if they were in that horde of people. Sterling's scent isn't one I'll ever forget; If he shows his face, I'll be able to pick it out of the crowd of his people.

Not knowing where he is or where my mate is makes me feel like I might combust and take everyone within a mile out with me. When I almost lost all control an hour ago and plans of tearing the town apart in search of Remi infiltrated my mind, Isabeau had grabbed me by the collar of my shirt before dragging me away like I was a child in trouble. She'd ordered

I pull my shit together and remember that Sterling plays smart, but I was going to have to play smarter.

So instead of ripping this town into tiny pieces, I've stayed put and waited for Sterling to show his hand.

I think I've aged twenty years since she was taken from me and each minute I'm apart from her the anxiety and fear take another year off my life. She's alive, that much I know, but for how much longer? Sterling wouldn't have taken her if he didn't have a plan in mind for her.

I've been leaning against this tree with my eyes closed, counting down the seconds for who knows how long, but the anxious pacing coming from my right finally has me opening my eyes. "You don't have to be here, man," I tell Ryker. "If I knew where my mate was, I'd be with her in a second protecting her myself."

Pruitt is stashed away in a secluded hunting cabin many, many miles away from here. Margot, Whisper, and an enforcer are there with her. She wanted to be part of the fight and be there for her pack, but she needed to prioritize the life of her unborn child. Which we all understood and supported.

"I'm where I need to be." Ryker stops moving to rub his face with a frustrated sigh. "Knowing that doesn't make it any easier, though. I want to protect my pack and get my sister back, but it's torture leaving my pregnant mate behind."

"I get it, dude."

Dropping his hand, he looks at me with an emotion I never thought he'd look at me with. Understanding. Solidarity? "When Nicolai took Pruitt and I didn't know where she was, I've never felt more terrified and helpless in my entire life. My world went dark, and I swear I thought I was dying."

I take low, steady breaths to keep myself under control. "That sounds about right."

"We'll get her back," Ryker promises. "And when we do, you'll never want to let her out of your sight again. You'll be like me and panic when she goes to the grocery store without you. Knowing Rem, she'll fight you every step of the way, but you won't care if she's mad at you because she'll be safe."

"I would give anything to have her be mad at me right now," I admit. I would take a thousand verbal lashings from her if it meant she was back in my arms.

Ryker's tattooed hand squeezes my shoulder. "We'll get her back," he repeats for me, but I think it's for himself too.

There's the faintest rustle of leaves overhead before Isabeau drops from the branches silently. Even when her knee-high, laced-up combat boots hit the dirt ground there isn't a noise. It's small things like this that made her Sterling's favorite.

"I counted just over one hundred and twenty of them," she informs the group of us keeping watch here.

There's more rustling in the trees, this time is much louder and there are a few whispers cursed. Winslow finally emerges from the dense foliage. "Will someone help me down? I don't have super-strength vampire ankles like she does and if I jump, someone will be carrying my crying ass out of these woods."

Ranger stands underneath the branch and raises his arms, motioning for her to jump into them. With a childlike squeal, she drops the five feet or so into his waiting arms. Once on the ground, she straightens her bulletproof vest and beanie on her head. Waving the binoculars she has in her hands, she says, "Something is wrong with those people. They look weird."

"You try growing up in a ten by ten foot, medical-grade jail cell while constantly being poked and prodded at the whim of a man who wants to use you as a weapon and tell me you wouldn't be a little weird," I respond dryly.

Winslow ponders something for a second before asking innocently, "I was tied to a bed, starved and drugged while a priest my grandmother hired performed an exorcism on me. Is that kind of the same thing?"

"Yeah, because you definitely came out of it fucking weird."

"I swear to God, this family is going to go broke paying for therapy," Ryker mumbles while rubbing his face with his hands exasperatedly.

"What do you mean they look weird, Winnie?" Ransom asks.

"There's something wrong with their eyes. It's like the lights are on but no one is home, if that makes sense. It reminds me of the patients that were overmedicated at the hospital. Or even the ones who got a *skosh* too much electric shock therapy."

Ranger looks at me like I am somehow the one with all the answers. "Does Sterling drug his people?"

I shrug my shoulders. "Not that I know of, but what do I know? It's been a long time since I was in the know on everything."

Beau pipes in, "She's right, something isn't right. They're too still. If they were just released from being captive all these years, they should be pretty fidgety. Nervous even, but they're standing perfectly still."

We all fall silent as we think over our options. It stays that way until Winslow, whose attention is suddenly on her chipped black nail polish, offhandedly throws out, "They could be spelled. Hexed even."

All eyes turn on her and when she brings her nail up to her mouth to chew off a piece of polish, she freezes in place and her two-toned eyes widen when she finds us all looking at her. "What? What'd I do?" She tucks her hands behind her back. "Why are you looking at me like that?"

"Why would you guess they're hexed?" Ranger asks.

"Probably because I was just reading one of Esme's journals about hexes, so it's just fresh in my mind." Esme is Winslow's aunt and the high priestess of this region. She's arguably the most powerful witch in America.

Ryker looks to the witch next to him. "How do you know for sure if someone is hexed? Is there a test or something we can do to find out?"

"You'd need to look at their palms and the bottom of their feet," Winslow answers like it's just an ordinary thing to say. When Beau passes her an incredulous look, Winnie scoffs, "Don't look at me like that. It's a real thing. If Sterling has hexed them to keep control over them, that means he would have cast an ascendency hex. To use those, you have to carve the spell into the palms or feet. It's how you control their movements. Think of them as his puppets and he's now pulling the strings. He would have needed a fairly strong witch to do something like that though."

Smirking, I nod my chin toward Winslow. "It's a good thing we know a high priestess then," I tell her before turning and walking away from the group. "Call Esme!" I holler over my shoulder.

"Where are you going?"

"I'm going to go snag me one of the weirdos across the way."

☾

Winslow was right. They're hexed.

It was fairly easy work grabbing one of Sterling's soldiers. I'd flashed in behind them and grabbed one of the ones loitering in the back. Before they could yell or move, I had my hand over their mouth and I was dragging them into the tree line, out of sight. The whole event took less than five seconds, but in that short time, I could still feel the power radiating off the large group of people. Sterling is a sick fuck, but he knows how to create powerful people. Like yours truly.

Now, back on our side of the territory fence, we have the young kid—he can't be more than fifteen—tied up and in the back of Ranger's gray SUV. He still wears all-white clothes that were customary at Sterling's facilities. The fit and style are similar to a pair of medical scrubs, but the material is softer than that. All of the captives that are here tonight are wearing them.

Isabeau, Ransom, and Ryker had stayed in the trees while the rest of us left to meet Esme up on the back road so she could examine him.

Imagine what a stereotypical psychic palm reader would look like and that's Esme. The flowing patterned skirts, the loose blouses and colorful shawls. She always has multiple bracelets on her wrists that make noise every time she moves, and she even has been known to wear charms and feathers in her hair. She looks like she should be selling homemade goat's milk soap at a farmer's market in New Mexico next to a man swearing his crystals cure cancer.

The high priestess parks her yellow vintage Volkswagen bug before hurrying across the road to us. "You think Sterling is dabbling in hexes now?"

"I don't think he is." Winslow grabs for the boy's restrained hands. I can smell the coyote shifter on him. Silver should affect a normal coyote shifter, but who knows what Sterling has made this kid invulnerable to. Just to be sure. I'd filled him with enough hellfire to keep him passed out. She exposed the boy's palms to Esme. "I know he is. Ascendency hex, right?"

Esme takes her reading glasses from the top of her mess of curly hair and drops them onto the end of her nose. "Well, I'll be damned. I haven't seen one of these in a long time. You're absolutely right, Winnie. This is an ascendency hex, it's been modified so it can work across a large group of people, but it works the same way. As long as the hex is in place, their master is in charge of them."

"How do we remove it?"

"The easiest way is to kill the one they're enslaved to, but seeing as that's easier said than done, the next choice would be to contain it before we can reverse it."

"Okay, if we can't get to Sterling, how do we contain it?"

Esme ponders over the question for a second before snapping her fingers as an answer comes to her. "A binding circle should do the trick."

I blink blandly at her when she doesn't offer any further explanation. "I'm sorry, some of us only have two ounces of warlock blood in them and magic is still pretty foreign to them. What the hell is a binding circle."

"Think of it as a vortex of sorts where magic ceases to exist." Esme makes a circular motion with her finger. "I'll cast my own spell in a fairly large area and once the hexed ones step foot into the circle, any magic in their system, whether it's their own or someone else's will stop working. The binding can't be broken until the original caster" —she points at herself— "me. Drops the shield. Once they cross that line they're stuck. Almost like magic magnets, theirs will adhere to the spell I cast, and it'll keep them in place until I say otherwise."

"Why don't we use this more often?" Ranger looks at the high priestess like she's been holding back on us.

"It only works on witches and people affected by a witch's magic. I wouldn't be able to bind any old wolf shifter or a vampire inside one."

"Gotcha."

"It's only going to work tonight because all of those people are hexed and have magic in their systems."

"This all sounds like a great plan, but how the hell do we get them inside the binding circle?" Winslow asks, her arms crossed. The bulky gear looks out of place on her petite body. "Are we going to set it up around them while they're just standing there?"

"You have to walk into a binding circle, one can't be formed around you."

"Okay, so we herd them inside?" Ranger questions.

I grin excitedly at him. "We use bait."

CHAPTER THIRTY-THREE
Jay

"When you said bait, I didn't think you meant us, you asshole," Ranger growls unhappily at me as we prepare for all hell to break loose.

"Did I leave that part out?" I cock my head to the side. "My bad. It's just a good thing you're fast because this is about to get hairy."

Isabeau cuts me a look as she swings a large gun over her shoulder. "That's putting it mildly. This is like poking a hornet's nest."

"I'm not *poking* anything," I scoff. "I'm sticking a bar of C4 in it and blowing it up. It's different." Okay, I'm not actually blowing it up, but I want Sterling to think we are.

Just like we are waiting for Sterling to make a move, we've deducted that he's waiting for us to do the same. And like I said, I'm tired of waiting and doing nothing. My mate is out there, and I need to get to her. For me to do that, I need Sterling to show his hand.

So, we're forcing the issue.

"Is Winslow all set?" I ask Ranger.

"She's up in a tree by the binding circle." I don't miss the slight grimace when he says, "She'll take care of any of them that don't go inside like we planned." It's easier for some to accept that sometimes in this world, we don't have any other choice but to kill. It's something Isabeau and I came to terms with early on.

"This is how we get your sister back," I remind him. *My mate back.* "And Winslow isn't alone out there. Most of the pack is there with her."

Only a handful are the lucky ones who get to be the bait.

"If you're fast in your wolf form, shift now. You're going to want to outrun these fuckers," I tell the people around me. On top of a few enforcers and other pack members, Ransom and Ranger are with me. Ryker is back at the location where Esme cast the binding circle. Like Winslow, he's in charge of either forcing people inside or eliminating the ones who get away.

Like always, Isabeau has the very important job of pulling the trigger tonight. "Ready, Beau?"

She has her feet planted and gun pressed into her shoulder as she looks through the scope at her target. "One sec."

"I just don't understand why we aren't shooting them. They're just standing there like sitting ducks," an enforcer I've never talked to complains to his buddy at his side, but the remark isn't missed.

"There are two reasons we're doing it this way," I tell him as I spin on my heels to face him. "First, we're trying to avoid as much bloodshed as possible. I don't know about you, but I think enough of your pack has died this year. There are about fifty more of Sterling's people here than I expected which means we are outnumbered. The more people we get into that binding circle the bigger chance we have at a fair fight. The second thing is not all of these people are going to be soulless monsters. Sure, some of them are beyond help, but if we can spare even a few of Sterling's creations, I vote we do it. No one deserves that life." I didn't used to be into second chances, but after Remi gave me one, I feel more inclined to do the same for others. "If you're worried you're not going to be able to fight, I wouldn't get too bent out of shape about it. Blood is going to be spilled tonight, don't you worry." With that, I return my attention back to the vampire. "Ready?"

"Ready," she responds calmly. "Everyone clear on what they need to do?" There's a chorus of confirmations before Beau nods her head. "Three... two... one."

At a speed that is too fast for the human eyes to track, Isabeau shoots off five rounds at five different targets. As each bullet hits its target, the night is filled with deafening explosions. Sterling isn't the only one who likes explosives. Isabeau also has a knack for them.

Using her power to walk through shadows, Isabeau had snuck over the territory fence to where the enemy was waiting patiently for us and planted five packs of C4 in various places.

Our thought is Sterling will assume we've thrown the first punch and he'll release the hold he has on his minions and the battle will begin.

With each explosion, the battle-like cries that come from his soldiers get louder as they are woken from their motionless state. The ground beneath us rattles as they charge through our fences and in our direction.

As their yells get louder, I can't help the morbid laugh that escapes me. I feel like I'm in a war movie and the enemy is charging at me with their muskets raised.

Ranger passes me an unamused look. "You really are twisted."

I salute him muckily before bringing my finger to my lips and whistling at the people around me. "Run!"

As a unit, we take off through the woods. Weaving and darting between the trees. The sound of our feet and paws digging in the earth is overshadowed by the roar of people following behind us.

If I wanted to, I could easily outrun all of them by miles, but I want them to follow me. I want to stay just close enough to tease them and make them think they're going to get to me, but really, I'm just out of arm's reach.

The binding circle was set up in a large, rounded clearing the pack usually uses as a pack meeting place during pack runs. The space is vast enough that we will have space if things go south.

"We're almost there!" Beau yells back at me, her black curtain of hair blowing behind her. "I can see the lights."

Watching Esme create the circle was an interesting sight to behold. She'd used an ornate, ritualistic knife to slice the palm of her hand before placing eight black stones around the parameter of the clearing. The stones were pitch black, making me wonder if they were onyx. These are questions I'll ask another time if given the chance.

Esme had walked around each of the perfectly spaced stones and whispered something I couldn't quite make out. I'm not even positive it was in English. While she chanted, blood from her hand poured over the stones. She did this eight times. When she was done with the eighth one, a glowing line, almost like a laser shot out of it, one by one, the pale orange line connected to each of the stones until there was a glowing circle shining on the ground.

In my peripheral vision, I see one of the hexed soldiers dart out of the horde of people. Her arm is outstretched in front of her as she picks up an immense amount of speed. Her nails have turned into talon-like claws as she reaches for the pack member running ahead of her.

"Beau!" I call out, getting the vampire's attention. She's closer than I am.

In a flash, she's pulled a throwing knife from her thigh and is hurling it toward the attacker. I look away before I see where it lands, but I don't have to look to know that Beau hit her target. She never misses.

The lights up ahead get brighter and with a last push of energy, we sprint toward them before abruptly moving to either side of the circle. The first wave of hexed soldiers don't have enough time to turn or change course. They skid across the glowing line on the ground one by one.

Forty or so of them are inside before the screaming and the yelling begins as they quickly discover they've been trapped inside. They run and bang against an imaginary shield, trying to get out, but it's no use.

As more are caught inside the circle, the pack members emerge from the shadows of the woods all around us. The looks on their faces tell you exactly what you need to know. This is their land, these are their people and they're going to defend each other and their home with their last dying breath.

It doesn't take long for the remaining hexed that are at the back of the horde to learn to not cross the line. They try to get their comrades out of the circle, but the shield doesn't budge.

Low growls cut through the night as their glossed-over

eyes bounce between all of the pack members now standing around.

As if it were planned, each opposing side barrels at each other at the same time and when they collide, it's like thunder booming as bodies slam together.

I knew this would be chaos, but to be in the middle of the madness is another thing. There are bodies and people everywhere. Claws and fangs of all different sizes are cutting through flesh. People are hollering in pain and others are shouting in victory as they take down their opponent.

I want to take pity on these people because under different circumstances, I could have been one of the ones out here forced to fight. Unlike the people who are coming at us like they're deranged, I know what it's like to be outside the confines of the ten-by-ten cells. I know what it's like to feel love and be loved. None of these people have that.

But if I take too much pity, everyone is going to end up dead. In the end, we need to survive if we're going to get any of these people help, so when they come at me with their claws drawn or power zapping from their fingertips, I show no mercy. I fight through them, taking down one after the other until my body is dripping in blood that doesn't belong to me.

Hot poker-like nails slice down my back while I'm busy breaking the neck of another demon. Roaring in pain, I drop the dead demon and face my newest attacker. The girl in front of me has her claws drawn and just like the paws of my wolf, they flicker with embers. I know without a shadow of a doubt that the girl in front of me is one of Sterling's failed attempts to recreate what he made with me.

"There can only be one," I tell the girl before my hand

grabs the back of her head and my palm slams into her mouth. Her screams of pain are muffled against my hand as I force hellfire down her throat. Her limp body joins the other demons.

I turn around to find my next opponent and find that one has already found me. A large muscular man with hair that hangs in his eyes is barreling toward me. I plant my feet and prepare for impact, but it never comes. When he's three feet away, a sharp blade *whooshes* right past my ear and into this guy's forehead.

Isabeau emerges from the chaos. Just like me, she's covered in blood, but unlike her usual calm demeanor, her features are overtaken with concern. She steps over a dead body and grabs my arm in a vise grip. "Jax!" she hollers over the battle. "We have to go."

"What?" I yell back as I slam my fist into someone fast before gripping their shoulder and filling them to the brim with hellfire.

"Sterling's not down here."

"I *know* that." I bend down and yank the knife she'd thrown from the large man's forehead. I toss it a few times in my hand before I send it flying across the space. Twenty feet away from me, it embeds into the throat of the woman Ryker is fighting. The tattooed wolf shifter turns my way and nods his thanks before continuing on.

"He's not down here, because he's up there." Isabeau's cold hand grips my arm and roughly turns me in the direction of the cliffs where Remington had screamed until she had nothing left. It feels like a lifetime ago. "I picked up his scent and I can hear them. They're up there."

I narrow my eyes in the direction of the dark cliffs,

searching for a hint of life or movement somewhere within them. It takes a second, but then I spot it. The faint dancing flame of a fire. It's as if he's signaling me, beckoning me to him.

Isabeau catches my arm when I step forward and begin to let my power wash over me. "Wait for me, Jax," she orders. "It'll only take me a few moments to get up there. Don't do anything stupid before then."

Don't do anything stupid, I swear those words are the kiss of death.

"I'm not waiting for you," I snap, pulling my arm away from her. "My mate is up there and I'm tired of fucking waiting."

Hold on, love. I'm coming for you.

CHAPTER THIRTY-FOUR
Jax

Facing the man responsible for all my nightmares while he's busy creating a new one in front of me is a special kind of hell. This new nightmare is even more terrifying than the one that's plagued me for over a decade. Even if I do make it out of this alive, I'm not sure I'm ever going to be the same. The sight of Remington, wrapped in silver chains and standing on the very edge of the cliffside with helplessness in her stormy eyes is an image I will see every time I close my eyes from now on.

As well as the smirking and scarred face of my father. There were always whispers about Sterling's burns, but I never saw them for myself. I always assumed they would have healed over time. Now that I'm seeing him for the first time in sixteen years, I find that he looks just as bad as when I first burned him.

He's aged pretty exponentially in those years as well, but the dark cloud that's always lingered around him has grown. It doesn't matter what age he is, as long as that dark cloud of evilness is alive and strong, he will be too.

"Remington," I call her name but keep my eyes on the

predator in front of me. I'm aware of William standing like a captor near Remi. It's like he's been tasked with watching over her. A useless task given the only place she could go is down. So, so far down. "Talk to me, baby. Tell me you're alright."

I know she's not alright, but I need her to tell me it anyway. Blood is dried on her pretty face and the skin around her eyes is bruised black and blue. She's pale and wobbly on her feet because of the silver chains she's wrapped in. "I'm okay." While I'm relieved to hear her voice, it does little to soothe the storm building inside of me.

"Of course, she's okay, I *barely* touched a single hair on her head," Sterling scoffs. His voice sounds different from how I remember it sounding, but if I had to guess, the burns are hindering his normal voice patterns. "But you know that quick temper you have? You inherited it from me."

"Thank God you didn't inherit any of his looks," Remi pipes in. Even in the worst of times, she's sarcastic. I'm relieved to hear it because as long as she's making those comments, she's fighting and she's here with me.

"Do you ever stop talking?" Sterling growls at her.

"Honestly? No."

Sterling gestures at William, a silent command transpiring between them. William nods once before taking a step toward Remi. Out of instinct, she shifts her body away from him, forgetting where she's standing. She wobbles in place and before I'm able to fully lift my foot off the ground to go to her, Sterling is raising his hand and *tsking* at me. "I wouldn't do that if I were you," he warns darkly. "If you take so much as one step in her direction or try using your hellfire to get to her, I will have William push her over before you have time to open your mouth to cry her name."

I grit my teeth and force myself to stay put as I watch Remi finally stop swaying. My palms are itching as the burn of my hellfire sets in. My chest feels tight as if something heavy is sitting on it, restricting my air. My wolf is going absolutely insane inside me. He's ramming against his metal cage with a force I've never felt before. With each hit, I can feel the metal crack and his chains loosen. For the first time ever, I don't feel the overwhelming sensation of shame or dread as he surges to the surface. For the first time ever, I need him. *She* needs him.

I have to pry my gaze away from her so I can return my attention to Sterling. I can't stop my eyes from roaming around his damaged face. The light from the torch they'd placed in the ground illuminates the carnage. Each imperfection and scar I left on his body are things I'm proud to have left. "I made myself a promise when I first left those scars on your body. I swore to myself that one day I was going to finish the job. I vowed that I would one day burn you so bad that there was nothing left of you but your corrupted bones. That was the price you were going to pay for killing my mother," I darkly tell him as white hot, angry power begins to seep from my pores. "But now that you've gone and touched my mate, I've decided that burning you alive would be too easy. It'd be a fucking mercy, and you and I both know you don't deserve that."

Sterling chuckles under his breath while shaking his head. "If you were to burn me alive, you would first need to conjure the flames of hell." His one soulless eye assesses me. "Tell me, Jax, have you been able to use the flames since you did this to me?"

"I don't need to use hellfire to burn you again."

"I suppose." His fucked-up mouth pulls in a cruel smile. "Though it would be more effective." Sterling shifts forward a few feet, but I hold my ground. "You had so much potential. I paved the road for you to become strong and ruthless, but all I see is the same little boy who cried for his mom. You've allowed trivial things like love and loyalty to weaken you. Your threats hold no weight when you're spewing that at me because of *her*." His gloved hand waves in Remington's direction.

She stands as still as possible on the edge of the rocky ledge. All it would take is one strong gust of wind or a small hiccup for our world to come caving in as she fell.

"You're wrong, Sterling. My threats mean something because of her. You created me and gave me life, but you are not the reason I still breathe. My desire for vengeance fueled me for a long time, but not anymore. If you take the reason I live away from me, I will kill you over and over again. I will make Kaius bring you back each time, only for me to kill you in a new and painful way. I will do this until you're the one begging to be set free. You will be the one begging for the sweet relief of death. You will regret the day you ever created me, and you will regret all the times you called me special!" My voice comes out like an angry roar as I begin to shake with rage.

Sterling begins to slowly pull the leather gloves from his hands. Finger by finger, he pulls at them before he's tossing them to the side. His right hand looks just like his face, burned and a mangled mess. From what I remember, his whole right side was burned.

"Do you remember what I told you happens to people that are no longer of use to me?" He asks surprisingly calmly as if he'd completely missed my outburst and warning. "You stopped being of use to me when you betrayed Nicolai and let Pruitt and her little pack kill him. The second you chose the Weylyns over me and my goals, you became useless to me. The second you started using your powers to assist the people who wanted to see me ruined, you became useless to me." Walking toward my mate, he tells me over his shoulder with a smile. "Remington was useful to me for only one specific thing, and now that she's played her role perfectly, I no longer see a reason to keep her around."

You know in movies when time slows to a crawl and sound becomes distorted, like it's coming from many miles away? That's what happens when he moves toward her, his scarred hand reaching for her.

I know I'm running at her at full speed, but as my world stops spinning and my heart stops beating in my chest, my legs feel as if they've been filled with lead and the dirt beneath my boots feels like quicksand slowing me down.

The constant noise of my wolf in my head falls silent and for a second, he ceases to exist. For the first time since I can remember, I'm alone in my cold, dark soul. I'm alone as I try to get to her.

I know William is still standing by somewhere, but he melts away into the shadows just like everything else. All I can see is her and her big, round scared eyes. Her lips move, words are said to me, but I can't hear them over the deafening silence in my head. But I still know what she said. I know it in my bones because the same words are on the tip of my tongue, but I've lost the ability to form words as my new nightmare comes true.

I love you.

The three little words that had the ability to fix my broken and battered soul are ripping me apart now. I always said she had the ability to cut me with her words, but those three little words are slashing deep, and I know now I'll never be able to heal from these wounds. They're fatal.

Before his scarred hand can touch her chest, her eyes flutter closed as if she's not strong enough to watch as it happens. I want to look away too, but I can't. I want to protect my mind from the horrifying sight, but I've never been able to look away from her. Now is no different.

Her hair billows around her head as the wind whips around her body as she falls in slow motion. Like an angel with broken wings, she falls from the sky and there's nothing I can do but watch as the owner of my heart and healer of my soul disappears from sight.

Like a rubber band being snapped, everything goes back to normal speed and my senses return, but I really wish they wouldn't have. I wish I never had to know what her screams sounded like as she fell or the heart-stopping, gut-wrenching and horrifying sound of her hitting the ground below.

I thought I knew pain, but it turns out that the pain I've felt up to this point has all been practice for the day I had to feel as the hallowed bond between me and my mate is ripped into ugly shreds.

It's a sick game the universe plays allowing a mate to live on without the other. No one should have to experience this kind of pain. If there was a God, he'd never allow mates to die apart. In life, we were tethered together. It should be the same in death.

As the bond disintegrates into ashes inside of me, my body gives out and I fall to my knees on the ledge she had *just* been standing on.

I can't breathe at first. The pain is so excruciating. It's the kind of pain that can't be eased or helped. I am forced to feel each and every excruciating second as I'm ripped apart. I realize as my body is so overcome with pain that it doesn't feel like mine anymore, that this is what people mean when they say hellfire causes soul-deep pain.

This is the kind of pain I've inflicted on others and now that I know, I truly don't know how they've survived it. Even if what I've done to others feels a quarter as bad as this feels, they should have died.

I want to die.

I want to jump over the edge with her.

I want to be with her.

I sit on my heels with my hands in my lap as my head drops back on my shoulders. Unable to hold it in any longer, a strangled scream rips through my chest and through the night air. In this moment, I don't care that Sterling or William are watching as I unravel into nothing. I allow myself to break and to feel the pain they've caused because I'm going to let it fuel me. The pain, the anger and the devastation are going to make me strong enough to kill them.

Remi is waiting for me, but I'm not leaving this world behind with Sterling still walking on it. I always said that no matter what, I'd find a way to kill Sterling, even if it ended up killing me. I was always okay with the possibility but now I'm at peace with it.

Either way, I will be reunited with my mate.

My scream dies when my voice becomes hoarse, and my lungs run out of air. Dejectedly, I hang my head as I resign myself for what's to come.

"What an absolutely disgusting show of emotion." Sterling clicks his tongue in disapproval. His voice flips a switch inside of me. The cold tendrils of grief that have encompassed me are slowly taken over by fiery, hot anger and stone-clad determination. "You should be embarrassed by that little display," he signs like he's at a complete loss for words. "I always wondered what your weakness was going to be, but I never would have guessed it would be a *girl*. Though, based on how you just... *crumbled*... I should have gotten rid of her sooner. Would have saved me a lot of headaches."

My palms start to heat as fire burns in my veins. Keeping my head dropped, I snarl darkly. "I warned you." My voice still sounds rough from the outpouring of emotion. My wolf chews away the remaining restraints and with each passing second, I can feel him rise closer to the surface. "I warned you what would happen if you took her from me."

"And I warned you even as a child what would happen if you turned on me." Sterling's response is cold and disconnected. "Get him off the ground," he orders William.

These two men, both of which I'm related to by blood, have shown me no mercy or decency and I'm about to return the favor.

William steps forward to follow his father's orders. Just as his fingers brush against the material of my shirt, I'm turning into a cloud of smoke. Reappearing behind him, I lock eyes with Sterling as I place my hands around William's skull. "I warned you," I repeat slowly.

Power burns in my palms as I push hellfire into my half brother's body. The air around me begins to hum and my chest rattles as the power grows strong inside of me. Stronger than I've ever felt it before. I feel like the sun is inside of my chest, expanding my ribs and burning me.

William screams as he's taken over by hellfire. My arms and hands tremble as waves and waves of power shoot out of them. It's like a seal has been broken and I'm tapping into a power source I didn't know that I had. William's body begins to shake and convulse. When he drops to his knees, I keep my hands firmly planted on him.

A faint light, like an ember coming to life starts to form on my palms. Similar to a single spark setting off a wildfire, a single ember is all it takes before the flames return.

William's cries fall silent, but he still shakes as the fire speeds through his bloodstream and nerves. He begins to turn bright red like he's been sunburned and cracks form in his skin. In the lines are more embers. Like the cracks in lava.

He's heated from the inside out to a temperature I've never been able to achieve before. William makes a gurgling sound in his throat a few times before blood pours out of his mouth and nose.

His skin bubbles and blisters before all but melting off his body. It's not a pretty sight, but it's one that I revel in. William is finally paying the price for the roles he played.

When the body finally completely catches fire, I stay put and allow the flames to build around me. They don't hurt me but they immediately burn the ground around us before spreading out.

Dropping the remains of his son, I raise my hands to be sure he can see what's happening. Like torches had been lit on my hands, flames shoot out of my palms and fingers. "You wanted me to control the flames of hell," I remind him. "Looks like you've finally gotten your wish."

With a roar, I let go of everything and let the anger take over. Like an explosion going off, flames explode from my body. It takes less than a second for the surrounding area to go up in flames. Like a virus, it spreads through the forest, setting tree after tree aflame. The ground is alive with fire as it eats through everything without remorse. Nothing is safe in its path of destruction, just like no one is safe in mine.

Smoke billows in the air around us as the world burns. It blocks out any of the light coming from the moon or stars. The bright orange flames light my way now.

Spreading my arms wide, I manipulate and push the flames until my enemy stands in the middle of a circle with me. Flames eight feet tall surround us and lock us inside together. I want Sterling to know he has nowhere to run.

I want him to know that he's trapped with no way out. Just like he's made so many other people feel.

Any other person would be cowering and searching for a way out, but not Sterling. He's too proud to allow his worry or concern show on his face. He may not show it, but beneath the scent of smoke, I can smell the faint tinge of his fear.

I grin at this because right now, Sterling is learning what I've always known. His creations, his ideas of perfection aren't the things that are going to save him. They're the things that are going to destroy him.

"Look at what you've created," I roar above the sound of flames. "Are you proud of me now, Sterling? Am I still *special*?"

Sterling's torn lips pull in an evil grin. His remaining eye begins to glow as his own wolf pushes forward. His fangs elongate, one is more prominent due to the missing portion of his mouth. "I should have killed you when I killed your mother, but I'll settle for doing it now."

His wolf rips from his skin with an angry howl.

Just like his human side, the wolf is equally as burned and mangled. The burns cover half of the large wolf's body. The flesh on the right side of his muzzle is nonexistent. All of his sharp teeth are exposed. Drool drips from his mouth onto the ground as he lowers his head and growls at me.

I grin to myself because Sterling is about to meet another one of his creations and this one is more vicious than I'll ever be. My wolf's ruthlessness is exactly what I need right now. His blind range and unwavering bloodlust will finally be something I don't look at with contempt.

I laugh darkly as I embrace my wolf and allow him to take over. I willingly and happily take the back seat and give him all the control. I won't remember what happens, but the next time I'm conscious Sterling will be dead, or I'll be reunited with Remington.

Both options are acceptable.

CHAPTER THIRTY-FIVE
Remington

The sun is warm on my skin and the breeze blows softly across my face. My eyes are closed, but there are birds chirping and leaves rustle in the trees as the wind blow through them. The ground that I lay on is soft and the hand that runs through my hair is comforting.

It's peaceful here.

I feel safe and warm, like everything is going to be okay.

A stark contrast to what I felt as I fell from the cliff. I didn't mean to scream. I wanted to be strong, but it tore from my chest before I could stop it. Poor Jax, he shouldn't have had to watch that.

I didn't feel anything as I hit the ground. I was falling and then I was here, in this warm paradise where everything feels like it's going to be okay. My eyes stay closed because I'm afraid the second I open them, the feeling of being at peace will be ripped away. I just want a minute longer to feel this instead of the pain I know will come when I finally accept what's happened.

I left Jax behind.

We promised what we had was forever and I left him

before we had our forever. It wasn't supposed to end this way, we were supposed to grow old and happy at each other's side.

We barely had any time and it's not fair.

I don't want to face just how unfair it is, so I'll keep my eyes closed and continue to feel at peace.

The hand stops running through my hair as a soft voice says my name, "Remington." I squeeze my eyes shut tighter and fight to ignore them. "You have to open your eyes, little bird."

Little bird.

I haven't been called that in over fifteen years, not since...

Recognition shoots through me and my eyes fly open to stare into familiar green eyes. She looks just as I remember her. I haven't seen her since I was eight years old, but it's like no time has passed for her. She's forever preserved the way she was when she died. "*Genevieve.*"

Pruitt's mom and my old alpha female smiles softly down at me. With my eyes open now, I discover my head is resting in her lap. "I can't believe what a beautiful young woman you've become. That *both* of you have become." I know without having to ask she's talking about her daughter. Her small smile falls as her eyes search my face. "You're not supposed to be here, little bird."

Her little birds, that's what she used to call Pru and I when we were little girls. She said it was because we were constantly flitting about.

Sitting up, I look around the space. We sit in a bright, sunny clearing. Purple flowers have blossomed all around us. It's beautiful, but something feels off. There's a coldness hiding just beneath the sunshine that's fighting to get in.

"This is it? Is this the afterlife?" I question. I don't know what I was expecting, but a forest that looks just like the one at home wasn't it.

"No." Gen shakes her head. "It's not. Think of this as the in-between. A waiting room before you move on."

"Why am I here?" I ask before I grimace and shake my head. "I know *why* I'm here. I died." *I'm dead.* That knowledge makes every nerve in my body burn with remorse. I'm dead and Jax is alone. "But why am I here in limbo? Why are you here with me? Shouldn't you be with Archer?"

Gen's face softens at the mention of her beloved mate. "Don't worry. Archer is with me. So is Addison and Noah. They're all waiting for me on the other side. I'm just here to keep you company until you go." She reaches out and smooths her hand down the side of my face tenderly.

"What do you mean *go*?"

She looks around the clearing. "This is all only temporary. Like I said, you're not supposed to be here. It'll all be over soon, little bird."

I stand to my feet, and she follows suit. "Where am I supposed to be?"

Genevieve just looks at me before placing a gentle hand on my shoulder. "I'm ashamed that this has all happened because of my family. I wish I could be there fighting with you all, but I'm proud of each and every one of you. You've all been braver and stronger than I ever could have," she says instead of answering my question.

"You've been watching us?"

She nods. "I look over you all when I can. It's been a blessing to watch each of you grow into the people you are now. My daughter..." She trails off like she can't find the words. "She's amazing," she finally utters.

I knew that Pruitt resembled her mom, but seeing Genevieve now, I didn't realize just how much they looked alike. Gen's blonde hair is tied into a long braid over her shoulder similar to how Pru frequently wears hers. Their eyes are the same shape and color. They both have the same high cheekbones I would knock Pru over the head to have. And they both have that warm, calming aura around them that makes you feel safe.

"Yeah, she is," I agree solemnly. "She's become a great alpha, but I have a feeling she'll be an even better mom."

Gen's face lights up at the mention of Pru's child.

The blue sky above us makes a loud noise similar to thunder. I jump in surprise, but Gen stays completely still like she knew it was going to happen. Tilting my chin, I watch as the blue sky bleeds away as darkness begins to seep in.

"What's happening?" I ask. The warm breeze cools, causing goose bumps to develop on my skin as it blows around us.

"Everything will be okay," Gen reassures me as there's another boom followed by a cracking sound. It sounds like glass is breaking. Staring at the alarmingly dark and thunderous sky, I watch as black cracks begin to form among the stormy clouds.

"No, something is definitely wrong." Can't she feel the eerie chill in the air?

"Sometimes darkness isn't always bad. Sometimes it's just righting a wrong," she comments vaguely as she watches me with knowing eyes.

The leaves that had been vibrant green just minutes ago slowly turn black before dissolving into dust. The purple flowers that had reminded me of Jax's eyes, also rot away into black nothingness.

Everything that was thriving and alive around us slowly disintegrates as darkness eats it. The wind picks up the black dust, making it swirl around us and stick to the white clothes we wear.

Genevieve remains calm and still, like she's oblivious to the sky literally cracking above our heads. "Genevieve! What's happening? We need to leave." *But go where?* I have no idea. I grab her hand and tug her. I don't know where I'm going to go but standing here watching everything fall apart doesn't seem wise.

Like a piece of stone, she's unmovable when I pull her. She pulls her hands from me. "No, you need to leave," she explains before stepping forward and wrapping her arms around me. Despite the chaos and darkness growing around us, her embrace fills me with light and that sense of peace I first felt when I got here. "You're not finished there, Remington. There are so many things that you need to do before you join us on the other side."

"I don't understand."

A disjointed voice begins to whisper in the wind. I try to find the source, but it's coming from all over. I can't understand what it's saying, but the longer it talks, the more the air around us begins to hum.

"Your time here is done. It's time for you to go."

The sky cracks again above us and the trees without their leaves begin to fall to the ground.

"It's time for you to go back," Genevieve whispers into my ear. "Let go of the things holding you down and allow yourself to be happy. Love when you can and love hard, because you deserve it, my girl." Her hand smooths down my back. "He's a good one, and I'm so happy you found him. You're going to live such an epic life with him."

My body begins to shake as foreign energy rushes through my bones. I gasp and my knees tremble. Genevieve's arms keep me standing. I try to talk but my body refuses to cooperate. My vision becomes hazy and dark and there's a buzzing in my ears.

Before everything goes dark and I feel like I'm falling again, I hear her whisper in my ear, "Tell my granddaughter I'm watching over her."

☾

COMING BACK TO LIFE IS HARDER THAN DYING. I DIDN'T FEEL anything when I died, but I feel everything as my body fills with life once again. My heart pounds wildly in my chest as my blood starts to circulate once more and my lungs heave painfully when I gasp for my first breath.

It's a jarring and abrupt experience that leaves you feeling rattled. Then again, it's something that shouldn't be done and therefore it shouldn't be a pleasant event. No one is softly coaxed back from the dead, they're violently torn away from whatever their afterlife was and thrown back into their body.

My eyes fly open and when I see the black, singed trees without their leaves, I think I'm back with Genevieve, but when Winslow's face leans over me and her teary eyes meet mine, I know I'm back.

"She's alive." Her voice comes out a hoarse cry, her bottom lip wobbling as she calls out to someone standing behind her. Her small, shaking hands grip either side of my face. "Thank God, I was about to be so mad at you."

Dread fills my chest as I stare at her. "Winnie, you *didn't*." If she was the one who brought me back, it means she gave up another piece of her soul. She can't afford to do that. It will destroy her. "Tell me you didn't bring me back. You know what the cost is."

Winslow shakes her head. "I didn't do it. I almost did it, but I didn't have to. "Her eyes dart somewhere off to the side, looking at something I can't see.

Groaning, I slowly pull myself into a sitting position. My recently repaired bones feel stiff when I move. All around us are burned trees, glowing embers still flicker in places. The scent of smoke is heavy in the air, making me cough as I choke on it. Off in the distance, I see bright orange flames dancing as they burn everything in their path.

Waving a hand in front of me, I try to disperse some of the smoke, but it's no use. As I cough again, my eyes finally lock on a familiar face everyone said I'd never see again.

He grins excitedly at me, his hand twisting on the top of his ornate cane. "I told you that you'd see me soon," Kaius tells me. "Did you not believe me?"

He tries to take a step forward, but the vampire that has apparently been holding him at gunpoint makes a warning noise. "Stay where you are," Isabeau snarls at him.

Her arctic eyes flick in my direction and I don't miss the look of relief in them when she looks at me.

"Kaius," I cough his name. "You did this?"

"Got here just in time." He nods joyfully. "Watching you fall from up there." He whistles low. "Was a magnificent sight to behold. I'd ask you to do it again, but I have a feeling it'd be one of those things that's only exciting the one time. Like when you eat at an amazing restaurant and when you go back, it's not as good as you remember. Kind of lackluster." Beau and Winslow stare at the necromancer with appalled looks. They're not as desensitized to his madness as I am. "Anywho, I came along just as these two did. You should have seen Winslow here try to bring you back." He clicks his tongue in disapproval. "She was doing it all wrong. That could have been disastrous for you both had I not stepped in. Lucky for you, I was able to snatch your own soul before it permanently flitted away to the far beyond." He makes a fluttering wing motion with his hands. That explains why I was in the in-between with Gen. Kaius's magic was keeping my soul tethered. "I wanted to make sure you came back as you and not like one of my other little puppets."

Uneasily, I frown at him. "Why would you do that? Why would you even go through the trouble of bringing me back?"

When I start to pull myself up from the ground to stand, Winslow wraps her arm around my waist and helps pull me onto my shaky legs. Even when I'm standing on my own, she stays close just in case I need more help.

He cocks his head to the side. "We had a deal, Remington. How am I supposed to get what I want and give you what you need if you're dead?" His eyes glance at his daughter. "Plus, I figured I owed my daughter a little gift before I went on my merry way. She was crying and just so distraught, snot was running down her face. It was not a pretty sight. I figured the easiest way to make that stop would be to just bring you back. And I didn't want to share my handkerchief." Kaius smooths a hand over the intricately folded pocket square in the chest pocket of is metallic sports coat.

The one thing that will remain true about Kaius is his motives will always and forever be selfish. He doesn't do anything with the greater good in mind. His actions will only ever serve him.

Winslow just stares at her biological father, but she doesn't say anything. Not that there is really much she could say in response to that.

"I'm flattered," I tell him dryly.

"That's an odd way of saying thank you, don't you think?" Kaius asks with his brows pulled together in confusion.

"You and I both know that you could have just had Jax uphold our end of the deal," I remind him.

"I have found that I enjoy your company quite a bit more," Kaius admits. "It will be such a pleasure and a joy to die by your hands." He pauses and looks around at the growing flames around us. "That is if your mate doesn't burn us all alive first."

"What?" I stutter. "*Jax* started the fire?"

"Yes, it would appear the demon has harnessed the flames just in time to kill us with them," Kaius mumbles.

Isabeau keeps her gun pointed at the necromancer as she turns her attention to me. "I tried to follow after Jax, but I got pinned by two shifters. By the time I was done with them, there were too many flames for me to get past. We all saw you fall, and I tried to get to you, but the flames slowed me down." She gestures toward Winslow. "And this one took off after me even though she was told to stay put."

"I thought I could help," Winslow defends herself. "We lost enough people, and I wasn't going to let anyone else in our family get hurt."

Our family.

They're my family, but they're not my person. I need to get to him. "Where's Jax?" I know he's alive. I felt the mating bond snap back into place when I took my first breath back hearthside. "I need to get to him." I turn around and stare up the cliff I had fallen from. The distance felt like eternity when I was free-falling from it, but it's roughly fifteen stories high if I had to guess. Kaius's magic not only returns souls to their body but repairs the body. I should be a bloody smear in the dirt right now, but I'm whole and in one piece.

"He's still up there," Beau explains. "With Sterling. They're inside the flames. There's no way to get to them without getting burned."

I stare at the flames dancing among the trees. "This is his hellfire?" I ask.

Beau nods her head in confirmation. "If it wasn't, I'd risk jumping the flames to get to Jax. I can heal from burns caused by regular fire, but no one can survive walking through hellfire."

Jax's voice floats through my mind, *hellfire is an extension of me. A piece of me. It can't hurt you because you're a part of me.*

"I can," I announce, determination replaces the stiffness in my bones. "I can touch his hellfire."

Kaius grins at me with a knowing look. "I knew it." He hadn't missed it when I'd accidentally touched him back in Seattle.

"Remington," Winslow says my name warily. "I don't think—"

I cut her off because I don't have time to debate this with her. My mate is up there fighting the man we should be facing together. "Get everyone back to the lake just in case the flames can't be controlled."

"What about the people locked in Esme's circle?" Isabeau asks Winslow. I have no idea what they're talking about, but I have to trust they've had everything under control since I was taken.

"Like Esme said, nothing gets in or out of it until she releases the spell," Winslow answers before looking at her dad with a skeptical look. "What about you? Where are you going?"

"Oh, don't worry about your dear old dad. I'll be close by," he promises with a gleam in his eyes before looking at me. "I want to watch the show for a little while longer."

He starts to walk away but Isabeau cocks her gun, stopping him.

"Let him go," I instruct her.

"You're sure?"

No, I think, but instead, I just nod my head once.

Kaius salutes us all before meandering away, cutting through the various fiery trees.

I wait for him to fully disappear before I look at the women who have become more than my brothers' mates. "I never thought I'd have sisters," I tell them. "But I'm really glad I can now call you mine." I squeeze Winnie's hand because she's closest. "Now, go. Get everyone away from the flames."

CHAPTER THIRTY-SIX
Remington

All your life you're told to not touch fire. As kids, we're dumb and ignore our parents' warning, but we quickly learn that they were right. Like most lessons, we learn it the hard way when we get burned, but we eventually learn.

That's why it's daunting to be standing in front of a wall of flames that burn hotter than the depths of hell. In my gut, I know that they won't hurt me, but the idea of literally walking through fire is something my logical brain screams at me not to do.

Up until this point, I was able to weave around the flames, but now I've reached a point where there is nothing but flames. Everything is burning and somewhere inside these flames is my mate.

Knowing he's in there gives me the final push I need.

Holding my breath, I lift my hand and slowly submerge my fingers into the flames. I still expect to feel pain, but just like when he tested his hellfire on me on the plane, all I feel is warmth and a tingling sensation under my skin. I also feel *him*. His energy.

Releasing the breath I was holding, I take off through the

hellfire. It's disorienting being inside of it, but I keep pushing forward as I climb the incline up to the cliffside Jax and Sterling are on.

I move as fast as I can. A few times my shoes catch on debris I can't see through the fire. By the time I make it up to the top, my palms and knees are scraped from catching myself on the rugged terrain.

There's a break in the flames before I come to a wall of them. I stand examining all eight feet of them. The rest of the flames behave like normal fire, it spreads and moves about, burning everything in its path, but these stay completely in place.

When a pained wolfish yelp comes from behind the wall of flames, I jump into action. I don't know who the sound belongs to, the noise is garbled by the rushing sound of flames, but it doesn't matter. If there's even a chance that it's Jax, nothing is going to stop me from getting to him.

I leap through the wall of fire and land inside what I can only describe as a bloody arena. The ground that was once dirt and grass is now red with spilled blood. The two gladiators that fight in the middle look like something from a nightmare.

I don't know how either of them is still standing. They both look like they've taken a thousand lashes with a whip and were then run over with a semitruck. And then backed over just for good measure. The blonde wolf's right ear is gone, adding to the rest of his disfigured appearance. Deep claw marks are raked across the black wolf's face.

Despite the horror show in front of me, I'm still hit with a wave of relief when I see that my hellhound is still standing.

He's injured, but he's alive and that spark of hope is enough to instantly make my tired soul feel stronger.

Or it did for a second, but when the ungodly looking blond wolf lunges at Jax and sinks his teeth into Jax's shoulder, the hope is replaced by a bloodthirsty vengeance I didn't know I was capable of feeling. "No!" I scream before my wolf flies out of me.

There have been so many times that stress or high emotions have hindered my ability to shift when I need to, but not now. My wolf explodes from my skin with a venomous snarl, the scent of her mate's blood only making her angrier.

Without hesitation or reservation, I barrel into the fray. I want to be able to greet my mate and revel in the fact that we are both here now, but there isn't time for that.

My body slams into the blond wolf, forcing him to release Jax's flesh. We roll on the bloody ground together. Nothing but a mess of legs and fur before coming to a crashing halt near the flames.

I scramble to my feet, not wanting to give him time to get over me and pin me to the ground. While he's still slightly dazed from the hit his body just took, I dive for his throat. My canines embed into the side of his neck. I rejoice and feel triumphant when I taste his blood on my tongue. I lock my jaw and shake my head violently to cause further damage.

He howls in pain and rolls to his back in an attempt to free himself. His paws kick out and try to shove me away. I hold my ground until the claws of his front paws slice across my chest. Pain rips through me, and I'm forced to let go of his neck as I cry out and retreat a step.

Behind me, I'm vaguely aware of the hellhound finally getting to his feet in slow, stiff movements. When he's finally standing, he limps forward a few painful feet, the wound in his shoulder affecting his mobility.

Sterling pulls himself off the ground and lowers his head while snarling. Blood-stained drool drops from his equally stained mouth. I can't tell if it's Jax's blood or from his own wounds. Most likely it's a combination of both. I don't know how long I was hovering in limbo while Kaius put my soul back into my body, but I know Sterling and Jax have been at this a while. Both are hurting and exhausted. Jax always said his wolf was volatile and savage, but Sterling's is too. Sterling also fought dirty by killing me right in front of Jax. That kind of distraction and pain is bound to have an effect on the hellhound.

Doesn't matter now, because I'm here and if Jax and I have proven anything, we're stronger together.

We need to end this.

Now.

I match his snarl with one of my own as I slowly begin to circle him. He follows my lead, watching and waiting for me to make my next move. Both Genevieve and Pruitt are powerful alpha wolves, it's not surprising that Sterling would also be one. He pushes his power out, letting me know he outranks me in the natural order. He wants me to know he's stronger.

I already knew he was stronger, but he doesn't know just how strong my determination is when I set my mind to a goal. He doesn't know the lengths I will go through to keep the people I love safe. As long as he breathes, he's a threat to my family and to the life I want to build with my mate. It simply won't do for him to be allowed to breathe any longer than he has.

A giant, unbelievably warm body brushes up against my side when he joins me in my slow, methodical circling. I want to turn into his body and revel in the sensation of having Jax close, but I force myself to keep moving while watching Sterling's body for any hints at what his next move will be.

Finally, having grown impatient and restless, Sterling dives at me. The hellhound is moving before I know what's happening. He leaps over me and lands on Sterling's back. His paws made of hellfire sear into Sterling's already burned skin as they land in a heap on the ground. Jax gets the advantage and pins the top half of Sterling to the ground. He tries to find an opening to sink his teeth into his opponent's throat or face, but Sterling is able to keep just enough space between them with his thrashing legs.

Diving into the mess, I bite his hind leg. My teeth hit bone, but I continue to add pressure until the bone starts to crack from the force. I rip at his flesh until his leg is nothing but a mangled mess hanging on by a bloody thread.

A sound comes out of Sterling that I can only describe as a scream, even though wolves don't have the ability to do so. I release the leg, planning on moving onto the other one, but stop when I look up and find Jax holding Sterling's marred jaw in his teeth.

He bites down until the bone splinters and is crushed from the hellhound's unforgiving weight.

When Jax lets go of it, it hangs almost completely detached from his body. Blood pours from his mouth and his tongue hangs helplessly out with nothing keeping it in place anymore.

The hellhound backs up until he stands at my side again. He turns his head just enough to lick lovingly at my muzzle before his gaze returns to the broken and quickly weakening enemy in front of us.

I want to stand here and watch as Sterling starts to look less and less like himself and more like roadkill, but we've waited a long time for this moment.

The blond wolf staggers, its mangled back leg making him uneasy on his feet. He stumbles forward but catches himself at the last minute. He's able to hold himself up for a few more seconds before, with a defeated whine, he crumbles into a sitting position.

I cut a quick, confused glance in Jax's direction, but he doesn't look back at me. Instead, he watches as the broken wolf morphs back into the vile man. The pained animal sounds transition into a groan of human agony.

In front of the wall of flames, Sterling sits on his haunches, his broken leg is at an unnatural angle. His jaw hangs limply from his already destroyed face and blood pours from the wound on the side of his head where his ear used to be.

He coughs on blood and does nothing to wipe away the droplets from his messed-up mouth. Sterling doesn't move or even attempt to get up. It's like he's finally accepted his fate.

I pull my wolf back and call upon the shift. The skin on my chest that had been cut burns in pain as my skin moves and manipulates itself as I shift into my human form.

I run my now human hand over my damaged chest and grimace when my palm comes back bloody. Wiping the blood off on my bare thigh, I stand to my feet.

Sterling watches me with a knowing, almost accepting look in his eye.

The hellhound stays close to my side, acting as a bodyguard. He growls a warning at me when he decides I'm too close to Sterling for his liking. Standing victorious in front of the man who wanted to take everything from us is a sensation I will reflect on for the rest of my life.

When all else feels like it's lost or things get hard, I will remember what we accomplished tonight.

I bend at the middle, resting my hands on my knees as I glare down at him. "How does it feel knowing you're about to experience what it's like to truly die? This time, there isn't a necromancer here to save you. You messed up by pissing him off." I look down at my bare body, the only wound is the one on my chest. "Thank you for doing that, it worked out well for me. I don't even have a scratch from my fall." I stand up straight and narrow my eyes at him. "You, however? There's going to be nothing left of your body. Even if Kaius felt inclined to bring you back, he couldn't because there won't be a strand of your hair left."

He gargles something in his throat, but I can't quite make out what he's saying, not that he could say anything that would make me change my mind.

"I want you to remember that this is a mercy," I tell him coldly. "I want you to remember that what you deserve is far, far worse than what you're getting. I want you to remember that your biggest mistake wasn't the horrific things you did in those labs to innocent people. Your mistake was coming after my family. I know that word doesn't mean anything to you, but to us it means everything. When you decided to come for us, you signed your own death warrant." I sink my fingers into the blood soaked and matted hair of the hellhound at my side as I say, "And while you burn and scream in pain, I want you to remember that there won't be a single tear shed for you. Your death will not be mourned by anyone. It will be celebrated." I grin darkly at him. "I warned you I'd dance in your ashes."

With that, I shove my hand into his chest just like he did me. Also, like me, he falls backward, the only difference is he doesn't scream while he falls. They come when he lands and the hellfire flames engulf him. His body thrashes and withers about while his pained cries fill the night air.

The sound of his screams falling silent is the sound of our victory. It's the moment when I feel the weight and the fear that has been haunting us for two years finally lift. It's the sound that gives me permission to truly look forward to tomorrow and the day after that without the lingering sense of dread.

Never in my life has silence sounded so good.

☾

I TURN MY BACK ON THE BURNING CORPSE AND FACE THE beast side of my mate. I know Jax isn't with me yet. He still has no idea that I'm okay—that I'm alive. Getting him back is my next priority.

Dropping to my knees in front of the wounded wolf, I smile when he instantly leans forward and presses his forehead against mine. A low, distressed whine comes from his throat as I smooth my fingers over his coarse fur. It's still sticky with blood, but I don't mind right now.

"It's over," I promise the wolf. "He's gone and I'm here." *Just like it should be.* "Everything is going to be fine."

I give him another minute with me before I pull back so I can look into glowing versions of Jax's eyes. "Can I have him back now?" I plead. "I need him." I need him like I need oxygen right now. Watching me fall was a terrible thing to witness for him, I'm sure, but watching him run toward me with that terrified look on his face broke my heart. I wish he'd looked away, so he didn't have to carry around that memory for the rest of our lives. "I need Jax back, he needs to know I'm okay." I'm desperate to ease some of the pain watching me fall caused him.

The wolf rubs his head against the side of my face once more before he lowers himself to the ground in front of me and drops his large head on my lap.

Just like Genevieve did for me, I run my fingers through the fur on his head until the fur melts away and turns into the perfect luscious locks of Jax's that I'm obsessed with.

The shift only takes a minute, but the seconds drag by as I wait for my mate to be fully with me once more.

Jax slowly comes to. He groans in pain as he becomes aware of the wounds that were inflicted all over his body while he was blacked out. I continue to run my fingers through his hair as I wait for him to right himself inside his mind.

I know the second he realizes I'm here because his whole body goes stiff, and he stops breathing. Unsure of what's going on inside of his head, I hold my breath and wait for his reaction.

One second, we're on the ground with his head in my lap, in the next breath, we're standing and I'm in his arms with his head now buried in my neck. My eyes burn and tears threaten to fall when I feel his breath shudder against my shoulder. I don't have words to give him yet, so I hold on to him and rest my head against his.

His arms tighten around me to a degree that's painful and I struggle to pull air into my lungs, but I let it happen for as long as he needs. I could stay this way forever and I'd be content.

We're both alive and breathing. What more could I possibly want?

After a minute of overwhelming emotion, Jax lifts his head so he can look at me. "Are you really here? Or did I die? I don't care which because either way I'm getting my wish." His beautiful purple eyes are damp as he stares at my face in wonderment. "I have you in my arms again."

I run my hand down his bloody face before dropping my forehead against his and whispering, "I'm really here. I'm okay. *We're* okay."

I instantly feel his body relax as the tension rolls off of him. "But how? I saw you fall." He jerks back in alarm. "Winslow? Did she do this?"

"No," I assure. "It was Kaius."

"Why would he—"

I cut off his question. "Because we had a deal." I pull back just enough that I'm able to look into those purple eyes of his. "Just like you and I had a deal. You promised me forever and I'm holding you to it." Every single beautiful messy moment moving forward is ours to share together.

"If you think I'm ever letting you out of my sight again, you're wrong. Knowing what it feels like to have our bond break..." He shakes his head and swallows hard as emotion clogs his throat. "That can't ever happen again. I won't survive it a second time."

I hold his face between my hands as I vow, "It won't. We're safe now." Gently turning his head, I point at where

Sterling's body is still in flames. There's barely anything left of it at this point. "See? He's gone. We won, Jax."

Jax looks at his dad's remains. The orange flames reflect in his eyes as he stares. He takes a minute before he says anything. It's as if he needs a minute to come to terms with what's happened. "Killing Sterling was my only goal for a very long time. I didn't allow myself to imagine the future because a part of me always assumed I wouldn't survive facing Sterling. I was okay with that fate because I knew no one would miss me. I wasn't leaving anyone behind." My heart breaks for the lonely boy Jax was for most of his life. "But now I see nothing but a beautiful life and future for us. I'm going to make you so happy, Remington Weylyn."

"I already am, Jax." I dip my head and press my lips to his. It's not a heated kiss, but it holds so much emotion behind it. It's a silent promise that what we have and what we are will remain. That together we will build a big, beautiful life, and we'll do it all at each other's side. "I do need you to do something though," I tell him against his lips.

"Anything."

"I need you to rein in the flames, hellhound." I can't help but smile at the nickname I gave him as a joke only to discover it's true. "You're burning down my home."

CHAPTER THIRTY-SEVEN
Jax

Having everything you've ever wanted when you're accustomed to having nothing is like finding yourself in a dream after living a nightmare for most of your life. I keep expecting to wake up and find myself back when Remington was dead and Sterling was alive.

I think that's why I haven't let go of Remi since we left the cliff and the ashy remains of Sterling and William behind. I'm afraid if I let her go, I'll lose her again. It's going to be a long, tough recovery before I'm able to move past the trauma of watching her die. I thought what happened with my mother was the worst thing I've ever witnessed. I was so wrong. Watching the other half of my soul parish will forever be at the top of that list.

While I extinguished the hellfire burning around us, I'd made her stand directly in front of me where I could see her at all times.

Calling the hellfire back to me was a lot easier than letting it go. All I had to do is picture it flowing back into my palms and safely back inside of me. It took less than a minute for the roaring flames that covered hundreds of acres of pack territory to return to me.

The devastation that it caused is severe. What was once a lush forest with trees taller than buildings is nothing but a smoldering black wasteland. I feel terrible that my power did this to the land that Remington's pack calls home, but I'd burn it all down if it meant I got the same outcome.

I care about the pack, but at the end of the day, Remi is my mate and only priority. I'm not sure there aren't any lines I won't cross to ensure that she's safe.

Remi doesn't know or understand just how horrific that experience was for me, and I pray to whoever might be listening that she never has to know. I told her I wouldn't survive it if it happened again, but I would bear it again if I could ensure she'll never feel it.

As we walk down to the lake where everyone should be waiting, I explain to her how we were able to trap a good portion of Sterling's hexed creations. Without the roar of the flames, the night is now eerily quiet. There are no signs of any distant battles or fighting going on. The remaining group that didn't make it into the binding circle is either dead or found a way to escape. Remington asks me what we're going to do with the ones we trapped in the circle, and I tell her the truth. I don't have the slightest clue right now, but we'll figure it out. The ones that can be saved deserve a life outside of captivity and experiments. How we're going to make that happen is unclear, but between all of us, we'll figure it out.

When we are close enough to the lakeshore to hear the voices of her pack and family, Remington's face lights up and that breathtaking smile I could stare at forever appears.

As we come through the tree line, someone shouts, "There they are!"

The crowd of pack members erupts into a symphony of relieved sentiments and cheers.

A pair of sweats are thrown at my chest from some unknown person in the crowd while someone I don't recognize walks up to Remi and hands her a large T-shirt to slip on. The garments are barely on our body before there's a flash of white-blonde hair and we're almost tackled to the ground as arms hook around both of our necks roughly.

"I'm so happy you're okay," Pruitt cries as she continues to hold us in the choke-hold-like hug. "I think I aged fifty years and now have a thousand gray hairs because of you two, but I don't care. You're both okay." Pru finally releases us and wipes at her eyes. "I could lie and say that they're just pregnancy hormones, but what's the point? I thought you were both dead."

Remi smiles reassuringly at her best friend and helps clear the tears from her face. "What? You thought I could leave you here to deal with my family alone? Not a chance."

Ryker comes up behind his mate and wraps his tattooed arms around his little sister. When he's done, he shocks me by turning to me. He gives me one of those quick man hugs where he hits me on the back once before pulling away. He then shocks me by saying, "I'm really glad she has you," before returning to stand by his mate.

I really might be dreaming. Ryker Weylyn just said something *nice* to me?

Each of the family members takes turns greeting us. Isabeau even breaks down and hugs both of us. Margot is a blubbering, sobbing mess, but we can understand what she's saying in between her choked cries.

Winslow, leaning against Ranger's side, pipes in after all the greetings are finished. "So, it's really over? He's dead?"

"Burned into nothing," Remi confirms. "He's never going to be able to hurt another person. Same with William."

"And just like that, we're the only ones left," Pruitt tells me with a soft smile. "The rest of our family is dead."

Our family.

It's still hard to wrap my head around the fact that Pruitt and I are related by blood. It does explain why I was able to trust and open up to her so fast.

Ransom laughs somewhere behind us. "Remi just had to one-up you, Pru. You mated her brother, so she mated your uncle."

Whisper shakes his head. "Oh my God, your family tree is going to be so fucked up. Your children's school projects should be fun. Honestly, I would tell the teachers that everyone is dead. It's easier to explain than this intertwined nonsense."

Everyone laughs at the human hacker who shockingly looks perfectly at home amid a pack of wolf shifters. I wonder what he's going to do now that this is all over. Or what any of us are going to do?

I know what I want to do next and I'm growing antsy having to wait for it. I want to give Remi time with her family so they can heal together. She needs that, but I just need time alone with her. I'll only ever need her.

Sawyer looks at Ryker. "And to think, all of this started because you decided to start hunting rogue wolves."

And that's the truth in all of this. All it takes is one choice, one decision for lives to be forever changed for the good or the bad. There's been a lot of bad, but standing here among this family, each of them with their mates next to them, I'm reminded of all the good.

Every drop of blood spilled, every scar slashed into my skin, every moment where I didn't know how I was going to keep going, it all brought me here. It brought me to Remington.

It brought me home.

"So, what now?" Winslow asks everyone, her unique colored eyes darting around to each of us.

"Now?" Pruitt grins while she reaches for her mate's hand. "We celebrate. We celebrate that we're still here and our enemy isn't. We celebrate the lives it cost us to get to this point, and we celebrate that from this day forward, we just get to live."

The pack's cheers turn into howls as everyone begins to shift around us. The wolves yip and bark happily before one by one they take off into the woods chasing each other. The sound of their joy fills the still night air.

The twins laugh and push at each other as they tear at their clothes and shift into large gray wolves. They tackle and play fight with each other for a second before they bound into the woods. Beau and Winnie smile at each other before walking into the woods side by side after their mates.

Soon it's just Ryker and Pruitt left with us. "Are you guys coming?" Pru asks, a hopeful gleam in her eyes.

Before I have to explain that my wolf doesn't get along with others, Remi jumps in and answers for me. "You guys go. Have fun with everyone for us." She turns her head and looks at me as she says, "I don't know if you guys heard, but I died tonight and that puts in perspective how precious time is. So, I'm going to go spend as much of it with my mate as I can." Her hand squeezes mine tight.

Ryker nods in understanding. "Okay, don't go far. We still have to figure out what we're doing with those people stuck in Esme's circle."

I can't fight the smirk that threatens to grow on my lips. "I'm not taking her far," I lie.

As Pru passes us, Remi reaches out and places her hand over her growing stomach. "Your grandma says hi," she whispers low. "And now I have to keep what you are a secret for four more months. Totally unfair." Pru looks at Remi with wonderment and confusion on her face, but Remi just smiles and promises, "I'll tell you all about it later."

Almost reluctantly, Pru follows Ryker into the trees.

Finally alone, I wrap my arms around Remi and rest my chin on her head. I breathe in her scent and allow it to calm the exposed nerves that are still inside of me. We stand quiet, just allowing ourselves a moment to revel in the calmness.

"Do you trust me?" I ask her after some time has passed.

Placing her chin on my chest, she looks up at me with nothing but love in her eyes. "With my life."

I smile, knowing she used the same answer I'd given her when she asked me the same question.

"Close your eyes and hold on to me," I instruct her.

Without question, she does as she's told.

My own eyes close and imagine the scene in my head as I call upon my power. As it begins to roar to life inside of me and the air starts to crackle with power, I order, "Whatever you do, don't let go of me."

"Never again," she promises before the power swallows us whole.

☾

I WANTED TO GO TO THE BEACH WITH MY MOM, BUT THAT option was taken from me. So, I brought my mate there instead.

Remington gasps and stumbles back a step when she feels the powdery white sand beneath her toes and the waves crashing softly onto the shoreline. Her head whips around, taking in the scenery as she works through her disbelief.

I could have warned her about what I was going to do, but I wanted it to be a surprise, and based on the look on her face, it was worth it.

When she first showed me that hellfire didn't hurt her, I considered the possibility that I could bring her with me when I used the flames to travel between places. The lingering fear that it would be too much stopped me from trying it. I changed my mind when I discovered she could walk through the flames without so much as growing warm. That's when I knew she could withstand traveling.

For the first time, I let go of her hand and allow her to wander away from me. We're on a small uninhabited island in the Caribbean. There is nothing here that can hurt her. Hell, no one even knows we're here.

She covers her mouth as she stares out at the beautiful water. The sun is starting to creep over the horizon and stunning pink and orange lines are forming in the sky. "I've never seen the ocean before," she breathes. "It's amazing."

"When I first was free of Sterling and Nicolai, this is the

first place I came. I sat on the beach for hours just watching the waves come in as I tried to come up with a plan," I explain. "And then every time I needed a place to think, or I needed to put some serious distance between us or else I was going to lose my fucking mind over the fact I couldn't have you, I came here." I spent hours pacing in the sand convincing myself that Remi didn't mean anything to me. It, of course, all fell apart when I saw her again. "Sometimes there are storms that happen out over the water. Each time lightning would strike, I would have to laugh because it's like the universe was taunting me. Your eyes have always reminded me of thunderstorms, and even halfway across the world, I couldn't escape you."

Remi turns away from the water. "That's because we were never meant to escape each other. We kept running, but we weren't really going anywhere. All we were doing was hurting ourselves, but not anymore," she declares. "There's no more running, no more bad guys after us, and no more hiding sides of ourselves from each other. Now we can just... *be free.*" She looks back at the water before smirking at me tauntingly. "Let's be free, Jax." She backs away from me as her hands grip the bottom of the white T-shirt she wears before lifting it over her head.

Completely naked, she takes off down the beach. Her laugh, full of joy and happiness, joins the sound of the crashing waves. I'm yanking at my sweats, bouncing on one foot as I pull them completely off my body before she has time to touch the water.

I run after her and watch as she dives into the waves without fear.

A few seconds later, I'm jumping in after her. The warm

ocean water washes over me, cleaning my skin of the dried blood that still coated my flesh. It also cleanses me of my past and the darkness that I've felt clinging to me my whole life.

Like Remi said. We're free.

I'm free.

We surface from the waist-deep water at the same time and before either of us has fully taken a breath, we're grabbing for each other.

She tastes like saltwater as our mouths crash together.

I kiss her like I'll never get enough of her. I kiss her like it's my last time because, after today, I'm learning that we truly never know what will be our last moments. I kiss her like she's my reason to get up in the morning because that's what she is. I kiss her like I'm trying to brand her with my mouth because the mark on her neck isn't enough.

A wave knocks into us, making her stumble away from me as she catches her balance on the sandy ocean floor. Not wanting that to happen again, I grip her hips and wrap her legs around my waist.

My hardening dick jabs into her flat stomach making her grin against my mouth. "Hard already?."

"For you? Always." I kiss down her throat until I reach the bite mark on her neck. I seal my mouth over it and suck lightly. Her head falls to the side as she moans softly. "What about you, love? Does that sweet pussy of yours want my cock?" My hand dips between us to tease her with my fingers. The pads of my fingers rub slow circles around her clit until her hips begin to swivel and mimic my pace. "That's it," I coax.

"Now, Jax," she pleads. "I need you inside me now."

I made a vow to keep her happy. How am I supposed to refuse her request?

Lifting her in my arms, I slowly bring her down on my dick until I'm buried deep inside of her. Both of us shudder and groan as white-hot pleasure takes us over. The world washes away, and all I can see or feel is us. My only focus and priority are the woman in my arms. She's the one who owns my heart and soul, and she's the one who saw the good in me before I was capable of seeing it myself.

There are a lot of things that I don't have the answers to yet. There are still so many unknowns regarding what comes next for us, but I know one thing for sure. We will walk through the mystery of life side by side, and we will find the answers together.

And we will continue to set each other ablaze while we do it because her flames combine with mine, and together, like a wildfire, they burn everything in their path.

CHAPTER THIRTY-EIGHT
Remington

Five Months Later

I'm happy.

Like deliriously and irrevocably happy.

I'm the kind of happy that's hard for other people to be around because I've been floating on a bubbly pink cloud of pure joy for months. If I was forced to spend time with someone like me, I would probably feel inclined to punch me square in the nose.

I'm happy and I'm *exhausted*, but in the best way.

Five months have passed since Sterling and everything he built was dismantled to the ground. Or I should say *burned* to the ground. After we figured out how to help the ones we'd trapped in the binding circle, we'd moved onto the few remaining breeding facilities still standing.

Kaius gave me the addresses and held up his end of the deal. Well kind of...

I'd walked out to my brand-new SUV one morning to find the list of locations pinned under my windshield wiper with a note from the necromancer.

Remington,

Absolutely immaculate work with Sterling. Bravo, my dear. It was a truly thrilling experience watching his final battle. A shame it's already over, but still a very satisfactory end.

As promised, here are the addresses. With news of Sterling passing, security will be light as the staff is starting to jump ship faster than rats.

Best of luck with your little crusade. Though I do want it noted, I still find this mission ridiculously tedious, and I firmly believe there are better things you can do with your time. That's just my two cents.

I'm sorry I couldn't tell you this in person. I know we had a playdate planned, but did you know they've found another tribe deep in the amazon that's never been contacted by the outside world? I think I may take a little jaunt down there and check it out. Hell, I just might resurrect their elders. I always thought being a god would be fun. I'll be sure to let you know if they build a shrine in my honor.

So, for the time being, I'm going to need a rain check on our plans.

I pinky promise not to get into bed with any more deplorable people in the meantime. I'll be on my best behavior, but I truly hope you'll be at your worst.

-Kaius.

After Jax got his fill of telling me *I told you so*, we'd taken the addresses to our new *permanent* resident hacker who verified that all the addresses were real places.

After multiple recon trips and an exhausting amount of planning, as a pack and as a family, we'd cleared out each and every one of the buildings. We saved every soul we could that was locked inside. Some of the staff fought back and protected the buildings like they were the last strongholds in the war, but many of them looked almost relieved to have been forced out of a job. They dropped their guns and walked out of the building with their white flags raised.

Whisper had been there the whole time, helping us through the high-tech security systems. He became just as invested in the cause as the rest of us. From what I've learned from being around him and the stories Winslow has told us, a lot of his hacker skills are used to right the wrongs of corrupt government officials or corporations. He likes to refer to himself as a cyber vigilante. He tells us that the Montana air has been good for his soul and plans on sticking around for a while. I hope he does. I've grown to really enjoy his company.

After the buildings were clear and free of any people, Jax had used his hellfire to burn them and everything inside them to the ground. There was nothing left that the humans could stumble across and begin to ask questions. Sterling may have been ready to let them know of our existence, but the rest of us aren't. We're content with how things are.

And yes, after all these months, Jax has retained the ability to control the flames. He says that night on the cliff, it was like the dam that was holding his power at bay broke and they've been free ever since. He doesn't know if it's a permanent change, but we're using them for as long as we can.

So many of the captives were women that were taken from their homes or right out of parking lots when they were walking to their cars. The ones that were mentally and physically ready to leave were reunited with their families as quickly as possible.

Many of the women took the children they had mothered with them as well. It was something that was never expected of them. They were given options and were promised the children would be well taken care of if they didn't have the ability to do it themselves. We had coordinated with packs across the country that had mated couples that were hit hard by the low fertility rates and were looking to adopt these special children.

In the end, we had less than twenty children that needed to find homes, the rest went home with their mothers.

There were a good handful of people that weren't ready to be reintegrated back into society or people who were still struggling with medical problems inflicted on them from Sterling's cruel experiments. There were also a few pregnant mothers that had elected to spend the remainder of their pregnancies with us.

All of my siblings had chipped in on a large Victorian-style home in town. Its tall hedges and big trees offer ample privacy. Winslow calls it a halfway house, and, in a way, I guess she's right. It was never intended to be a permanent option for the rescued people but a place they healed and recuperated.

We knew when we bought the property that it would eventually be empty once we were able to rehabilitate everyone. Five months later, we're so close to having everyone ready to leave the nest. We're still waiting for a couple of babies to be born, and a few of the women have such bad post-traumatic stress, they're afraid to leave their rooms. Winslow spends a lot of time working with them as she's healed from her own trauma. Plus, she's a really good listener and somehow always knows what to say. She's so weird, but she's also so wise.

Our pack doctor, Dr. V, put her private practice on hold to

work with us as we get these souls back on their feet. She's helped us endlessly to help nurse all of them back to health. Even though I hadn't graduated from nursing school, she gave me lots of hands-on experience and even offered me a job at her practice if I ever want it.

I don't know if I'll take her up on her offer, maybe one day when I'm ready to settle down.

After traveling to the beach with Jax, I realized just how much of the world I wanted to see. While I no longer feel suffocated by my family or my home, the desire to leave and explore the world with my mate is strong.

The pack environment also isn't a conducive place for Jax's wolf. He doesn't like or understand a pack's structure. For the sake of Pruitt and his relationship, Pruitt can never be Jax's alpha, and therefore, being a true member of the pack isn't likely. It's a fact that we're both at peace with. He's not a pack member officially, but he's a member of our family which is even better.

We've been living at the loft in town and over the past few months, we've slowly been making it our own. It's small and needs some TLC in places, but that's okay. I'd live anywhere if I got to live with him. Soon it's going to be a place we just stay at when we're in town.

Tomorrow we're leaving the only state I've ever known and we're going to take a page out of Kaius's book and go on an adventure. We don't know exactly where we're going or when we'll be back, but the not knowing is what makes it exciting. We're going to figure it all out together just like we do everything else.

Giddiness fills my chest like a swarm of cheerful butterflies as I tip my head back and allow the autumn sun to warm my face. I want to savor this moment because it's perfect. We've been having a lot more of those kinds of moments now that things are finally starting to settle. Without the looming threats and monsters lurking in the shadows, we've been able to truly enjoy the small moments like this.

Opening my eyes, I scan them over what used to be a lush forest. Months later, the ground is still black, and the trees are still gone. But like my pack and my family, it's starting to heal. To grow again. Bright green sprouts are peeking out of the burned soil. Soon this part of the territory will be good as new. Better even.

I'm shifting the blanket on my lap when I sense him. After five months of being mated, I can sense his power when he uses it to travel. I can feel the shift in the air, the slight humming energy before the faint scent of smoke appears.

He sits down behind me, his legs on either side of mine. Closing my eyes once again, I lean back and nestle up against his warm chest. My lips tip up when I feel his lips skim across the mark he left on my neck. Touching, kissing, or just looking at his mark is his favorite thing to do. It soothes him, I find.

Jax has nightmares and more times than not, he flies awake next to me, gasping for breath and his eyes glowing as his wolf pushes forward to protect him. He doesn't admit it, but I know he's dreaming about watching me fall. After he catches his breath and settles a bit, he always reaches for me, pulling me tight against his chest where he then caresses the mark on my neck until we both fall asleep again.

I wish there was more I could do to help him heal from that night, but if this is what he needs, I can live with it.

Jax's arms snake around my waist as he asks, "Are you happy, love?"

He asks me this every day, usually when we have a quiet moment alone like now. Jax promised to make me happy, and he takes his promise very seriously. Every day for five months I've given him the same answer. Even when we were in the thick of rescuing all those people, it was the same. "Happy and so, so in love."

And his answer is always the same too. "Tomorrow is going to be even better," he vows, and then he kisses my cheek.

He's always right. Each day I spend with him, I feel lighter, and I feel more at peace.

I feel whole.

I used to take for granted feeling like this, but now I know better. I know how fast things can change and how easy it is to let the darkness in. I submerged myself in it until I couldn't breathe, but Jax stood by me and, like a torch, his flames led me home.

So, from now on, I'm not going to take a single second for granted.

Happiness is hard to come by, so when you find it, hold on tight and fight like hell to keep it. No matter what, you deserve it. You deserve to be happy and to be loved.

I look down at the sweet bundle of newborn bliss in my arms. "And you are," I whisper to my niece. "You are so incredibly loved."

Jax turns my head so I can look at him as he says, "And so are you."

EPILOGUE

Remington
Three Months Later

The crisp Grecian morning air prickles my skin and makes my heart happy as I stand on the deck of our villa overlooking the ocean. After two weeks here in Santorini, I've decided it's my new favorite place we've been too, but my answer might change again after another two weeks of traveling. I've pretty much said that about every place we've been to the last three months. Each beautiful city is new and exciting. I find something to like in all of them.

I especially enjoy that I get to explore each of these uniquely beautiful cities with the man I never thought I could have but is now the man I'm never letting go of.

He's been to so many of these places already, but when

Jax visited them, he wasn't there for leisure. He was still following whatever leads he could on Sterling. It's as if he's getting to experience everything for the first time with me.

I never thought I'd be so content to be away from the pack or from my home, but I've found so much peace in traveling the world that I'm not in a hurry to get back to Montana.

Plus, it's hard to miss my family when I talk to them multiple times a day. With a family this big, I'm talking to someone different all the time trying to stay up to date. I usually talk to Pruitt the most because I'm admittedly obsessed with my niece. How could I not be? She's the perfect combination of my brother and best friend. I think the universe had a wonderful plan in mind when it gave my big, scary, tattooed brother a blonde-haired little girl. I think they knew he needed something to soften him, and holy shit has she. Ryker Weylyn is a pile of mush for his daughter.

"Look!" Pruitt squeals happily over the FaceTime call as the camera flips around and my cute as hell niece is back on the screen. "See, I told you she was waving."

She's not, but when someone tells you that their baby is doing something, you smile and nod. "Hello my sweet, River!" I wave back at the screen. River's not actually waving. The four-month-old has recently discovered her hands and is clearly fascinated with them.

It was hard as hell to keep what Genevieve told me from Pruitt. All day long I had to fight myself to not announce to the world that I was going to have a niece. The girly clothes I purchased in mass quantities were strategically hidden so Pru wouldn't see. Pru had of course broken down and pleaded with me to tell her, but I'd refused. She had said from the beginning she didn't want to know what she was having, so one of us had to be strong.

Pru got me back by keeping her name selections a secret. My brother and sister-in-law had surprised us all when we discovered they'd stuck with tradition and gone with an R name.

River Genevieve Weylyn.

"She misses her aunt and wants her to come home." Pruitt turns the camera back around so she can show me her pouting face.

I laugh and shake my head at her dramatics. "Oh really? *River* told you that?"

"*Yep*, I'm now fluent in baby babble. It's a skill I'm adding to my resume right after *'curse breaker'*," she jokes before turning serious. "But really, when are you coming home? We miss you around here. Doctor V said she could use your help at the halfway house."

"There are five people left there. I have full faith that between Winnie, Doctor V, and Doctor V's staff, they've got it covered for the time being."

Five people... It's an absolute miracle that's all that's left. Everyone still feels guilty about the lives that were lost that night when they had to fight Sterling's hexed people. There were just so many people who were beyond saving. Their minds were gone and all that remained were the monsters they were created to be.

Jax and Isabeau keep saying it was a mercy that those souls were put to rest, and the rest of us are clinging to that.

As if I'd summoned her myself, Winslow's voice comes through the phone followed by a door slamming. "Pru, I need to borrow some baby formula."

Pruitt's head whips around to look at the witch who now stands behind her. "What? Why?"

"Erin had her baby last night, but now she's gone. She left the little boy in a laundry basket for us to find this morning," Winslow explains with a sad sigh. Erin was one of the women who'd agreed to stay at the halfway house until she had her baby. She was a quiet and reclusive leopard shifter. Most of the time, we had to talk to her through her bedroom door. Winslow has spent many hours sitting on the ground outside the door, trying to coax her out to no avail. "I know we told the women that we'd take care of their babies if they decided they weren't capable of raising them, but it still makes me a little sad he doesn't have a family now."

"We'll find him a home," I tell her. Winslow's head turns as she searches for the source of my voice. "I'm on Pru's phone."

Winslow finally looks at the phone in Pru's hand. "Oh hey! I thought I was hearing voices again." She puts her hand over her heart in relief before walking closer. "You look all tan and pretty. Where are you now?"

"Santorini still. We're moving on to Croatia tomorrow I think," I explain quickly before going back to the more pressing issue. "I still have the contact info for the packs who were looking to adopt, I'll reach out to all of them. Don't worry, we'll find him the perfect family."

"Ranger and I are going to keep him for the night I think." Winnie reaches around Pru to scoop River up from the playmat. "It's just for a night, it shouldn't be terrible, right?"

Pruitt just laughs. "No, it's great, if you don't mind not sleeping, and baby vomit in your hair."

I'm laughing at Winslow when she looks down at River

and cringes when there's the faintest scent of smoke in the air. There's a smile on my face before I feel his arms wrap around my middle and his face bury in my neck.

"Jax!" Pruitt exclaims. "Tell your mate it's time for you guys to come home!"

Jax chuckles softly before kissing the side of my neck and lifting his head. "Why would I do that when I have her all to myself right now?" he asks Pru with a devious grin on his face.

Pru's rebuttal is cut off when Jax ends the call. The phone is barely out of my hand before I'm being lifted off the ground and placed on the railing of the balcony. Unable to stop myself, I glance down below me. It's a long way down. Ever since falling from the cliff, heights haven't been a friend of mine, but Jax's arms are holding me in place, and I know without a shadow of a doubt he'll never let me go.

"I don't know how I'm ever going to be able to share you again," he tells me in that slightly rumbly voice that makes my insides quiver. "I just want to keep you all to myself for the rest of our lives."

I don't need much convincing. Exploring the world together for the rest of our days sounds like heaven to me. "Okay."

☾

Two Months Later

MY RECEPTION ON THIS BOAT IS TERRIBLE AND THE EMAIL I'M trying to read won't load past a certain point but based off the small amount I'm able to read, it would seem I need to talk to my sister-in-law.

We're in Iceland and we're supposed to be whale watching, but I'm caught up in what's going on at home instead. I click her name and wait for her to answer. The phone rings for a second and there's brief pause as if she's picked up before the line goes completely dead. With an annoyed huff, I stuff the phone in my pocket.

If this problem didn't revolve around the future of a child, I would let it go and let them figure it out. I also can't ignore the massive amount of responsibility I feel to find each of these kids a home. The only reason I felt confident leaving home five months ago was because everything was settled and planned. All the infants and kids had homes lined up. But of course, nothing can be easy. No one can follow the set path, least of all Winslow.

She's always marched to the beat of her own drum, even when she's the only one who can hear the rhythm. Winslow hears and sees a lot of things that we can't.

Searching the fairly large boat, I look for my mate amongst the human tourists. I find him leaning against the door of the cabin with a mischievous smirk on his face. Unless that look is worn within the parameters of our bedroom, it usually means he's up to no good.

Walking up behind him, I poke him in the side. "What are you staring at?"

Jax turns his head just enough I can see the corners of his mouth curl even more. "One wrong move, or strong gust of wind, and she's going in the water." He points across the boat where a girl is posing on the railing while her boyfriend takes a multitude of pictures of her.

"You're supposed to be watching the whales," I remind him.

He shrugs, "I saw one, but now I want to see one swallow an Instagram model like she's *Pinocchio*."

I want to scold him and tell him how horrible he sounds, but I can't because I would also find it hilarious to watch her fall into the ice cold Atlantic. Jax's sick humor is rubbing off on me. Reluctantly, I look away from the disaster waiting to happen and tug Jax inside the cabin and into the bathroom that's roughly the size of an airplane's

"What are we doing?" He analyzes the snug space before smirking at me. "Really? You want me to take you in here? It'll be tight, but I never back down from a challenge."

Laughing, I push at his chest and shake my head. "No, that's not what we're doing. Though it does sound fun."

"Then what are we doing? I know we promised to be there for each other and never be apart, but I don't think we need to hold each other's hands while we go to the bathroom, Remington."

"Shut up, you idiot." Sometimes I just can't deal with him. "We're hiding in here because we need to go home." We can't disappear in thin air in front of a boat full of people.

"*What?*" He drawls, clearly confused. "Why would we do that?"

"Because I think my sister-in-law is stealing a baby."

☾

WE MATERIALIZE IN THE MIDDLE OF WINSLOW'S LIVING ROOM just as she's coming around the corner from Ranger's office. When she locks eyes with me, she makes a surprised squeaking noise and turns quickly back around like she's going to flee from us.

"*Uh uh*, don't even think about it, crazy cakes!" I yell after her. "Get your ass back here and explain to me why the leopard clan in northern California emailed me to express their disappointment that they won't be adding Erin's baby to their family. What the hell, Winnie? This is the third placement you've rejected for him. This was the perfect placement too. He would have been with his own kind, and the couple who were going to take him were great."

She glances behind her with a nervous look before tucking her hands innocently behind her back and rocking on her heals. "Oh, hey guys, what a nice surprise. What are you doing here?" Winnie asks, completely ignoring my question.

"Cut the shit, Winslow." I cross my arms. "I have places I need to be. Whales I want to watch and disgusting black licorice I need to eat." What is it about Icelandic people and their black licorice? It's *foul*. Haven't they ever heard of a Snickers bar?

She stands there, trying her best to keep her face impassive, but unfortunately, Isabeau is the master of that look. Winnie can try as hard as she wants, but she still looks like a deer caught in the headlights.

Jax plunks down in the armchair that's between us. His head whips back and forth like he's watching a tennis match as he waits for one of us to break our tense staring contest.

The shrill sound of an infant crying down the hallway has her breaking my impatient stare with a defeated sigh. "Those families were all good people. I actually liked all of them, but I couldn't give Jasper to them. They weren't right for him."

"Jasper?" Jax repeats for me, cocking his head.

"Yes, that's what we've been calling him. I don't know where it came from, but it fits him." The soft smile that forms on her mouth doesn't go unnoticed as she talks about the baby.

"How could a clan of other leopard shifters not be right for him?" I question. "He would have fit right in there."

The baby—*Jasper*—also has warlock genes, but we won't know what kind of power he possesses until he's much older. The clan in California wasn't concerned about his mixed DNA. None of the gracious people that took in the kids cared, all they saw were children that had rough starts to life and needed homes. The selflessness I witnessed over the past nine months has been heartwarming. The outpouring of support for the victims of Sterling has been astronomical. People were appalled when they learned what had been going on in the shadows, and so many wanted to help.

Ranger appears from the hallway with a small infant in his arms. "They weren't right because they weren't us."

Winslow's face lights up when she sees them. Like a magnet, she's drawn to the admittedly adorable pair and glides across the space to stand closer. "We were trying to buy time until we were sure, but now we are." She runs a finger down the little boy's face, her signature chipped black nail polish in place.

I have a feeling I know where this is going but need to confirm it. "Sure of *what*, exactly?"

"He belongs here with us." Winnie looks over her shoulder at me. "I don't know how to explain it, but when I look at him, I know he's ours. I wasn't sure I wanted kids or was ready for them, but the idea of passing him off to one of those other families made my heart hurt."

Ranger shifts the baby on his chest. This is the second time in two years I've seen my brother with a baby, and just like last time, he's a total natural. He's at complete ease holding such a fragile life in his hands. Ranger's face sets with determination. "He's our son. Jasper is our son."

I look between the two of them for a second before throwing my hands up in frustration. "Well fuck, you guys. If he already had a home, I could have stopped looking for one for him weeks ago." I drop my hands and rest them on my hips. "Send a text or something next time so I don't have to come hunt you guys down."

Winslow gives me a sheepish apology, but it's clear she's irrationally happy right now and can't be bothered to feel that bad. I can't blame her, I too, am that happy.

With a long exhale, I walk toward the new little family. "Alright, hand him over so I can meet my new nephew."

☾

Three Months Later
Jax

THE KNIFE FLIES THROUGH THE AIR RIGHT IN FRONT OF MY nose before sinking into the bark of the nearby tree with a *thud*. With an amused smirk, I take another bite of my apple before turning my attention to the knife thrower.

"You missed."

"I never miss," Isabeau argues, and just to prove a point, she throws another knife. This time it pierces the apple in my hand. The piece of fruit flies out of my grip and ends up impaled on the same tree. "See? I find it rude you would insinuate otherwise."

Frowning at what was once my snack, I tell her, "It was a joke, but I know how those have a tendency to fly over your head."

She flips a knife around her hand in a move I can only assume would slice my fingers off if I tried it. I'm not a novice when it comes to weapons, but I'll never be as skilled with them as Beau is. There was no point in training me in the art of knives or firearms when my weapon was my flames. Though my flames haven't been used as a weapon since the night Sterling died.

There hasn't been a reason to. For the first time in my life, I have peace. For the first time in my life, there aren't men out there that want me dead or people I want to see dead.

"I understand jokes, I just don't find you funny." Beau tucks the blade safely in the leather holster on her thigh. "What are you doing back here? I thought you guys were supposed to be in…" She pauses for a second, thinking over her answer. "I want to say Australia."

It's been eight months of traveling the world with my mate and I'm still not ready for it to end. Every day is new and exciting, and every day Remington wakes up with a smile on her face because of it. I know what it's like to see her struggle to smile and now that she does it so freely and easily, it's something I'll never take for granted again. It's also something I'll do everything in my power to protect.

As long as she's happy traveling and seeing all these amazing places, we'll continue to do it, but the second she decides she's had enough, we'll find the place we're supposed to settle down. Whether it's here in Montana or somewhere tropical, I don't care. I just want to be in the place that makes her smile the most.

"Argentina," I correct. It's hard to keep it all straight. I'm not even sure where we're going to be next week. "And we're back because Winslow and Pruitt kept sending Remi baby pictures and I think she was feeling left out."

Beau shakes her head, and a small laugh escapes her. "How did we get here? How are we these people?" she questions aloud, a twinge of disbelief in her voice. "I was the girl who needed nothing and no one, but now I'm a mate and wife. And an *aunt*. The oddest part of all of this is I enjoy it. I enjoy being a part of this family."

I jokingly tell her, "You're growing soft, Isabeau."

Those eyes, the same color as an arctic glacier narrow at me. "Take that back."

"It's okay, because I am too." I was the boy who didn't think he'd live past the age of sixteen and now I'm the man who has nothing but a bright future ahead of him. "But I think it's okay that we are. Our edge kept us alive, but we're not fighting for our lives anymore, are we?"

"No, I guess we're not," she relents.

"What are you going to do with all this time now? Maybe you can find a hobby. What are your thoughts on knitting?"

She walks over to the blades stuck in the tree. "If someone makes me knit, I *will* stab them in the eye with a knitting needle."

"Bowling?"

The unamused look she passes me answers my question.

With our enemies dead or gone for the time being, we all have nothing but time to figure out what our lives are going to be. I, for one, am curious to see what we're all going to be doing years from now when the last of the dust has settled and the events of the past two years are nothing but a distant memory.

I'm also excited to see what mischief my mate and I can get into. Between the two of us, I'm sure we can find all kinds of trouble to get into.

☾

Eight Years Later
Remington

WHEN YOU'RE YOUNGER, YOU HAVE AN IDEA OF WHAT YOU think your life will be. You hold onto that image, and you cling that dream. When someone asks you what you want to be when you grow up, you see the perfect life you've created for yourself in your head.

And while you're doing that, the universe is laughing at you and your best made plans. It laughs because it has something better in mind for you. It laughs at you because it knows that the life you envisioned in your head will look lackluster in comparison to what you're really going to get.

Had someone told me all those years ago when my world was so dark and bleak that this is where I'd end up, I would have laughed in their face. Then I would have cried because I wouldn't have thought it was possible.

But standing here today, in the backyard of my childhood home, I know it's all possible. All those dreams and wishes have come true.

"River!" Ryker calls across the yard to his daughter that looks so much like Pruitt it's remarkable. Her hair is a couple shades darker than her mom's white-blonde locks, but holy crap, they're twins. Just like Genevieve and Pru were. "Give your brother a turn on the swing!"

"Grandma said I could use it!" The little girl, who inherited her attitude from her dad, yells back. There's the cutest scowl on her round face.

Jax made the mistake of telling her once that she was the cutest little angry person he'd ever seen, and she did *not* take it well. Her blue eyes had lit up with so much fury, I thought they were going to burn the house down. My mate had then, of course, made matters worse by bursting into laughter when River stomped her foot in frustration.

"Yeah, and your *dad* is telling you to let Ruger have a turn." My brother crosses his arms and stares down his daughter, daring her to argue with him more. It's a nice show, but everyone here at this family barbecue knows that Ryker will fold like a cheap lawn chair for his daughter.

Ruger was born just eighteen months after River. I thought Pru was going to kill her mate when she found out he'd knocked her up again. She'd called me in hysterics while I was in Japan. The tears were a mixture of joy and panic. After twenty-four hours passed, the panic was gone, and Pru was just as happy as Ryker was. If it was up to Ryker, they'd have a baseball team of kids. Pruitt, however, is content with the two that she has.

While River looks like Pru, Ruger looks like the rest of the Weylyn's with our dark brown hair and blue eyes. He got his mom's calm nature though.

"I really should buy another playset so there's more swings," my mom comments from where she's taking the plastic off a bowl of cut-up fruit. The long picnic table is covered with different dishes she made. Just like how she liked to entertain the pack, she loves to entertain her growing family. She goes overboard with everything she does. We had planned on this being a lowkey summer barbecue, but I'm pretty sure I saw fireworks in the back of my dad's car when we pulled in.

"Don't you dare," Pruitt orders my mother. "You spoil them too much already."

"That's the job of the grandma, right?" My mom is an amazing mother, but she thrives as a grandmother.

Winslow walks up with a bright red popsicle in her hand. "Jasper threatens to run away to grandpa and grandma's house all the time. If he keeps climbing on top of the roof and refusing to come down, I might consider it." As a leopard shifter, my nephew has an innate instinct to climb things. It'd be funny if it weren't terrifying to see an eight-year-old teetering on the roof of a two-story house. Also due to his leopard nature, he's sneaky as hell. You look away for two seconds and that kid is long gone.

My mom laughs. "No, the other perk of being a grandma is I get to hand them back to you at the end of the day."

Isabeau and Ransom walk up, swinging a little girl with curly dark hair between them. "I thought that was the perk of being the fun aunt and uncle?" Ransom asks. "We get to fill them with sugar and then hand them back to you when the sugar crash happens."

Winslow narrows her eyes at Ransom. "Please tell me you didn't give her candy again."

"He didn't, Mommy," Isla promises before letting out a high-pitched squeal when Beau and Ransom swing her again.

"Good," Winslow sighs in relief. "I love you but you're a tiny terrorist when you have sugar."

Isla giggles before shaking her tiny head. "No Mommy, Uncle Ransom didn't give me candy, but Aunty B did." She sticks out her tongue to show it's stained bright blue. "It was boo-berry."

Winslow grimaces when she looks at her four-year-old, before shooting daggers at Isabeau.

The vampire shrugs her shoulders innocently. "What? You said I can't show them my knives. What else am I supposed to give them to make them like me?"

I scoff. "That's a load of crap! You know you're their favorite even without bribery."

I always thought that the favorite aunt position would be mine, but Beau has somehow dethroned me and I'm okay with it. She and Ransom have been clear from the start they aren't interested in having kids of their own, but they play big parts in their nieces' and nephews' lives. Isabeau even dressed up and went trick-or-treating with everyone last year. I never in a million years thought I'd see the vampire with kitty cat face paint, but it happened, and I have photographic proof.

Isla wiggles her tiny body until they put her on the ground. "I'm going to go show Dad."

"That's fabulous idea," Winslow encourages as her daughter hightails it across the yard to where Ranger and Elias are grilling. "Maybe he'll deal with the mess Aunty B created."

"It was *one* piece of candy," Beau defends herself as she drops the dark sunglasses on top of her head onto her face. She still wears her leather corseted outfits often, but over the years she's learned to relax a little more. Today she's in a pair of leather leggings and a white T-shirt. Even with the casual outfit, I know she has at least three weapons on her person. I'd bet money she has a dagger in her boot. "Stop acting like it's as bad as that sleeping elixir your dad sent."

"Stop referring to Kaius as my dad," Winslow groans. "He was a glorified sperm doner and nothing more, and now, may he rest in pieces." She unenthusiastically crosses herself before sticking the melting popsicle in her mouth.

It took Kaius five years to decide he'd finally had enough. On a boat, off the coast of Nova Scotia, we had our not so heartfelt goodbyes before I killed him. There were no frills or fuss, it was quick and dirty. When it was done, we secured his body to an anchor and dropped him into the Atlantic. He kept his end of the bargain, and so did I. He seemed thrilled at the prospect of learning what comes after death. I'm sure he's causing chaos in the afterlife as we speak.

Prior to his death, Kaius had somehow learned Winslow was now a mother to Jasper. He sent the creepiest box of baby related items. There was a baby rattle made of human bones and an ominous bottle of liquid that said, *'for when it won't stop crying'*. It's the thought that counts or whatever, but those items went into the trash immediately.

Or so I'm told. I wasn't here when it happened. At that point, Jax and I were still living the nomad life and traveling. It wasn't until this year we finally came back. For the time being anyway. The small loft apartment in town is where we're calling home as of now.

In those seven years that we were away, the last of the people living at the halfway house had received the help and support they needed to start new lives. We're still in contact with most of the people we helped and stay up to date with what they're up to. We remind each of them every time we talk that if they need it, there's always a room waiting for them here. We always assumed we'd sell the property we bought to house them all, but we like the idea of keeping it just in case someone needs extra help. We want all the survivors to know that they'll always have a home if they need it. We'll never turn our back on the people and kids that suffered because of Sterling.

Looking around my parents' back yard, I search for my mate and find that he's nowhere to be found. Excusing myself, I walk across the lawn toward the tall trees. Halfway across, the football Ryker and Sawyer are throwing flies over my head.

"You couldn't have waited like *two* seconds?" I roll my eyes at the pair.

Sawyer's response is to pelt the ball at my brother's stomach. Ryker cusses him out, but in the end, they're both laughing their asses off. Both are well into their thirties now, but you'd think they were still seventeen. It's hard to believe that I'm barreling toward my thirtieth birthday as well. Time is moving too fast, but hell if I'm not enjoying every second of it.

I walk into the trees and instantly know he's close. My spine tingles and my wolf perks up. It doesn't matter how long we've been mated; she still gets excited when he's near. She especially likes when Jax allows his wolf side out. With all our traveling, we've found great secluded places where he feels safe enough to shift.

Following his smokey scent, I stop at the base of a large tree. I know they're up there even though I can't see them.

The faint sound of their whispered voices and hushed laughs come from the branches way up above.

I should have known that the pair would have disappeared together. It's their go-to move at family functions.

Shielding my eyes from the bright sun, I peer up into the leaves. "Boys! Stop being anti-social and come back to the house."

There's some rustling and the tree shakes as they move into view. After a second, two faces come into view. "Hi Aunt Remi!" Jasper waves down at me with a big smile on his face. The kid is going to be a heartbreaker one day with his shaggy blond hair and warm brown eyes. At eight, he's already a smooth talker. The girls aren't going to stand a chance against him.

Next to him is my equally handsome man. Jax has always been good looking, but with each passing year, he gets hotter. It's truly unfair.

"Your mom is going to wonder where you are soon," I tell the young leopard shifter. "Why don't you head back. I think we're going to eat soon too."

Just like his dad and uncles, Jasper is never one to turn down the offer of food. At a speed that would make most people nervous, he climbs down from the tree. His little claws dig into the tree trunk as he slides to the bottom. He can't fully shift yet, but his claws and eyes have recently started to shift.

I ruffle his hair as he sprints pass me. Winslow and Ranger were right, Jasper belonged with them. I think it was fate that he became a member of this family.

In the faintest cloud of smoke, Jax appears in front of me. Grinning, he tips my chin so he can press a sweet kiss to my lips. "Hi, love." I will never get tired of the way his voice makes every nerve in my body come alive. His touch has the same affect, which is why I lean into his palm when he cups my cheek. "The trees are completely grown back. You'd never know I burned any of them down."

"I knew they would, they just needed time to heal." Like all of us did. The scars, both physical and emotional, left from that time are no longer open and raw. They're healed and barely visible. We both still have nightmares occasionally, but they're few and far between now.

Violet eyes clash with mine. It's like he's looking into my soul as he searches my eyes. I know what he's going to ask before he opens his mouth, but it still makes my chest squeeze with joy each time he does. "Are you happy, love?"

With gentle movements, Jax pulls the fabric down so he can get a better look at the bundle secured to my chest. It's been two months since he was born, but still, my eyes burn with emotion each time my mate looks down at his son.

Dash Whitlock was the gift that finally brought me home after seven years of traveling the globe. Once he's a little older, we'll be back on the road, creating more memories, just the three of us, but for now, we're enjoying our time here with our family.

I gently trace my finger down my sleeping son's face. "Happy and so, so in love."

Jax dips down and kisses Dash's head before promising, "Tomorrow is going to be even better."

The End

Did you enjoy Fire Bound? If you could take five minutes to leave a review on either Goodreads or Amazon, it would mean so much to me. Reviews help authors by making their books look more appealing to prospective readers. Thank you!

ACKNOWLEDGMENTS

Boy oh boy, where do I even start?

I can't believe I've written the final words to this series. When I first wrote *Wolf Bound*, I didn't have any expectations. I just wanted to be able to say "I wrote a book". To my utter and complete shock, people actually read it and they seemed to enjoy it.

So thank you so much to the readers for making dreams, I didn't really know I had, come true. Because of you guys, I'm on a career path that challenges me every day, but also makes me happy. That's something I wasn't sure I would ever find and I'm so glad I have. Telling these stories brings me so much joy.

Also because of this career, I've been able to meet some of the coolest and best people. I dedicated this book to my tribe, but I'd like to thank them even more.

Greer, I can't even sum into words how much I adore you and cherish our friendship. Your endless support and encouraging words always get me through when I feel like giving up. I love when we're spiraling together, but eventually talk each other out of it. We're a true dream team.

Ramzi, you're my twisted sister and best friend. You've been there for me when I've needed either a helping hand or a swift kick in the ass. Thank you for answering all of the questions and showing me the way. I honestly couldn't do this without you. I'm so, so excited about what's to come for us.

Cat, you are talented and magical. You're also my favorite human. Thank you for always making time for me and making me the most beautiful things.

Ash, thank you for reading through my dumpster fire first drafts and helping make my stories pretty. Thank you for your endless support and always calling dibs on my MMCs. It makes me happy to know I'm creating men worth calling dibs on!

Bre, thank you for taking the time to beta read for me. I know you're very busy chasing after your little baseball team of kiddos. I absolutely love your feedback.

Lee, thank you for always checking in on me and making sure I'm working. I love that you hold me accountable. Also thank you for putting up with my cliffhangers.

Thank you Christina for helping me keep all this shit organized. I couldn't disappear into my writing cave if I didn't know you'd be there picking up the slack!

To my street team, thank you for posting and sharing all my stuff. Also thank you for taking the time to read and review my books! I appreciate you all endlessly.

To Ellie and Rosa at My Brother's Editor. Thank you for always dealing with my last-minute nonsense and endless errors. Thank you for making my words pretty.

Lastly, to my family. Thank you for supporting me in everything I do. Without your support and grace, I wouldn't be chasing my dreams. Also PS: Dad, please never read these books.

ABOUT THE AUTHOR

Kayleigh lives in Denver Colorado, just two hours away from some of the best skiing in the world. A luxury completely lost on her considering she avoids snow at all costs. Well, she avoids *outside* at all costs—she's what you'd call an 'indoor cat'. She much prefers to sit inside on her computer all day drinking massive amounts of caffeine. She'd have an IV drip of the stuff connected to her if she could.

When she's not writing, you can find her binge-watching Netflix like it's her job. Or at the local Mexican restaurant, because the girl loves tacos and margaritas.

f facebook.com/kayleighkingwrites
◎ instagram.com/kayleighkingwrites
a amazon.com/author/kayleighkingwrites
g goodreads.com/kayleighkingwrites
BB bookbub.com/profile/kayleigh-king

READ THE REST OF THE SERIES

Wolf Bound (The White Wolf Prophecy, Book One)

Pruitt and Ryker's Story

Soul Bound (The White Wolf Prophecy, Book Two)

Winslow and Ranger's Story

Shadow Bound (The White Wolf Prophecy, Book Three)

Isabeau and Ransom's Story

Made in the USA
Middletown, DE
07 September 2021

47788672R00265